# Mary Peters

**Other Maine books from Islandport Press**

*Hauling by Hand: The Life and Times of a Maine Island*
by Dean Lawrence Lunt

*Nine Mile Bridge*
by Helen Hamlin

*The Cows Are Out*
by Trudy Chambers Price

*Those Damned Yankees*
by Clarke Canfield

*In Maine*
by John N. Cole

*The Story of Mount Desert Island*
by Samuel Eliot Morison

*Here for Generations: The Story of a Maine Bank and its City*
by Dean Lawrence Lunt

*A Moose and a Lobster Walk Into a Bar: Tales from Maine*
by John McDonald

**Children's Books**

*Titus Tidewater*
by Suzy Verrier

*When I'm With You*
written by Elizabeth Elder
illustrated by Leslie Mannsman

# Mary Peters

by Mary Ellen Chase

ISLANDPORT PRESS

NEW GLOUCESTER • FRENCHBORO • MAINE

Islandport Press
P.O. Box 10
Yarmouth, Maine 04096
www.islandportpress.com

First Islandport Press Edition, November 2005

This revised edition of *Mary Peters* reprinted by Islandport Press
Inc., by arrangement with Simon & Schuster. *Mary Peters* was
originally published by The Macmillan Company, 1934.

ISBN: 0-9673231-5-X
Library of Congress Card Number: 2005935098

Book jacket design by Karen F. Hoots/Mad Hooter Design
Cover illustration by Maitland de Gogorza
Book design by Michelle A. Lunt/Islandport Press
Photo of Mary Ellen Chase courtesy of Smith College

# Other Islandport Press books by Mary Ellen Chase

*Silas Crockett (1935)*

This stirring tale recounts the sweeping changes that took place
on the Maine coast during the nineteenth and early twentieth
centuries. By offering superior historical detail, authenticity and
great writing, Chase's classic novel is considered one of the most
distinguished books in Maine history.

*Windswept (1941)*

"John Marston first came into possession of Windswept, its
hundreds of rough, unkempt acres, its miles of high, rockstrewn
coast, its one precipitous headland, cut by the fierce tides into
almost a semi-circle within which his house was later to be built,
on Advent Sunday in the year 1880. He was fourteen years old at
the time. The day, in fact, chanced to be his birthday."

—excerpted from *Windswept,* coming in 2006

To
Margaret Eliot Macgregor

*Thou wert the morning star among the living*
*Ere thy fair light had fled.*
*Now having died thou art as Hesperus giving*
*New splendour to the dead.*

—Plato, in Shelley's translation.

From *The Brothers Karamazov*

"You must know that there is nothing higher and stronger and more wholesome and good for life than some good memory, especially a memory of childhood. People talk to you a great deal about your education, but some good, sacred memory, preserved from childhood, is perhaps the best education. If a man carries many such memories with him into life, he is safe to the end of his days, and if one has only one good memory left in one's heart, even that may some time be the means of saving us."

# Table of Contents

# About Mary Ellen Chase

Mary Ellen Chase was not only born and raised on the coast of Maine, she was molded by it; its history, its character and its spirit never abandoned her whether she was standing in the classrooms of Smith College or wandering through the meadows of England, another land she loved dearly. Her longtime companion, Eleanor Shipley Duckett, put it succinctly when she wrote: "Maine made and shaped her."

Less succinctly, Chase herself wrote: "To have sprung from Maine seafaring people; to have spent my childhood and many of my later years on a coastline unsurpassed in loveliness; to have inherited a wealth of thrilling history and tradition; to have been born at a time when great ships, built by Maine people in a hundred seacoast villages, had been for nearly a century making Searsport and Rockland, Belfast and Thomaston, Wiscasset and Calais better known in Canton, Singapore, and Sydney than even New York and London were known; to have been brought up with men, and with women, too, who knew the Seven Seas too well to be bounded in their thoughts by the narrow confines of their own native parishes;—such an inheritance of imperishable values imposes a debt which cannot possibly either be underestimated or even fully discharged."

Mary Ellen Chase was born in the village of Blue Hill on February 24, 1887, the daughter of a country lawyer and schoolteacher and the granddaughter of a sea captain. The second of eight children, she could trace her ancestral roots to the original eighteenth-century settlers of Blue Hill, which is located at the head of Blue Hill Bay between Penobscot Bay and Mount Desert Island. She had a strict upbringing and her childhood was steeped in literature and books and religion through the Congregational Church. She attended Blue Hill Academy starting in 1900 and graduated from the University of Maine in 1909. Her college education was interrupted briefly while she taught in one-room schoolhouses in Buck's Harbor and West Brooksville.

Following graduation, she traveled west, teaching first in Wisconsin and then Chicago at Miss Moffat's School for Girls in 1912. She also took her first fledgling steps toward professional writing when she sold her first story, "His Place on the Eleven," a story about football, to *The American Boy* in 1909 for $17.

She moved to Montana to recover from tuberculosis in 1914 and shortly saw the publication of her first book, *His Birthday* (1915), a 48-page children's book about Jesus' sixth birthday. During the following two years she wrote other children's books, including *The Girl from the Big Horn Country* (1916) and *Virginia of Elk Creek Valley* (1917).

In 1917, she began working toward a doctorate at the University of Minnesota. She received her master's degree in 1918, and in 1922 she received her doctorate and became an assistant professor of English at the university.

The year 1926 was an important one for Chase. She published *Mary Christmas*, her first novel, and she moved back east to begin three decades of teaching at Smith College in Northampton, Massachusetts.

In 1932 she published *A Goodly Heritage*, her first of three full-length autobiographical books that touched upon her beloved Maine and her hometown of Blue Hill. (Chase followed with *A Goodly Fellowship* (1939) and *The White Gate* (1954).)

### The Maine Novels

In 1934, she published *Mary Peters*, a novel set in Maine that essentially launched her career as a successful novelist and firmly established her credentials nationally. "This is not a novel, but a symphony," crowed Robert P. Tristram Coffin in the *New York Herald-Tribune*. Its success and the success of the Maine-based books that followed established her reputation as a leading author of the regional novel.

Elienne Squire wrote in her biography of Chase, "She discovered in the demise of a region not only a meaningful relationship to twentieth-century realities, but the source of a country's strength and ongoing spiritual heritage. Chase carried the chronicle forward, elevating the regional novel to its highest level by paying homage to the past."

*Mary Peters*, set between 1880 and 1920, discusses the shifting nature of some seacoast towns during the sometimes wrenching decline of Maine's position as a great sea power and the arrival of out-of-state rusticators to Maine. It was a shift that Chase obviously regarded with deep sadness.

In *Mary Peters*, she wrote: "There was something immeasurably sad to her in the sight of a grandson of a shipmaster in the foreign trade shingling the roof of a summer cottage for his livelihood . . . something sadder in the knowledge that the strangers, who by their demands supplied that livelihood, knew little and cared less for the boy's history."

In writing *Mary Peters*, Chase was greatly influenced by Sarah Orne Jewett's *Deephaven*, which also depicted the deterioration of a once-prosperous coastal port. Chase followed *Mary Peters* in 1935 with *Silas Crockett* (reprinted by Islandport Press, 2003), an epic that follows the lives of four generations of a Maine seafaring family and also chronicles the changes along the coast.

As with *Mary Peters*, Chase carefully researched *Silas Crockett* to maintain historical accuracy; she even took the family name Crockett from a sailor who let her hold the wheel of an old steamboat, *Catherine*, that once plied Maine waters. Biographer Perry D. Westbrook wrote that *Silas Crockett* "epitomizes an era in American cultural history." And the Baxter Society, in association with the Maine Historical Society, named *Silas Crockett* as one of its "One Hundred Distinguished Books that Reveal the History of the State and the Life of its People."

While Chase considered *The Edge of Darkness* (1957) the final installment of her "Maine" trilogy, *Windswept* (1941), which made her rich and famous, was deeply rooted in the state as well, but explored deeper issues.

Of course, Maine was not her only subject. She also wrote the novels *Dawn in Lyonesse* (1938), *The Plum Tree* (1949) and *The Lovely Ambition* (1960), as well as several books about the Bible, including *The Bible and the Common Reader* (1949), *The Psalms for the Common Reader* (1961) and *The Prophets for the Common Reader* (1963). She was also hired by John D. Rockefeller Jr. to write a biography of his wife, *Abby Aldrich Rockefeller* (1950).

Ultimately, Chase wrote more than thirty books, as well as dozens of essays, articles and short stories. Still, Chase is best remembered for her contributions to Maine literature and her wonderful descriptions both of Maine's glorious past and the powerful forces that transformed it, not always for the better.

Her work gained her significant recognition as both a writer and lecturer. In 1959, Chase received the Hale Award for distinguished writing by an author with New England connections. She also received an Honorary Doctor of Letters from the University of Maine and Bowdoin College, Honorary Doctor of the Humanities from Colby College, Doctor of Letters from Northeastern University and Doctor of Letters from Smith College.

Through it all she never forgot her roots.

She once wrote: "I am daily grateful that I was born of good, simple New England stock, had seafarers among my ancestors, was one of a large family, and can forevermore count Maine as my home. To these circumstances I owe whatever I have accomplished; and whatever honor there is in that accomplishment is not my own but that of the State of Maine."

Mary Ellen Chase died in a Northampton, Massachusetts, nursing home in 1973; she then returned home for good. She is buried in her hometown of Blue Hill, in a family plot that overlooks the coast of Maine.

Dean Lawrence Lunt
New Gloucester, Maine
October 2005

# Foreword

*By Mary Ellen Chase*
Excerpt from the *Colby Library Quarterly*, March 1962

Among all my novels, I am most fearful of those about Maine, largely, I suppose, because I am conscious of failure not only in myself and in whatever small power I may possess over words and their elusive ways, but also toward the rich heritage which I have been given, either by happy chance or by the Grace of God.

*Mary Peters* was born in my mind at least twenty-five years before Mary, her mother, Sarah Peters, her father, who was captain of the *Elizabeth*, the officers and sailors of the ship, and the village of Petersport had any shape at all beyond the dim dreams and visions. I suppose its beginning goes back to my grandmother's stories when I was a child in Blue Hill. My grandmother, Eliza Ann Wescott Chase, who was born in 1827 on a farm ten miles north of Blue Hill village, went to sea for eight years between 1852—when she set forth on a disastrous honeymoon with my grandfather, Captain Melatiah Kimball Chase—and 1860 when my grandfather retired from his job as master of three successive ships. His ships sailed to Mediterranean and South American ports and even to the Far East during those wonderful years when our American Merchant Marine, largely of New England origin and genius, became famous throughout the world. One of my grandmother's favorite stories, which she always told us on Sunday afternoons, was of the port of Cadiz in Spain. It was a snow white city, she always said, rising from the blue water, gleaming in the Spanish sun, like some New Jerusalem awaiting tired, seaworn exiles from home. I first learned from her, I am sure, the meaning of a symbol; and although I myself have never read *Mary Peters* because I lack the courage, I think it begins with the words: "Mary Peters first saw Cadiz in 1880. She was nine years old then."

My grandmother always hated and feared the sea, and with ample cause. Yet she understood what it had to give women of her generation who loved their shipmaster husbands too much to remain at home while they sailed upon it. And this perception she somehow managed to convey to me as a child—this understanding of its gifts as well as of its terrors, this sense of a great and various world beyond our own small harbor and our own Maine hills.

Cadiz thus became a symbol for me, too, remaining always in my mind, together with my grandmother's memories of long hours on a quarterdeck while the benign tradewinds blew; of gay, fearless days in one port or another; of this sailor and that; of strange harbors and tongues; of gallantry and cold and danger; and, above everything else, of a life bigger and wider and more full of meaning than that of my inconsequential childhood. She also taught me to see the sky, especially at sunset when many-shaped clouds lay above the horizon, in terms of the foreign harbors which she had known. "That looks like Riga on the Baltic," she would say, "with the dark hills beyond." Or: "There's Marseilles. I can almost hear the clatter upon the piers."

The University of Maine contributed more than a little to *Mary Peters*. I knew the Searsport Colcords there, Lincoln, Joanna, and Maude, all of whom had been reared at sea. They gave me the material for Mary Peters' lessons there, for they had all prepared for college in a ship's cabin under the teaching of their respective mothers and of well-read ships' officers, like Mary's beloved Mr. Gardiner.

My own voyages across the Atlantic contributed perhaps most of all. I crossed it in 1921, 1924, and during the four summers between 1930 and 1933 when *Mary Peters* was at long last beginning to be written. From the decks of whatever ship I was on I studied the sea and the sky; took careful notes on every phase of the weather, on every flight of birds; observed colors or their lack; saw a rainbow in both sky and sea; let no detail of fog or wind or waves escape me. The sad episode of the drowning kitten happened before my very eyes in 1921. I went to Marseilles, spending hours along its untidy waterfront, and more hours looking at London Post. I went to Genoa, Naples, the Piraeus and Athens, the Balearic Islands. I never went to Cadiz, for I have learned that symbols do not often bear exploration.

As to characters in books, it is difficult if not impossible to describe their creation. I think it is safe to say, however, that no character in pure fiction is ever founded upon an actual person. Bits of conversation, tricks of speech, the odd use of hands, a pair of eyes, episodes and events, countless mannerisms—these, of course, all help in the creation of people in books; yet the people themselves remain the mysterious creation of the author, or of some Power quite outside him. He is rarely if ever sure of just how or whence they came. *Mary Peters* (whose name is that of my great-great-grandmother) is an idea more than she is a person. She is modelled upon no one, nor is any other character in her book. She was created solely for the purpose of showing how a childhood spent largely at sea might help to form a mind and an imagination invulnerable against time, chance, and tragedy. I hope she does this.

# I
# The Sea

# The Sea

## 1

Mary Peters first saw Cadiz in 1880. She was nine years old then. She had awakened early to the swift knowledge that the ship was quiet, not plunging or rolling, not pitching or swooping, not whining or groaning in her bolts and beams or rattling her gear, not even perceptibly swinging to the tide, but instead, still, tranquil, idle. She had awakened also to the querulous cries of gulls, to their dark shadows wheeling across the mist-dimmed glass of her port, closed only the night before because of bad weather. Slipping into her clothes and not stopping even to wash her face and hands in her tin basin, she had run quickly up on deck, where now she stood with her father and stared, round-eyed, at the dazzling whiteness of this strange city. Its high, encircling wall which kept the sea out, its domes and spires, turrets and pinnacles and minarets reaching upward, the confusion of its many homes, even the sunswept lines which marked its narrow streets—all white beneath a sky of Spanish blue.

Standing there on that June morning with the tantalizing, many-odoured land smell once again after long days in her nostrils, with the gulls circling, screaming and swooping after galley refuse, and the ships of many countries anchored here and there in the still harbour, she thought of all the white things she had ever known in her short life. There was the white of Monday sheets on Maine summer fields, weighting down the buttercups and daisies, which made wet, shadowy spots against their whiteness; there were blossoming syringas and lilacs against white Maine doorways and the freshly painted spire of the church at home, on the hill above the sea; and there was the crisp whiteness of a rare party-frock with flounces and ruffles and lacy furbelows, which, fashioned for her during a brief sojourn to wear at Ellen Kimball's birthday party, had been done up in newspapers by her mother and left

3

behind (with many yearnings and a few secret tears on Mary's part) as being neither suitable nor necessary for a little girl at sea.

But these images of the land which she summoned up from some deep, shadowy recess in the back of her mind, where land things always stayed, inevitably gave place to fresher, clearer pictures of white things at sea. There was the continual white wash of the ship, lounging past their bows, hurrying aft as they cut through, churned astern into white foam, following them on and on; there was the sudden, quickening sight of distant, spreading canvas against a clear horizon, seemingly the whitest thing in a vast, unpopulated world; and there was the strange, incomprehensible coming of fog, heralded only by the breaking into white caps of steely, perhaps not unquiet, waves and the sudden lowering of the clouds to shut them in. Then the first wraiths of silvery mist like spray above the sea began to thicken as though they were joined by innumerable sweeping hosts, and within but a few minutes they were slipping, a phantom ship through a universe of phantoms, even their own sails but dark and indistinct blots against the clinging whiteness.

There was the white of infrequent snow, which sometimes on a winter voyage came swirling from a black sky to fall athwart a gray ocean, making the scoured surface of hatchways dingy and smudgy by contrast and heightening the grime of mildewed and weather-stained sails. Again and again, just before she went to sound sleep at night in her narrow berth—a sea sleep which carried one millions of miles from the earth—she glimpsed through her porthole the white circles of foam on a black sea, which only the foam made visible, while she murmured a drowsy prayer for themselves and for all others doing business in such great waters. And as for the white of her party-dress in its tightly closed drawer so many hundreds of miles away, was it whiter than the white of nightdresses and petti-coats and drawers which were washed on sunny days and hung in the rigging, there to billow and flap in the wind and to prove how gray or yellow the colour of canvas really was?

But Cadiz was whiter yet, she told herself, as she stood there gazing upon it on that June morning. There it was, projecting so far into the Atlantic that it held as it were its own harbour in the great hollow of its outstretched hand. There it was, seemingly a dream city where everyone was asleep or at least under a spell of some kind and quite unaware of storms and fogs and high winds which had made heavy running for them under upper topsails nearly all a long voyage. There it was, secure and sunswept and quiet, holding the sea at bay with its white wall.

That shining whiteness she was never in all her life to forget. Although she saw it then for the first and the last time, Cadiz ever afterward was to remain in her mind through many and varying years as the imperishable symbol of security, stability, and quiet order—a place both unassailable and unafraid, a place where one actually knew where one was in a wide, colossal world of uncertainty, a still harbour which had, as it were, miraculously caused to cease the creakings and groanings, bangings and slattings of wood and iron, rope and canvas, all the multifarious and incessant uproar of a ship making small way in bad weather. Flashing upon her tired little mind and longing eyes in one ecstatic vision of pure delight, it was not unlike the beatific vision of the City of Heaven to the Apostle, transcending in jasper bulwarks and blazing emerald streets all earthly perplexities and sorrows. Here, to Cadiz, although she little realized it then, she was in spirit to return, not once but many times, as to some ancient, long-established truth, no tool of time, no prey to uncertainty, but rather impervious to chance and necessity, invulnerable against the anxiety, suspense and sorrow of the life she was to live.

Doubtless the first, tenacious impression of the city became more deeply rooted in her imagination by a more tangible acquaintance later in the day. The ship's carpenter, a bow-legged, grizzled man named Ellis, discoursed at length to her and her brother John on what manner of town it was as they followed him about his tasks during the morning. He had a way of looking up harbours and ports of call in a fat book he owned and then divulging his knowledge to chance and patient listeners, much to the scorn of the common sailors to whose casual lives ports meant nothing at all except drink and women and subsequent flat pockets. He was inordinately proud of his first name which, being Vespasian, was seemingly a constant call upon meet and requisite intelligence. He did not love a ship or the sea, though he hailed from Searsport, that home of ships and deep-water captains; but he had a fancy nevertheless for odd nooks and corners of the world, and a ship provided ways and means of satisfaction. He had, too, a quaint, philosophic mind, not uncommon to ships' carpenters whose business it is to set things straight after confusion and disaster and to keep things in working order.

John Peters at this time did not love ships either. He looked upon voyages in them as painful interims between haymaking at home on hot July days, trout-fishing, and a friendly life with animals on his uncle's farm. Perhaps this common distrust of the sea bred a sympathy between the boy and the slow-voiced, deliberate Ellis. At all events John adored him and followed him here and there about the decks, holding his tools or willingly running forward to fetch something from his shop, which smelled of fresh shavings, paint, and newly greased iron.

"As I make out from my book," he said to the children while John hung on his words and Mary, to whom breakfast had meant a half-hour's deprivation, still gazed across the water, "it's an old town and a wicked one. King Solomon himself used to trade here to get presents like ivory and gold for his seven hundred wives. And you children ought to know how long ago that was even if you can't get to Sunday school as all children ought. Perhaps he came here himself; anyhow, he sent ships and ships. And Hannibal was here, too, stopping a great while to get his elephants and men all together to cross the Alps on Rome. When you once get home to school again, you'll learn about it. And the Romans—they built a wall, too, not this one you see but centuries ago and now all underneath the sea. The Romans—they were great folks for walls. I don't rightly know how many they built, but there was a sight of them all over the world. And the Romans lived here in great numbers, as I make out, because they loved luxury and sin and too much to eat. That city there, for all it looks so quiet, children, was once as gay and wicked as Sodom and Gomorrah, which the Lord destroyed, cut off, root and branch. And then the Moors came and built some of those white, heathen towers you see to try to drive out what Christians there was left, and there was wars and rumours of wars in these parts. Oh, there have been great goings-on for centuries in that old city! Climate's a mighty powerful thing on people and nations, children," he concluded, sucking on his empty old pipe, "and too much sun and warmth is just as bad for folks as too much fog and cold."

Could there be too much sun, Mary wondered, too much sun anywhere in the whole world? Without sun the city could not shine, could not send up into that shimmering sky those thin lines of light from its many spires. Was it a bad thing to be warm, to be gay even, and once in a long while to eat whatever one liked? Even now little red-sailed boats were coming from the shore laden with fresh fruits, oranges and grapefruits, plums and apples, pineapples, bananas, and great clusters of white grapes which jeweled the water with a riot of liquid colour. Others would come with fresh fish and meat, bread and nuts and wine, new cheese and butter. Her father and mother would bargain and buy for both cabin and fo'c'sle, and as they resumed their long voyage at sundown, there would be a blessed change from the fare of kegs and tins and barrels.

John's eyes watched Ellis smooth with his plane a bit of splintered rail, but his mind pondered Hannibal's elephants. How large a stretch of level ground would it take to line up even fifty elephants? How much larger a piece for them to charge across? Acres of land where one could walk and run, solid earth where one need never fear strange qualms in one's stomach, persistent even after months at sea. And if elephants for an army, then horses as well—great kindly beasts which champed and munched, wheezed and snorted in their stables, snuffled in their grain-bins, and blew out jets of water when they were thirsty after long marches. Such horses would take hundreds of men to curry and card and brush them and blacksmiths with blazing forges to see that their shoes were right. And if horses, then cows and goats and sheep, for an army must be fed. And great, lumbering racks of hay following after the whole army host and drawn, perhaps, by scores of yokes of stout red oxen, like Star and Bright at home.

Were there nooning trees in Cadiz, he wondered, when that great wall was built, for workmen to rest under in the middle of the day, to eat their lunch away from the hot sun, and to drink cold swipes of molasses and ginger water, brought out to them by some women as his aunt brought pitchers to the Maine haymakers? Or in those old times were they worked all day without any rest at all like the children of Israel under King Pharoah?

That afternoon they went ashore with Ellis and the second officer, who, having sundry commissions to perform, left them to their garrulous conductor. Their feet felt too large in their stiff shoes, which got caught now and then in the cobbled streets, and little streams of water ran down their backs under their warm clothes. Used as they were to the cleanliness and order of the ship, the narrow hot streets with the beating sun upon them and incalculable bits of filth everywhere about were somewhat disarming. But the whiteness prevailed in glaring white walls hung with roses and red trumpet-vines, and all manner of strange, unknown flowers, which sent down heavy perfume upon them and made them quite giddy at times with the heat. There were dirty children in almost no clothes at all who laughed at Mary's straw bonnet and short hair, and perhaps more at her round, serious gray eyes. There were countless beggars, whose hope of good and easy prey must be continually and roughly thwarted by Ellis, and innumerable goats with dirty, matted hair, and donkeys with red panniers and bells, which tinkled softly whenever they raised feet or tails against the black swarms of sticky flies. In a crowded marketplace of many wares and unfamiliar tongues they spent some hoarded pennies after much irritated gesticulation over their value on the part of Ellis and some stray Spanish words which he had picked up somewhere, to their great admiration and to the amusement of the vendors. John purchased a china donkey with red panniers for coins and a cork in the bottom of each for release when overloaded, and Mary a brooch made of flower mosaics in every imaginable colour.

Later when the sun dropped lower and more people began to emerge from the white, closely shuttered houses, the three of them walked on a great promenade which bordered the sea wall and from which they could discern among hundreds of odd craft their own ship, the *Elizabeth*, the familiar tangle of her spars and ropes, and note with pride how well she looked as she rode the harbour water.

"And it's good and lucky for you, children," said Ellis darkly, holding a hand of each, "that she's there and your home with good Christian parents to bring you up the way you should go. What would you do, I want to know, if you was left here in a wicked place like this?"

But his own delighted preoccupation with all the arts of evil which he saw everywhere displayed denied his pious concern even as it lent spice to him as a companion.

Here on the wide promenade they passed all manner of persons, grander than those in the crowded town but perhaps fully as wicked. Dark men with plumed hats and sashes, some of whom had guitars hung about their necks, escorted dark, beautiful ladies who seemed to laugh most of the time, throwing back their heads and showing their white teeth. One of these in a fit of sportiveness, quite alarming to the shrewd eyes of the vigilant Ellis, tucked a rose in the black band of Mary's bonnet, tilting up her chin with a jeweled forefinger and bursting into a peal of laughter at the child's staid surprise. When she had passed by with the two amused gentlemen who accompanied her, she turned back to laugh again and to wave her hand. There were veiled ladies, too, mysterious and distant, and bearded, rather disheveled men in white and brown burnouses. There were black priests in flat black hats going about barefoot upon their somber business. There was music from brilliantly arrayed bands in open green parks and nearer occasional music from strolling players who picked at or blew from every sort of odd instrument strung somewhere about them. And always there were the sun and the blue, lounging sea and below in the harbour the clamorous desperation of hungry gulls.

They joined the second officer on the quay as the sun went still lower and rowed home across the great, encircling bay, in and out among the many boats, music still drifting out to them above the steady rhythm of their locks and oars, above the cries and calls and clatter from decks and galleys. On board there was the familiar bustle of getting underway, for they had no cargo for Cadiz, being bound east through the Canal for Java where their voyage would end, some time or other, one never said when. Just before dusk they slipped out on a full Cadiz tide when the great tower of San Sebastian had already begun to stream forth its beacon and the harbour vessels to hang their lights. Mary stood on the quarterdeck while the sailors ran round the capstan to bring up the anchor, drowning in their raucous chanties the now distant music from the shore.

> *The ship went sailing out over the bar*
> *O Rio! O Rio!*
> *Turn away, love, away*
> *Away down Rio!*

As they made for open ocean she watched the bright lights of Cadiz pricking the dusk like mellow, hanging fruits. It might be a wicked city, but it was beautiful and serene. The heat and dirt of its narrow streets were forgotten once and for all time, and only her vision of the morning remained.

The dark blue of the sky fell nearer; a star appeared; the *Elizabeth* caught the light wind and lay over like a swooping gull to the foaming water. And Cadiz with its incredible whiteness soon lay far astern like some drifting, crumpled flower across great stretches of sea.

2

Unlike her brother, Mary Peters did not dislike or mistrust the sea. Perhaps, indeed, as a young child she thought little of it so far as definite sentiment was concerned, merely taking it for granted as children everywhere are likely to take for granted those familiar places and associations in which they have long found themselves. Her father's ship was to her quite as safe and substantial a home as her grandfather's big brick house and the limitless waters on which it sailed as natural and secure a setting as green Maine fields and rocky pastures. Indeed, for some nights after her infrequent returns home she slept restlessly in a great four-posted bed with feathers and a bolster; and several days always elapsed before she could correctly measure the distance between her feet and the ground and become accustomed to its sudden and level solidness against the soles of her shoes.

Also unlike her brother she had been born at sea, or at least in the harbour of Singapore, they having arrived just in time for her to be washed and dressed by a brown woman instead of on the high seas by her father and the second officer. The women of the last century who had taken as husbands for better or for worse the masters of ships in the foreign trade knew well they were at the unsolvable mercy of wind and weather and accepted their lot with gallantry and humour. To bring forth at home or at least in port was, of course, best if manageable. If not, one took the chance and made no fuss about it.

As a matter of fact, it was Ellen Kimball who should have been born on the *Nautilus* in Singapore, for it was her father who had contracted for the voyage. But he, alas! was unequally yoked with an inland wife who at the last moment nervously conceived the fantastic notion of carrying a nurse aboard, a proposal which had been received by that portion of Petersport society representing the sea with much comment, hilarious and even bald. And it all ended in a quick and generous exchange of masters, with Sarah Peters studying her private calendar, packing their chests and bags, and leaving John to his grandparents. Ellen Kimball was born safely and decently in a bed at home while an equinoctial gale tore at the shutters and the nurse thanked her lucky stars she was where she was; and Mary Peters on the same day but one uttered her first and lusty cry in the close, hot cabin of the *Nautilus*, confirming her tired mother's healthful notion that things usually turned out well enough if one just didn't get too much worked up over them.

Sarah Peters had, in fact, sufficient and eloquent occasion to remember that voyage of well over one hundred days had even Mary been out of the reckoning. With internal evidence prophesying that her time was shortened and with nasty weather proving a bit irritating, she had been sewing late one afternoon on Mary's things when she heard confused and stumbling steps on the companion-way. The door burst open to let in the first officer and the warm, sickening smell of fresh blood. He asked in a thickened voice if the captain was in the chart room, and as he turned thereto, suddenly bending his back, she saw a hatchet well-lodged between his shoulder blades. She became nurse then to a dying man, dragging out the hatchet with her own hands and getting him extended on the cabin floor with pillows and brandy while her husband felled to the deck with a bar of iron the two sailors, jail-birds from Liverpool, who had stirred up the mutiny.

They buried the first officer at dawn in a blue, smoke-like mist so clinging and heavy that they lost sight of his canvas-wrapped body before it hit the water with a smacking sound. She herself, large with new life even as she stood with death, read from the New Testament while the officers held their caps in their hands and kept wary eyes on the dim fo'c'sle.

"I am the Resurrection and the Life, saith the Lord. He that believeth in Me though he were dead, yet shall he live, and he that liveth and believeth in Me shall never die."

She asked of Death where was its sting and of that cold, deep grave where was its victory, although she well knew that the abiding-place of both would be long in Petersport where his mother lived and her own sister whom he was to have married once that voyage was over. Then she said a prayer as they committed him to the water, unused as she was to praying aloud in words, because she wanted them to know that he had been buried with a prayer.

"Receive, O Lord, the soul of this, Thy servant, which we now give into Thy keeping."

Her high, strained words went out into the blue mist like blunted arrows.

He had been a young man with an enviable record at sea, and the *Nautilus* had been his first charge as chief officer. He had had an odd, quick way of extracting intense pleasure from the most ordinary things, flying fish, queer bits of seaweed, the sun when it was cut into a perfect half by the horizon and the water.

Mary had been but three weeks old when they resumed their voyage. Except for some months in her babyhood and a term of school at home now and then, she was to sail until she was fifteen and ready for the Petersport Academy. She throve at sea. She grew brown and ruddy with lithe, strong arms and legs like a boy's. Her brother throve well enough also so far as his body was concerned, although he never outgrew sea-sickness in a certain sort of motion. But in his mind he was always for the land, much to his father's chagrin. He had a passion for farm animals and missed them intolerably when he was absent from them; and although they tried all manner of substitution in the way of pets, goats and monkeys, rabbits and even dogs, pets did not thrive at sea. Instead they were forever causing major tragedies which John bore but ill, so that they came more and more to alternate his voyages with stays at home. And when he was fifteen and Mary but eleven, he unpacked his chest for the last time with a warm, engulfing pleasure at his heart and began his Latin grammar in the red brick Academy.

Perhaps the first and clearest of those manifold impressions and images which her peculiar environment was to inscribe upon her sensitive imagination arose naturally enough from the sea itself and those incalculable, ever-present, seemingly capricious forces of weather which governed it. Surrounded always by watchful,

prophesying eyes, accustomed as she was to the daily scrutiny of
the chart at nightfall to note what progress they had made and
where they were on a wide expanse of white paper designating a
wider ocean, she grew weatherwise long before she could remember it. She knew the skies, those gray, brooding skies of certain
mornings, close upon them, breaking later in the day to move
upward and make the distant ocean blue long before they themselves had reached it. She knew those pale, solitary days when the
sky was wan and dappled and the sea almost the colour of thin
milk, when a rare sail seemed almost an intrusion upon their own
solitude in the immensity of space, and when, if one were ever
lonely, one was lonely then. There was a certain clearing at evening
which she learned to love and watch for, when the sun went down
in yellow splendour, purpling the steely sea and looking like some
vast conflagration until the amber and saffron clouds parted to sail
slowly away and leave a space of purest light in which a star would
come if one waited long and patiently enough.

On such evenings when the waves were tipped and then suffused with colour the flying fish would sometimes come, leaping in
perfect rhythm through wave after wave, down and up again, in
and out. She knew the cold, undistracted winter skies of northern
voyages, far, far above them, careless of them all, with Orion calmly
pursuing his hunt, red Aldebaran, and Sirius, brightest of all; and
buttoned high in her blue reefer, she watched them as they moved
night after night toward other skies, unhurriedly giving place to
other constellations. Ellis taught her their names when he was
aboard and the dictionary how to spell them; and she inscribed
them painstakingly in a logbook of her own which her father
made for her and in which, along with a careful copy of his chart-
ings, she entered sundry matters of her own observation. The
southern, tropical skies, she early discerned, were more intimate
and familiar, cloudless, bending close over them, their stars like

mellow lamplight and their great orange moons almost fragrant in their richness.

She learned something of winds, too, upon which they were utterly dependent and, as she grew older, the art of being undismayed before them and their indisputable power. She grew used to that sudden shudder of the ship from bow to stern, from main truck to keel, before an unexpected blast and her plunging about like some startled beast until she was trimmed to it and knew where she was. And she knew, alas! the days when there was no wind at all and they wallowed about on a calm sea in obedience to strange undercurrents. Then the ship gave up her magic and much of her dignity also, whining and rattling in her rigging as though she were, indeed, out of temper, slatting her canvas like a peevish child. She knew and loved those long days when they had once caught the Trades and ran before them, mild days of sun and blue sea and steady wind sometimes lasting for weeks on end. Then the ship came into her own again with no need of apology for her behaviour. She made time with filled sails, dipping between the easy waves, yielding herself and all she was to wind and water; and on her decks was the delightful, unbroken monotony of all things going well and little to do. In the morning the sailors holystoned and scoured, and the water carriers with great buckets followed after, sluicing over the scrubbed portions which almost immediately dried in the sun and wind. In the afternoon her mother sewed on the quarterdeck or read aloud, while forward the sailors lounged and smoked, spliced rope or worked at the spunyarn winch, now and then singing those songs which hang about a sailor's world, framed no one knows where, but common to the Seven Seas and lingering in the very air above them:

# The Sea

*Oh, Boston's a fine town, with ships in the bay,*
*And I wish in my heart it was there I was to-day,*
*I wish in my heart I was far away from here,*
*A-sitting in my parlor and talking to my dear.*
*Then it's home, dearie, home, it's home I want to be,*
*And it's home, dearie, home, across the rolling sea,*
*Oh, the oak and the ash and the bonny el-lum tree,*
*They're all a-growin' green in my own countree.*

*My name was Robert Kidd, when I sail'd, when I sail'd,*
*My name was Robert Kidd, when I sail'd,*
*My name was Robert Kidd, God's laws I did forbid,*
*And so wickedly I did, when I sail'd.*

*My parents taught me well, when I sail'd, when I sail'd,*
*My parents taught me well, when I sail'd,*
*My parents taught me well, to shun the gates to Hell,*
*But against them I rebell'd, when I sail'd.*

*Come all you young and old, see me die, see me die,*
*Come all you young and old, see me die,*
*Come all you young and old, you're welcome to my gold,*
*For by it I've lost my soul, and must die.*

*We had one lady fair on board, Bridget Reilly was her name.*
*To her I promised marriage and on me she had a claim.*
*She tore up her flannel petticoats to make mittens for our hands,*
*For she could not see the sea-boys freeze on the Banks of*
    *Newfoundland.*

Of rains she remembered longest those sudden, violent rains
of the tropics, coming to cut a still sea which had extended sometimes for days on every side like a mass of hot, solidifying grease.

How welcome it was! How they brought out every barrel and keg and bucket to be filled to the brim with fresh water for washing or even for drinking if their supply was low! Best of all were the days when it rained for hours. Then they would close the scuppers and catch the rain on the deck. Sometimes it came in great warm sheets, pelting the deck planks with heavy drops and then splashing and swirling when it had once covered them, veritable inches of rain swashing about with the motion of the ship. She and John then shed their clothes down to their lightest underthings, scrubbed and washed and rolled about with shouts of laughter. The sailors brought from the fo'c'sle their dirty shirts and dungarees, the cook the galley cloths and table linen, and there was much scrubbing with stiff brushes and strong soap. And as they slid on before the now freshening breeze and the sun came out once more, hotter than before, their clothes dried in the rigging and they themselves felt a new cleanliness and respectability.

And as she grew older, there came sliding imperceptibly into her mind, becoming so much a part of her that it could not even be called a thought, the understanding that they themselves were a part of the element in which they moved. Their world, self-contained and regulated as it was, was in turn contained and regulated by a world of sky and wind and water. The ship took her pulse from the great, unseen heartbeat of the sea which sent a tremor from its very depths into them, now slowing, now quickening at its mighty will with which they themselves must be in harmony. They moved, floated, drifted at large with Eternity. They talked surprisingly little of things ashore. As a danger from storm or wind when it was once past seemed of small importance, so the affairs of a more confused world which they had left behind them faded into a background of relatively small significance. A port was always a surprise, welcome often to be sure and sometimes memorable, like Cadiz, but always startling in its concrete return to things they had half forgotten.

3

Not that life on a ship did not have its own concrete aspects also! From the time when the sniffing tug came alongside in New York or San Francisco or Liverpool until, after perhaps a three-months' voyage, they had reached their port somewhere or other, they were regulated by a discipline far more concrete and rigid, surely far more certain, than that discipline commanded by the forces outside themselves. From dawn to dawn the mathematical routine went on, drowsy men even while she slept leaving wheel and lookout to others whose turn it was to take them. Her own hours were regulated also, and with little variation she did the same things day after day.

In the morning after breakfast was over and the cabin had been set to rights, there were lessons, beginning at nine, ending precisely at twelve with only time to wash ink or pencil marks from one's hands before dinner. These went on, six days out of seven, and throughout all the months of the year, it being wisely decided that interruptions in port and furloughs at home more than equalled the vacation periods of land children. Moreover, without the companionship and competition of a real schoolroom progress was felt to be slower; and lastly Sarah Peters held herself in no high regard as a teacher although she did her utmost, conferring earnestly with school authorities at home and mapping out conscientiously just what her child (or children) might reasonably be expected to accomplish. What was more, perhaps indeed even the *most* important factor in the whole situation, if a child were working quietly at his books, he was out of mischief with no time hanging heavy on his hands as sea-time well might if it were not properly arranged.

They studied at the big table in the dining room beneath the skylight with the tumbler-rack hung like a chandelier over their

heads, making more or less of a clatter in rough weather; and they
recited what they had learned to their mother in the main cabin
between eleven and twelve when the steward was busy with his
preparations for their dinner. Their mother sat with them while
they worked, darning or sewing, both to be at least partially ready
for their questions and to see that they attended strictly to the
business at hand. During the four years after John left for home
and the Academy, Mary was a solitary pupil except for one blissful
six months when a little girl from San Francisco made the voyage
around the Horn way to Liverpool and back again. She became
Mary's room-mate and constant, beloved companion, doing her
lessons, too, in precisely the same manner and never once getting
over the delightful strangeness of it.

It was pleasanter, at least in her earlier years, when John was
there, even though he was much farther advanced in his books
than she, and even though he became irritated and kicked and
hitched about a bit over mighty diagrams of Longfellow and the
parsing of words in "Snowbound."

"I don't see it at all," he would say petulantly to his mother, or
at least as petulantly as he dared, trying her out of the corner of
his eye. "And boys at home have sentences, not 'The Psalm of
Life.' There isn't a paper long enough in the whole chart room for
all these verses. And it's a horrid poem anyway. I hate poems!"

Problems made him scowl the most, not so much over their
difficulty as over the matters with which they dealt. When A and
B were mowing a field with C to help them now and then for a
few hours, Mary knew that he was more homesick than actually
puzzled over the reckoning of time had they worked all three
together. Nor did he like any better the imaginary sectioning of
apples in common fractions when their own supply had long since
run out, or problems in percentage which had to do with a
farmer's profit and loss on the sale of sheep and horses and yokes

of oxen. History he loved and learned easily, dreaming over Daniel Boone and Ponce de Leon until his mother called him sharply back to the narrow world of the cabin and the green felt table.

"John, you're staring into space again. Please keep your eyes on your book."

And John, remembering cautiously that one did not answer back on board ship even as little as one ventured to do so on land:

"I'm just thinking. The teachers at home all tell us to think and think. You can't learn without thinking."

She herself rather liked her lessons than not, even when she must do them all alone. More than John she developed early a sense of mental as well as of physical order together with a stubborn tenacity which made her hold on to baffling, difficult things until they were straight in her mind. She did not like to put away her arithmetic and slate with a perplexing sum to which she had the wrong answer. It was somehow out of keeping with the only life she knew well, like a rope loose when it should be tight or an idle, slatting sail which should be filled with wind. There was always, too, approval to be won, the surprised approval of teachers and supervisors at home when they examined her progress between voyages, the quiet approval of her father, who devised clever ways of making study more exciting. When at ten she had mastered long division sufficiently to put 1492 into 1,000,000,000, to multiply the divisor by the quotient, and, adding the remainder, procure the dividend without a single erasure or mistake, he framed for her a diploma of his own which proclaimed her ready for fractions and which was, moreover, signed by the officers, first, second, and third, after they had witnessed her examination, standing straight and serious as though on duty behind her.

"This is to certify," the diploma read in her father's neat printing, "that Mary Bartlett Peters has passed with credit from Long Division to Common Fractions and has been duly examined

therein by the undersigned. 13th January, 1881. Lat. 42° 58' N.
long. 14° 24' W.

William B. Peters, *Captain.*

Rufus Nichols, *Chief Officer.*

John C. Pendleton, *2nd.*

Nathan Osgood, *3rd.*"

And always during the morning she could be sure of the
afternoon when, once her hair was brushed and a cleaner apron
on, she could read, curled up on the bench in the main cabin or
in a corner on deck. There was always some sort of library aboard,
sets of novels more or less complete, odds and ends of books of
every conceivable sort, good, mediocre, and poor, pious books in
those days of tracts from Seamen's Societies, books on elementary
medicine, *Black Beauty, Uncle Tom's Cabin, The Wide, Wide World*,
collections of sentimental poems designed for Christmas gifts, a
complete Shakespeare in one volume, textbooks long outdated, a
few of the popular stories of the eighties, full of tears and rather
diluted passion and depicted by such novelists as the Reverend E.
P. Roe and Mrs. Amelia Edith Barr.

She read, or at least sampled all of them, never getting
enough, and always cherishing the exciting possibility of an
exchange. For not infrequently when two captains met in some
harbour, Valparaiso or Hongkong or San Francisco, they would
quickly decide to swap libraries in order to ensure at least a partial
diversity in fare. Whereupon, without the trouble of examination,
after that casual manner bred by the sea, a boat from one would
transport its books to the other and take a chance on what it
might carry back across the water to its own shelves.

At four in the first dog-watch when the weather was good
there were games on deck, jackstones, and ball and jump-rope
before supper. After supper the chart was brought out and examined as to where they were, what the ship had done, and how in

general she was behaving. Mary loved the chart study and added her prognostications to those of the officers, always pleased that her father took or at least pretended to take them seriously. Comparisons were made then of other ships on the same sea on other voyages to the same port, and more prophecies were uttered in spite of the fact that one never knew what was ahead.

The second dog-watch was the time for swapping of yarns and tales of many good ships of their own time which they met at sea, sometimes overhauling them to the great pride of all on board, often seeing them in port, quiet, the beautiful tracery of their rigging etched against the sky. She grew accustomed to their names and business, British clippers in the emigrant and wool trade, carrying passengers to Sydney or to Melbourne and wool back home again. She knew the *Samuel Plimsoll*, the famous Aberdeen iron flyer, built in 1873, which had made many a passage from Plymouth to Melbourne in under eighty days, and once had herself seen her nearing London, heavy with Australian wool and ore. Some ships were unlucky, she knew, from their very launchings, like the ill-fated *Loch Ard* whose manifold dismastings in gale after gale were but dark prophecies of her final destruction five years later with fifty souls on board and whose story hung like a sinister shadow over more than one ocean. Such a ship the sailors termed a "killer." There was that grisly, oft-repeated tale, current in the eighties, of the *Cospatrick*, sailing from London in 1874 with over four hundred passengers for Auckland and burning off Cape Horn with only three survivors to relate a story unequalled among the many she knew for its hideousness. Of her boats only two had left her without mishap, carrying between them eighty-one persons without food or water. Men and women died then, one by one, as days succeeded one another, and their blood was sucked and parts of them were eaten by other crazed men and women who died, too, in their turn. That these things

were true or had been true even while she sailed, she knew full
well; and yet as she heard them in the peaceful dog-watch with all
things going as they should, they became but stories, not frightening her overmuch when at eight the crew marched aft for orders
and one began to think of prayers and bed.

There were rules, too, for children as well as for men and officers, and they were unquestioningly obeyed. Talk with sailors was
forbidden. Tools and sundry bits of gear were never to be touched
without permission. Children kept strictly away from fo'c'sle and
galley and did not go forward for walks and games unless attended
by one of the officers or by the carpenter or bo'sun. There were
places designated for one's own possessions, and there, and
nowhere else, they were kept in neatness and in order.

On Sundays discipline somewhat relaxed, especially in good
weather, and only the necessary work was done. Sarah Peters held
rigidly to the custom of Saturday-night bathing, and there was as
thorough a scrubbing in a tin tub in one's cabin as before the
kitchen fire at home. In the morning there were clean clothes in
every cabin; forward there was much shaving and sometimes hair-
cutting by some good-natured sailor who extracted payment in
tobacco if dimes were scarce; and all over the ship an air of added
decency prevailed. Instead of lessons the children were quizzed for a
full hour about Bible stories, how old Methuselah was when he at
long last died, full of years, and what King David said when he was
told of Absalom's tragic end. They memorized a Psalm also, set for
them a week ahead, and learned, if they were wise, a verse each day.
Before they could have their dinner, they must recite it; for in the
seventies and eighties parents still believed that children had souls
and were concerned on sea as well as on land over their salvation.

*Oh that men would praise the Lord for his goodness and for his*
*wonderful works to the children of men! . . .*
*They that go down to the sea in ships, that do business in great*
*waters,*
*These see the works of the Lord and his wonders in the deep.*
*For he commandeth, and raiseth the stormy wind which lifteth up*
*the waves thereof.*
*They mount up to the heaven; they go down again to the depths;*
*their soul is melted because of trouble.*
*They reel to and fro, and stagger like a drunken man, and are at*
*their wit's end.*
*Then they cry unto the Lord in their trouble, and he bringeth them*
*out of their distresses.*
*He maketh the storm a calm so that the waves thereof are still.*
*Then are they glad because they be quiet; so he bringeth them unto*
*their desired haven.*
*Oh that men would praise the Lord for his goodness and for his*
*wonderful works to the children of men!*

4

The souls of sailors, too, had a way of resting somewhat heavily
on the mind and conscience of Sarah Peters during the twenty
years which she voyaged with her husband. Not that hers was an
overly pious nature like those common to many New England
village women of the seventies and eighties. She had seen the
workings of too many strange faiths in too many lands to be
entirely circumscribed in one way of thought and behaviour.
Nevertheless, her heritage remained sturdy enough within her to
cause some little anxiety now and then over at least a few individ-
uals among those multifarious crews from every country beneath

the sun who shuffled up their ladder or gangplank for a voyage and ran down again in diverse ports of the world probably to be seen no more.

With some few exceptions they were as fortuitous and incidental a lot as the earth produced, their ways as trackless and past finding out as the uncharted ways of birds which sometimes appeared hundreds of miles from land, circling about for an hour, settling now and again upon the waves, and then disappearing into fog or sunshine. They were of every age and every description. Hardened, tattooed old tars, sometimes as valuable as they were profane, bunked in the fo'c'sle below mere lads in their teens whose mothers, she thought, must be worrying about them somewhere in the world. From Maine and Nova Scotia, Denmark and Ireland, Brazil and Spain and Portugal, they belonged in truth to no country and seemingly knew no anchorage. Rumours of decent food, lenient officers, lucky ships lured them aboard; and more persistent rumours in port of better fare, better treatment, and better luck lured them elsewhere.

She early learned their ways ashore from a less concerned husband and grew inured to what would have caused righteous horror in her friends at home. She saw the women who lingered about the quays and piers of every harbour, the cheap, filthy lodging-houses of the nearby streets, and the drinking-places which would take their money and fire their long-denied and ready passion. These things did not make her overly anxious as they would have made a land woman of her inheritance and generation. They were but inevitable clauses of that prescribed code which governed a common sailor's life; and she knew them for what they were, just as she knew for what it was that code of dull respectability which governed nine-tenths of the life ashore in Petersport from whence she came and in hundreds of other God-fearing towns and villages.

It was, in fact, not so much a moral or even a religious urge
that prompted her concern over their shifting fo'c'sles, but rather
something different, at once deeper and less tangible. Had she
remained at home, she would, true to her heritage, have laboured
and prayed for their conversion through the grace of God to a
new and better standard of living, their eschewing of women and
liquor and foul language; but since she had not remained at home,
the insistence of that heritage had become mellowed and leavened
until imperceptibly she had come to value the imagination of man
quite as much as his soul (if there were, indeed, any difference
between them!) and to hold a beautiful thing quite as necessary as
one which was called good in the somewhat limited connotation
of her day and generation. Life was strong and abundant in this
New England woman. She had bequeathed its strength and plenitude to her daughter; and in both the sea had wrought its steady,
intangible nourishment, the power and security of which only
later years on the land would reveal.

Sarah Peters did not analyze these things. Scrutiny into oneself
or into one's motives played no part either in her time, or above
all in the flexuous, drifting yet necessary environment of the sea.
She knew only that the life within her could and sometimes did
blossom into moments of unimaginable, incredible loveliness,
glimpses of the Eternal in time, rare moments which came and
went, which could not be sought or asked for, but by which one
steered one's course, wholly alive only while they lasted.

It was her hunger for such moments in others that caused her
anxiety. She hated to see the stray chance of them choked, cloaked
out of sight by hours and days of sordidness and sin. Doubtless
seeing in certain of the men (as such an imagination is forever
bound to do) possibilities which did not really exist, unable to recognize that *ex nihilo nihil fit*, she was quick to discern signs of
respect in them, crude graciousness, an interest in the children

with whom they must of necessity have little to do, generosity and instinctive kindness. She liked to recall those saddened, frightening days as they crawled toward Singapore in 1871, days and nights when she had paced her cabin in pain and wondered if Mary would ever wait a few hours longer. Mary had presents then, both before and after her arrival, odds and ends of whittling and carpentry, bits of jewelry and embroidery searched out of dunnage bags and surely intended for quite another purpose. A birth on a ship is lucky, and Mary's birth on the *Nautilus* tended just then to minimize the superstition that death is always the heaviest cargo any ship can carry. For the return voyage not a few of the crew signed on, coming aft a few weeks later, shaved and in clean dungarees to view the baby and to bespeak in their silent courteous manner no little admiration for Sarah Peters herself.

Knowing it was the last thing they welcomed, she never asked questions as to where they hailed from or what manner of family appendages they had left at home; but she had a smile for them as they changed watches or worked on the main deck. Home crews she liked best, New England men and boys from Gloucester and Marblehead, Bath and Boothbay and Rockland; and although these often faded out like the others from voyage to voyage, scrambling down the ship's side with dunnage bags on their shoulders and not even so much as a glance astern, she sent some thoughts after them to stay their wandering hearts. Next to them she inclined toward northern sailors, Swedes and Norwegians, Icelanders now and then, well-set, blue-eyed fellows who kept their clothes cleaner, worked better, and were generally more stable than the others.

Perhaps her inclination toward them dated from the return of her first voyage in 1866, as a bride. Among the sailors who had shipped in Liverpool was a Swedish boy, hardly sixteen, one would have said, from his smooth cheeks and long, ungainly legs, which waited for the rest of him to catch up with them. As he passed aft with the others of the crew at nightfall for the relief of the watch, she scanned his white face and knew that he was afraid. She came on deck one day in a high, sudden wind just in time to see him ordered aloft, and her heart stood still at the terror in his eyes as he hesitated a moment before springing to obey. She wanted to cry out in protest to the mate who had sent him there, but, remembering in time that such stern commands were a part of this relentless life which she had chosen, she ran below instead to pray frantically in her cabin and listen to the mad slatting of unmanageable canvas. When, unable to remain longer, she had again run to the deck, she was just in time to see him fall from far above, like some great flapping bird, catching here and there for one instant on blocks and stays before he struck the deck with a ghastly splintering of bone and tearing of muscles. He had not had time to be afraid, her husband said, in a vain attempt to soothe her, for she had seen his face. When they had gathered him up, like some refractory parcel of odds and ends which refuses to be put neatly together, and had made ready to sew him into fresh canvas, she herself had run through the shrieking wind to the fo'c'sle and demanded to see his small possessions. Among them she found a prayer-book, quite unused, in his own language and some clean handkerchiefs worked with his name in red cross-stitch:

JON ANDERSON

The men who were sewing with their great needles, which whined through the new canvas, stopped until she had stuffed the book and the handkerchiefs inside. And later when the deck was washed and he had been quietly dropped over the side, she sat in the creaking cabin beneath the swaying lamp and dictated a letter to the sailmaker, also a Swede, to be sent to his mother whose own letters she had found in his dunnage. No reply ever came to her. Her stark news seemed to have gone into a void as limitless as that which he had entered. But she prayed always thereafter that wherever he had gone, he might at least be unafraid, having, as she told herself ironically, surely worked out his own salvation in accord with the Scriptural command "with fear and trembling."

Nor was life before the mast usually so ill-starred and sinister. A fo'c'sle existence was a many-hued one not the less because of the steady influx and efflux of new and mysterious material. As they grew older, the children shared their mother's curiosity in the variety and diversity of types and characters upon whom they were dependent and who contributed so largely to the interest of their life.

Ellis, whom Sarah and William Peters had known as children, and who sailed with them as carpenter whenever he would, played the part of a busy and garrulous newsmonger, revealing all manner of fo'c'sle tittle-tattle as he worked upon the main deck or dickered at odd jobs about the after cabins.

"There's a Portugee feller for'ard, ma'am, that's got what you'd never in the world think of tattooed into his back. It's a picture no lady should see and that no man's any the better for seeing. I'm only telling you the truth. 'When you come to die,' I says to him, 'and want your sins forgiven,' I says, 'don't let the priest see your back.' 'Oh,' says he, in his queer lingo, 'I've seen 'em as would thank me for turning such a back as mine on 'em. They can't see such things every day! But when that time comes,' he says, 'I'll seek out the best I can get, for by the Lord I'll need him!'

"You'd never once think, would you, children, when you see that young I-talian there what he does half his off time a-sitting quiet in his bunk? You see him all good-natured and smiling and soft-voiced and hear him playing on his flute evenings so you'd never guess in a month o' Sundays what's occupying his mind and what he's up to. Now whether he does what he does for an outlandish kind of joke just to make other folks feel queer and crawly in their insides or whether he's actually got a serious purpose in his head, wicked as it is, it's hard to say. Lord knows he says it's serious enough, but when he says it's serious, he smiles just as if it couldn't be as serious as he says it is. Well, as I say, time will tell, and if it tells what he claims it will, it's going to be a mighty serious time for him. What does he do, you say? He sharpens a knife round and round on a piece of stone, not a whetstone but a stone he says is bound to add poison to any knife it sharpens. First, he spits on this stone, which is round and blood-red and fits into the palm of his hand, and then he grinds that knife on it till the stone is dry again. Three times he spits, and it's no secret he's keeping. He says right out with a smile on his face that he's sharpening it for a girl in Valparaiso that did him dirt once. 'Good Lord, man!' I says to him, 'you've shipped wrong! We're bound for the Java Straits,' I says. 'Valparaiso was last voyage but one.' 'There's time in plenty,' says he, letting his smile get away from him in the nicest sort of laugh. 'I wait well, and the knife's not ready yet.' And when he's dried up three lots of spit on that red stone with turning the knife round and round, he locks up both of them in a safety-box he has and hangs the key round his neck on a dirty string he wears, and there it dangles with the head of the Virgin Mary."

Mary walked forward one night in the second dog-watch with Ellis, holding close to his hand, and saw the Italian who was so calmly waiting for fate to take him toward Valparaiso. He was sitting with his back against a capstan playing his flute, his black eyes dreaming over the immeasurable miles of smooth, clear water. It was a still, spring evening with amber clouds drifting so low that one could see the pale blue sky behind them—a land evening when one sometimes thought of meadows and marshes with the sound of peepers and tree-toads. Mary fancied the notes of his flute floating out across the amber water, round and clear like soap-bubbles. She stood listening and staring at him until he became conscious of her and smiled at her with his eyes, making the flute then play a dance tune so that the soap-bubbles came faster and faster, bounding away in incalculable numbers. Later in bed she thought of the girl in Valparaiso and wondered what it meant to do dirt to people so that they sharpened knives on round, red stones with poison in them. She knew Valparaiso with its great harbour in a half circle like an ox's horns and wondered again in what house on its spur of hills the girl lived whom he would find some day.

There was an Irish sailor named Michael who had sailed twice with them and whom she remembered because of his right hand on which only the index finger remained. He had a superstition about his name, which was that of an archangel, and would never allow it to be shortened lest it incur the anger of the archangel and bring him ill luck. He could do incredible things with his one finger, curving it around the handles of the heaviest buckets or clinging with it aloft in the most perilous of positions. It was extremely ugly to look upon, but he was unconscionably proud of it and of the service it could render him. He carried three packs of grimy cards pinned securely in a pocket of his shirt and dealt them out on the fo'c'sle table, so Ellis said, with great dexterity. First, he dealt one pack in a circle, the next in a square, and the third in a five-pointed star. And try as they all did to mix them, the Jack of Hearts was sure to show up in precisely the place he said it would, now in one, now in another. Foolish as it seemed, the rest were afraid of him and his mad skill with the cards and forbore to shorten his name lest he work some curse upon them.

Sailors, Mary learned, believed all kinds of nonsense and imbued with it even stout New England boys who should have known better. They did not like to see birds circling far from land, believing them to be the souls of drowned mariners and capable of bringing the worst of luck. Some of these belonged especially to Mother Carey, the horrible witch-wife of Davy Jones, who had combed her hair with the largest bones of the sailors before she turned the smaller into birds to circle about over all the seas for years on end and never see the land. They hated sharks with malevolent hatred and felt that they did themselves and any ship incalculable service if they caught one on a great hook baited with salt meat and beat him to a cruel death. Certain black Atlantic fogs depressed them into moroseness; and a sun-dog might well bring any number and manner of disasters.

Usually impervious to their easy credulity and in point of fact often no seaman at all was the sailmaker, a practical necessity to every ship. Whatever his name might be, he went among the crew by that of Sails. Like carpentry his trade begat within him a certain philosophical outlook on the world. Not only did he put in order disordered things, but he was in league and partnership with mighty forces. He was the ally of the wind which without him was as useless as was his toil without its good favour. Like cook and carpenter he worked in no shifts, his time being dictated by circumstances and he himself the arbiter of it. He smelled of tar and hemp, beeswax, resin, and fresh canvas; and the hard skin of his knotted, calloused fingers was seamed and corded like the rope of his new reef-points. He sat for hours on the deck, tailor-fashion, repairing and patching, setting at naught the Biblical warning against new cloth upon old. Across the front of his shirt he wore a leather bib into which he stuck his great needles, and on the palm of his right hand was his thimble, encased in leather and securely strapped across the back.

Once when John was twelve his sewing and repairing had been used for quite a different purpose. Mary never forgot that day, young as she was. John, jumping rope on a slippery deck when there was a roll on, was hurled suddenly against a sharp angle of the companion-way. She had never seen such a gush of blood as that which weltered the deck from the gash on John's head or such awful whiteness as that which swept her mother's face and stayed upon it. Her father held John's head between his hands up there in the sun and wind. Even the sailors stood about in consternation with the officers. The medicine chest in the cabin supplied some tough string, which looked for all the world like thin wire; and it was the sailmaker whose fingers drew the awful, blood-filled hole in John's head together. For days she heard her father's quiet voice saying to John, "Steady, old man. Just a moment now. No fellow screams, you know, aboard a good ship."

Mary remembered the sailmaker afterward, whoever he was, as a slow, quiet man who took pride in his work and liked to read when he was free. She remembered the steady, crunching stabs of his great needles in and out of the heavy canvas and the whine of waxed thread as he drew it through—sounds which she sometimes heard through the open skylight as she did her lessons. She remembered, too, the calm, intent look on his face as he stood at the taffrail with short legs wide apart, gazing aloft at their filled sails whenever they ran before a fair wind.

## 5

John Peters would have been happier at sea could his life there have included the friendly company of animals. He might even have tolerated with better grace than he did the absence of horses and cows and the warm, homely smell of barns at supper-time, had the cold nose of some dog sniffed about his knees or nestled in his hand as he studied in the cabin. Dogs did not take to the sea, at least on the *Elizabeth*. They yelped and whined the first days out, obviously afraid of wind and water; and when they had once understood that there was no escape, that stretching on hearth-rugs and digging up old bones were now no more, they developed a nerve-racking mood of startled expectancy, trembling at sudden noises and never once relaxing into that stupid, blissful indolence so enviable in dogs. If they survived the voyage and were not humanely left ashore in some new and strange home, they invariably sickened and died once the *Elizabeth* had put to sea again. Puppies were no better. Even into one of four weeks, brought dotingly on board by John in an egg-basket, there had mysteriously been already injected the desire for companionship in kind, the need of green fields and rabbit-holes, of cats on back fences, and of hens to chase. It was pitiful to see these wants staring at one and be unable to supply even a meagre substitute.

The hope of a dog relinquished once and for all before John was ten, rabbits were tried. These were crass, unfeeling little beasts, and their failure at acclimation could certainly not be accredited to overly sensitive emotional natures. They had their home in the carpenter's shop in an elaborate house with sliding doors and shuttered windows built by Ellis and John, and quite unappreciated by its tenants who much preferred to sniff about for potato parings among piles of sawdust and shavings. They ate canned food when necessary without protest, gazing indifferently at nothing at all; but they were forever found wanting in the matter of rearing a family. Conceiving and bringing forth quite in accord with their prodigal habits on land, they were nevertheless a prey to a wholesale infant mortality which in one voyage alone wiped out three successive litters.

"This voyage has had nothing but death notices at breakfast," said Sarah Peters with vigour to Ellis, who thereupon, once they had reached San Francisco, presented John with a billy-goat and four bales of hay.

This creature provided makeshift chores for John, but, after the perverse and ingrowing character of goats, responded in no wise to his care and afforded no outlet for his affection. Its fixed, glassy, yellow stare above its ever-rotating jaws and its mincing tread were not warming to any heart; and no one felt regret when John tethered it in a Maine field and left it there.

Sailors sometimes provided diversion in the birds and beasts which they now and again carried about with them as mascots and talismans from which they refused to be separated. These purveyors of good fortune were usually parrots or monkeys of some species. Sarah Peters was not inclined to leniency toward them, violently forbidding them entrance to family quarters either on deck or in the cabins. Her moral nature rebelled against the filthy tricks of the monkeys and the profane and ribald language of the birds even though she often could not understand it; and as a good housekeeper she could not tolerate the chance of insect life of which they always gave outward and vigourous sign. It was quite enough, she said, that she had been called upon to endure the constant presence of rats which no New England housewife would put up with for an hour.

Rats were the best sailors imaginable. They were, indeed, the one animal which seemed to thrive on a life at sea. There was no ridding a ship of them. Even when terriers were sent into an empty hold in port for the express purpose of a general massacre, a goodly number always escaped to return again with the new cargo. They came and went through the cracks of tightly closed hatchways; they scuttled across decks in full light of day. It was nothing to be awakened at night by one or more scurrying across one's bed. Clothes and shoes must be put away securely in drawers against their certain depredations. Cats, poison, and traps were alike useless. They intimidated the first by reason of their numbers and were cunning enough to evade both the last. Bad as they were in ordinary temperatures, they became insufferable when the ship once slid into the tropics. There as, smitten with heat, she began to give out her odours (her own and those of whatever cargo she carried, wheat, guano, oil, hides, wool), the rats swarmed from the hold through all conceivable apertures and crevices and made themselves at home in cooler, more airy quarters.

Once in Valparaiso when Mary was eleven, the little daughter of the shipping agent to whom the *Elizabeth* was bound came on board to spend the night as Mary's guest. She had never been on a ship before. She was a dark-eyed Spanish child with quick, light steps, and, almost hysterical with excitement over so novel a home, she explored every cranny of every deck with Mary following after, quite bewildered by so much effervescence and by her own uncommon duties as hostess. She wore a pair of new red shoes, the like of which Mary had never seen before. They buttoned high up her leg and were finished at the top by a turnover cuff of shining black leather adorned with little black tassels. It was easy to see they were her especial pride, for she looked at them often as they whisked her about the ship, glancing now and then at Mary to see whether she were properly impressed by their beauty and elegance.

Mary was so impressed, in fact, not alone by the shoes but by the tremendous significance of a guest of her own, that, although she had been warned by her mother to close Gracia's things at bed-time securely in a drawer, she could not bear thus to divulge or even to suggest such a disturbing family secret as the presence of rats. Instead she trusted to luck and to a frantic prayer that all might be well. The consequences of her faith were humiliating in the extreme! In the morning the red shoes were no more than a network of frayed strips of leather surmounted by a few melancholy tassels and held limply together here and there by vanquished black buttons. Gracia wept as unrestrainedly as she had laughed the day before, refusing to eat her breakfast; and Mary, plunged headlong into an abyss of remorse and shame, wondered what on earth their two fathers found amusing in so tragic an occurrence. She willingly gave Gracia her best pair of boots, black with staid tops of felt, her chagrin not lessened by her recognition of the contempt with which they were sulkily put on. And it all ended with Mary fervently wishing never to have a guest again and with Gracia sullenly asking herself how she could ever have looked with ardour and envy upon a childhood spent at sea.

It may easily be imagined that not a member of the officers' mess on the *Elizabeth*, except perhaps John himself, looked with any degree of confidence upon a new pet when, upon the beginning of what was to end as his last voyage, he was presented with a kitten. Ellen Kimball was the donor. She had given a party on the occasion of her tenth birthday, and John and Mary had attended, the latter in the white party-frock which now must needs be lengthened to meet the requirements of two years' growth. They had taken Ellen as a gift a Javanese basket filled with candied Eastern fruits, odd nuts, paper flowers which opened miraculously in water, and some tiny packets of spiced tea. And Ellen's mother's practical mind had seen fit to return the basket which Sarah Peters could certainly use, she said, for any number of odds and ends, sewing appurtenances and the like, always in the way in a ship's cabin.

Ellen herself brought home the basket after supper, still clad in her party dress of sprigged pink mull with silvery ribbons at sleeves and waist. She was a mature child for ten years with a somewhat hard prettiness and a shrewd way of getting what she wanted. She was observant, too, and by keeping her eyes and ears open learned things of which other children of her day and generation were quite wholesomely ignorant. Even at ten she was beginning to push her scraps of information as far as they would go, putting two and two together and cherishing the result in her imagination after she went to bed at night.

She thought of John as she followed the country road to the Peters house, peering every now and then into her sagging basket to see if its contents were safe. He had grown bigger than she had any idea of during the months he had been from home. His tanned face at fourteen was taking on the lines of the faces of older boys, and he had a shy seriousness which piqued her and made her want to discover his thoughts and learn whether he liked girls or thought them useless and silly as did most of the boys she knew. Moreover, there was about him the glamour which always hangs about a comparative stranger and which in the last century was always accorded a boy returned from a foreign voyage.

She stopped at the gate and called to him. She did not want Mary to come running out on the doorstep as she might well have done and spoil their conversation. When he came shyly down the driveway and looked at her inquiringly across the white pickets, she gave him the basket, giggling at his surprise as it suddenly hung heavy from his hand.

"What—why, I never, Ellen! It's a kitten!"

"Yes, my mother sent back the basket to your mother, but the kitten's mine, and I'm giving it to you."

"Oh, thank you. Do you mean to take away with me—to sea?"

She tossed her head and looked at him archly.

"Of course, I do. I don't give presents away to be left behind, if you please. Besides, you'll be saving it from being drowned. My mother was going to drop it in the brook tomorrow."

His hands closed tightly on the gray kitten which he had lifted from the basket and which was already nestling in the hollow of his neck. Even Ellen Kimball never quite forgot the startling pity in his eyes.

"Drown it? She can't drown one when it's—it's grown like this—when it's old enough to be a friend. It's cruel. If they must be drowned, it's got to be when they're just born and don't know anything."

"Well, I suppose she can if she wants to. *You* couldn't stop her. After all, when cats have kittens so often, you can't keep them all, can you? There's plenty more she's going to drown, but I've saved this one for you. It's the nicest of the lot. I heard my father say its father must be an Angora it's so fluffy. The rest are smooth and skinny, so perhaps it doesn't matter."

"It does matter. It matters terribly."

"Well, don't cry about it. Didn't I save the best for you? And I fooled my mother, too. She doesn't know I went to the barn and found it."

He stood silently fondling the kitten until Ellen felt neglected.

"Remember," she said a bit imperiously, "it's not Mary's kitten. She hasn't any part in it at all. I'm giving it to you—as a keepsake—to remember me by when you're far away out at sea."

"Yes, I'll remember," he said, still as much to the kitten as to her.

She fidgeted uneasily with the latch of the gate until he looked at her. Then something all at once came over him—a feeling he had never had before and did not know at all. Suddenly he was seeing Ellen in a new light, as a rather irritating little girl with long curls to dip in the inkwell of his school desk, not as Mary's friend and confidante, but as someone who cared enough for him to save a kitten from drowning and to give it into his keeping. Suddenly, too, he felt strong and protective, able to look out for Ellen and the kitten, to protect all girls and helpless animals.

"Remember, John," said Ellen again a bit impatiently, as though she had not gotten the rejoinder she expected, "it's a keepsake to remember *me* by."

He looked at her again, still that strange new strength within him, and saw that her cheeks were pink and soft.

"I'll not forget, Ellen," he said. "I'll take care of it. It won't be drowned with me."

And then, without the least intending to do so, he found that he had kissed Ellen on the cheek and that she had gone away with a queer little smile and left him alone by the gate in the September twilight.

From the start the kitten set at naught all prophecies and mis-givings by proving herself the most adaptable and best of ship-mates. She grew fat on canned milk, caught mice at an incredibly early age, and even had the astonishing temerity to threaten rats with a foretaste of the future. She slept on the table before John's open arithmetic, lay across his knees at meal-time, and shared his berth at night. She had an irresistible way of arching herself around one's ankles when she wanted attention, purring with incredible distinctness. She liked nothing so much as to chase a spool down a sloping deck, retrieving it with her paw before it reached the trough below the rail and pushing it up again to where John waited. She had a face like a wide-open flower and round eyes which remained blue and candid instead of becoming sinister and yellow like those of most kittens. For once John had a friend at sea who asked of life nothing more than his companion-ship, and he himself throve mightily thereunder.

The tragedy occurred off Cape Horn, that place of many tragedies, on a cold morning above a cold gray sea swept with fog. The *Elizabeth* was lying low over the water making good speed before a smart wind. No one ever knew just what happened. The kitten was jumping about before school-time on the main deck aft pursuing her favourite spool when a great, curving wave, breaking unexpectedly over the side, carried her back with it into the sea. John saw her terrified face for an instant lying on the receding back of a gigantic swell. Mary saw it, too. Then it was lost in the burst of spray which pelted the water like the most dismal of rain.

Late that night after John had stolidly refused all comfort from parents and officers alike, Mary heard him crying in his berth, a whimper now and then, and stifled sobs above the creaking of wood and straining of rope and canvas. Spent with her own tears of grief and sympathy and heavy with approaching sleep, she yet could not leave him to suffer all alone. In her long nightgown she crossed the swaying floor and sat silently on the edge of his berth, not knowing what to say, afraid to touch him, trembling with cold and pity.

"I'm sorry," she stammered at last, putting her hand upon him. It was neither right nor enough, but it was all that she could think of.

He turned even farther from her, flattening himself against the white cabin wall.

"Go away!" he said roughly. "It hurts worse when people are sorry."

Mary clambered shivering into her own bed to lie again wide awake and think of the gray kitten against the immensity of gray water. Since drowning was to be its portion, would it have been a happier fate to die in the pasture brook together with its brothers and sisters in a well-weighted meal-bag? Or was it better to be swept quickly away by a great wave in whose pathway you happened to be? Ellen's mother had doubtless chased the other kittens, bag in hand getting breathless and irritated, becoming flushed with determination and hatred. They had been frightened half out of their senses, scurrying about the woodpile, trying to hide in the hay-loft and grain-bins, anywhere to escape Mrs. Kimball bearing down upon them. One could not even try to escape the sea like that nor could one be angry with it. There it was, that was all. Even at ten she somehow understood that it was too vast to be loved and too indifferent to be hated. There it was. She knew, too, that their tears, those in her mother's eyes and in her own, even John's as he sobbed in his berth, were not because of the sudden snuffing out of the kitten's little life but rather because of its helpless face against the gray, pitiless sea.

From then on the voyage seemed interminable, around the Horn and up the long, stumbling slopes of water toward Rio. John was sullen over his books, irritable and moody, the poorest of companions. She was not sorry when they once again reached New York in early spring and started homeward.

John was not sorry either. He had made his last voyage. Ill-starred as it had been and inundated with an anguish he would never forget, it was nevertheless his last. He noticed the green mist of the awakening elms as he had never done before, the grains of yellow pollen trembling on the willow catkins, the rushing saw-mill streams, the snug farms within encircling hills, house and woodshed, toolhouse and barn all safely hitched together. He saw the oxen ploughing in the damp furrows and remembered suddenly how one's feet stumbled among the clods behind the plough-handle and how warm and wet one felt within one's shirt. He remembered with a smile the coat of brown soil on his feet at night and how his aunt supervised the scrubbing of them in a pail of warm, soapy water in the woodshed before she risked his tired body between her clean sheets. In his imagination he saw the tiny green shoots of corn pricking the earth in orderly rows beneath the warm May sun, the dry birch brush they would set for the peas just beginning to trail, the vigilant watch for potato bugs. He saw the blue green of the oats in the first July days, heard the sharpening of scythe points on whetstones and the rasping clutter of the mower before the falling grass. He spied the yellow pumpkins half hidden among the stalks of corn and saw the patient tread of the horses on the thresher between open barn doors. And he knew that when he came home from school at night over frozen, rutty November roads or through a December snowstorm, he would see through the early darkness the warm glow from the windows of farmhouse kitchens and the forms of women moving from sink to stove and cupboard, getting supper for their men-folks. Above all, he knew that the sun would rise over one familiar hill and set behind another, instead of appearing day after day over one limitless waste of waters only to set below another.

Ellen Kimball remained in his mind only as a fear, the fear lest she should suddenly speak of her gift to him and he should cry before her. To her credit she did not speak, having promised Mary in an early confidential talk to keep silence. But what was in truth more powerful than Mary's request was the memory of his kiss at the picket gate. She set great store by the kiss which was her first, even though John had seemingly forgotten it. In her own mind at least it gave her among the girls of her age a certain distinction in knowledge and experience which she did not want to lose by incurring his displeasure.

6

Mary Peters did not honestly miss her brother in these later years at sea. She shared with her mother a warm, secure contentment in that he was happy and at home, and in the secret places of her own mind cherished an intense relief that she no longer felt obliged to combat his recurrent homesickness. They heard from him now and again in one port or another, his letters being sent on by their agents in steamships which overhauled their slower passages. He did not like his Latin overmuch though at its worst it was better than the poetry he had to learn for Friday afternoons. He had thought Friday afternoon reciting would be given up in the dignity of the Academy, but a new preceptor was determined not to relinquish it. Much to his disgust, he had had to learn "The Burial of Moses" and "Curfew Shall Not Ring Tonight" and deliver each before the whole Academy with appropriate gesturings which embarrassed him. He discovered that these two poems were greatly in fashion, the whole school thinking it extremely odd that he had escaped them even in his few terms at the village school. He hoped he would soon be rid of poetry though he feared it kept right on throughout the Academy. He would thank them all very kindly if they would bring him some seeds of foreign grains

and vegetables, for he intended in the spring to fashion a hot-bed
from some windows which his uncle had discarded, and he wanted
to try some new and odd things even though his uncle said they
would never grow in Maine soil.

Now that he was gone, life on the *Elizabeth* was less interrupted. Days succeeded one another in ceaseless monotony and
yet each with its own quiet, unperturbed excitement. There were
still her lessons, but they were more quickly learned without John
to fret at her elbow, and they became more interesting as she
passed beyond her twelfth birthday and began to do her hair in
one long, heavy braid. She even tried some Latin quite by herself
in her father's old grammar and learned to decline *mensa* and at
length to write quite correctly *The queen will give a white rose to
her beautiful young daughter.* There was more time for reading, too,
without John begging for checkers and jack-straws. They swapped
libraries in Liverpool the year she was twelve with the captain of
the *Emmeline Stevens* from Boston. Among the unfamiliar volumes
were *Jane Eyre* and *Wuthering Heights*, over the reading of which
her mother hesitated before giving a dubious consent. She never
forgot either of them, the terrifying passion of the latter returning
again and again to her memory whenever a high wind whined
aloft at night and sudden spray dashed over her closed porthole.
From the *Emmeline Stevens*, too, came a new book, which had
been making a continued stir in the world for ten years and more.
It was called *Lorna Doone*, and she and her mother read it aloud
on a memorable voyage while they ran before the Trades through
weeks of perfect weather and seemingly were destined to have no
single mishap or even setback for eighty long and perfect days.

She took to memorizing stanzas in those years when she was
alone. She was perplexed over her brother's hatred of the exercise for
she herself found inexpressible pleasure therein. Among the books
which they had gained by the timely exchange in Liverpool was one

entitled *A Garland of the Best Verse*, which she conned over and over, filling her mind and delighting her ears with its words and rhythms. Once she had learned a poem, she gave her memory a final and exciting test by copying it with the punctuation complete and exact in a little blank-book of clean pages which she kept close at hand on the shelf above her bed. She divided the poems into groups as suitable, she thought, for certain weathers and seas and times of day. There were the stirring ones fit for robust days of high yet steady wind when all hands were watchful and busy, eager to get the utmost out of the *Elizabeth* by wise yet bold and gallant sailing:

> *"O Caesar, we who are about to die*
> *Salute thee!" was the gladiators' cry.*
>
> *Thou, too, sail on, O ship of State,*
> *Sail on, O Union, strong and great!*
> *Humanity with all its fears,*
> *With all its hopes of future years,*
> *Is hanging breathless on thy fate.*
>
> *Lars Porsena of Clusium*
> *By the nine gods he swore*
> *That the great house of Tarquin*
> *Should suffer wrong no more.*
> *By the nine gods he swore it,*
> *And named a trysting day,*
> *And bade his men ride forth,*
> *East and west and south and north*
> *To summon his array.*

There were those which sprang to her mind on evenings in the tropics when the sea on all sides was a luminous amethyst and the sky flamed with unbelievable colours:

# The Sea

*The splendour falls on castled walls*
*And snowy summits old in story,*
*The long light shakes across the lakes*
*And the wild cataract leaps in glory.*
*Blow, bugle, blow, set the wild echoes flying,*
*And answer, echoes, answer, dying, dying, dying.*

*Helen, thy beauty is to me*
*Like those Nicean barks of yore*
*That gently, o'er a perfumed sea*
*The weary, wayworn wanderer bore*
*To his own native shore.*

And there were others which must be said so slowly, with such lingering over each lovely word, that they belonged only to those calm, tranquil, cloudless evenings when the ship slid almost imperceptibly through a still, clear sea, the almost foamless waves of her wake rolling idly together again into quiet water:

*This is the ship of pearl which, poets feign,*
*Sails the unshadowed main,—*
*The venturous bark that flings*
*On the sweet summer air its purpled wings*
*In gulfs enchanted, where the Siren sings,*
*And coral reefs lie bare,*
*Where the cold sea maids rise to sun their streaming hair.*
*O swallow, swallow, flying, flying south,*
*Fly to her and perch upon her gilded eaves*
*And tell her, tell her what I tell to thee.*

On bitter nights in some northern or far southern sea when the decks were treacherous with frost and ice and the shrieking wind tore in the rigging and the ship pitched about like some angry beast, she snuggled deeper into her blanket, reciting stoutly to stifle the fear in her heart:

> *Blow, blow, thou winter wind,*
> *Thou art not so unkind*
> *As man's ingratitude.*
> *Freeze, freeze, thou bitter sky,*
> *Thou dost not bite so nigh*
> *As benefits forgot.*

There were other poems which she recited also in bed at night as she grew older, her love for them enkindled and animated by the books she read and by those inescapable fancies which are the guerdon or the bane of awakening adolescence.

> *For the moon never beams without bringing me dreams*
> *Of the beautiful Annabel Lee,*
> *And the stars never rise but I see the bright eyes*
> *Of the beautiful Annabel Lee,*
> *And so all the night time I lie down by the side*
> *Of my darling, my darling, my wife and my bride*
> *In her sepulchre there by the sea,*
> *In her tomb by the sounding sea.*

> *I arise from dreams of thee*
> *In the first sweet sleep of night,*
> *When the wind is sighing low*
> *And the stars are shining bright.*
> *I arise from dreams of thee,*
> *And a spirit in my feet*
> *Hath led me—who knows how?*
> *To thy chamber window, Sweet!*

# The Sea

*A Garland of the Best Verse* was not the only impetus to her growing love of poetry and her ambition to commit to memory as much of it as she could. In the September that marked her thirteenth birthday there joined them in New York a new first officer, Mr. William Gardiner by name, a young man of thirty who had been to sea as a boy, gone to Harvard College, tried school-mastering for a season, and then returned to his first and irresistible profession. When he had boarded the ship and she heard him on deck giving his crisp, sure commands as they got underway, she understood, even while she set the things in her cabin in order, that something new and exciting was coming into her life.

She was not, first of all, unaware of his good looks. He was tall with a fine carriage, and he wore his sea clothes well. He had a lean, tanned face. When he consulted with her father or thought quietly by himself, he had a way of holding his chin firmly between the thumb and forefinger of his left hand, so firmly indeed and with such pressure on his cheeks that bright spots of red were visible when he at last released his hold. His eyes were blue and steady, with that expectant yet tranquil gaze peculiar to eyes which have looked more upon seas and skies than upon trees and streets and many people. He had his own books on his cabin shelf and a little blossoming plant on an iron bracket which he screwed into the wall next his porthole. He told Mary, as she passed his doorway while he was screwing it into the hard wood, and could not resist a shy glance, that his mother always kept geraniums and other plants all over the place at home, and that he had rather liked them himself since he was in knee-breeches. In their first days out she cherished an almost desperate hope that everyone would like him as much as she did and was unspeakably relieved when she overheard her father saying to her mother that he felt sure he had drawn a first-class man. He had been doubtful, they knew, about too much book-learning in officers, who needed instead to be practical and quick and put up with no nonsense whatsoever. Mr. Gardiner proved not to have the least patience with nonsense, but he was at the same time decent with his men and had the gift of getting himself liked as well as respected by both sailors and under-officers.

Now meals became far more interesting affairs, almost occasions, for which one prepared in odd ways hitherto unthought of. Mr. Gardiner had always something to say or to tell, drawing this story or that observation out of his mind quite as a juggler draws one surprising thing after another from a bag full of tricks. Used as she had been for years to the grave and sedate courtesies of the silent Mr. Nichols, it was days before she could accustom herself to this new and delightful state of things which, she told herself gratefully, could not possibly cease, at least until they had made New York once more and perhaps not even then. Lessons now had a goal, which was dinner. Moreover, they provided answers to the questions which Mr. Gardiner might ask concerning them, or questions which she might shyly ask of him. Reading, too, possessed an added lure, for Mr. Gardiner was given to asking her about one book or another, whether she remembered this or that in *David Copperfield* and whether she could say "And what is so rare as a day in June?" as he was still able to do from "The Vision of Sir Launfal."

Sometimes now she changed her dress before dinner instead of afterward as the program had been, her mother wisely making no comment on this innovation. At home and in New York before she sailed she had noticed the new way in which some girls, scarcely older than she, were doing their hair in front, allowing the short, loose hairs above either temple to escape the severity of a round comb and instead arranging them, with the judicious help of water, in a drooping wave on either side of the forehead. After much practice and with many misgivings lest her father tersely comment on her altered appearance, she summoned courage to come to the table one noon, her heightened colour only enhancing the new line of her hair. Her father, engrossed in other matters, was mercifully unmindful although she could hardly eat her dinner from nervousness. She hoped fervently after she had gone to bed that evening that she was not the prey of vain imaginings in thinking she had seen approval in Mr. Gardiner's face when he passed her the potatoes.

The young mate, on his part, found things vastly fresh and appealing in the little girl whose grave, clear eyes always answered the enthusiasms of his own. He liked Maine coast people, his own family having come from the tide-waters of the Kennebec, and he counted himself lucky to have his first voyage under his new papers with such a captain and in such surroundings. In his off hours he got out his Shakespeare and read *A Midsummer Night's Dream*, *The Merchant of Venice*, and *Romeo and Juliet* with Mary and her mother, each taking a given part. Mary never forgot those hours on the sunny deck or beneath the uncertain light of the cabin lamp. Life blossomed then for her through words and pictures she had not known before, Shakespeare, except for the excerpts in *A Garland*, having seemed hitherto a hard, dull book designed especially for grown-ups. She had occasion to remember their reading far longer than had Mr. Gardiner, unless, indeed, the good memories of this world make easier and less confused our adaptation to another. But that such pastime remained a good memory to him also is certain. For during the last dreadful hour of his life, among thoughts of greater concern and a labyrinth of lesser matters, he caught himself now and again repeating to his chaotic mind in Mary's voice rather than in his own:

> *Night's candles are burnt out and jocund day*
> *Stands tiptoe on the misty mountain-top.*

A schoolmaster himself, he proved of welcome service to
Sarah Peters whose sense of inadequacy, now that Mary was nearing the Academy, was beginning to prey upon her. An odd fifteen
minutes with him could set straight the most disordered task.
Mary felt sure that there was nothing in the whole world which
he did not know. Latin became a new and enthralling engagement
now that she did not have to rely upon the imperfect memory of
her busy father, who had himself proceeded but little beyond the
grammar before relinquishing it for the sea. Before eight weeks
had lapsed, she had travelled from *mensa* and the queen's roses to
such a formidable sentence as, *Since it was not unpleasing to the
young prince, his father, the emperor, sent him into other lands in order
that he might learn the manners of many men.*

But it was rather as an interpreter of the one environment she
really knew that Mary Peters longest remembered Mr. Gardiner.
He became the voice of her half-formed thoughts, making clear in
words what she had dimly felt within her. Moreover, he had that
delightful and reassuring way of assuming that her understanding
was quite equal to his own. Something of a scientist himself and
quickly observant of all about him, he opened her eyes to things
she had only half seen before. God Himself out of any sort of
whirlwind could not have rebuked Mr. Gardiner as being unmindful of the treasures of His creation!

Their first voyage to the Indies and south to Rio took them
through those strange, undulating meadows of the Sargasso where
the ship in great easy swells lifted herself to settle again into what
were seemingly depths of green, amber, and yellow verdure. That
drifting, nomadic vegetation, one thousand miles from land, shifting now and again in obedience to mysterious impulses so that
they found themselves all at once in clear, weedless water, had prevented the sailors of Columbus, he told her, four hundred years
ago from despair and mutiny. Leaning over the lowest edge of the

rail, Mary and Mr. Gardiner drew in their odd harvest to the deck
and examined it there for whatever spoils it might conceal.
Clinging tenaciously to the fronds and bladders of the weed were
tiny crabs and shrimps, seahorses, snails, and odds and ends of
unknown shellfish, most of them in the yellow-brown of their
own anchorage. This for the never-failing amusement of the day.
At sunset on those clear evenings the dolphins played around the
ship. Although she had seen them scores of times, their leaps and
curves, their sliding from water into air and back again with
scarcely a drop of spray, the green, gold, and blue of their sides—all
took on new magic with Mr. Gardiner beside her. When darkness
came, there came with it luminous fishes, spotted with brilliant
points of light or else seemingly ablaze with bellies of flame, moving through the clear water or glowing among the weed. Now
and then they spied a circular fish upon whose head a tiny
appendage bore, as it were, a globe of light, flashing ever before
him like a beacon upon the dark mazes of his voyaging.

Pacific waters were even more miraculous. They might
become suddenly purple through incredible numbers of jellyfish,
which, once night had fallen, were like gliding globes of fire. They
sheltered somewhere to divulge, no one ever knew when, brilliant
red porpoises rolling along their absurd and stupid way through
deep blue waves. They were the home of whales more idle and
playful than those of Atlantic seas, spouting and churning about
sometimes in considerable companies. And in their Eastern harbours one was sure to see those strangely bellied water snakes with
keels and tails like fish, not mighty fearsome creatures like those in
*The Ancient Mariner* but small, sinuous, swimming in tiny circles or
drifting through still water, slender, gaudy shapes, black, banded
with green and gold, sliding away on some mysterious, subtle business of their own.

On a morning while they were still in the Sargasso waiting impatiently for wind he called her from her lessons to see a bewildered robin who, far from land and kind, had perched in desperation and hunger upon their taffrail. Fear making it overbold, it flew to the deck for crumbs, staying with them in the sun all day long. The next morning it lay dead in a secluded corner. Mary herself found it there when she had run early and hopefully to the deck to give it breakfast. She was unashamed of her tears as she showed its poor, ruffled little body to Mr. Gardiner, for he had a gentleness about him which made her sure of his own sorrow. He told her then of a Roman poet named Catullus who gave a sparrow to Lesbia, the lady he loved, and how when the sparrow died, he wrote a poem about it which said in one simple line what had happened and how he felt about it:

> *Passer mortuus est meae puellae*
> My lady's sparrow is dead.

She copied the Latin, which even she could read, in her blank-book and said it over often to herself.

Mr. Gardiner's gentleness, although it could always be depended upon in such sad moments, was not perhaps uppermost within him. He loved the sea and sailing-ships with a tenacious, almost jealous love, and just as bitterly he hated the inroads upon them of ships propelled by steam. Whenever they saw smoke darkening a clear horizon or were overhauled by some freighter or passenger steamer, plunging surely along, dependent only upon the coal in her bunkers and the great, filthy engines in her bowels, Mr. Gardiner's rage burst forth in the volleys of an overworked volcano. Mary half dreaded, half welcomed these explosions which not infrequently heightened the atmosphere at dinner or supper.

"There's no help for it, Mr. Gardiner," said her father, though the gleam in his eyes said also that he liked Mr. Gardiner for his fury. "It's coming whether we like it or not. In twenty years there'll be mighty little call for us. The world's being made over by those engines into a new one so you might as well keep calm."

"It'll be a poorer world, sir," cried Mr. Gardiner with a mighty thump of his fist on the table. "You can't tell me you don't believe that!"

"You and I believe a lot of things that the world don't take much stock in, Mr. Gardiner, and if you stick twenty years more to this business, if those engines let you stick twenty years more, you won't get so hot about things. Sailing takes the heat out of a man about things that are going to come anyhow."

"Does it?" cried Mr. Gardiner, not noticing that Mary was offering him the bread. "Well, it hasn't taken it out of me yet, sir!"

"No," said her father. "You're young yet, but it will. Maybe in twenty years you'll be on the bridge of one of those steamships, only a bigger one than you and I have any idea of. You'll be in white ducks waiting for a pilot to take you into port, and at night you'll dine with rich New Yorkers who'll feel honored to be asked to sit at the captain's table."

"Never!" cried Mr. Gardiner again. "Never in this life! I'll stick to sailing so long as there's a decent ship afloat. I'd rather go down in a ship like this, sir, than face such a future!"

"Well," said the captain folding his napkin, "we won't look forward to going down, Mr. Gardiner. I've sailed most seas for thirty years, twelve of them in this ship. There've been close shaves, perhaps, but I've never had to face going down in her or any other. And there's always school-mastering, Mr. Gardiner. Mary here says you're a good teacher."

Mr. Gardiner might have remembered Mary then, but he forgot her long enough to give his last shot which Mary always knew was bound to come in one form or another.

"Steam may revolutionize the sea, sir, but it won't make men and you know it."

"It *has* revolutionized the sea, Mr. Gardiner," said her father, starting for the companion-way. "You're behind the times. And I suppose there'll be men of some sort made somehow even though they're not the sort we like the best. Better save your energy, Mr. Gardiner. There's a blow on, and the sea's getting up."

It never seemed necessary for Mr. Gardiner to save his energy. He always had enough and to spare. After one of these conversations his commands were more crisp and sure than ever. He kept the under-officers and sailors tearing about at top speed to fulfill them while he himself walked swiftly up and down the decks, now here, now there, his eyes and mind sharpened for the slightest detail which did not satisfy him. It was as though within himself as well as on the ship he longed to demonstrate the intrinsic worth and value, dignity and grandeur, of the enterprise they were engaged upon, as though he had no life at all apart from the planks of the ship beneath his feet and the ocean she moved upon. He knew a sailing-ship for what she was, no insentient thing but a being who like Antaeus from the earth drew her life from the sea. Scorning to set at naught the wind by the harnessing of steam, such a ship became the ally of wind and waves even while she was subservient to them. She lent herself to both, and while she was dependent upon them, she was likewise glorified by her wise use of them, as the sun is apprehended only by the light of the sun and as God is the only approach unto Himself.

Something of the essence of these great matters made itself manifest in Mary Peters' imagination during those last years at sea in the companionship of Mr. Gardiner. She became aware that they who did business in such great waters were not only dependent upon them but in a larger sense one with them, obeying the laws which they obeyed, moving as they were moved. More and more clearly she understood that she herself, Mary Peters, now getting ready to leave the *Elizabeth* for the far more terrifying walls of the Petersport Academy, was only a tiny part of things that moved ceaselessly on and on whithersoever they must. The wind rose and they flew before it or, by the quick use of all their wits and strength, lent themselves as best they could to its willfulness; it died, and they waited as patiently as might be. They prophesied, knowing full well that their prophecies might well come to naught. What wonder that the mind of a sensitive child framed upon such surroundings and such perceptions should become that of an observer, an onlooker upon life, rather than that of one who longs to shape all things in accordance with his own preconceived designs?

Once on a sunny afternoon when they were in mid-ocean running before a fair wind they spied a ship miles away on the horizon. Her hull had already sunk below the curve of the sea, but her sails still caught the light and flamed there like some great, distant beacon. Mary stood by the rail with Mr. Gardiner silently watching as she had watched so many, many times before. The white expanse of sail was sinking from sight, but the glow remained. At last their eyes could discern but a single spot of white and then only the tiniest prick of light as though it were an evening star. It seemed long minutes before that point of light vanished, and even after it had gone some vestige of the glow remained before they were again alone with sea and sky.

"That's it, Mary," said Mr. Gardiner then. "That's what this life is that you and I know. There couldn't be a better symbol of it. It's hull down with everything that's tough and hard about it. It's only the sails and the glow on them that we'll remember. That doesn't go out. You keep it in your mind even after the sea has taken it.

That's what brought me back to ships, and that's what you'll remember all your life."

<h2 style="text-align:center">7</h2>

One noon in the October of Mary's last year at sea, two days after they had dropped anchor at Liverpool, her father made an announcement at the close of dinner. It seemed a simple remark enough, yet something in his making of it and in her mother's reception of it made the cabin somehow pregnant with meaning not untouched by mystery. Mr. Gardiner felt it, for, with a quick glance about the table, he excused himself and went toward the companion-way. Mary remained where she was, silently folding her napkin, half expectant of a summons to go, half aware that she was supposed to remain where she was.

"Jim Pendleton's in the Mersey," her father had said. "I met him in the offices this morning."

Her mother had made no reply at all, but the sudden heightening of colour in her face and the startled way in which she had fingered the tablecloth made Mary conscious of her surprise, perhaps displeasure.

"Where's he been?" asked Sarah Peters, when they were alone, after a long, not too comfortable silence. "Where's he been all these years?"

"Sailing," said her father. "To Melbourne mostly. He's touched New York now and again. I knew. I've seen notices of the ship here and there. To tell the truth, I've seen him once or twice though I've never said. He's aged a lot. I didn't like the looks of him too much this morning. But he's still a good master. You could tell they thought a lot of him up there by the way they talked."

"He always was," said Sarah Peters. She was looking at her husband now with her eyes large and bright, but Mary somehow knew that she was thinking of her. "He always was bound to land on his feet whatever he did or wherever he went."

"I don't know about that," said the captain of the *Elizabeth* slowly. He drew his pipe from his pocket and began to fill it with uncommon deliberateness, pressing the tobacco with his blunt middle finger more and more firmly into the bowl. "We always used to think so, but I guess these last years haven't been any bed of roses for him. He looks bad—and old. His wife's dead."

"Oh," said Sarah Peters. And then, after what seemed hours to Mary sitting there, "I'm sorry for that. When?"

"Last spring," he said. "She was sick a long time, years I guess. She died in Paris while he was away. He's got his boy with him. I saw him this morning."

Mary saw the colour again deepen in her mother's cheeks.

"How old is he? Somehow I can't keep track of time."

Her father paused before replying as though considering his answer.

"It's not—that one," he said. "The oldest died when he was five. This one's sixteen or just going on that. He's not a bad-looking boy. There's something rather nice about him. He's a little lame, I think—got some sort of hitch in his walk, though I couldn't make out just what was wrong. Good-mannered and rather shy. I think you'd kind of take to him. He speaks English with a Maine accent. His father's seen to that."

"What's his name? Did you ask?"

"Yes. He's named for his father."

"Is he—a Pendleton?" asked Sarah Peters.

"No, I can't say he is, at least in looks. He's tall like his father, but thin and small-boned. He looks French all right."

Silence again around the table. Mary rose as if to go.

"You needn't go, Mary," said her mother.

She sat down again with a queer tingling in hands and feet.

"Jim's got a notion—" began her father.

"He always had notions," said her mother quickly. "What's this one?"

"He's got a notion," began Captain Peters again, sucking on his unlighted pipe, "that he wants the boy to go back home to school. He don't want him to stay in France. There's not many of his mother's people left, and Jim don't fancy those that are, I take it. He wants him to go back with Joel and Mattie and go to the Academy and maybe to college. He says he's bright and likes his books. He don't take to the sea."

"He's no Pendleton then," said Sarah Peters. "But perhaps it's just as well."

"Perhaps it is. But there's Pendletons and Pendletons. We've got no copyright on them in Petersport. Jim's got another notion that I might as well tell first as last since it concerns you and Mary here."

Mary sat on, acutely uncomfortable and unable to tell why.

"Well?" asked Sarah Peters.

"He wants to see you. I don't see why myself or what would be the use after all this time, but he does. He says it's just as you say, of course, but I can see he wants to talk to you."

"What is there to say? I'm sure I've nothing."

"Jim always had plenty to say," said Mary's father, scratching a match at last. "I guess he hasn't changed in that respect. But I made no promises. I just said I'd ask you and let him know. You decide as you think best. Only, if I know anything, you won't have to see him more than once. He's a sick man."

"Well," said Sarah Peters slowly, "he's always got what he wanted, and I don't know as I mind seeing him. I'm sorry he's sick. There's a lot of water flowed under a lot of bridges since I knew Jim Pendleton. He can come if he likes and bring his boy. I don't know that I mind—any at all."

"When?" asked her husband. "He's sailing Friday. It's Wednesday now." He rose from the table.

"If he's coming," said Sarah Peters, "he may as well come. That's one thing there's no use waiting for. Send the boat if you like and tell him. They can come for supper tonight."

Mary sat quietly with her mother while her father went on deck. The steward came to clear the table. He carried away the dishes, removed the cloth, and spread the green felt. When he had gone out and closed the door, Sarah Peters looked at her daughter whose eyes fell before her mother's steady gaze. The cabin all at once felt hot and close although the day was sharp and cold.

"Mary," said her mother after what seemed an interminable silence, "I've thought for a long while that I ought to tell you about some things. And I guess now is as good a time as ever. You see, there are things that girls of your age ought to know. I don't know just how to tell them to you, but there *are* things. My mother never told me—things were different when I was a girl—and I never knew things I should have known till I was married and found out about them. And then all at once I understood about certain things that had concerned me more than I knew they had."

Mary did not, could not speak. The cabin was filled with portentous, acutely embarrassing knowledge suddenly loosed from her mother's mind to hang over the table above their heads. She felt hot all over and as though she were going to cry.

"I don't want you to find out things the way I did," her mother went on. "If you'd lived at home, in a town, like other girls, you might have seen and heard things for yourself. Maybe it would have been better for you, but there—I don't know. Anyway, you're growing up. You're not a little girl any longer."

With her mother's summary words all the shining, quiet days of her past seemed suddenly to Mary as though they were shut out of sight very much as the hatches were battened down over the ship's tight cargo. She felt commanded to face another life of which she knew nothing. She wanted desperately either to escape from it all or else to learn quickly what its mysteries were which her mother knew but could not seem to tell her. Suddenly without any reason at all she saw again the kitten's helpless face against the gray sea and knew that she must cry.

"There's nothing in the world to feel bad about," said Sarah Peters, although she knew at that moment that there was the lot of men and women throughout the world. "I don't mean to frighten you. It's just that boys and men are different from women, Mary. You're going home next year to school, and you'll see things you haven't seen before. I wish you didn't have to see them, but you *will* have to. You'll see girls behaving foolishly and letting boys take liberties with them, and you'll have to learn that nice girls can't do it. Sometimes men are selfish, and sometimes women lead them on to do things they shouldn't do. And then there's tragedies and sadness. People are sorry when it's too late, and babies are born when they're not wanted."

Mary was sobbing now with her head in her arms on the table. She could not look at her mother, who felt with some justice that she was making a bad mess of things. In the eighties such conversations, if they were held at all, were seldom marked with success. Sarah Peters in reality had intended no such conversation until they had returned home ready for school. To be sure, the necessity for it some day had been lying in the back of her mind, a sinister necessity which had, now and again, sometimes when she awoke at night, prompted her to plan for it, to rehearse words, against the time when it must come. It had, in fact, been precipitated by her husband's announcement, and now there seemed no turning back. She moved from her own chair to that of Mr. Gardiner next to Mary and laid her arm across the girl's shoulders.

"Don't cry," she said. "There's not a thing to cry about." She paused, sharply conscious of her own incompetence, wishing fervently she had not put her hand to this unwieldy plough, realizing suddenly how little of her own life and her quick joy therein lay in what she was trying to say. "You've seen some things for yourself, young as you are. You've seen how the sailors go off with cheap women when they go ashore, women that take their money and do them harm. I can't explain it all, but you'll know by and by. There are beautiful things in life, Mary—I don't want you to think there aren't—but I'm afraid there are ugly things, too, and sometimes they're all mixed up together."

Mary cried on. Some great sorrow lay deep within her, thick, heavy, stifling. It was made up of all the sorrows everywhere throughout the world, and there was no escaping it.

"Perhaps I can explain better," said her mother at last after another painful silence, "by telling you about the man who's coming here for supper, the one your father's just been talking about. He grew up in Petersport and went to school with your father and me. I—loved him when I was a girl—or at least I thought I did— more than I ever loved anyone. We were going to be married. He went to sea. Sometimes going to sea is not the best thing for young men, especially for a young man like him. He met a French woman in Brittany somewhere, not what people call a very good woman, I'm afraid, and he loved her more than he loved me. He came home and told me, and that was all there was to it. He didn't tell me all there was to tell—I suppose he couldn't—but afterward I found out that she had had a child, and that he was its father. He went back to her, it was the only thing he could do, and they were married, after a while. Then the next year I married your father. You'd probably hear all this some time. People don't forget things at home. So I might as well tell you myself since it's all come up this way."

Mary's mind suddenly became a confusion of images. She thought of the young Italian sharpening his knife for the girl in Valparaiso who had done him dirt. She remembered for no reason she could understand the beautiful woman in Cadiz who had tucked a rose in her bonnet. She thought of Heathcliff in *Wuthering Heights* and of Catherine's broken heart and of Annabel Lee whose high-born kinsmen had borne her away from her lover. She thought of Mr. Gardiner and knew that he could never treat anyone so monstrously, no matter what the cost. Sarah Peters' blundering confidences had not been so ill-timed after all, for in her sudden romantic sympathy for her mother, she at least partly forgot her own dilemma.

"I'm sorry he treated you so," she stammered from the safety of her arms on the table. "Why do you let him come here? I don't want to see him."

"Nonsense!" said her mother, somewhat relieved at this turn of affairs. "That's past and gone. He's paid for it all. People pay for things in this world, Mary, don't forget that. Sometimes they pay too high a price for foolish moments that they can't help. You'll understand things better some day. He's not a bad man. He's had trouble, your father says he's ill, and he wants to see someone from home. Wash your face now and read a bit, and don't worry over what I've told you. And when you're puzzled over things you don't understand, you can ask me, and I'll tell you the best I know how. You can wear your new dress tonight if you like, and while your father and I talk with Captain Pendleton, you can tell—young Jim about the school at home and other things he'll like to know."

Mary sat on at the table after her mother had left to make plans with the cook for supper. Through the open portholes there drifted the sounds of harbour activity, the calls of the stevedores loading or unloading cargo at the nearby wharves, the steady clacking of cranes and winches, the whistles and snorts of passing tugs. Through the filthy harbour water oars, rattling in their locks, rose and fell rhythmically. Gulls screamed, swooped downward with a hiss to rise again with a mighty beating of wings.

In the cabin itself all was quiet. Mary felt, perhaps not entirely unpleasantly, that she had entered upon a new existence. She thought that the tears for her childhood, which her mother had told her was past and gone, should by all rights continue to flow, but they did not. Her face was hot and flushed, but dry. Genuine as had been her distress, real as had been the sorrow that engulfed her, they had now given place to a sombre regard of herself which, although solemn in the extreme, was not without its pleasurable features. Even her mother's disclosures of the dark things that might beset her when she entered upon life at home and in the Academy had temporarily assumed a less tragic importance. What was mainly concerning her at this moment was the thought that such suffering should have made unmistakable inroads upon her appearance. Such bitter knowledge, she told herself, ought to make her look as old and experienced as she felt, so that Mr. Gardiner might look upon her with surprise and sympathy, wondering what had wrought such a cruel transformation. Crossing to the cabin mirror which hung above the drawers for linen and silver, she studied her own expression to see if it recorded such sadness as she felt and decided as she stared into her own eyes that she did look somehow different. She still tried to convince herself that she was outraged over the unkind appearance of Captain Pendleton, who had, she felt sure, broken her mother's heart, but somewhere deep within her there bubbled a secret excitement which would not be disowned. She planned to meet Captain Pendleton with great dignity, to look at him in such a way that he would realize she was no longer a child but a young lady who understood all that had happened in years gone by and who was a faithful and discerning ally of her mother. Young Jim did not play a great part in her consciousness at the moment. She was sorry he was lame and hoped he might not be too shy at conversation should they be left alone together.

After half an hour of sorting out emotions and convincing herself that she was a new creature, she washed her hot face with great care and did her hair. She arranged it in the new way, adding a touch even more mature by turning up her heavy braid and tying it in her neck with a black ribbon. Her new dress she was glad to see was longer and made her look undeniably older. She could not read, her heart beat too quickly, and besides, there was far too much to think about. She would have liked to search out Mr. Gardiner but was held back by the fear that she might be unequal to the occasion or that he might not recognize that it was an occasion at all.

It was trying to her new sense of maturity to discover, when she once stood on deck with her father and mother awaiting the approaching boat, that she felt extremely shy and ill at ease. Her mother seemed calmness itself and her father quite as usual. If their worlds like her own had been turned topsy-turvy, they evinced no sign of it. When their guests had ascended the ladder and were exchanging greetings, she was quite too perturbed to play the role she had so carefully decided upon, and, when she thought it all over later, felt sure that Captain Pendleton had not been so impressed as she had hoped.

He was a tall man with a thin, anxious face. After her own embarrassment had claimed her time and attention, she tried to discern therein some repentance or shame in his greeting of her mother, some regret or affection in her mother's face; but whether there were nothing of the sort or whether her own discomfort had dulled her perception of it, she could not tell. Nothing was certainly apparent save cordiality and easy friendliness. She wondered with a quick sense of disappointment if certain stories she had read were wrong, and if people were doomed to forget even close things after many years. And then she was obliged to abandon such puzzled querying and greet the boy who stood beside his father.

He was a slight boy with brown eyes, close-cropped dark hair, and mobile features. He walked with a distinct limp, one thigh seemingly insecurely set. She liked him at once. He was shy like herself, but in some odd way his shyness was from the first moment no stumbling-block or hindrance. Instead, it seemed to recognize and make friends with her own on the easiest, least exacting terms. When they walked off across the deck together until supper should be ready, she felt peculiarly comfortable and in no urgent need of Mr. Gardiner upon whom she had depended to manage the conversation. Leaning against the rail, they watched the great harvest moon rise above the chimney-potted homes and dishevelled quays of Liverpool without each worrying the other with the fear that there was nothing to say. After a time they found their tongues and talked of what manner of place a Maine Academy was and whether Mary had been in Paris and why, if a fellow hated mathematics, he should have to learn them anyway. When Mr. Gardiner joined them, Mary had so far forgotten her predetermined manner before him that he was entirely unconscious of any tragedy or sadness whatsoever in her life.

Supper was the easiest possible meal. The men talked mostly, of ships and ports and cargoes, and of persons they had met here and there in all places under the sun. Mary and young Jim listened, and Sarah Peters saw that everyone ate plentifully and was satisfied, without any betrayal, so Mary thought, of anything that might well be going on in her mind. Captain Pendleton talked a great deal, telling stories with quick movements of his hands to illustrate them or to move them along more rapidly, and not by any wild reach of her imagination could Mary detect the least embarrassment on the part of anyone.

Whether, indeed, Captain James Pendleton and her mother talked together of their past in the hour after supper while she and Mr. Gardiner and young Jim sat on deck and her father busied himself about the *Elizabeth*, she never knew, although she later imagined all manner of dramatic, chastened dialogues between them. And that night, after the boat had returned Jim and his father to their ship, and she was at last in bed, she fell immediately asleep in spite of a melancholy determination to review in every minutest detail a most momentous day and to see herself as one who had resolutely put away all childish things.

While her daughter slept, Sarah Peters lay awake and thought, her thoughts detached from herself, from her body which had responded to emotions once astir within her, now dead. Like Mary she thought she ought to feel things which she did not feel. The trouble did not lie with her memory, sufficiently acute to recall all manner of situations and happenings which had once mattered intensely and now lay numb and inert, not even any longer within her heart but only in her mind. It was as though she rehearsed the sorrowful confusion of some stranger, as though she read objectively some one else's sorrow which she could not make real to herself. Was time kind or cruel, she wondered, thus to smother or at least to transform its offerings? While James Pendleton had sat opposite her in the cabin after supper, speaking remotely of matters that had once been of such burning consequence to them both, she had not been able to summon from within her one solitary pang, one hurt in the least commensurate with the concern she felt over his own present sadness, which had to do with another woman recently dead, or with the wave of tenderness which had swept over her when she saw his boy who was lame.

# The Sea

Was the trouble with her, she wondered, that she was callous and hard, not like other women who seemingly kept and nourished old sorrows and regrets? Had her years at sea with the long, ceaseless monotony of their recurring, unvarying days been instrumental in blotting out the more concrete, more concentrated past? She was not at forty-five insensitive, impassive to emotions. That she knew full well. Life beat fervidly within her, spending itself over this and that—Mary sobbing at the table, the purple of southern seas, the blossoming plant in Mr. Gardiner's cabin, the discarding of old, familiar garments, a kitten drowning in a cold ocean, birds far from land. Some lamp within her, by whose glow she lived, was always rekindling itself, lighted by one odd thing or another.

Was it not, perhaps, she thought at last, as the freshening odour of the incoming tide scattered at midnight the acrid harbour smells—was it not that another world of love lay beyond mere desire, the tangled, importunate, mysterious desire which she had long ago felt for James Pendleton but which was now no more? And that this other world was one, not of passion so much as of tranquillity and tenderness, of depths far exceeding those of the first, of life more abundant, of love more perfect? Might it not be that she had all unconsciously entered into this other world where old pain was not and where new pain, occurring as it must in the rhythm of life, was somehow allayed by a longing to protect those who suffered, by a quickening companionship with all things that must live?

Once this thought had penetrated her understanding, she felt a sense of calm and comfort. She lay relaxed in her bed, her mind at peace with her body as minds must learn somehow to be. The rising water slapped the sides of the ship. A church tower somewhere ashore struck the hour that began yet another day. Men's voices broke the stillness, resounding across the harbour from some late mission for the conversion and anchorage of unstable seamen's souls:

*Time like an ever-rolling stream*
*Bears all its sons away;*
*They fly forgotten as a dream*
*Dies at the opening day.*

That was true, she thought. Life never stopped. It went on in flux and reflux, in its own measured rhythm, old desolations recurring in new, less desolate guises, new sorrows taking the place of old, gaiety coming with its sudden, bright surprise and going inexorably again, sure some day to return though in different form.

The tide was the symbol of it all. The love of her girlhood had lapsed and ebbed, forsaken her shores. Now it had come flooding back, unrecognizable at first but now clearly seen as tenderness and pity. Mary's bewilderment and anguish, which she, blundering in her own embarrassment, had been unable to make easier, more simple, would recede to come back again now and then through the years in less piercing disguise.

Nothing was ever final; nothing was ever lost.

8

In the late August of 1886 they reached San Francisco after a voyage of three months and more around the Horn, a long, wearisome voyage of head winds and high, stubborn seas, of fog and cold and lurid dawns which foretold more trouble and proved all too true to prophecy. Even Mr. Gardiner proclaimed himself tired, dead tired, and more glad than he had ever found himself in all his life to see the Golden Gate which would admit them after the necessary preliminaries to the wide, glistening harbour of the city with its range of purple hills, tumbling eastward toward yet higher ranges.

Mary was glad, too (her moods followed Mr. Gardiner's with almost startling accuracy), and yet in all her gladness there was a deeply buried sorrow. For this was her last voyage. No longer would she watch with him the disappearing canvas of ships, or do her Latin in the hope of praise, or study the curves of dolphins or flying fish on clear, quiet evenings. Once they had landed, even before the *Elizabeth* had been repaired and reloaded, she and her mother were to board a train which would carry them across miles of unfamiliar land, mountains and deserts and prairies, back east to Petersport and its white-columned Academy.

She could not even begin to imagine what life would be like without Mr. Gardiner. Lying in her berth at night with the ship behaving so badly that she creaked in every joint and rivet and pitched about until one was ready to scream from irritation, Mary confessed to herself with no small amount of condemnation that even absence from her father did not, could not, constitute her main regret. Share as she might her mother's anxiety over an odd seizure which had kept the Captain of the *Elizabeth* in his cabin for four harassing days and left him drawn and white, she could not seem to direct the ache in her heart as it obviously should be directed. In vain Mr. Gardiner promised a Christmas in Maine and exciting days now and again in home ports. She knew with a hideous sinking within her body that things would never be the same again.

Change to a child reared as she had been was in itself portentous. Not that change was unknown to her in its larger, less personal aspects, but it was known with a difference. Changes at sea were not cleavages in one's life. Their mutations and variations were all a part of one's life itself. They were imposed by, were, in fact, a part of vast forces whose very nature was continuity and changelessness, however much they shifted, whatever were their deviations. Even a child did not so much submit to them as she was carried along with them in their endings and beginnings, their

perpetual flux and reflux. But changes wrought by human agencies, by human decision, were different, more revolutionary, more
invasive. They left one without defense, with the terrifying necessity not only of subservience but of adjustment as well.

Just living was lonely enough anyway, she told herself, perhaps
not unconscious of the ironic philosophy of her thought, but, nevertheless, in genuine distress as she gathered together her possessions from drawers and lockers and chests, some to be reluctantly
thrown into the sea, more to be carefully labelled and cherished.
Her throat ached and her eyes filled with tears as she sorted this
and that. There was the little brooch she had bought in Cadiz;
some frail, translucent shells which she had gathered on tropical
beaches; the diplomas her father had printed; old hair ribbons and
laces, which her mother said she no longer needed; a feather from
the dead robin in a tiny box; her own precious books which
should never be on the close, narrow shelves of any other ship in
any other far harbour. The worst of it was one could never know
another's fears and sorrows. They must be borne alone. One held
certain deep things in one's heart, which was tightly closed, battened down as the ship's hatches were battened down over her
cargo, tightly packed away, remembered by nobody as they sailed
from one port to another. She could not tell her mother of her
fears—fears of the Academy where others would study the same
lessons and do better with them than she, fears of teachers who
would expect quick answers, fears of boys and girls who already
knew one another and who would hold in common knowledge
of persons and things with which she had had little or nothing to
do. She could not tell Mr. Gardiner of her sorrow at leaving him.
Even if there were words to say it in, which there were not, she
could not say it because it could not be said.

All these things lay in deep and painful confusion within her
on the last afternoon when the tumbled outlines of San Francisco

rose out of a gray distance, peopling its dark hills. She stood by the rail and watched its lines sharpen as they drew nearer, sailing over a dark, melancholy sea. A stiffening wind from the mountains was holding them back, disabled as they were from ugly winds already. Mr. Gardiner was too busy to give her so much as a word as she stood on the deck in her land clothes, shivering in the unseasonable cold. Neither he nor her father liked the looks of things. The mountains of the Coast Range were dark and forbidding, and a sickly green light lay over everything.

Once the necessary entrance formalities had been executed, she and her mother were sent summarily ashore, not waiting for the *Elizabeth* to dock or anchor. The blue waters of the channel, often so touched with yellow sunlight as to deserve its name, now ran gray and cold. There had been no time for leave-takings and, in fact, no necessity for them as they were to meet again the next day at latest. She sat beside her mother in the close cabin of the tender, her hands stiff and unwieldy in unaccustomed gloves, a symbol of the freedom she had lost forever. The carpeted corridor of the hotel on Market Street, which on other landings she had thought so elegant, the red-velvet chairs, the hurry and confusion of the great lobby, even the food at supper, so much better than they had known for weeks on end—all these but deepened and concentrated her sorrow. While she slept but restlessly beside her mother in a great black walnut bed high up above the city street, the gathering storm sweeping from the hills smote upon her dreams as it smote upon the harbour waters and the sea without.

The ship's agents brought them the news in mid-morning after her mother had stood seemingly for hours at their window, scanning the sea-front. The *Elizabeth*, which had never known in a score of years irremediable disaster, had been blown down the coast to meet her untimely and ignominious destruction on an island reef. Mr. Gardiner need no longer fear lest his fate should be white ducks and rich New Yorkers. The world had been made over for him in one brief and terrible night, not by engines but by those very forces which had given him his life and to which he had in turn given himself. His body was not found.

They waited for what seemed a limitless succession of interminable days before they could board the train homeward. Somewhere, far forward, among boxes and bales, casks and crates of extraneous, lifeless material lay the body of the captain of the *Elizabeth*. It was some scant comfort to Sarah Peters to be told by San Francisco doctors that he had died of heart failure long before the sea had washed him back into his own cabin.

Mary wondered what such comfort could be but was relieved for her mother. Remorse tormented her that her own great grief was elsewhere. It was wrong that it should be so, but it was true. She saw Mr. Gardiner tossed about by gray, relentless waves, beaten against brown rocks, floating at queer, gruesome angles through clear, sunshot water, lying hideous and swollen at the bottom of the sea.

Her mother, quick to sense her pain, did her utmost with consolation.

"There's a difference in people, Mary. You mustn't forget that. He wouldn't have wanted to be here, on this train, like your father. He gave his life to the sea from choice, and he would have wished—*did* wish, I'm sure, to die in it and leave his body there. Your father was different. He went to sea because young men from home, the best young men when he was young, did— because his family had. He would have wanted to be carried back home, but Mr. Gardiner, never!"

The words brought some measure of comfort to the girl's mind, but the images persisted in her overwrought imagination.

On they went, snorting over mountain passes, rumbling through canyons, toiling over stretches of cactus-strewn sand. Skies were high, bright, cloudless. The huddling red sandstone bluffs of the desert, in which, some friendly passengers told them, cave-dwellers once had lived, gave place at last to wide, windswept prairies, billowing like the sea before the Trades, some open with herds of plunging cattle, some fenced and shorn and set about at regular intervals with freshly bound sheaves of grain like little huts. Purple thistles and waving yellow cornflowers relieved the cindery wastes on either side of the track. After four days, during which Mary had seen more land than in all her life she had known existed, they came into the fat corn country of Iowa and Illinois, with yellowing pumpkins among the ragged, wholesome shocks, with slow, willow-bordered streams open to the sun, with black, fertile roads straight like long lines of ink, sometimes marked by high, lumbering wagons heaped with green stalks of corn. Boys rode upon them, stretched in drowsy content beneath the warm September sun; and Mary thought of John who awaited their return with a sad, bewildered heart. In yet another day they were among the close, friendly New England hills with a red maple already here and there among the hemlocks, with familiar boulders by shallow, rushing streams, and white houses among high, narrow fields.

They did not talk much throughout those long days. There seemed little to say. They watched the land flowing constantly past their windows, each filled with her own stifling thoughts. Mary loved her mother with a great, pitying love and strove mightily to anticipate her need of things to make her less tired. She became grateful as the days came and went that Mr. Gardiner was not lying ahead there beside her father. She could not imagine him inert, white, still, his quick life stopped. Once, when they had halted on a siding for an hour to await the passing of a western-bound express which was late, they walked back and forth almost the length of the train, avoiding only the car which was far ahead. Their quick steps, back and forward, forward and back, seemed to set free some of the thoughts that swept and surged about in Sarah Peters' mind.

"I hope you'll learn more than I did, Mary—in the Academy, I mean, and from your books. Things you learn help in times like this. Last night I tried to recall something which I learned, or at least heard when I went to school years ago. There was a preceptor there who used to tell us things that I remember I liked. He talked to us in a class we had. Once, I remember, he told us about a philosopher who lived years ago, Plato his name was. I've never quite forgotten one thing he said—about pleasure and happiness meaning only that pain and sorrow were absent, and the other way around. He said people could never know happiness unless they knew pain as well—that life was like that. I've known many times that he was right, and I know it better now. This pain won't last always for us. Pleasure will come again and then perhaps more pain. I guess that's the way things have to go with everybody."

It was a windy day. Mary was to remember afterward how the wind swept along the sides of the track, how it bent the masses of goldenrod and frail asters, how it blew her hair about and fluttered her mother's long black skirts. She took her mother's hand then and held it against her hot cheek, and Sarah Peters cried a bit as she had not done before and felt better.

John met them in Boston, tall and lanky, uncomfortable in his best clothes. He was no longer a boy who fretted over his books and wanted to be amused. Mary found herself looking to him to manage things for them, and realized suddenly that women turned to men because of something seemingly stronger within them.

She felt a new sense of safety as they journeyed northward through the now familiar towns and villages. Now and again they skirted the sea upon which she was to sail no longer. She thought she ought to hate it as she saw the surf pounding the brown ledges and ringing distant lighthouses with white spray. It had killed her father. Mr. Gardiner lay somewhere within its waters.

But she felt no hatred. One could not hate that which had been all the life one knew.

Her first night at home in the red-brick house with its white gate she dreamed of Cadiz, its towers and turrets mounting on its headland, its sunswept streets and walls, all white and shining as she had known it years ago. Her father was with her on its broad promenade above the sea. He had a guitar held by a red cord around his neck which embarrassed him so greatly that he turned all at once into Mr. Gardiner.

It was wonderful to walk there with Mr. Gardiner in the dazzling sunshine with the broad leaves of palm trees swaying in the light wind and a riot of flowers clambering up and down every white wall they passed. They stopped now and then to look at the harbour below them, blue and strewn with all manner of ships. She told him she thought he was dead, but he laughed at her with the old, steady look in his eyes which she had known and loved. Then with a mighty thump of his brown hand on the white balustrade of the promenade he swore he would sail ships all his life, ships with never an engine inside them, ships that spread their canvas until they dropped below the horizon in a last glow of light. A Spanish lady drew near them then with a flower in her hand and tried to kiss Mr. Gardiner, but instead he turned from her and kissed Mary in a kiss that lasted longer than she had ever supposed a mere kiss could last.

When she awoke, she was crying into her pillow. The east was streaked with pale light. She watched the dark hills of Mt. Desert, which on the south enclosed the harbour from the open sea, soften and grow blue before the sunrise. Beyond them, out of sight, lay the world she had known. Near at hand tumbled small, uneven fields bounded by stone walls aflame with goldenrod. An old, untended orchard sprawled over a neighbouring hillside. Gardens in the rangy disorder of early autumn interspersed the meadows here and there. Rock-strewn, fir-clad pastures mounted the harbour hills. A cock was crowing somewhere. She had left the sea and was at home.

# II

# The Village

## The Village

## 1

Petersport in the late eighteen-eighties was as typical of Maine seacoast society as any one village or period is ever typical of another in a like environment. Change was upon it, inevitable but as yet, at least in its longer effects, not wholly recognizable. Its docks, which twenty and thirty years earlier had echoed to the sounds of mallet and hammer, were now deserted, its piers rotting. Less than half a dozen of its families which from the early years of the century had won a deserved name and fame upon the sea were now actively connected with it. The War of the Rebellion had taken its toll of men and of ships and had rendered ocean trafficking precarious; iron and steel had taken the place of wood in ship construction, demanding the erection of docks near the source of supplies; the dispiriting inroads of steam were steadily increasing.

The Peters family was among the last to leave the sea even as it had been among the first to take to it. Perhaps its shipmasters and chief officers hung on with greater tenacity because they saw more clearly what was happening than could those whom they had left behind at home and wanted to drink deep while drinking was still possible. From the vantage ground of Shanghai or Liverpool or Valparaiso their perspective was less impaired. They knew too well that the old days were past, those days when foreign ports were household words and when a man's vision and wisdom and humour were supposed to be compatible with his journeyings over the watery face of the earth. They saw what was happening in other and farther places and related it by means of wide experience to their own hearthstones. They noted the spread of industry, the imposition of new tariffs, and the consequent lack of need for so many imported goods. They were business men as well as sailors, and they knew that one could not sail away heavy and with impunity sail home again light. But they hung on with others of like tradition and nurture as long as hanging on was possible with any profit whatsoever, scorning to go "into steam," playing a losing game for the glory and the fun of it, because they hated the notion of settling down within a small compass, of adjusting themselves to a confinement foreign to the only training they had ever known.

The village itself was far less aware of these matters just as one who is used to the care of a sick person cannot feel the same surprise over his condition as one who sees him suddenly after a long absence. It was proud of its seafaring history, regretful that its docks had fallen into disuse. From one of these the three-masted schooner *Magnolia*, first of its kind, had been launched in 1833; and there was no schoolboy unaware of this distinction. It recognized the social superiority of its retired captains and took pleasure in their stately homes, built, furnished, and renovated with the proceeds of battles against storm and wind. When the best of its young men (and, as time went on, of its young women) sought larger fields of enterprise, it regarded them rather with pride and favour than with concern as to who should take their places at home. And when in the late seventies certain professors from Harvard College and some Boston business men bought its best points and headlands and erected modest homes with wide verandas and perhaps a tower or two in the early style of the summer cottage, most of its inhabitants rejoiced in this turn toward prosperity, delighted in this new contact with the outside world, and, naturally enough, could not for a moment glimpse any unfortunate developments therefrom.

Once again it was those who had been farthest away who saw most clearly what was happening near at hand. But partly because men and women bred to the sea were inured to change more basic and fundamental, partly because the very necessity of the life they had led had tended to make of them spectators of time and of existence rather than participators therein, this stealthy beginning of coast metamorphosis did not rest too heavily upon them. Once at home with their ships scrapped or in dry-dock or, with lofty spars removed, destined to end their days in the new barge traffic of harbour, lake, and river, they gave themselves up with philosophic humour to whatever their coast towns and villages provided.

It was not unpleasant then to receive within their homes a college president whose learning was in no whit superior to their experience hewn out of a hard school. They knew the world, cities and harbours and many races of peoples, the manners of many men; the best of them had read and thought, bringing to bear upon their books and their minds a shrewd intelligence which no amount of training in a college or a university could better. They were men of taste and appreciation. The white gates which led to their beautiful doorways with fan-shaped shutters and studdings of brass were hospitably opened to the early "rusticators" who sought their shores and made the hearts of mere tradesmen rejoice; their door-stones of solid slabs of Maine coast granite were set about with rare Pacific shells; within their libraries were Persian rugs and Chinese tapestries, mahogany, brass, and old silver, and sets of books from London stalls. Portraits of themselves and stirring pictures of their ships hung upon their white-panelled walls. They laid their tables with damask cloths and set them with East Indian china. They could talk of anything under the sun. Once they had faced the future which had driven them from the seas they ceased to trouble overmuch about it. Like the present it would soon become the past in which they really lived.

They scorned patronage from anybody and in truth merited none. They were the best of the coast, representative of the best inheritance it could provide, and they knew it.

2

Like scores of other coast towns and villages similarly situated with the sea before it to the south and hills and ridges toward the north behind its mounting fields and pastures, Petersport could and did lay no small claim to beauty. Beyond its landlocked harbour, shaped like the horns of the oxen which still ploughed its high, rocky fields, beyond its outer bay rose the hills of Mt. Desert, blue in a west wind, purple before a north, pale gray when a northeaster troubled the seas. From the summit of its hills Penobscot Bay, strewn with islands and lights and traversed by white sails, reached oceanward. Ponds, which no one thought of calling lakes, were set low among its wooded slopes. From one of these a brook, which would elsewhere have been termed a river, tore seaward, twice halted on its way to furnish power for saw-mills, which on foggy April mornings when the spring was in the air shrieked their raucous music in the ears of Mary Peters, setting out for the Academy with her Greek and Latin books in an ample red-plush bag. Coastwise schooners, the last to fall before the conquest of steam, loaded staves and edgings, tied with yellow cord which smelled of tar, and fresh planks of spruce at its wharves; and fishing boats came in at dawn with cod and haddock at three cents the pound.

On the three steep hills which led north, west, and east from the one main street with its blacksmith shop, its few stores, its post-office and its dishevelled waterfront, rose the homes of its more substantial citizens with wide spaces between them where their lawns gave place to fields and to flower and vegetable gardens. Here lived the sea captains, the doctor, the two ministers, the preceptor of the Academy, the leading grocer, the postmaster, the lawyer; here, too, lived certain elderly and middle-aged ladies, widows and daughters of seafaring men of the clipper-ship era, women who

throughout the last century on the coast of Maine placed an unde-
niable stamp upon village life and thought. There were two white
churches as lovely and gracious in their architecture as they were
cramped and forbidding in their theology, one on West Hill, the
other on North. Over the long hill to the east ran the road to the
world outside, to the railway town eighteen miles away where
there was one train a day. A yellow stagecoach rumbled along this
road daily during the summer months with four labouring horses
and a driver in a red coat who, even as late as the eighties, sounded
a horn as he put on his creaking brakes and held back his horses
for the rutty, lumbering descent of the hill. He brought the mail at
noon and carried back after dinner with his outgoing bag any
chance and adventurous passengers who were taking the train.
Most journeyings (and they were few enough) were taken by boat.
At the steamboat wharf, situated on the left of the two harbour
horns, the coastwise steamer from Rockland, which made connections at dawn with the larger Boston boat, docked three times each
week from April to December when the ice closed in. The snow
closed in also, such snow in the eighties that the stage-driver, now
in a yellow pung with buffalo robes and hot soapstones, left the
warmth of his kitchen fire but three times a week and fervently
thanked the Lord when he could "get through" his eighteen miles
in five hours.

This long eastern road, once it left the village proper and
before it began its slow mounting of the hill, passed through certain outskirts of the town where lived the less substantial of its
people—labourers of sorts, fishermen, those who had once
worked at its docks. They bore the same names as the others, were
presumably of the same stock, their progenitors having come one
hundred and fifty years before like those of the others from Salem,
Newburyport, and Andover. There was not a foreigner among
them, not so much as an Irishman or a Scotchman. They were

Bartletts or Osgoods, Barretts or Woods, Hinckleys, Parkers, Stovers, Grindles, Merrills, Lords, Peterses or Wescotts with the rest—all English by race and tradition. Of whatever factors had contributed to their less important role in Petersport society—inheritance, intermarriage, health—they were ignorant; and in the eighties there were no public agencies either to inform or to strive to better them. They lived a respectable existence. Their women did the washing and the spring cleaning of larger houses; their sons went to sea on coastwise schooners in the summer and in the winter worked in the woods; their daughters rejoiced and were glad as the summer hotel business began to afford them in its dining rooms an easy and exciting livelihood.

The hill roads to the north and west led to the country, a Maine coast country of well-fenced farms and pastures and woodland. Here the people were of the same stock likewise, but families which for generations had followed the land rather than the sea. Their sturdy, low-built houses, many of them over a century in age, sat well back from the country road often beneath the slope of some northern hill. They were "story-and-a-half houses," painted white or yellow, with a bedroom, where their guests were housed and their children were born, downstairs behind the parlour, and sloping chambers above. They had long ells for kitchen and buttery which were in turn hitched to woodhouse and toolshed, carriage-house and barn. Their front yards, frowsy with scythe-cut grass, were intersected by gravelled paths or white clapboarded walks leading to austere front doors shaded by lilacs and syringas; their back yards where chamomile and rabbits'-foot clover flourished gave space for a woodpile, a pump or a well-sweep beside which milk-pans aired in the sun, a barrel for catching rain-water beneath the eaves, and in good weather for sundry vehicles—buggies, hayracks, and raking machines. In their garden plots, wired against the depredations of fowls, they grew crimson peonies, bleeding-hearts, fuchsias, marigolds, and nasturtiums. Grassy orchards lay before or behind their homes with now and then beehives beneath the apple trees. Their fields and vegetable gardens were small in compass; their soil was not fertile; but they themselves were for the most part independent and secure and as proud in their inheritance as those who had known Hongkong and Calcutta. Their wood-lots supplied their winter fires; their pastures and fields fed their stock; and if their cash resources were small, their cellars and storehouses demanded only labour and a modicum of decent weather to burst with plenty. When their sons and daughters had exhausted the resources of the district school, they gave them fall and spring terms at least in the Academy. On Monday morning they drove them down to some village room, the backs of their wagons bulging with well-cooked food, hams and cold pork and chickens, hogshead cheese, pies and doughnuts, tarts and cake and ginger cookies, bread, butter, pickles and preserves, enough to nourish mind and body until Friday at four o'clock when they would drive them home again.

The Academy was on West Hill just below the Congregational church and immediately adjoining the churchyard. It was an old building. Its red-brick walls, white cupola, and four white pillars had been erected in 1790 under the aegis of the church, which had established it for instruction in the ancient languages, in mathematics and history. In the eighties, although it was no longer under ecclesiastical supervision, it still taught the same subjects with English literature added and certain studies supposedly scientific. It had the reputation of being one of the best old-time academies on the coast and pointed with pride to former preceptors now on the faculties of Harvard and Yale and Princeton.

Its preceptor in 1886, when Mary Peters with quaking heart opened her Harkness Latin grammar and stared also for the first time upon the Greek alphabet, was a certain Mr. Bates. He wore a cutaway of good black stuff, a gold scarfpin in a true lover's knot, and parted his hair low on the left side. His trousers were tight and inclined to shortness, showing sometimes his homeknit stockings of good gray wool and always the felt inserts of his pull-over black boots. He taught the Classics with as much gusto as good taste would permit, and on Sunday mornings undid his scarf of seemly Scotch plaid in black and gray in the chilly gallery of the Congregational church preparatory to singing tenor in the choir. He came from Bowdoin College and dined every month at the two parsonages. His scholars called him Sir and deplored their inadequacy in attaining his high standards.

His two lady assistants made up in dignity what they lacked in solid training although they had attended the new normal school in Castine and were themselves sturdy Maine products. They wore their hair high on their heads in soft loops securely pinned to their crowns; they had crimps across their foreheads and fine curls in the back of their necks above the ruching of their high collars. They wore dresses of good wool in brown, navy blue or green, fashioned close and high in the neck and across the breast, long dresses edged with brush braid against fraying and often trimmed with a velvet panel on the left of the skirt which was exposed by the looping up of the overskirt. They suffered uncomplainingly from narrow waists which they drew in as they dressed in the morning and took pride in the new attached bustles which, ingeniously hitched to their long black underskirts of alpaca or farmer's satin, lent a formidable appearance to their backs as they bent over desks or wrote upon the wooden blackboards. Beneath these underskirts they wore quilted petticoats, of farmer's satin above the knee, of quilting from knee to ankle against Maine cold. Below these, for the sake of complete modesty, each wore a short knitted petticoat often self-made from red yarn and designed to cling tenaciously to discreet winter underwear. To guard their gowns from the ravages of chalk or from the dust of their classrooms they often wore aprons of black sateen with ruffles cut in points and outlined as were the pockets with red feather-stitching. And because the heat from the stoves in the back of the rooms rarely reached their platforms, they were glad on winter days to slip into a house-jacket or a sacque, so popular in the eighties, crocheted and tied at neck and wrists with jaunty bows of ribbon. When they left the Academy at night, each wrapped herself in a long cape of padded plush or a coat with epaulettes and large buttons from high collar to the bottom of yet another skirt. Reserving for Sundays their high hats of buckram covered with stockingette or beaver and lavishly trimmed with crown bows of velvet with perhaps an ostrich feather curling across the brim in front, they draped their heads in bead-trimmed knitted hoods, which looped below their chins and which were daringly called "kiss-me-quicks" by the fashion expert of *Godey's Lady's Book*. Each owned and carried on Sundays a tiny sealskin muff with a piquant bird in brown velvet perching upon the side most exposed to view.

They boarded in one of the best houses in town, it being considered an honour in the eighties to house the teachers. They shared a large bedroom with an ornate black walnut bureau, a commode with a splasher behind it worked in ducks and cat-tails, an air-tight stove, two Boston rockers, and a great double bed into which they got at night in their high-necked flannel gowns. Before they could settle themselves for a well-earned sleep upon their feathers, Miss Tapley must do up her front and back hair in lead curlers, which operation she essayed with the lamp lowered because she was shy before Miss Farnsworth whose hair curled naturally. Miss Farnsworth was younger than Miss Tapley, being only twenty-six to the other's thirty. She had a lover in Wiscasset, who taught in the academy there. She kept his letters in her Bible on the table at her side of the bed, and each night as soon as she thought Miss Tapley was asleep, she secured the latest, with as little crackling of the paper as was possible, to put it under her pillow. Sometimes when certain audacious words of his, staring boldly at her from his lined paper, caused her breath to stick in her throat for a minute, she concealed that letter in her bosom and actually taught with it lying there, proving that her heart was like all others in all ages and places even though it was not so recognizable beneath its layers of wool and flannel, stout alpaca or bombazine.

Sometimes, too, when the words of her letter came suddenly between her and the parsing of all words in the opening lines of *Paradise Lost*, Miss Farnsworth wondered with heightened colour in her cheeks if she were really a good example to the young of Petersport. For she and Miss Tapley and the serious Mr. Bates were supposed in the eighties to be just that very thing. Miss Farnsworth and Miss Tapley taught in the Sunday school. Refusal to do this would have marked them as unprofessed Christians, a stigma which they themselves could never have borne and which would never have been for a moment tolerated by most of the village. They were the somewhat subdued "life" of the games held after the Thursday night suppers in the vestry of one church or the other. They chaperoned candy-pulls and husking-bees and Hallowe'en parties; they frowned upon dancing and upon kissing games; and if on sleighing parties their watchful eyes had reason to suspect the holding of two mittened hands beneath a buffalo robe or horse blanket, they felt in duty bound to speak to the girl concerned, for it was a maxim of the eighties that "a young woman could and should control any such situation."

Miss Farnsworth felt shy in the face of such intrusive reminders, for with the letter from Wiscasset hidden deep against the her who was really she, she knew that she herself would have welcomed, had in times past welcomed, was eager again to welcome, indeed to participate in, such froward indulgence. She usually left such one-sided

conversations to Miss Tapley, who, if a meaning glance in the semi-
darkness or a pregnant clearing of her throat were not instantly
efficacious, relentlessly administered them the next day after school.
Miss Tapley was for the moment at least whole both in conscience
and in heart, although she herself in the winter of 1886 was a prey
to vain imaginings concerning a copy of Longfellow presented to
her by Mr. Bates, who had said on the fly-leaf that he gave it to her
"with deep regard."

Although the two churches would have been shaken to their
foundations by such a diagnosis, they also unconsciously nourished
and even now and again satisfied the heart-pangs of Petersport
young men and maidens. Of the two the Congregational was tacitly felt to be a bit superior. Distinctly the upper levels of village
society sat in its high-backed white pews, looking out through its
clear, many-paned windows upon its churchyard and its surround-
ing fields. In Maine in the eighties one would prefer to be a
Congregationalist rather than a Baptist just as one preferred to be
a Republican rather than a Democrat. Its theology, however, dif-
fered little from that of its neighbour on the opposite hill. Both
solemnly upheld the full-armoured Christian life as adjured by the
Apostle Paul and both made it as unattractive an existence as possible. But the young who sat on Sunday mornings before their
pulpits knew well that each afforded other more exciting consola-
tions, approved by their elders simply because they were sponsored
by the church. If one must sit with one's family on Sunday mornings, there were the Sunday evening services where one might sit
elsewhere, casting one's eyes and thoughts wherever one chose.
Better still there were the Tuesday evening meetings conducted by
young people themselves. These were testimonial meetings where
a young man's piety was encouraged in outspokenness by the sur-
reptitious, hopeful glances of the girl who sat beside him, meetings
of sentence prayers sometimes understandable by some one else

concerned quite as well as by Heaven, meetings of hymns more sprightly in their rhythms and more melting in their words than "The Church's One Foundation" and "Nearer, My God, to Thee." Moody and Sankey were in those years highly esteemed, and they without the shadow of a doubt fed youthful hearts quite as much as they saved youthful souls.

The annual revival held each January, when with the cold and snow spiritual life was ebbing and when emotions needed warmth and expression, was itself instrumental in the discovery of affinities and in the promotion of shy advances. More than one young man was urged forward to the mercy seat, once the call was given at the close of the nightly meeting, quite as much by the thought of the pleasure and relief of the girl whom he hoped to see home as by the deplorable condition of his own inner life. On such nights tender words were exchanged at gates and on cold door-stones, for the transition from the state of one's soul to the state of one's feelings seemed easy and natural now that emotion of one sort or another was in the air. Even Miss Farnsworth after a week of such meetings felt things loosed within her and wrote to the young man in Wiscasset words and sentences she could never have written in October or in March; and Mr. Bates once called formally upon Miss Tapley twice in the seven days to discuss the miraculous conversion of the worst boy in the Academy and to wonder what they two might do together to avert the backsliding which they feared.

The eighties were years of free church suppers on Thursday evenings when certain ladies "entertained" two by two and when every housewife of the respective parishes strove to outdo her neighbours in culinary art. At two o'clock they gathered in the vestry carrying in their hands their cakes and pies, doughnuts and jellied tarts, covered with spotless napkins, and over their arms their sewing-bags of embroidered plush and velvet. When they bore their offerings into the church kitchen where the white-aproned hostesses awaited them, they always apologized for them, deprecating the fact that the cream for their Washington pies would not whip properly or that they had suffered unforeseen difficulties with their doughnut fat.

By two-thirty they were seated in a great circle in the outer vestry, plying their needles for the August sale. It took months for Sarah Peters' ears to become accustomed to their incessant chatter and for her bewildered eyes to take account of the variety and multiplicity of their handiworks. They made ample aprons of percale and sateen with rows of feather-stitching or cat's-cradling; they embroidered splashers and tidies and lambrequins; they fashioned ingenious penwipers in bags of satin or velvet, worked in gold-pointed stars and disclosing at their openings some shreds of black serge or felt for the wiping of the pens. These were designed to hang jauntily on a hook at the end of one's desk and add a piquancy to the usual employment of desks everywhere. They crocheted bags and breakfast caps, thimble cases, bed-socks, and hoods for every head; they knit gay wristers for men-folks and leggings for children. From cross-stitching on canvas they designed watch-pockets, jewel-bags, and footstools. They made yards of crochet in cable stitch which they sewed in all sorts of intricate designs on table covers and sofa cushions and bureau scarfs. They shirred and they appliquéd, tatted and smocked, hemstitched and beaded on net. They made pincushions in the shape of tomatoes and carrots, oranges and lemons; emery bags by stuffing acorn shells; picture-throws from left-over scraps of silk. Blotters were covered with wide ribbon securely pasted down and ornamented by a smart bow of a contrasting shade. Mandolin and violin cases, so popular in that day, were elaborately fashioned from red and green shirred velvet, the colours alternating from one side to the other. They made tulip lampshades over sarsenet foundations in pink or nile green, shades of net and lace or white China silk, and for the lamp mat accompanying such a creation they used silk or crochet of the same colour. Hair and hat ornaments were popular. If they could not be sold in Petersport, the summer people would buy them. They made aigrettes of feathers, satin butterflies, silk flowers and birds and great bows of tulle, mounted on invisible wires. They quilted innumerable quilts and bedspreads with geometrical designs in patchwork. And as the crowning triumph of their art and perseverance they made in the winter of 1886 a hanging bookcase with three black walnut shelves, held together (or apart when hung) by gold cords and ornamented by valances of crimson plush embroidered in silk crewels and finished with innumerable fluffy balls. For this they planned to sell lottery tickets, knowing well that its charm would tempt many a heart and pocket.

At six the work was put away and the men and children gathered for supper. The air was warm and clinging with the smell of beans and brown bread and coffee; the long tables were set. Children of the "entertaining" families waited on them, standing in a seemly fashion with bowed heads while the pastor asked the blessing. Beans were passed from one to another in great dishes, yellow-eyed beans, pea beans, and natives; glasses and cups were kept filled; men asked jocularly for Ellen Hinckley's apple-pie or Susan Osgood's molasses doughnuts and pretended to abjure all others. The young people in the corners of the room waited for the second table when they might eat together and for eight o'clock when their elders would depart and leave them to their games. Young men who were connected at least for the time being by ties of affection with the "entertaining" families might help with the dishes. In the kitchen there would be sly bandying of words, shared bits of left-over cake, snatching of dish-towels, and sometimes in the numbers crowding about the kitchen sink a contact of hands which seemed unavoidable. Such delightful comradeship

manifested itself later in games where choice was a factor and again
when company home was proffered. So that at ten o'clock when
girls in freezing bedrooms took off one layer of apparel after another,
they had reason to bless the church of their fathers for something
besides religion as had also the young men who wound the
kitchen clocks and banked the fires before they ran upstairs to bed.


3


Within this compact, securely established community Sarah
and Mary Peters felt like strangers in more ways than one,
although neither admitted her feeling to the other. Neighbours
and relatives had opened the big brick house high on its hill above
the church and the Academy, had cleaned and dusted and straightened, laid fires, washed curtains and made beds so that those who
came back might feel at home and so that Captain William Peters'
body might rest in a seemly, tidy parlour during its last night in his
birthplace. Men in appropriate black clothes had watched the
night through in an adjoining room while Mary upstairs dreamed
of Cadiz and woke to tears and while Sarah Peters in her room
across the hall had not slept at all. John in his room at the back of
the house had wondered whether he ought not to be downstairs
with the others and had wished fervently that things might be
over so they might all settle down once more.

Things were over the next day, the funeral in the church, the
burial in the yard. It was a clear September day, Mary was to
remember, with a high northwest wind which deepened the harbour water and bent the cemetery grass, tall again since its early
cutting for Memorial Day. When they returned in their carriage to
the house, Ellen Kimball, whose father had died the year before,
came with them and sat with Mary on the haircloth sofa in the

parlour, talking in subdued tones of any topic that mercifully presented itself and knotting and unknotting her handkerchief in embarrassment over a difficult situation.

Ellen was not easily embarrassed and this unwonted mood sat heavily upon her. She did not feel at home with Death in such close proximity and so much in evidence. She herself seemed of no importance, and she was not at her best when she was forced to play a minor part. Nor did any of them for that matter seem of the least importance—Mary sitting there on the sofa in her high-necked black dress, John drumming on the window panes of the dining room and wishing he were in his old clothes on the farm, Sarah Peters wondering in her kitchen why on earth people were so stupid as to cook everything possible for you when the one thing you really wanted was to do things for yourself.

Ellen was undeniably pretty, and the black ribbon at the throat of her white dress set off her fair complexion. She looked older than her years. Mary was torn between her own embarrassment at not being able to find things to say and her relief at Ellen's presence which at least prevented her from being left alone with her mother and John. She had a curious feeling that in spite of Ellen's proffered sympathy and self-proposed company, she was really thinking of John and wishing he would join them. If John should come in, she felt sure that Ellen would talk in a more spirited fashion even though she felt it necessary to lower her voice in deference to Death, which still seemed to be secreting itself in the heavy folds of portières and window hangings, lambrequins and velvet table covers. Once when John passed through the room on his way to the staircase, glancing at them with a shy half-smile, Mary was conscious of something happening suddenly inside Ellen's body. Something inside her had tightened all at once like a rope suddenly strained by a wind-filled sail or like the tremor the ship sometimes gave before she plunged ahead upon a new course.

She herself was not wholly unacquainted with such a sensation. She herself had felt her heart at once tighten and quicken when Mr. Gardiner had been late for dinner and when he had comforted her about the dead robin; but she felt oddly sure that the tightening inside Ellen was somehow of a different sort, with which she as yet had had nothing to do, and she found herself vaguely uncomfortable before it.

"Is John really going to college?" asked Ellen when they had completed a rather stilted conversation concerning new handiwork for picture frames which his passage through the room had interrupted. And then, without waiting for Mary's answer,

"I don't think he'll take to it much, do you?"

"Why not?" asked Mary. "When Mr. Bates called last night, he said John was well prepared. He said there couldn't be any trouble at all."

"Oh, I don't mean about lessons," said Ellen hastily and, Mary thought, with more than a suggestion of superior wisdom. "He's smart enough even if he just won't ever show it. But college isn't all lessons. It's mixing with people, too, and making friends, and John won't mix. He—he's offish, Mary. You ask anyone if I'm not right. You don't know him half so well as his friends here do—you've been away so much."

Mary felt suddenly jealous for John and furious at Ellen.

"What do you mean by offish?" she asked tartly. "I don't know that it's anything against a boy if he's just shy."

"I didn't say it was anything against him," said Ellen with a shrug of her shoulders irritating to Mary in its further suggestion of an experience wider than her own. "Of course, it isn't. But he *is* offish. Ask anyone you like and see what they say. Mr. Bates might not say so, but what does he know about young people? He's thirty-five if he's a day and thinks of nothing but Latin and Greek. What I mean by offish is just that John won't enter into games and things. I've only just been to Academy parties this last year, but I've seen that much already. He's so afraid that a forfeit will be called on him that he gets red all over." A giggle almost escaped her, but she recalled it in time, remembering suddenly that she was with Mary in the role of a comforter.

"Maybe they're silly games anyway," stammered Mary, and found herself blushing to the roots of her hair.

"Well, if it comes to that, maybe they are," agreed Ellen with an expectant eye on the staircase through the open door. "But it doesn't do to act so if most people want to play them. And John's as offish about them as—as Mr. Bates would be if anyone ever called a forfeit on him which I can't imagine. It's hard on a girl when a boy refuses to play up in forfeits. Once you've been home a few months, you'll see if I'm not right."

She turned suddenly on the slippery haircloth of the sofa and faced Mary with an odd little glint in her round, lusterless blue eyes.

"He needn't act so bashful all at once anyway. He didn't used to be like that. I could tell you a thing or two about your own brother, Mary, if I'd a mind to."

Mary felt a desperate need for a change in subject and cast about for a substitute.

"Are the lady assistants nice?" she asked after a none too comfortable pause.

Ellen's reply was quick and sharp.

"What does John think? They've taught him for two years."

"I don't remember his ever saying."

"I'm sure he never has. That's another way he's offish. He never says what he thinks. Well, I have my own opinion if he hasn't. Miss Tapley's strait-laced and always ready to jump on you for the merest suspicion, but Miss Farnsworth is nice and understanding and doesn't fly off the handle at every little thing. They say," Ellen lowered her voice impressively, "people say Miss Farnsworth is engaged to be married."

"Who's they?" asked Mary bluntly, but relieved that the conversation was becoming at least less personal.

"Oh, one and another. She gets letters often in the same handwriting from the same place. They notice at the post-office. And she writes at least twice a week to a young man there. I know his name only I don't think I ought to tell it all about everywhere. But it isn't just the letters. It's the way she acts now and then in literature class especially. We girls all notice. Whenever we read a poem that has to do with love, her cheeks get pink and her voice takes on a different tone somehow. Last year it was as plain as day how she was affected when we read 'Annabel Lee.' I just love that poem, don't you?"

Tears sprang to Mary's eyes then, but she was spared either Ellen's comment or her mistaken sympathy. For just at that moment when she was striving to push the tears back where they belonged, the latch of the gate clicked to let through Mrs. Kimball's ample and black-clad figure. Mrs. Kimball had come for supper, bringing with her more food in jars and bowls and nappies. She brought with her, too, in her somewhat flurried manner and high, quick voice, the unmistakable evidence of news.

This she successfully concealed until after supper although it stirred uneasily within her and made the atmosphere even more tense than it would otherwise have been. She called Mary and Ellen from the parlour to set the table and herself joined forces with Sarah Peters in the kitchen. She was a large, square woman with prominent features and crowded teeth in a large mouth. The center of her upper lip had a mobile droop in it which Mary did not like. Whenever she looked at it, she thought of Mrs. Kimball chasing the kittens, doomed, no matter how they scurried to hide themselves away, to end their terrified lives in the pasture brook. Beside Sarah Peters' spare figure and finely cut face Mrs. Kimball was relentless, insensitive, perhaps a bit cruel. But she was a good manager of the most dreary affairs, and she infused into the tired house an energy it had not felt for hours.

"I'm glad you're getting acquainted with your own kitchen," she said heartily to Sarah Peters as she slammed the oven door upon the scalloped potatoes she had brought. "There's nothing like work when props are knocked out from under you like. Don't I know? Haven't I gone through it all myself? After Warren died didn't I go to work the very next day after the funeral and put up a hundred jars of fruit? Some of my neighbours thought I was crazy not to sit moping around or not to go through his things the way some folks would. But I knew better and so must you. My mother used to say there was nothing like good hard work and lots of it to mend a broken heart, and she was right."

Sarah Peters tried not to wince at Mrs. Kimball's blunt reference to the state of her heart and was helped by her half-humourous questioning of herself as to how she could possibly find sufficient work to do now that her neighbours had cleaned her house, done up her curtains, filled her shelves with preserves, washed her own pots and pans. Even getting supper was denied her since it had, in fact, been cooked elsewhere and was this moment warming in the oven.

Supper itself was not the easiest of meals. Sarah Peters abstractedly served the food. John, called officiously downstairs by Mrs. Kimball, was the epitome of embarrassed silence, and Mary herself was acutely uncomfortable without quite knowing why. Ellen knew quite well the cause of the petulance which gnawed within *her*, but she bided her time and at the moment ably seconded her mother who pleasantly felt the responsibility of the situation squarely upon her. Moreover, Mrs. Kimball knew that she was concealing that within her which, divulged later in secret to Sarah Peters, would substantially enliven matters, at least for herself.

"In two weeks wanting three days," said Mrs. Kimball, generously buttering one of her own hot raised rolls, "you girls will have birthdays. Ellen and I have a plan for that, Sarah. We say, why not join in a nice party at our house? Naturally you wouldn't feel like having one for Mary herself this year—I mean, just now with things happening like this—but Mary can come with Ellen and I'll tend to everything. You needn't have a mite of care of anything at all."

"It's kind of you," said Sarah Peters, "to think of Mary's share. But I don't know. Maybe it's too soon after—"

"Nonsense! People won't think a thing of it, sensible people won't. And it's a good way for Mary to get acquainted again. She's almost a stranger to the young folks."

"Remember, mamma," interposed Ellen, "that this is going to be a real grown-up party with supper around the table, not just refreshments, and games in the evening. Remember, you said I could invite older boys and girls. You'll come, John?"

"I'll be gone, I think," said John, stirring uneasily in his chair.

"No, you won't. Mr. Bates said you didn't have to go till the twenty-second, and this will be the night before."

John, feeling himself securely caught, said nothing.

"You'll have parties and parties in Brunswick, John," said Mrs. Kimball, "so you may as well get used to them. This can be a sort of farewell one to you, too. And I hope," she continued, an obvious tone of importance creeping into her voice, "that the Wilburs will still be here so Grace can come. They're the nicest people, Sarah. You'd never know that old Bowden place on the point for the way they've fixed it up. They've built a porch all around it, so far out they can actually catch flounders at high water, and they've put in a bathroom and all sorts of new things. Asa Bowden would fair turn over in his grave, I say. They must have a heap of money to do all they've done. But there, they're common as common. Mrs. Wilbur sewed for the fair just like one of us, and then turned right around and bought and bought. And Mr. Wilbur gave so much to the church fund that Mr. Bean's salary this year is no problem at all. Fact is, we're even thinking of raising it to seven hundred though there are them that think it would be an outrage. And Grace is such a nice, pretty girl, just seventeen, isn't she, Ellen? One day in Sunday school she asked Ellen down there and came for her in her own carriage. Ellen had a lovely time and came home with so many ideas for a new dress that I declare I about went crazy trying to make it like Grace's. I think Grace would love to come, don't you, Ellen?"

"Probably," said Ellen. "Only maybe she'd think it sort of plain compared with New York. I don't know."

"Of course, she wouldn't. Don't you go getting crazy notions! She's too much of a lady to have such thoughts. Don't her mother come right into my kitchen and talk with me just as if I was like her with lots of help around? The Wilburs and those other folks on the point have brought a lot of life to this village, and we ought to be thankful."

"Who else will come to the party?" asked Mary. It was the first word she had spoken during the meal, and, inappropriate as it seemed to her, she felt she must say something.

"Oh, we'll decide together the first of the week," said Ellen. "The trouble's going to be drawing lines. We don't want school to open with half the town mad at us."

"Maybe someone'll come that you're not expecting."

Mrs. Kimball could not resist offering the suggestion but remained impervious to Ellen's questions.

The Peters family was glad when supper was over although the Kimballs were conscious within themselves of a pleasant sense of mastery. Ellen's careful gleaning from Mr. Bates of the date of

John's departure had assured his presence at her party, and their professed association with the New York Wilburs had in their own minds at least placed an enviable stamp of distinction upon them. What was more, Mrs. Kimball cherished her news to be soon divulged after the manner current among women in Maine villages in the eighties when they dealt with matters presumably not fitted for younger ears.

The occasion seemed meet and right while the girls and John were clearing up after supper. She and Sarah Peters sat down in the sitting room, the oblong centre table between them with its tasselled velvet cover and its lamp of Dresden china. Mary, setting the table for breakfast and putting away the dishes which John was drying for Ellen in the kitchen, saw them there and knew by the way Mrs. Kimball was leaning across the table toward her mother that some intimate conversation was in progress. Nor was she above loitering a bit with the cups and plates to learn if she could from Mrs. Kimball's discreet undertone what was making her mother seemingly so intent on her knitting of winter socks for John.

"I thought you might as well hear it from me, Sarah. You'd know anyway tomorrow. . . . Yes, at sea, two weeks out from New York. . . . They buried him there. . . . I suppose it was just as well though it's always seemed heathenish to me. . . . No, I don't know what. I guess he was failing up generally. . . . He's too young for that, but I guess, if the truth was known, he's lived a life! . . . Yes, the boy's coming here. . . . I don't know—in a few days, I'd say. . . . Lame? Well, I never. I don't envy Joel and Mattie. Get your own raised up and off your hands on their own, and something else is sure to be put on you to do. That's the way things are, I guess."

So Captain James Pendleton was dead, too, and young Jim was coming to Petersport. Mary paused in the dark passageway between dining room and kitchen to feel suddenly sorry for him, less for his father's death and his own closed life perhaps than for this new one which awaited him and upon which she herself was about to enter. She remembered him as he stood by the rail of the *Elizabeth* watching the lights come out and the harvest moon as it swung above the busy river harbour, set about with the dark outlines of the ships he and she had known. She wondered how he would take to Petersport shut in among its hills and more how Petersport would take to him.

Later when Sarah Peters relayed to her children Mrs. Kimball's news as they got the house closed and ready for the night, she betrayed no feeling whatsoever. Indeed, she had none. Her life had made surprise practically impossible; and she had become used to the swift pulling down of curtains over one thing or another.

## 4

Young James Pendleton proved the sensation of the village, the nucleus of its revolving thoughts, impressions, and opinions. Coming suddenly out of a past which everyone thought securely closed, he relivened memories, unearthed half-forgotten incidents, instigated a hundred points of interest and conjecture. He was the talk of the town for months. In appearance obviously unlike his father except for the set of his head and shoulders, he must perforce resemble his mother, a mysterious woman as unfavourably thought of as she was completely unknown.

It has always been difficult for an outsider to fathom the Maine coast attitude toward a foreigner and especially toward a foreign marriage. Perhaps some odd hangover from provincial England has dictated it; perhaps the very tenacity with which men of English tradition settled its coastline, learning its precarious harbours and conquering its stubborn soil, has bequeathed a jealous suspicion toward the newcomer, the barbarian. Whatever its cause, it still exists among coast people, and in the last century it was both active and ungenerous. Maine men might and did sail the Seven Seas; they might be at home in foreign ports and conversant with foreign merchants; they might fill their homes with foreign wares; but when it came to marriage, they married into native stock. And if, as infrequently happened in order that the exception might prove the rule, some captain or officer completely lost his senses and married abroad, he righted his mistake somewhat by having at least escaped alliance with a woman of Latin race.

James Pendleton had married a French woman. That was all anybody knew, and that had been quite enough to incur the suspicion of many of his townspeople, especially of the land element among them. Rumour had it that the woman had not been any too respectable; but whether rumour in this instance was based upon the distrust accorded her race in general or upon the somewhat volatile nature of James Pendleton in particular, no one was in a position to say. His brother Joel, the postmaster of Petersport, whose lack of imagination had kept him at home from boyhood, and his wife Mattie knew or at all events pretended to know as little as any one else. They received his son with decent cordiality into the old Pendleton home on North Hill and after two months knew him as little as they had on the day of his arrival.

He talked easily but said surprisingly little and proffered less than little to his aunt's careful but shrewd questions about his home and his mother's family. Mattie Pendleton was foiled from the start in her attempt to discover what lay behind his careless, pleasant ways. He was clean but untidy, willing but negligent and forgetful, consistently polite to the point of annoyance. He read omnivorously, lounging in his uncle's favourite chair until he was tartly reminded of the fact when he at once became distressed and apologetic. He had brought French books in his outlandish-looking trunks and boxes, and when his aunt carried them distastefully

to his unkempt room, which with exasperated sighs she attempted
to straighten daily, he had a good-natured way of returning them
one by one to the sitting room table and leaving them there for
callers to gaze upon with disapproval. He spoke English with his
father's voice and accent and was surprisingly quick at picking up
odd coast phrases current at the time. He had an extremely irritating way of dreaming for long fractions of time, slumped in a chair
or gazing upon the harbour as he leaned against the window
frame, smudging with his coat sleeves the white paint or his aunt's
carefully polished glass. This habit put her, as she said, "completely
on edge," pestering her not only by its idle uselessness but by the
uncomfortable feeling it gave her of being outwitted and baffled.
Whatever could he be thinking about, she asked herself again and
again; and since she had been sturdily reared on the maxim that
Satan was unquestionably lord of all forms of idleness, she always
came to the conclusion that behind her nephew's dark eyes (in
themselves distasteful to her!), behind his lean, vivacious, mobile
face some mischief was brewing to further the disgrace his father
had already brought upon the family name. As to the cause of his
lameness, no one knew, least of all his aunt and uncle. Whether he
suffered from it no one knew either, for he was uncommunicative
and nonchalant in the face of all querying. He had a passion for
music which Petersport could neither understand nor nourish. He
was forever twanging a guitar or playing a fiddle in his room at
night and singing to them strange words which his aunt distrusted
because she had not the remotest notion of the meaning they
conveyed. Without the least permission and apparently with no
idea that he was doing anything extraordinary he ransacked the
square piano and tuned it so that he could strum upon its yellow
keys. His aunt's persistent probings into his mother's religion (for
she feared the worst!) left her entirely unsatisfied. He made no
objection to attending church and sat docilely enough between

his aunt and uncle, his dark eyes on the minister's face in respectful attention. He was not like his father, the congregation said, more interested in him than in the sermon, and yet in some indescribable, perhaps none too complimentary way he was.

The one redeeming feature of his presence so far as his uncle and aunt were concerned was the punctual and generous payment for his board and keep. This came the first of each month in a check from a New York law firm into whose hands James Pendleton had evidently placed his affairs and those of his son. To Joel Pendleton's careful inquiries, demanded by his wife, reply was summarily made that there were sufficient funds for the boy's care and education and that the firm alone had charge of their disposal. Young Jim himself received from the same source twenty dollars monthly for his pocket, a sum which his aunt thought more than enough to send any young man straight to perdition. He was as careless about money as he was about his neckties and shoestrings and was forever leaving bills and loose change about the house, a habit irritating beyond words to his aunt, who, like most of her neighbours, kept her money for church beneath the newspaper in the right-hand corner of her topmost bureau drawer, her money for the missionary society in an old teapot, and her money from the sale of eggs in a pink cup on the kitchen lamp-shelf.

Largely from curiosity, partly from interest and pity, the boy was invited here and there about the village during the first few weeks after his arrival. He dined, sombrely enough, at the two parsonages. He took tea staidly with Miss Abbie Wood, who read *The Atlantic Monthly* and passed upon books for the Ladies' Social Library, and with the Misses Stover, who hoped he would join the church and do well at the Academy. He had supper far more genially in the homes of sea captains who had known his father and grandfather. These men recognized his intelligence, talking with him of ships which he had not much liked but had known and telling him tales of their own youth in ports and on oceans which he knew. They might deplore his father's lack of sense but, like seafaring men everywhere, were not greatly concerned over his lack of morals. They confided to one another and to their wives, if they had them left, that the boy had a rough course to steer with Joel and Mattie Pendleton and gave him a friendly hand when they met him about the village.

Had such men wielded either through numbers or by force of interest in village concerns any real influence in the shaping of that mysterious and insecure phenomenon termed "public opinion," the lot of young James Pendleton in Petersport might have been an easier one. But here as elsewhere on the coast, as the nineties waited just around the corner, those who had left the sea remained in mind peculiarly there rather than at home. Home affairs were matters of speculation, sometimes of amusement, but rarely of active interest. Men who had known the world at large found it not only difficult but idle to join lodges and discuss village politics. Men who had waited humourously for most of their lives upon time and space could not bring down their minds to trifling activities within a small compass. They sat by their fires in the winter and in the summer walked the disused piers, swapping yarns with the ever-decreasing few who had lived the lives they knew; they counted their money, giving generously enough to this and that, secure in the knowledge that they had enough to last them through; they watched the weather by glass and wind and water and received as their just due the respect accorded them by their townspeople who had not known the earth as they knew it. But they lived in a past, going, all but gone, and allowed those who had stayed at home to place their stamp, more solid if less gracious, upon the community.

5

If James Pendleton, Jr., was the cynosure of the maturer eye
and mind of Petersport, he was even more the centre of attraction
for all its young. He arrived in time for Ellen's grown-up party
and nearly disrupted the occasion by merely being there. Was he
shy or merely taking all things in as he sat at Mrs. Kimball's
bedecked table and ate her pressed veal and hot rolls, mashed
potatoes and jelly, ice cream and cake? Was he interested or super-
cilious, defiant or only embarrassed as he joined in games odd to
him, impeding their progress either by his initial lack of understanding or by everyone's curiosity over how he would behave?
Ellen herself was partly excited over his presence which added
such glamour to her party and beside which that of John seemed
suddenly extremely dull and undesirable, partly incensed that he
paid so little attention to her. In games where choice was necessary, he chose either Mary or Grace Wilbur, Mary for John
Brown's Body and Spin the Cover, Grace for all games where forfeits were exacted. Ellen's brain even at fifteen was subtle, or at
least cunning enough to note a difference in his treatment of the
two. He seemed to depend on Mary to make him feel at home;
but with Grace he assumed a haughty manner as though he could
demand of her whatever he liked. Whether he kissed Grace in the
dark hall whither they were sent together as a post-office forfeit of
five minutes, Ellen would have given her new dress to know. But
she was left in galling ignorance just as, ferret though she did, she
never discovered how long he stayed on the Wilbur porch after he
had climbed before the astonished gaze of all of them into the
Wilbur carriage which came for Grace at ten o'clock. Mrs. Wilbur
could have told, supplementing her information with the time it
had taken her usually dependable coachman to drive the three
miles through the woods to their summer cottage. But after a

somewhat harassed night, spent in gloomy cogitations over the "actions" of the younger generation in contrast to the impeccable behaviour of her own, she thought better of her impulse. The less summer visitors partook of village affairs the better, she concluded, and confined her opinions of the new arrival to Grace herself, who after her mother's onslaught tearfully packed her bags for New York with at least the pleasurable knowledge that she was older and wiser than before and that there was not one thing her mother could do about it.

It was only in Sarah Peters' house on the hill above the church that Jim Pendleton felt really at home. He was forever mounting the hill at odd hours during school-less days to squeeze himself into the children's old highchair in her kitchen, his long legs wrapped around its rungs. He watched her at her baking and, now that John was gone, filled her woodboxes and swept her porches. On many afternoons as soon as school was out he walked home with Mary, carrying her plush book-bag and seldom saying a word as they climbed the hill together, his left leg jerking about in a sort of half-circle before he could place it on the ground. He kept his curious, silent dependence upon Mary who liked him and found herself far more at home with him than with her brother. She helped him now and then with his lessons toward which he maintained an annoying indifference. Two years older, he was supposed to be ahead of her in all subjects, although his desultory schooling here and there had proved the exasperation of the meticulous Mr. Bates, who expected a seventeen-year-old boy to be where he ought to be and not distributed over the whole tidy curriculum. If on these afternoons he was not invited to supper, he usually stayed anyway, never for a moment thinking, to Sarah Peters' acute discomfiture, that he should first go down her hill and up another to apprise his aunt of his intended absence from her well-regulated table.

Sarah Peters, in spite of herself, tempered her annoyance with mercy. She could not divorce the notion from her mind that the boy was in some unorthodox way connected with her and that she owed him kindness and understanding. The first was easy to give him. It welled up within her, not to be withstood. The second was more difficult. She felt it like the first within herself and knew it was born and nourished out of a common past of which relatively few of her neighbours knew anything at all. She never could look at him steadily as he held her skein of yarn for her, moving his forearms rhythmically to keep pace with her winding, without seeing distant harbours, smelling confused land-smells, feeling the rhythm of ships pursuing their wide ways over the oceans of the world. But he did nothing to help her in her understanding. Probe as she would, she got little, at least in words, from him.

"Are you happy here, Jim?"

"Of course. Why not?"

"I mean in Petersport. Do you like it?"

"Well enough. It's all right."

"Is it like what you thought it would be?"

"I don't know. I suppose I never thought much about it."

His answer was what she might have expected. People reared as he had been did not think much of the future.

"Didn't your father ever tell you about it—how it was when he was young?"

"I don't think so. I don't remember that he did. He wanted me to come back here, and here I am."

"Do you like the people here?"

"They're all right, I guess. I like you and Mary. I don't think the others like me much."

"What a silly notion! Of course, they do."

He raised his eyes from the skein he was holding to confound with the knowledge within them her own pretense.

"No, they don't. You know that. They don't like—outsiders. But I don't care. I can come here. It doesn't matter—one way or another."

Once on a day when it was snowing in great silent flakes and they were alone, she took a daring plunge, her heart quickening as she did so.

"What about your mother? Did she know you were coming here? Did she want you to come?"

She waited fearfully, thinking she had invaded his seclusion, wishing she could take back her questions. But if at first he was perturbed, he did not show it.

"I don't know. I don't think she much cared—if she knew. It was father who managed things."

Encouraged by his seeming ease, she went a step further.

"You've never told me about your mother. I wish you would. What was she like?"

The boy's reply was brief although still he showed no embarrassment.

"She was not like you," he said, and, the yarn being just then wound, he went quietly into the room across the hall where Mary was doing her lessons.

Although perhaps it did not bring assurance in its wake, Sarah Peters' understanding of him progressed most rapidly on the winter evenings when he brought his guitar or violin to the house and stayed far too late.

Mary was following the prescribed custom of Petersport for its young ladies in taking music lessons, Miss Farnsworth supplementing the local music teacher who was advancing a bit beyond her pupils through some months at the Conservatory in Boston. Miss Farnsworth could play hymns and waltzes, polkas and funeral marches, and was not averse to an extra half-dollar which came her way for each lesson administered on Saturdays. On these winter

evenings Jim Pendleton hurried Mary along through her laborious
reading, wondering why she must hesitate before mere notes,
impatient at her uncertainty and ignorance. He played with her
until he could bear it no longer and then flew off on wild improv-
isations of his own, on the piano which nettled him by its bad tone
or preferably on his own violin and guitar. Then and then only did
the places he had known and even the thoughts he had thought
flash before him until Sarah Peters was frightened and troubled and
went to bed wishing he were anywhere but in Petersport.

"Here is Cape Horn in a storm, Mary!" he would cry, and
thunder forth crashing chords from the old piano, which shook
and creaked in helpless protest, until Mary was bewildered and
embarrassed and wished he would go home.

"Here are the Straits of Java at sunset."

He swept his guitar then, picking from its strings such tremulous, vibrating notes, such haunting, lingering echoes that still,
tropical seas came suddenly into being with flaming clouds above
them. Mary thought of the young Italian and the notes of his flute
sailing away above the quiet water. Stars came out then, such stars
as Petersport would never know; purple shores lay in the distance
with dark, shadowy palm trees; and a great orange moon began to
describe an arc on the horizon and then a circle as it swung higher
into the eastern sky.

Once after Hongkong had come into being from his violin
and she had seen again its yellow harbour water, its drifting, laden
sampans and heard the hoarse cries of their vendors, she asked him
in a sudden, stirring impulse to play Cadiz on its high peninsula.
He could not, he said. If he had ever seen it, he could not remember at all what it was like; but if she would tell him, he would try.
Standing in the middle of the room with his violin on his shoulder, he waited for her to tell him and became again irritated and

impatient when she found to her surprise and chagrin that she could not tell him so much as a single word.

6

John Peters did not like Bowdoin College. He did tolerably well in his studies but made few contacts and never once seemed to realize why he was there or what it was all about. He stayed on through his second year mostly to please his mother, but he spent his vacations arguing with her as to the wisdom of her desire for him. He followed her about the house pressing these matters. In the morning it seemed to her hours that he stood in his old overalls, which smelled of hay and manure, with an armful of wood held above the kitchen woodbox.

"I'm sorry, mother, but you can't make a scholar out of me. It's no good. I get my lessons well enough, but it's hard work and I hate it. Now take chemistry. I thought I'd like it better than Latin and history and all that, but I don't. I stay shut up in that laboratory two afternoons a week, and where do I get? Nowhere! Make a scholar out of Mary. She likes it. I can't be a doctor or a minister, mother. I know I can't. And there's fewer chances at sea all the time even if I liked it. Why can't I be what I want to be? I'll make a good farmer, and what's the matter with farming? I'd be happy at that. You want me to be happy, don't you? And it's foolish to spend what little money we've got on making me finish. If you'd let me quit in June, I could take what it would cost the next two years and make my first payment on uncle's farm. He's quitting anyway to go out West with all that new land there, and he'll sell cheap, the stock and all. And I'll get a start, a better one than most fellows. I'll be twenty-one, mother, in June. Can't I do what I want to do?"

Sarah Peters rolled out her cookies with deft sweeps of her arm, creased the brown dough with the blunt edge of her knife, cut them with quick, circular twists of her cookie cutter, and felt herself giving way. When he proffered the argument for happiness, she had no answer. She wanted him to be happy in his own way. She looked at him standing there, his wide, shy, blue eyes set honestly in his ruddy face, his shock of fair hair, always unkempt, his big strong hands curved about the sticks of white birch wood, his strong, healthy body. On the left side of his head just above his temple she could see between the thick locks of his disordered hair the scar of his fall ten years before on the *Elizabeth* and was tortured again by the memory of his suffering and her fear. She offered her last point while he arranged the armful of wood neatly in the box and while she spread the cookies in her well-greased pan.

"What about your friends? Won't you be lonely way up there in the hills? Aren't there boys in college you'd take to more? Life's a long thing, John, and you have to think of your future, you know."

"I have thought of it. I've thought and thought. What if you don't care much for friends, mother? I know you think I'm queer, but I don't care much for friends. Leastways I haven't made them at college."

He looked at her, growing more red and shy. She could see his heart beating in his throat and the sudden deepening colour of the scar upon his head. All her fortifications fell at that moment.

"Maybe I am queer. They all said so at the Academy. Ellen's always at me about it. I like animals the way most folks like people. I can't explain how it is. I just know, that's all. If I have horses around and cows and—things, I'll be all right. And I might—marry somebody some day, perhaps. Farmers do. And then I'd have a home of my own." He paused by the woodbox, his back toward her, trembling with embarrassment. "And I wouldn't be way off somewhere—away from you—the way I'd probably have to be if I finished college and went into something else. I'll stay here nights—I promise—as long as you want me. I'll—I'll do anything, mother, if only you'll let me have my way."

The die was cast and she knew it as she washed up her cooking dishes, keeping her distraught mind firm on her oven. She watched him through the back windows of the kitchen as he swung his axe above his chopping-block, cleaving the circular white birch sticks with sure and steady swing, splitting the fir and spruce into thin, knotted yellow lengths for her quicker fires. These he would pile in the woodshed before he returned to college, the hard wood in one orderly row, the soft in another. The chips and bits of bark he would gather in a big basket ready for her hands on cold, sharp mornings.

He was like her in only one way that she could see: he liked getting things finished and he had a passion for work that was more than joy. Love might hurt him, but work with his hands, never! It would soothe and heal, fulfill, give him his birthright. She could not keep it from him. From a long and tenacious perspective she knew him and his race better than he would ever know himself. Out of his struggle with his land, his dogged, rock-filled soil, his jagged ledges, his persistent trees, he would win what others of his family had won from their fight with the seas. Like the best of his race he could not be managed for long. He might be independent, determined, severe, hard even, but, like the oxen ploughing his fields, straining and stumbling through the heavy soil, he must be given his head.

She realized gratefully as she set her kitchen in perfect order and hurried upstairs with broom and dustcloth that she did not lack understanding of him. She herself shared his passion for work, for completion, for perfection of a given task. Only with her, as it might later be with him, she worked for a purpose; and this purpose was the freeing of her spirit. Once her house was in order her mind was clear, her imagination unimpeded. She could review her life then, each incident of it falling without confusion into its allotted place, each impression clear and unimpaired, each decision accepted for what it was without the nagging of regret. Life still blossomed for her into moments of loveliness although most of them now were either in retrospect or else made possible in the present by the synthetic powers of the past. But just as she could not sit down to her sewing in an undusted room or work at her gardening with her beds unmade, so whatever joys she knew reserved their ecstasies until she herself was in order. Memories remained unencouraged on Monday mornings, and the crimson peonies bursting beneath her sitting room windows unnoticed until her ironing on Tuesday was done and spread for airing.

Whether the work of her neighbours freed and translated them in like fashion, she could not know nor did she much care. Like her they cleaned and scoured, baked and brewed, pickled and preserved, but whether their jars upon jars of jelly, piccalilli, chili sauce, and preserves, carefully labelled and standing upon their cellar shelves, bore any relation to that which gave meaning to their lives, she could not tell nor had she any means of knowing. She knew, sometimes, with a despairing sense of her own inadequacy that she could not feel toward one of them in their snug homes as she had once felt toward the least of the sailors now and again on board the *Elizabeth*. There she had been irrevocably bound to all souls by a common destiny, conscious that they moved together, whither or no, through the common medium of the sea. Here she was conscious of no common destiny, no chance, no dependence. There were no other women of like age and experience in the village, and had there been, they would doubtless, after the manner of their kind, have found confidences difficult. And the several older women who had once followed the sea seemed at least to have settled down as she could not do into the reliable, dogmatic grooves of life ashore.

Sometimes momentary rebellion swept her as she sat with the Ladies' Circle and sewed for the August sale, obviously the focal point of every woman's mind during the winter. She could not get used to the calm certainty directed toward small events, the minor irritations and anxieties over this and that, she whose life had been so largely spent in the inevitable drift of great forces, outside one's decision, independent of one's desires. She was a failure at participation, she concluded, either in work or in thought; and she sewed all the more ardently, determined to make up in manual and material co-operation what she lacked in other more fundamental ways.

Out of moments of such rebellion came a deeper understanding of her son, a more voluntary willingness to let him have his own way. She began to see that his passion for the land was deeper than inclination or resolve, that it was rooted in the soil itself and thence in some mysterious manner had passed into him just as the sea had bred in his fathers and forefathers the same mysterious, invincible alliance. Beside such a force mere decision was paltry and inconsiderable; and she gradually relinquished her plans for his future without a shadow of regret.

7

Neither did Mary Peters participate well or easily in matters which seemed of such burning import to her schoolmates, the choosing of a class motto, the forming of new clubs, the delicious speculation over this or that new romance within their midst. These things were forever eluding her, or she them (she never knew quite which), and she seemed always pulling herself back to necessary attention. She did whatever the others did: she coasted and skated and went on sleighing parties; she gave her share of candy-pulls and sewing-bees; she went to church suppers and Sunday-school picnics; and on Saturday mornings she learned the ways of her mother's kitchen and how to make pie-crust and layer-cake, apple butter and hogshead cheese.

She was popular enough among her associates, rather looked up to, perhaps a little feared, partly because of her mind which was always ahead of other minds of her own age, partly because of her appearance. She was beautiful at seventeen with a loveliness that waylaid people, startling them simply because they were not expecting it. There was, indeed, seemingly nothing to startle anyone in her quiet, almost still face. Her gray eyes were not in themselves surprising nor the irregular line of her brown hair nor the sure, high carriage of her head which somehow accentuated her high cheek bones. No one would have paused over her colouring, which was easily eclipsed by that of Ellen or of a dozen other girls, or over her mouth, sensitive and thoughtful though it was. The surprise lay in the sudden transformation of skin and features by a singular radiance which lay either behind them or quite outside them. In her face a light was repeatedly enkindled, sending a glow into her cheeks and lips and remaining in her eyes so that even thoughtless persons paused and wondered what it was. At such moments she was like a daisy field in full sunlight or like the glow on the sails of a disappearing ship. Perhaps the very source of this peculiar transfiguration was responsible for the increasing sense of insufficiency she felt in the people whom she knew. For except when she was at her books or on walks by herself when no one could suddenly call her back to things at hand, she was conscious of a want which she did not fully understand but which was always there.

She loved study with a passion. When in her second year in the Academy she had been promoted to geometry, she could hardly wait to get home at night to sit down with ruler and compasses and clean white paper before her propositions and theorems. She measured and drew, lettered and bisected. She sat scrutinizing her problem, questioning, pondering, until all at once tantalizing, half-formed possibilities like recurring beams of light would gleam fitfully in her mind, never to be entirely lost sight of, until together they could be made to glow in an illumination of understanding. The result was intoxicating to her, and she would work for hours to experience it. She loved, too, the neat piling of her book, paper, and tools at the far corner of the table, suggesting by their very orderliness that she knew beyond a doubt what had been required of her.

Even better she loved her Greek and Latin, her history and literature, although sometimes, instead of dispelling her want, these had a way of bringing it more potently into being. In them she lived again something of the life she had known as a child. They were forever granting life to illimitable thoughts and fancies, stretching on and on like the sea, until they were out of sight, transcending her grasp. Yet although she could not follow them, she knew where she was with them whereas with people she never knew. When in her third year she reached the *Odyssey*, there was the sea again, barren and unharvested, wine-dark at night, its ways darkened when the sun had sunk. There it was, the vast and heaving deep, cut by swift and dark-prowed ships, moving over its broad back. There were its havens, like Cadiz; and there, in language beautiful beyond mere words, were its hollow, sounding caves where nymphs lay in love with Poseidon, lord of all.

She could not understand how the imperturbable Mr. Bates could take it all so calmly, insisting on cases and tenses and never once saying how magnificent it was. The members of the class, too, seemed to Mary inert and sluggish enough, labouring on through line after line and reckoning ahead the passages likely to fall to them. Ellen did not study Greek. She and her mother thought it not a sensible subject for girls and only tolerated Latin because in the eighties a social superiority was attached to it. Sometimes,

indeed, Jim flashed Mary a glance of comprehension, and not infrequently, when he was at the house, he asked her to read some lines
to him because he liked the sound of them. But these cases were
but occasional, and she was conscious of disappointment.

English literature was less torpid than Greek in its results. It had
a way, unless too difficult, of proving congenial to the diverse
thoughts and feelings of everyone concerned; and now that Miss
Farnsworth, in Mary's third year, had definitely decided to marry the
young man from Wiscasset once June had set her free, her presenta-
tion of the subject was far more emancipated. To Mary, Shakespeare
brought back Mr. Gardiner and the long, quiet reading in the dog-
watch of clear, favourable days. She got out her old copybook filled
with the verses she had culled from *A Garland* and said them over
again, adding now to them the lines about "the quality of mercy,"
which Miss Farnsworth strongly recommended, Hamlet's soliloquy,
and the ravings of poor Ophelia about her flowers:

> *There's rosemary, that's for remembrance; pray, love, remember;*
> *And there is pansies; that's for thoughts.*

And when she found definitions about life, she wrote them
down, too, aware that something deep within her responded,
whether it was called a walking shadow, or a fitful fever, or a poor
player, or a tale told by an idiot.

She became aware, too, as the months succeeded one another
and the end of her life at the Academy lay not so far away that
that which had given meaning to her years at sea was somehow
deeply hidden within the thoughts of books, ready to give the
same secure meaning to those who could take it. People who had
said great and beautiful things in books and poems had said them
not so much out of their own thoughts as out of that which had
made their own thoughts possible. It was all very puzzling but

there it was, trembling on the edge of her understanding and seemingly caught for a light-filled instant and held when she recited at Miss Farnsworth's command or better still said over to herself as she climbed the hill from school:

> *We are such stuff*
> *As dreams are made on; and our little life*
> *Is rounded with a sleep.*

She would have liked to share her reading and her thoughts with her mother, but a certain austerity in Sarah Peters and a corresponding reticence in herself made this seemingly impossible. There was an understanding between them, which, perhaps by its very existence, made them uncommunicative. Their rare moments of confidence were awkward, even painful, and neither encouraged them. But each cultivated toward the other a courtesy bred of affection and a quick sensitiveness to the other's thoughts and feelings.

Perhaps there is no finer sentiment than that respect with which certain responsive, though reserved natures regard others of like mind and spirit. It is the most invincible of those hardy, deep-rooted parts which make the New England character at its best. In its essence it is an emotion rather than any state of mind; and it at once stabilizes and enriches as more volatile emotions can never do. It assumes the presence of values in others and is as tenacious of their preservation as of its own. It is at the basis of whatever is aristocratic and permanent in the New England tradition; perhaps, indeed, it is itself the tradition. Such respect was strong within Sarah and Mary Peters, establishing between them a mutual consideration and making less necessary the expression of affection which each might have welcomed could it have been attained without the shattering of insurmountable barriers.

Singularly enough, or perhaps again not so singular, she found
her best companion in studies an old captain, her father's uncle,
Caleb Peters, who lived on the brow of their own hill. He occupied quite by himself the back rooms of his house which had
known better days. Now that he was well past eighty, the past gave
place only to the weather for supremacy in his thoughts. He had
sailed all his life from early boyhood to seventy years. He had
known whalers and emigrant packets, tea and wool and gold-rush
clippers; he had known ships as he had never known his wife and
children. His prime had coincided with the years of the big ones,
the fifties, when the docks of Rockland and East Boston,
Portsmouth and Nova Scotia had rivalled those of Liverpool and
Rotherhithe and of the stout, porridge-eating builders of
Aberdeen. He had dined with Donald McKay and his brother
Lauchlan; he had known James Baines and the Duthies, William
and John and Alexander. He dared pass judgment on world-
known masters like Bully Forbes and Bully Martin; and once he
had supped in Hongkong with Captain Anthony Enright in his
cabin on the tea clipper *Chrysolite*. He had watched with skepti-
cism the launch of the *Great Republic* in 1853. He had known
every ship called *Golden*—the *Golden Light*, the *Golden Eagle*, the
*Golden West*—all Down-East clippers built for the gold rush to
California, and he said their names over to anyone who would listen like a priest invoking Heaven. He still deplored as a recent disaster the selling of American ships to Great Britain in the financial
panic of 1857!

Like many men of his type and training he had a reverence
for learning, not because he himself had directly felt its influence
but because he himself in his voyaging over the world had been
close to its sources and its wisdom. The language of Homer was
not dead to one whose ship had coasted in the Mediterranean,
picking up for Liverpool from Patras and the Piraeus cargoes of

currants and citron, hides and olive oil. He told Mary how he had conducted his crew in shifts to see the Parthenon by moonlight.

Mary could not bring her books too often to his fireside. He sat with his black skull cap well over his bald old head and showed her plates he had of Liburnian biremes, of triremes and quinqueremes to supplement those in her history, of Flemish carracks and Portuguese caravels. He refought the Battle of Salamis with the best ships he had known and ventured a prophecy on Trafalgar had things been managed differently. He lived so completely in the past that he never for a moment suspected it was not both present and future. Loneliness did not seem to touch him nor the thought of Death which must be around a nearby corner, although nearer were Sumatra and Ceylon, Martinique and Valparaiso, and even the ancient, unharvested seas of Homer.

Mary never left his neat and shipshape kitchen or sitting-room without an odd sense of security about him. He was the one person she knew who did not seem to want anything in all the world. She had a responsible feeling, not uncommon to youth toward age, of not wishing to disillusion him; and once when she had read somewhere that Zeus has two urns of sorrow for one of joy, she was careful not to repeat it to him lest it might disturb his peace. She could not share the concern always voiced about him on church supper evenings when the women who entertained sent him a generous basket, packing it with tart prophecies of the evil hour when he should set himself on fire by puttering around at night with his old logbooks and papers. Reasonable as were such fears in view of his habits, he seemed to her somehow removed from all disaster.

Was it that the abundance of his life had been such that it could not know depletion, that instead it kept filling all his needs through its own fullness? Or was it simply that extreme old age dulled the wants of youth? She did not know. But when she descended the hill on her way homeward, looking seaward to the dark outlines of the Mt. Desert hills beneath the stars, the thought of Cadiz, almost due east in the straightest of lines, so filled her mind that there was no room for any other thought.

8

In spite of his disproportionate urns the chief of the gods outdid himself in September of 1889. For at the beginning of Mary's last year in the Academy, Hester Wood came from Barrett's Bay and overflowed her life with joy. Now, like great-uncle Caleb she, too, wanted for nothing.

Barrett's Bay was a small settlement ten miles toward open water. Its school was poor, and Hester's parents felt disposed to give her a year of greater advantages before her entrance into Castine to train as a teacher. They were further disposed, moreover, to leave her in Petersport for complete terms, to board her in a respectable family, week-ends and all, instead of driving for her on Friday afternoons and returning her on Sunday evenings.

Mary fell in love with her at first sight and spent a week of anguish before she felt any assurance that Hester might return her affection. To her, Hester was every desirable thing in the world that she herself was not. She was fair (fairer than Ellen who was acutely uncomfortable at the knowledge) with dark brows and lashes to accentuate her fairness. Her eyes were such a deep blue that when she widened them suddenly as she had a fascinating way of doing, they seemed almost purple. She was lithe and slender with lovely hands and feet, which Jim Pendleton had a steady way of watching, sometimes to Mary's annoyance. She loved pretty clothes, which her mother, even in Barrett's Bay, had known how to make her, and she always looked surprising no matter what she had on. Her face seemed always alight, not like Mary's which waited for something to enkindle it. She was like windflowers and hepaticas starring the woods, like wild plum blossoms bordering a stony field. She was, in fact, the epitome of freshness like something quite unspoiled; and before she had been three days in Petersport, she had the Academy at her feet. She was as unspoiled in nature as she was in appearance, so kind and gracious to forlorn and homesick boys and girls in the first weeks of school that Mary's conscience smote her for her own neglect and selfishness. When Mary brought her home one afternoon at four o'clock, Sarah Peters felt as though a nosegay had blossomed on her very centre table and asked her to supper so impulsively that Mary was startled. And when at Thanksgiving the woman, in whose home Hester lived, fell ill and she must seek lodgings elsewhere, Sarah Peters set up an airtight stove in her best room and sent John to fetch her possessions.

Now life quickened for Mary like a stream finding its way into sudden sunlight. She experienced every hour a fresh baptism of her spirit. She was a new creature, how new no one but herself could understand. She could not tell Hester how she felt nor did she want to tell her. Instead she indulged herself in the luxury of her new, intoxicating thoughts. She assigned poems to Hester as she had once assigned them to the moods of the sea, saying to herself as she watched her watering the geraniums in the sunny window that she was the Three Graces all in one or that her face might have launched even more than a thousand ships. Old familiar objects about the house took on new meaning as she dusted them, and dish-washing became something to live for with Hester flourishing the dish-towels and bursting into laughter over Mr. Bates' serious ways. It was easier to talk with people now that Hester was so often at her elbow, easier to enter into games, easier to have patience with Jim, who actually seemed to have discovered somewhere a new, if not too fiery, eagerness to complete at last his irregular and haphazard course at the Academy. The glow in her face came more often now and stayed for such long intervals of time that at length it grew into a steady illumination at which Sarah Peters rejoiced until in the very nature of things she found herself fearing lest it might go out.

They studied together at the table in the sitting room beneath the lamp. The wonder of a companion was always kindling itself anew in Mary's mind. They read their history in silence and then recited it each to the other until they had it clear. They did their Vergil together, looking up words in a common dictionary, making their translation smooth and good, pausing to share their confidences.

"Do you see how he could have done it, Mary? Deserting her like that when she loved him so? I don't. Maybe men did such things long ago easier than now. Do you suppose they did?"

"I don't know," said Mary. "Perhaps."

"I think they must have. They could always say like Aeneas that Apollo told them to. But that didn't make it any better for Dido. And—and the worst part," her face coloured and she dropped her eyes, "was the way he left his clothes and his arms in their chamber where they—had slept together. That part is the worst of all."

Mary coloured in her turn. "Yes," she said, "but it's beautiful even though it is terrible."

"But it's more terrible than beautiful. And the way she had to bear things all alone, not telling even her sister when the wine on the altars turned to blood and when the screech-owl cried at night from the tops of the houses. I'll feel sorry for her all the days of my life, Mary, even until I'm old. I know I shall. All our lessons tonight seem full of sad things. I felt like crying when we read about the Crusades. Do you think all those were justified with people dying of hunger and sickness?"

"People seemed more willing to die for things then," said Mary. "Maybe they had visions more easily than people do now. That's what it says, 'Led on by a beatific vision, they willingly endured privations and sufferings.' "

"Well, it may have been all right for them, I mean for the older ones. But what about all those little children? Nothing can ever make me think that was right! Do you suppose little children could have a vision of God all by themselves? I don't! I can't forget how they were sold into slavery and died by hundreds. They were just babies, Mary. Do you realize that? Think of their poor little feet on those hard roads, walking and walking for days and weeks. I can't get them out of my mind. Besides," she finished, a bit embarrassed, "besides, I don't understand what a vision of God means. Could you love God enough to die for Him—even now, Mary?"

"No," said Mary. "No, I'm sure I couldn't. Maybe people or maybe God was different then. At least He seemed more real then, I think." The colour mounted again in her cheeks. "I—I might love somebody on earth enough to die for—them. But that's different. I suppose that wouldn't be the same."

"No," agreed Hester, unaware of Mary's beating heart, "no, I'm sure it wouldn't."

John liked Hester. Mary could see that, silent as he was. When he came in at supper-time after a long day on the farm, he always looked expectant. Now that she had come, he washed in his room instead of in the kitchen, carrying the hot water there even on cold nights and changing all his clothes before he came downstairs. He did not fall asleep so often over his paper or book as he had used to do, and now and then he unbent enough to suggest a lunch before bedtime. Hester had a way of asking him about his day, what he had done and how his animals were. She knit him some wristers for Christmas, and he had a habit, not unconscious, Mary thought, of drawing them off when he came home in whatever room she happened to be. Once on Saturday morning when Mary was making his bed and giving his room its weekly tidying, she found concealed beneath the cover on his bureau a handkerchief of Hester's. Her heart performed queer antics within her as she stood there with it in her hand. It was crumpled and a bit soiled as though it had been carried for a long time in a pocket. She had a strange feeling that she had had no right to touch it and replaced it carefully, refraining from changing the cover on the bureau lest John might notice and know that someone had discovered his secret. That afternoon as she went into the pasture with Hester and Ellen for hemlock boughs to decorate the church, she could not tell from the many feelings within her which was uppermost.

John did not like Jim Pendleton; that, too, was obvious, even to Jim. Whenever he came up of an evening as he frequently did, John was manifestly uncomfortable. If he did not go to bed early or sit in the room with his mother, he remained silent and uncommunicative in a corner of the sitting room. It was not that Jim was unfriendly; he was genial enough unless they annoyed him with their ignorance of his music; it was just that he and John were cut from different patterns, that each inwardly suspected the make-up of the other. In Jim's indolent nature the suspicion was not deeply rooted enough to breed anything save indifference; but in John's it smouldered darkly, breeding all its restless children.

Sometimes in long afternoons on the farm when his morning work was done in the barn and his wood was cut, when his paths were shovelled and there was nothing else to do till chore and milking time, he sat alone in the kitchen of the farmhouse, now gradually becoming his own, and thought and thought. He would feed his one fire and then sit before it with his feet in the oven, listening to his aunt's old clock tick away the hours and watching from his frosted windows the winter sun swiftly moving down the southwestern sky toward fir-clad ridges and crusted snowy fields.

Now and again he paced the wide, yellow floor-boards of the old kitchen, smoking his pipe which his mother did not like at home, or rearranging his stiff, unmanageable hair before the mirror above the sink to see if he could improve upon its appearance. He had no attractions to compete with Jim's, and he knew it. Even his strong, perfect body did not count for much, for girls always felt sorry for a boy who was lame, and pity often started other feelings. He had not needed to finish college to realize that. Pocket money helped, too, and good clothes and music, none of which he had; and above all else the ability to keep awake at night. It was humiliating the way sleep fell on him wherever he was after a day in the woods with his axe or even after a puttering day in the barn and toolhouse. Sometimes he would be nodding at half-past seven with painful jerks of his head, his eyes closing just as Hester asked him a question. No one could ever know his disgrace when his mother called him to his senses or how, after he had once gone to bed unable to bear longer the inroads of sleep, he would lie awake a whole hour cursing himself.

The worst of it was that, even as he hated Jim, he, too, felt sorry for him. He could not conceive of what life would be without the free and splendid use of every bone and muscle. He wondered, as he hung his lantern on a nail above his patient row of cows, placed his pail and stool and dug his head into the warm side of the first to be milked, whether perhaps Jim's infirmity might not account for some stories he had picked up from the men about the village. Even he who heard little and said less had gathered quite by chance that Jim now and again hung about a house on the eastern outskirts where a girl lived. Whether his mother or Mary knew this, if it were true, he did not know nor had he considered telling them. For he had an innate understanding that, true or not, it did not really concern them. Men looked upon women as women wished they should; and his honest soul could find not one flaw in Jim's attentive regard, even in his affection, for Mary and Sarah Peters. Hester threw quite another light on the matter, but it was only fair to say (and comforting to his perturbed heart) that thus far she had seemed to care more for Mary than for either of them. It was the future he dreaded with the dice so loaded against him.

9

Mary and Hester continued as the winter went on each to penetrate and permeate the other's life. But there was a difference in their attitude each to the other which Sarah Peters was quick to discern. Hester found complete satisfaction in Mary's companionship. She asked for nothing else if Mary were but with her, found every pursuit delightful in which Mary participated. But she did not love as Mary loved. That, she was all unconsciously reserving for another time, for some one else not yet thought of. There was a completeness in Mary's love for Hester that startled and vaguely disturbed Sarah Peters for she knew that sorrow lay in wait within it. Hester lived in Mary's imagination, transcending everything she thought as well as everything she did. There was no help for it, and Sarah Peters knew it. Mary would love again, and yet again, whether a person, an object, or a thought; and her love would inundate her like a full spring tide. She watched Mary on Sunday morning in church sitting beside Hester and understood that she was thinking not of God or of the armour of righteousness, but of the new life welling within her and freeing her spirit.

On winter nights after they had put away their books and gone upstairs to bed, Hester came to Mary's room and sat in her flannel nightdress on the foot of Mary's bed, well wrapped in comforters and blankets. Sarah Peters heard them talking in low tones together and understood that the days were not long enough for their confidences.

"I don't know what it is about Ellen, Mary. Some days I think I like her lots, and then again I'm not so sure. You can't talk to Ellen about anything *really*, now can you?" Mary stared into the darkness where Hester's face was outlined against the footboard and felt for her words.

"Maybe it's not really Ellen," she said. "Maybe it's because you can't talk with many people about things that—that really mean the most."

"I don't think it's that. I think it's because Ellen never thinks about those things. She's always thinking about herself and what people think about her. She's always trying to impress some boy or other, and she wants people to be always planning things for her. My mother says you never get anything that way. I can talk with you, Mary. You're my best friend in all the world. I shall always want to talk with you—years from now when we're both grown up in homes of our own, I'll always be coming to see you. I know I shall. Won't it be awful if we don't live near together?"

Mary caught her breath at the awfulness of it. For some reason she could never dream about the future as Hester could. She seemed always now holding close to the present. Even the wide reaches of the past had for the time become faded, much to Hester's astonishment. She could not understand why Mary who had been all over the world and had seen things that she had never seen did not talk more about it.

"Didn't you miss your friends terribly at sea, Mary?"

"No, I don't think so. It's hard to remember exactly. Some things you remember so clearly you could never forget, but not that, about missing friends, I mean. Things were so different at sea. Somehow you never thought of missing things at home."

"Wasn't there ever anybody to talk to? I mean except your father and mother and John? I mean to tell things to?"

"Yes," said Mary, "sometimes."

She thought of Mr. Gardiner then and of how Hester had come to take his place and make her life again surprising and bountiful.

"Well, my life seems just nothing compared with yours. But anyhow I have you. And if you go to Castine, too, we'll be there together. I keep thinking about it and what fun it will be, really going away to school together. I wish we could go to college. More and more girls go all the time, but my father thinks four years are too many to spend just at books, especially when you haven't much money. Wouldn't you like to go to college, Mary?"

"Yes," said Mary. "I'd rather go than anything, but I'd hate to leave mother all alone so long. I don't know. I guess I don't plan as you do, Hester. I'm—I'm just happy the way things are now."

"So'm I. But I can't help thinking of all the years ahead and the good times we'll have. It's fun to think of the years unrolling themselves way off somewhere and coming nearer and nearer all the time. Won't it be queer some day to write down 1900? It just doesn't seem possible, does it? In 1900, Mary, we'll be twenty-nine years old. By then I suppose we'll be married, don't you?"

"I suppose so. Most girls are."

"You're sort of queer, Mary, even though you're nicer than anyone I've ever known. I don't believe you ever think about such things. I'm afraid I do. I wonder who I'll marry and how many children I'll have. I hope the first one will be a girl, for I've set my heart on naming it for you."

It was early in January that the first cloud threatened to dim Mary's complete happiness. But it was so tiny and so ephemeral in nature, it passed away so quickly and seemingly left so little a mark, if any at all, upon Hester that for a time she pushed it out of her mind as being of no consequence. She had come suddenly into the sitting room one Saturday evening from setting the table for breakfast to see Jim bending over Hester's chair. She had some new music on her lap which, he had said at supper, either she or Mary certainly ought to be able to play for him; and he with his elbows on the back of her chair seemed studying it with her. But when Mary turned from the table to the door and stood there for an instant quite unperceived, she noticed something in his face she had never seen in it before. He was not looking at the music at all. Instead his eyes were on Hester's neck as it rose from her round white collar, and his lips were unmistakably against one of her yellow braids of hair which she wore coiled about her head. What was more, Mary surprised him in the act of moving his hand from the chair to press it against Hester's shoulder.

Whether Hester herself was conscious of his lips on her hair or the momentary resting of his hand against her shoulder, Mary did not know. She knew only that both coloured visibly and moved at once toward the piano to spread the music on the rack. Jim was more petulant than ever about the tuning of his fiddle; both Hester and Mary played worse than usual; and the whole evening, with John staring moodily at them from the sofa, seemed heavy with suppressed feelings of every sort. And yet when Hester brought her quilts and curled up on the bottom of Mary's bed for their customary half-hour of talk, Mary could discern nothing at all singular or even different in her manner. Nor were the ensuing days anything but reassuring. Whatever mad mood Jim might have been in, Mary concluded, Hester was no party to it and might, indeed, have been quite unconscious of it all.

During the last week in January the two churches buried their divergences and united in their annual campaign for the saving of souls. The most persuasive of evangelists was imported; meetings were held every evening; and before two days and nights had elapsed, the emotional life of the young had been stimulated to a high degree of intensity. Mary dreaded this annual maelstrom of heart-searching, embarrassment, bewilderment and uncertainty. The atmosphere at school was bad enough with spiritual confidences exchanged in corners, with Mr. Bates clearing his throat and mopping his brow as acts preliminary to his own encouraging words for souls "on the verge of coming forward," and with everyone in so sensitive a state that tears were likely to flow upon no provocation at all.

Her own peculiar situation in regard to salvation did not make matters any more comfortable. She had been away from home when most girls of her age had taken the decisive step, approached the mercy-seat, and there-upon, after due allowance had been made for backsliding, had been safely received into one church or the other. Her life at sea had not nurtured the necessity for any such definite decision as that about which people in every January talked so earnestly. Such a decision was at once beyond her comprehension or her need although she was actually ill at ease in the knowledge that she more than any other girl in the village was expected to "take her stand." Ellen had been saved at fourteen and annually felt herself aroused to an agreeable, even cosy assurance of that salvation, singing confidently each evening and concerning herself during the day at school in intimate talks with the boys she knew who were still recalcitrant.

Sarah Peters was silent on the matter, never attending the meetings, avoiding the church until it had once more settled down into more quiet, less disturbing paths. She had saved her own soul too many times after too many different ways to be either sure or ardent about any one method. She thought sometimes as she saw Mary's lighted face or gazed in memory beyond the Mt. Desert hills that she knew something about the grace of God; but she was unable in January to relate her knowledge to this other indispensable grace which seemed attainable only by means of such a painful upheaval of one's nature and such inroads upon one's identity.

One morning while Mary and she were working alone in the kitchen, she ventured to speak because she knew the girl was suffering. She was cleaning her pantry, and, while she busied her hands in washing shelves and replacing her jars and cans, she could talk with greater freedom from within its narrow confines.

"I don't want you to be worried over these meetings, Mary. Don't think I mind what you do one way or another. Only don't think your soul is full of sin just because you're feeling all upset. I know how you feel. I went through it all myself when I was fourteen, and I can't say it's any memory I cherish. I joined the church then like most of the others. The church is a good thing, but I don't think these meetings are. I think myself there ought to be other ways of filling up the church."

She wrung out her cloth in soapy water and washed yet another shelf. She was trying to put into words for Mary's sake what would not seem to go into words. "I've never been sure at all about how souls are saved, Mary. I think they're saved at—at odd moments when you're not expecting it. And they keep on being saved all your life."

Mary, washing her cooking dishes at the kitchen sink, was crying quietly, glad that her mother was securely in the pantry, sure she would not come out to confront her tears.

"They're saved by—by thoughts you have that are sent to you every now and then, I don't know how. And by people you care for. (Mary thought of Mr. Gardiner and then of Hester.) And sometimes just by things you see like some of the things we used to see when we sailed—things we weren't expecting. (Mary thought of Cadiz and light flooded her face once more.) It's a bad thing to be always expecting things, Mary, but it's a good thing to be—well, sort of ready for them." She replaced her cans in order on the clean shelf, the spice cans and the coffee, the jars marked salt and mustard, saleratus and soda. "And sometimes—I know it sounds foolish, but I believe it's true—sometimes you save your soul when there's no other way to do it just by setting things right with your two hands."

Mary did not forget her mother's words, but the momentary light went out leaving her face dark again and her mind a torment during the week of revival. For now, in addition to her own bewilderment, she saw that Hester was going where she could not follow, and her heart beat wretchedly within her. Hester's heart was wretched, too, but only because she felt upon it a grievous weight of sin. Her impulsive, affectionate nature was shaken by the appeals and the pleadings, by the hymns that were sung and by the urgent testimonies of the redeemed. Now when she came into Mary's room at night, she crawled into bed beside her, instead of sitting swathed in comforters at the foot, and wept out her spiritual woes on Mary's shoulder. She grew nervous and thin and could not eat, so that in a way it was a relief when on the night of the last meeting she gave herself up and stumbled forward to the mercy-seat.

Mary knew that evening by the tightening grasp of Hester's hand upon her own that she could withstand it no longer. They were sitting in the back of the hot, crowded vestry, having decided late and against Sarah Peters' good advice to go. Jim, moody, perhaps brooding over his own sins, sat on the other side of Hester. The evangelist had sounded his last threatening appeal; the final and most efficacious hymn was nearing its last tremulous stanza:

> *Just as I am, Thy love unknown*
> *Has broken every barrier down;*
> *Now to be Thine, yea, Thine alone,*
> *O Lamb of God, I come,*
> *I come.*

Hester went then, tears flowing down her crimson face. Mary felt instinctively that she must follow her down the aisle, that she must save Hester from all those embarrassing, tortuous by-products of divine grace. She felt that she could not leave her there in tears among all those fluttering, relieved souls who, once the meeting was over, would crowd about her, asking her intimate questions, praying with her, rejoicing over her new cleanliness. She almost rose to her feet but remembered suddenly that she could not go unless she were inwardly ready, and she knew that she was not. And then as she sat in misery watching Hester's shaking shoulders against the bench where she knelt so pathetically alone, she saw in amazement that Jim had shifted his lame leg after a manner he had when he was about to stand. In another moment he had stood and in yet another he was limping down the aisle after Hester.

While the after-meeting, which was always held by a few of the faithful ones over those who had come forward, went on, Mary escaped out-of-doors and walked up and down before the church in the cold. The land was wrapped in snow. The stars were bright, only dimmed now and again by the northern lights which swept up from the dark hills and illumined the sky, spreading from the north to touch the ice-covered harbour. Mary knew that far beyond the Mt. Desert hills they touched the open sea, bringing suddenly into being on its dark surface pools and lakes of flame, and that somewhere out there ships moved in their strange glow. She wished that she were there, feeling again beneath her feet the dipping of the ship in a wide freedom, there where emotions were less concentrated, less bewildering. If she were there, she thought, the awful ache in her heart over Hester might be swept away by the wind and the sea.

After fifteen minutes Ellen came out of the church in her blue hood and fur jacket. She did not seem to be in either a chastened or a pious frame of mind, and Mary surmised that something had displeased her. She preferred the stars and the lights to Ellen and was so short in reply to Ellen's questioning that she was soon alone again. The questions in fact reflected Ellen's irritation quite as much as her concern.

"Aren't you ever going to decide, Mary? Everybody expects you to and still you don't. Why didn't you tonight with Hester? What's standing in your way?"

"Everything," said Mary, surprised at her sudden anger and not looking at Ellen at all. "Everything. Only nothing that you would understand, so please don't mention it to me again, Ellen— ever—all your life."

There was great and widespread rejoicing over Jim Pendleton's conversion. Only the remnant of the sea-faring population kept its tongue well within its cheek. His had been tacitly regarded as the one most needy soul in Petersport, and his sudden and unlooked for repentance occasioned a joy felt to be but an echo of that experienced in Heaven over the proverbial one sinner as against the ninety and nine. The silence he himself maintained toward the whole matter was, it must be admitted, somewhat disarming. He had had nothing whatever to say as he knelt beside Hester nor did anything in his manner suggest spiritual fervour. And when he appeared before the committee of the church, again with Hester, as a necessary preliminary to his joining it, his evidence, which was to substantiate his reception of grace, was pitiably negligible. Nevertheless he was admitted to the communion of the faithful, the committee being impressed by his need, if not by his enthusiasm, and confiding sadly to one another that with times changing as they were the church should concede to young people as far as possible.

Sarah Peters made no comment on the supposed change in Jim. Indeed, she saw no change whatever. He preserved the same indifference and at times indulged himself in the same moodiness.

But she felt the appeal in him that she had from the first, and, in spite of John's dislike, he was always welcome to her house. He was at his best with her, and she knew that, if he loved anyone, it was herself. He could not do enough in odd, sudden ways for her comfort, spending his money on this and that for her kitchen and sitting room and bursting now and again when they were alone into confidences about this or that person who annoyed him or about his life at sea with his father. He still hated questions and she asked him none, either about his soul or his behaviour.

She hoped now that January was over that the saved and the unsaved might take up existence again in more orderly fashion. She had always trusted to time to right things.

## 10

Things did settle down after January was over. Sarah Peters watched them through February falling slowly back into their accustomed places. She saw Hester becoming less conscious both of sin and salvation, lifting her head like a wilted flower placed at last in generous water. She saw Mary forgetting her wretchedness, bending in delight over her books again, laughing with Hester over the latter's ill-timed and confusing discovery of Mr. Bates with his arm actually around Miss Tapley in a darkened hallway. She saw John so busy with his seed catalogues and his budget for new spring ploughing and planting that he grew oblivious of his scorn over Jim's conversion and even, for the moment, of Hester's presence with him at the sitting room table.

She was not, however, unaware of a subtle change in Hester, a change emotional rather than spiritual. She wondered if Mary noticed it, too, and concluded gratefully that she did not. There was a new restlessness in Hester as the spring came on. She was dreamy and vivacious in turn, less absorbed in her lessons, laughing suddenly at nothing at all. She was variable in her behaviour, capricious like a spring wind. She would delight John in the early evening by her interest in the new land he was to plough and then quite forget him at eight o'clock in her concentrated practising of accompaniments, obviously for Jim. Once on an afternoon early in March when John drove down from the farm for her at four o'clock to fulfill the promise she had made to go with him to see his twin calves, he found she had forgotten and had gone for mayflowers with Jim. No number of embarrassed apologies could ever set it right with John. Even in February she suddenly decided to drive the ten miles to Barrett's Bay every other week-end to see her parents; and instead of their coming for her on Friday and returning her Sunday evenings, Jim took upon himself the responsibility of transporting her at least one way in a carriage hired in the village, a stylish carriage with red wheels, which set John to mending his broken fences with fury in his heart.

Nevertheless, in spite of her absences and her sudden distractions in mind, she was still to Mary the perfect companion. And as the spring days came on and the saw-mill began its strident cries on misty April mornings and the smelts and alewives filled the brooks on full night-tides, they found life more thrilling and complete than ever. Plum and wild cherry blossomed in the fields and thickets; lambkill made the pastures violet; Canada mayflowers starred the pine woods like candle flames. John's apple trees grew pink with prophecies of bloom. Mary and Hester filled Sarah Peters' crocks and pails with each in turn; they carried armfuls to Uncle Caleb on the hill; and on Saturday afternoon when Hester stayed in Petersport, they banked the pulpit of the church with spring.

They found an old field botany among the books in the house and began looking up the unfamiliar flowers they discovered, taking ever-new delight in rare ones now become friends, pressing them between the pages of the family Bible. Ellen was intolerant of this pastime. She found it irksome in the extreme to pause on walks for the purpose of identifying this and that and to Mary's delight seldom accompanied them.

Now the ice had left the harbour; the shores were again clear. The blue water extended once more thirty miles to the Mt. Desert hills. The high pastures dried in the spring sun. Fir trees put out their green tips. Mary felt new life springing up within her, and in Hester she felt that life expanding into a fullness which even she herself could not experience. Hester grudged the hours indoors. She dreamed from school windows and, once they were free at four o'clock, flew out-of-doors like a thing possessed. Looking at her running along the wood paths, Mary was forever thinking of beautiful, timeless maidens like Atalanta or Daphne with gods or men in swift pursuit. Hester was constantly planning this or that, more excursions to the woods, a picnic on a harbour island to which they would row themselves, early risings for walks before breakfast. She sang about the house, ran up and down the stairs, could scarcely sit still even to eat. She was a whirlwind and a fire all in one; and Mary, watching the glow in her cheeks and the shining in her eyes, thought she had never seen anyone so lovely.

Best of all, she had Hester almost completely to herself. John, engrossed in his fields, was late each night in returning home, and, as spring went on, Jim came less and less to the house. Sometimes when they returned from their endless walks, they found him with Sarah Peters, watering her flower-beds for her at twilight or sitting silently while she sewed. But he had a way of leaving when they came in, conveying the tacit and none too courteous assumption that he had not come to see them at all. He was moodier than ever, neglectful of his studies and seemingly forgetful even of his music. Mary could not keep the notion from her mind that Hester was uncomfortable in his presence. Something in her seemed to die when he was about. And on alternate Fridays when he appeared suddenly to drive her home, she seemed, as the weeks went on, as reluctant to go with him as she was unable to stay.

One Saturday morning in May, scarcely an hour before the boat docked for freight and any chance passengers for Boston, Jim mounted the hill in his best clothes to tell them good-bye. Standing silently in the doorway with his hat in his hand, he took their amazement as casually as he had apparently taken or, indeed, made his own sudden decision. He had no plans, he said briefly, but he was sick of school and he had given up college. He was of age and could do what he liked, and he did not like to stay longer in Petersport. He might work in New York. He did not know.

Mary was alike too stunned by his news and too embarrassed by his sullenness either to remark or to question, but Sarah Peters walked with him to the gate. She had the feeling that she could not let him go without an attempt at least to pierce this black obscurity in which he moved. The lilacs were blossoming above each of the white gate-posts; the sun was bright and high. He made as if to raise the latch, but she placed her hand upon his arm, detaining him. He turned and looked at her then, his eyes searching hers as though he could never carry away enough of what was in them. Then, as though what was there was at length too much for him, his own dropped. She still kept her hand upon his arm.

"Are you running away, Jim?"

"Yes, that's it. You always know."

"I'm not reproving. I'm just asking. Sometimes it's the best thing to run away."

"Well, I'm running. It's the best thing to do. I'll only make a mess of things if I stay here any longer."

"Is—is the mess made already?"

He was to hate himself, did hate himself as he stood there because of his reply, but he made it:

"No, but it would be made if I stayed. That's why I'm going. I'll make a mess of things all my life."

He raised the latch of the gate and went through, closing it behind him. But before he turned to go down the hill, he faced her once more with the white pickets between them.

"I'm running away, but I'm not hiding, remember. You'll always know where I am. I'll write you. You've been good to me. I hate leaving you."

She watched him from her doorway as he limped down the hill, past the church he had joined three months before. She wondered as she watched how far people could be held responsible for the moods which gripped them and for the messes they made. But since she could not answer her question and knew of no one who could, she went back to her housecleaning, glad that it was a Saturday.

## 11

It was impossible to discover how Hester felt about Jim's sudden departure. He had always been the one subject upon which she was consistently uncommunicative. When she returned on the Sunday afternoon following with John who, an unwilling substitute, had driven to Barrett's Bay after her, she said little or nothing about it. She ate her supper, more silently perhaps than usual, looking especially lovely, Mary thought, in a new blue challis dress which her mother had made for her. While they washed the dishes, Mary ventured the suggestion that Jim had already confided his plans to her, but she was met with a denial at once so fervent and so inexplicably angry that she was startled. John on his way to his farm could have told her that the denial was an honest one. He had seen Hester's face when she came to the door to greet him.

But John was a young man of few words and about this matter more than any other kept his own disturbed counsel.

That evening instead of attending prayer-meeting as usual they walked at Hester's suggestion along the lower shore road to watch the moon rise over a full spring-tide. Mary felt somehow that Hester was gathering herself together, striving to imbue herself with a vitality at that moment peculiarly depleted. She was trying to act herself when she was not herself. It made an embarrassment between them of which they were both acutely conscious but which they could not seem to bridge. They walked for the most part in silence, mentioning only this and that—the way the tide was inundating the lower meadows, the perfect reflection of some schooners in the outer bay, the suspicion of mist around the moon when once it had cleared the eastern horizon. They went farther than they had intended, Hester demurring whenever Mary proposed a return, so that darkness had quite fallen and the moon was sailing high and white over the full sea before they started homeward.

Even then they waited on the summit of the hill they had just climbed. It was a favourite objective of theirs, the goal of many of their longer walks, and they paused as they had done so many times before. The tide was in flood. Seemingly they had caught it at just that mysterious instant when it had ceased to flow and had not yet begun to ebb, in that strange, quiescent cessation of any motion at all. Mary knew it had not paused, that the moment between flow and ebb was instantaneous, and yet the impression remained. It was as though time were not, or as though standing on their hill-top they had conquered time, were living moments which could neither be added to their lives nor yet taken from them. There was no sound at all except for the high singing of the peepers from brooks and marshes. Beyond some quiet, misty fields the sea extended before them, full, light-swept, complete, holding time for a motionless moment, the sorrow of the world blotted out, made as nothing.

Mary, swept by an emotion she could not put into words, took Hester's hand. She did not clasp or hold it. It lay within her own hand, its palm against her own. She was conscious in those moments of the world standing still for her and Hester. There was nothing to fear, nothing to plan for, nothing even to remember. And then suddenly, beyond and below the fields, somewhere from a group of fishermen's cottages which they could not see, there came the distant crying of a child.

Time began to move again then along its resistless, perpetual way, the tide to turn, the world to become alive once more with all its pain. A wind stirred the grass and swept through the firs. The child cried on somewhere in the darkness. A nameless fear seized them both standing there. Hester's hand clasped Mary's, no longer still upon her own, but tense and dependent. She was crying herself.

"I can't bear it, Mary. It's so terrible. Where is it? We ought to do something."

"We can't. It's down there somewhere in those cottages. We can't do anything. We don't even know who lives down there."

"It sounds so lonely. I'll never forget it! I'll hear it all my life, I know I shall. It makes me afraid, Mary. Aren't you afraid?"

"Yes," said Mary.

She held Hester close for a moment and then started running with her down the hill, away from the crying. She was afraid, not for the child, its punishment, its sickness, its loneliness, for whatever it was crying, but of some other greater, less tangible fear. They ran in silence, stumbling down the rocky, rain-cut hill, not stopping until they were far away from the sound, then hurrying along the shore road, through the silent village, up the hill past the silent church.

Some time in the night Mary woke suddenly. She had been dreaming of the child, but as she sat up in bed, she thought, so clear had been her dream, that she heard the crying near at hand through the open window. She listened, still in fear, but all seemed silent and secure, and she fell asleep again, glad that the sky was growing light above the Mt. Desert hills and that a song-sparrow had already awakened in the nearby pasture.

## 12

They graduated in June. They wore dresses fashioned by Mrs. Wood's skillful fingers at Barrett's Bay and by Sarah Peters' in Petersport. They were dresses of white muslin and lawn, shirred and smocked and tucked. They were smooth and narrow in the waist and hips with long, flowing skirts, yards upon yards of skirt which just cleared the ground enough to show their neat black shoes. The sleeves were leg-of-mutton, then so popular, sleeves which were pleated at the shoulders and billowed out in folds above the crinoline giving them shape and fullness, and which had wide, deep cuffs of shirred ruffles. More ruffles bordered their elaborately smocked yokes which reached to their high-ruffled collars. With these creations they wore hats of white leghorn, so twisted out of their natural shape, so bedecked with bows and feathers and birds that they had much ado to keep them in place on the very tops of their pompadoured heads. All the other girls of their class were similarly arrayed. A popular monthly of the day in a poem quoted by the *Hancock County Courier* as befitting this and like occasions elsewhere within its domain called them "demure phantoms of sky and air" and prophesied that the "stern praeceptor" under whom they had been trained must forever hold in higher esteem their purity and beauty than any of the learning he had given them. Whether this was true of Mr. Bates, who, sitting in neat black with the two pastors and his lady assistants in the pulpit of the Congregational church, conducted the exercises, no one knew except himself. It was perhaps excusable that his eyes should stray at frequent intervals from the phantoms to Miss Tapley, who wore an elaborate gown of gray India silk, brocaded in pink roses, the skirt made in the new waved design with panels on the hips and the bodice pointed in front and edged with deep ruffles of rose. She looked self-conscious enough beneath her high hat trimmed with ostrich plumes. She carried a rose parasol, which some thought affected and showy, especially since she held it in her left hand so that Mr. Bates' modest garnet ring was much in evidence on her engagement finger. Propinquity had been the tool of fate which had at last settled Mr. Bates' equally modest future for him; and Miss Tapley need no longer think with rancour in her heart of Miss Farnsworth, now a matron of a year in Wiscasset.

Hester left for home as soon as things at the Academy were over, and John found time, even at the expense of his new cultivator, to drive her to Barrett's Bay. She was to return in late August for the church sale, she and Mary having been named for the lemonade booth. They would then discuss nearer plans for Castine, Hester being already entered, Mary still undecided.

Summer came on. The small and experimental plot of wheat which John had planted did well against all prophecies of older farmers; and his two peach trees, which he had insisted might be made to grow in Hancock County as well as in Knox, proved themselves to be at least holding their own. He cut his hay in hot July weather and in the long, still evenings lay on his haycocks and smoked his pipe, watching the fireflies glimmering in the thickets and listening to the whip-poor-wills' restive calling through the moist darkness. He gathered his hay into his barns, receiving great forkfuls from the boys who pitched it into the loft, storing it tightly away himself beneath his rafters. And while the great empty rack was backed out of the doorway by his straining, sidling oxen, he stood for a moment in the high opening of the loft to survey his work and the yield of his acres before he swung himself downward to land just in time with a great clatter on its lumbering floor. Mary read and walked and gardened, put up numberless jars of strawberries and blueberries and raspberries, and dreamed of Hester's visit in August.

This year the summer people had come in still greater numbers. New cottages began to rise on points and headlands of the inner and the outer bay. Boys who had planned on college began to see a more immediate and profitable livelihood in carpentry and masonry, and storekeepers made closer contacts with Boston and New York for delicacies unknown in Petersport. In church on Sunday mornings city fashions and faces were much in evidence. These proved a bit harassing to the preachers, who well knew they could not compete either in matter or in manner with metropolitan pulpits, and more than a bit embarrassing to villagers whose dimes and quarters in the contribution boxes were hidden out of sight by the crisp bills of the visitors and whose best clothes looked tawdry in comparison with those of the sojourners in their midst. Mail-time in the village square became more and more a social function at which the summer dwellers of the eastern shore met those of the western to arrange for sailing-parties and luncheons. They wore smart clothes and either drove their own carefully groomed horses in stylish carriages or were transported in tasselled surreys with coachmen, sometimes black, and always correctly liveried. At twelve o'clock, Mary thought, as she descended the hill in the hope of a letter from Hester, the village no longer belonged to its rightful owners. She felt shy in the presence of these strangers even though they paid no attention to her as she wove her way among them to the post-office window.

Sarah Peters did not feel shy among them. As persons they meant nothing to her in one way or another. But their invasion of the coast meant not a little in that it marked a change as summary and sweeping as it was inevitable. They themselves were not the cause of it; perhaps instead they were a result. Change, she knew, was a law of life and time, moving no one knew how or why, triumphant over what seemed to be its causes. And change was remaking the coast even as it had remade the life upon the seas.

Like all persons who cherish values within or without themselves she cherished the seafaring heritage of Maine. It was her own, descended to her and to others through many generations, and she could not hold it lightly. She had been born into a family and married into another in which foreign ports were household words, in which men and women and even children bridged the Seven Seas in their thoughts. She wanted passionately that those thoughts should remain, and she saw them fading into obscurity. There was something immeasurably sad to her in the sight of a grandson of a shipmaster in the foreign trade shingling the roof of a summer cottage for his livelihood. There was something sadder in the knowledge that the strangers, who by their demands supplied that livelihood, knew little and cared less for the boy's history. The coast to them was beautiful; they came to it for health and pleasure; but the traditions which clothed its rocks, filled its harbours, and gave meaning to its high, stony fields and pastures were not inherent in them. These strangers in another decade would be purchasing for their summer homes the houses built by sea captains; and in yet another decade the last remnant of that sturdy, irreplaceable race would have vanished. Even now the few who remained were looked upon as delightful oddities, their homes, their pictures, their humour, their knowledge and wisdom as things to be sought after because they were uncommon. She resented the way these visitors had of calling Uncle Caleb a "character," their inundation of his house to see his maps and charts and to hear his stories. She knew that the line of demarcation between natives and sojourners would grow until two alien peoples shared her coast. But because she was in the grip of something inevitable, as she had, indeed, been for most of her life, she accepted conditions as they were, only keeping her own thoughts clear and tenacious. And just now she with every other woman in Petersport was bending her energies, outwardly at least, to the August sale which could not successfully be without the generous and interested patronage of the strangers within their gates.

This year the sale was later than usual, partly because dog days had proved excessively trying with heavy fogs, partly because the plethora of sewing was late in completion. The date was finally set for the 30th of August; the place, which moved in yearly rotation from one church to the other, was the Congregational vestry. There, from sunrise until two o'clock in the afternoon when the selling actually began, every able-bodied woman, young, middle-aged, and old, spent her every ounce of energy. Tables were set up and laid with white cloths; booths were erected, their wooden framework concealed by fir and cedar; freezers of ice cream, tiers of cakes, pounds of homemade candies were stored in the kitchen. The two pastors in their shirt sleeves proved that they could do with their might whatsoever awaited them. Deacons with hammers in their hands and their mouths filled with tacks and nails were for once, in spite of the apostolic command, completely in subservience, not to say subjection, to their wives. Clothes baskets laden with every species of handiwork under the sun awaited the noon hour to be spread upon the tables chosen for aprons or underwear or household furbishings. Children with armfuls of goldenrod and asters ran across the adjoining fields to be received at the door by the members of the committee on decorations and sent back for more and yet more.

Mary within her fir-trimmed booth was covering her mother's largest crock with bunch-berries, inserting them ingeniously between many rows of twine so that the gray of the crock should be quite invisible. She was waiting impatiently for Hester, for whom John had driven early that morning, wondering where on earth they were. She was eager for Hester's admiration of the red berries, an idea of Mary's own quite new to former fairs. She did not want to place her cups and glasses until Hester should lend her suggestions. And she wanted above everything else just to see Hester for whom letters had proved but a dreary substitute.

Ellen, festooning the edge of the fancywork table with work-bags of every description, added to her impatience.

"John's taking his time, I should think. It's too bad you have to do that all alone. They ought to have been here an hour ago."

Mary inserted the last bunch-berry at noon just as the clock was striking and was standing a bit in front of her booth to survey the effect when she saw John come through the open door. He came straight toward her and with his every step she saw the anxiety which strained his tanned face. He did not waste time in preliminaries.

"Hester's sick. I think she hurt herself coming up. Her hat blew off down by the Salt Pond bridge, and before I could stop and get it, she jumped out after it right over the wheel. She acted crazy when she did it. She caught her foot somehow and fell in the road. She said she didn't hurt herself, but she must have. She began to be sick right away—to her stomach, I mean—and she kept it up all the way home. We stopped and stopped I don't know how many times. She looks awful. She's gone to bed, says she's sorry she can't help you. She's white—and crying. I'll go get mother."

Running up the hill from the church, Mary reached home before John could drive his mother there. Hester was sick. That was apparent. She lay in her bed, all the colour gone from her cheeks, her face a bluish white, her eyes tightly closed as though she was afraid they would betray the awful spasms of pain that threatened to tear her in pieces. She turned her head toward the wall when Mary entered and made no response even to her kisses. To Mary giving them softly on her white cheek, her customary reserve broken, it was as though they were as nothing. About the sunny, tidy room lay Hester's clothes in complete disarray—her blue challis, her graduation frock which she was to have worn at the lemonade booth, her pink gingham which she had worn running through the wood paths and in which she always seemed to be laughing, her shoes which somehow Hester marked as her own shoes and nobody's else after she had worn them even for a day.

Sarah Peters' face underwent a strange and sudden change when she looked at Hester, when she saw and felt her quivering body. Mary saw the terror mastering it and herself grew white with fear, then whiter with swift and dreadful understanding. But there was no time even for fear. At her mother's command she ran to the kitchen to build a hot fire and to place on the stove kettles and pans for hot water. John was sent for the doctor and then, once he had come and Sarah Peters had stood on the stairs for a moment of tortuous indecision, to Barrett's Bay after Hester's mother.

The doctor kept Mary out of Hester's room.

"It's not right," he said to Sarah Peters, "for young girls to see these things. They've got to live themselves, remember."

Sarah Peters wondered for a fleeting instant while she knotted sheets and wrung out towels in boiling water, while she fetched and carried at the doctor's curt orders, whether Mary would ever live more than she was living in those hours. She passed her in the kitchen, to and fro on her swift errands, asked her for this or that, saw her suffering face and shaking hands. They did not speak as they worked, nor did they speak to John as he kept the fire going, standing between times in the sunny doorway with his back toward them.

Ellen tended the lemonade booth at the sale. The ladies at the fancywork table decided they could spare her best for that. She looked pretty in her white graduation frock beneath her fragrant booth, and she knew just what to say to all the young men in flannels who wanted lemonade for themselves and their friends. Her crock covered with red bunch-berries was much admired. Mrs. Wilbur and Grace and Grace's new husband, who was on Wall Street, said they had never seen a more original idea. They should copy it themselves with Ellen's permission for their next afternoon party. Ellen dimpled as she gave it and concluded she did not at all object to her unexpected transfer from the fancywork.

By three o'clock the sale was in full swing. Business was rushing. Evidently this was to be the sale of sales. The church drive was thronged with carriages. Horses tied to the white fence strove between the panels to crop the churchyard grass. Coachmen lounged about and waited. Young men and girls ate their ice cream and cake as they wandered among the graves, read the quaint inscriptions, and admired the view across the harbour to Mt. Desert. The tide was coming, and the sea was full and blue before a southwest wind. Within the vestry gentlemen in white from Baltimore and Cleveland and New York bought things they would never use in an impulse of generous patronage. The lottery tickets for a log-cabin quilt were sold twice over in half an hour. A bachelor from Bar Harbor who was visiting the Wilburs won it amid shouts of good-humoured raillery. Fancywork disappeared as if by magic, and seemingly every servant in every cottage was that evening to be presented with a new apron.

Mrs. Kimball behind the underwear table was storing up compliments and studying her every rejoinder.

"I never saw such stitches, Mrs. Kimball! How *do* you do it?"

"Do it? I've done it all my life. There's not a machine stitch on my daughter's graduation dress. That's Ellen in the lemonade booth. I always say handwork gives a tone to things. Maybe everybody don't know it's there, but *you* do all the same even if it's out of sight."

"But the time it takes! Judge Ramsey, I insist you examine this beadwork. It couldn't be done on Fifth Avenue. And all home talent! It's amazing."

"I'll never wonder again what you ladies do all winter in the cold. I shan't worry any more about you. I've always heard that Maine air makes energy. Now I know it."

"My dear, you can't do better than to get some of Edna's wedding underwear right here. Look at these handkerchief flounces on these petticoats. Mrs. Kimball says they hemstitched fifty handkerchiefs for one skirt and I can well believe it. And joining them in that adorable way! It's positively a lesson to all us lazy people!"

"Are you ladies willing to divulge the secret of this superb coffee? An egg you say with the shells left in? And watching till it boils up. Well, I'll have to wait for next year. My cook would never do it in the world."

By four o'clock the sale was over. The salaries of both ministers seemed assured. Surreys and buggies and carryalls were stirring the August dust on the shore roads east and west, and in the vestry kitchen women in ample aprons were clearing up and congratulating themselves on a wholly successful venture.

At four o'clock Mary Peters, standing white and breathless at the foot of the staircase, knew that Hester had died. She knew it by the moments of terrible silence in the room above, the door of which had been opened into the hall so that Hester might breathe all the air there was. The sun, lying warm on the white phlox in the garden, streamed through the doorway behind her and flooded the hall with light and warmth. The tall clock ticked on. It had ticked on through many deaths in that old house. It held within its polished case, framed by some old clockmaker, long since dead, the slow, resistless accent of Eternity.

After the moments of silence there was movement in the room above. Staring upward, she saw her mother leading Hester's mother across the hall into her own room. Hester's mother was moving her arms about wildly as though by the mere action of her body she could beat off that which had broken her spirit. The doctor came down the stairs then, passing her without a word. She heard him speak to John in the kitchen. Then they walked together out the back door toward the barn where country men felt more at home when speech was not easy.

She did not see Hester again, lying quiet in the sunlight. Nor did she see Hester's dead baby. Sarah Peters washed and dressed it, tiny and unready though it was either for life or for death, putting on it some of the clothes Mary had worn after she had uttered her first cry in the cabin of the *Nautilus* in the harbour of Singapore. It was a little girl. She washed and dressed it in Hester's room, carrying hot water there after Mary had somehow moved from the staircase into the sitting room to sit by the table in complete numbness of mind.

That night at eight o'clock after they had made a bed for Hester in John's spring-wagon, which he brought from the farm, they carried her and the baby to Barrett's Bay. Mary sat between John and Hester's mother on the high seat. Sarah Peters stayed behind in the silent house because she had not dared withstand Mary's decision to go with Hester. She sat in the dark of the sitting room so that she might not be compelled to see callers who might well have heard at least part of the truth about Hester. She knew she had a secret to guard for the sake of Hester's mother, who, even in her shock and grief, was shaken with dread lest anyone should know what had really happened to her daughter.

The night through which they moved to Barrett's Bay was kind to Hester's mother. The wind shifted suddenly to the east and a fog came rolling in, clothing the dark hills with an impenetrable whiteness, obscuring even the fullness of the moon. It insinuated itself into the roadside thickets, making them mounds of dark whiteness. The taller trees were blotted out as though they were not. One would not have known their presence had not now and again some great drops from them fallen into the road or struck the wagon with heavy, final thuds as though they were more solid than water. The high shrilling of the August insects was muted to a dull monotony; and the sound of the horse's feet was heavy and sombre even against the many stones and ledges. When they came to the bridge over the Salt Ponds where the tide made up into the marshes so that at its full there were two sedgy lakes, no water at all was visible through the obscurity in which they moved. Only the sound of swishing reeds and grasses, bending before the force of its ebb, and its hurrying over the rocks beneath the bridge told them that there was any tide at all. Mary could not even see John's face nor that of Hester's mother beside her. There was no silence, she thought, comparable to the silence of fog. It weighed upon them, shut them in, sang in their ears.


13


When she and John drove back at midnight, the full moon had at last conquered the clinging whiteness. The trees were freed once more. From the roadside thickets white wraiths of fog were moving. The horse's feet were again sharp and clear; the song of the crickets was high. On the Salt Pond bridge they caught the acrid scent of the flats beneath the still reeds and grasses, saw them bare and waiting for the morning flood. The stars were a pale white before the radiance of the moon.

Mary knew that elsewhere, too, the moon was high, or rising, or waning. She knew that over the sea it had this very night freed patient ships from fog. She knew that in these hours it had already sailed serenely above birth and death, love and hatred, fear and longing, in a thousand far corners of the earth, in Liverpool behind its muddy river, in Cadiz white on its high impregnable hill. She knew that numberless hearts had seen in its tranquil unconcern either the fulfillment of their joys or the cruel antithesis of their pain. Sitting there beside John, she thought these thoughts not in any effort to heal or to free herself but rather in a desperate attempt to escape from the tumult in his own mind of which she was acutely aware. She thought she ought to speak to him, try to say something, but all at once she remembered the night off Cape Horn after the gray kitten had given up its little life, and she could say nothing.

Sarah Peters was waiting up for them when they drove into the yard at one o'clock. She stood in the back doorway before the mellow lamplight of the kitchen. She had hot food ready for them and the table in the dining room as graciously set with her best old china as though she were giving a party. There was a fire burning in the fireplace, a soft-wood fire that snapped and crackled as it ate into the yellow spruce sticks.

When John had put up the horse and washed his hands and Mary had folded her mother's shawl and put it in its appointed place high on the shelf of the closet, they sat down to eat, neither daring before their mother's eyes to refuse, impossible as eating seemed to be. Sarah Peters ate, too, cutting her cold ham with firm, deliberate slashes of her knife which told them both that eating must be accomplished whether or no. She made no comments while they ate, asked no questions, but when they had finished and John made as if to rise from his chair, she spoke for the first time since they had returned, sitting there behind her tea-things, as inescapable as the coming tide.

"I've got something to say to you children. You're worn out, I know, and it's probably not the time to say it, but it has to be said some time or other, and now's the only time I know. You can cry, Mary. It's good for you. Cry away. And you, John, can stay on the farm a week if you like without coming home. But now's my time and you have to listen to me.

"Probably I'll never speak to you again like this—so far as I know I never have spoken like this—but this time you'll have to listen, and it wouldn't be a bad notion if you understood at the beginning that I know more about some things than either of you. You've been through a terrible thing. I know that. I'm not pretending you haven't. I don't know why people have to go through terrible things. Nobody knows and nobody ever will know. There's probably a reason only we can't know it, and the longer I live, the more I realize we aren't supposed to know it because if we did, we might be more full of rebellion than we are. But there's something more terrible than what you've gone through, and that is the thoughts that you keep in your minds about it."

She looked at them both sitting there, Mary with her face buried in her hands, John with his head turned from her staring sullenly at the curtained window, and gathered her forces to go on.

"I know what's in your minds. Maybe I can't do a thing to straighten them out, but I'm your mother, and I've got to try. You're thinking, Mary, because you're young and don't know, that Hester was treated cruelly and that she's paid too dearly a debt she never owed. The first is wrong, and so is the last. I won't say she hasn't paid too dearly. She has. But debts in this world aren't often contracted singly, and people sometimes have to pay to the uttermost farthing. And you, John, are thinking that this mess sits squarely on Jim Pendleton's head and that you'd like to kill him for it. Well, you're wrong, too."

An ember from the crackling fire snapped out onto the braided rug, and John turned in his chair long enough to grind its light into the woolen strands with a savage thrust of his heel which left a black mark on the blue and gray fabric.

"The sooner you get that thought out of your head, John, the better for you all your life. I'd know you were wrong even if Hester hadn't told me herself, upstairs, this afternoon. She told me things before you brought her mother, but I didn't need that she should. I knew them anyway. There are forces in this world that no one's really to blame for, forces that take people and hurl them along before they know they're taken, forces that beat them in spite of all they can do. I'm not saying they ought not to know or that they ought to be beaten. I just say they *don't* know and they *are* beaten. And sometimes even when they do know, they know too late.

"And all sorts of things determine those forces, race and inheritance and bringing up—things that a person can't be held responsible for. I'm not excusing Jim Pendleton, I'm just trying to explain him. They loved each other, he and Hester. Maybe it wasn't the sort of love you—had for her, but it was love all the same, and love always takes its toll, whether of happiness or misery, often of both. I want you to know another thing. Jim didn't know this was going to happen, and she didn't until a little while ago. She should have, but she didn't. You think, John, that he should have protected Hester. You're probably right, he should have; but when another person is swept by the same force that you are, protection doesn't play much part in what you think and do. You think you would have taken care of her. Probably that's true. I hope it is. You're different from Jim. You haven't in you the things that will make his life a hell for him. But I'd rather you had them all, I'd rather you made a mess of everything you touched, than to have you hard and without any pity for the things that make up this world!"

Her voice rose in the quiet room, and her son shifted uneasily in his chair.

"Everybody has waked up too late about this thing. Hester's mother thinks I should have known and saved her. I suppose I should. Perhaps I think she might have prepared Hester better herself for things she would have to meet in life, given the sort of girl she was. Jim waked up too late and went away, hoping he was in time to save them both. He'll pay for this, you may be sure of that. Hester's had the easier way out."

The clock in the hall struck two. Sarah Peters pushed back her chair as though she had had her say and then suddenly leaned forward within it, her hands clasped against the table.

"There's another thing. You've got to get out of your heads the notion that they did a wrong and sinful thing. Youth is hard until it comes up against the very thing it condemns. It was ill-judged and unwise, but it wasn't wrong, at least in itself. It was wrong only in that it has brought suffering and pain to themselves and to others. Hester hasn't died in disgrace. Don't keep that thought in your heads even if it never leaves her mother's. When the next century comes along and I'm perhaps dead and gone, you'll see people looking at things like this differently.

"And in spite of all this village will say, if it ever knows, and it will know for there are plenty here to ferret it out, Jim Pendleton's not branded as a bad man. He'll be a better one from now on. I'm sending for him to come. He needs me. You needn't either of you see him—it's better you shouldn't. I've always cared for him, and I care for him more now this has happened; I want you to, after a bit. I don't think it's too much to ask."

She raised her head proudly and looked at them both, and at last they returned her look, both of them sitting miserably before her.

"At least, I don't think it's too much to ask of you with all you've had since you were born and with the sort of people you come from. We ought to realize that we've had a different life from most in this village. We've known the world, all parts of it, and we can't be shut in by these streets and hills. If you children are, then you're unfair to what you've seen and known. You've got your land, John. It ought to teach you things even if your life at sea didn't. And, Mary, you and I have had enough in our lives to keep us from being cramped up in our minds. This thing will leave a scar, I know that, but the best way to handle scars, after you've seen them straight, is to remember things big enough to wipe them out. That's the only way I know to steer one's course in this world. And we've been face to face with the biggest things there are, things so big that the memory of them ought to leave no room for small thoughts. Remember those days in the doldrums when we waited and waited for a wind to fill our sails. Well, it came, didn't it? After we'd waited till we thought we couldn't wait any longer? It came, and we went on again. You'll go on again, too, if you just get your thoughts straight and wait long enough."

She rose from the table and with laden hands moved toward the kitchen. Neither John nor Mary Peters ever forgot the way she held her head as she did so or the look in her eyes.

# III

# The Land

# The Land

## 1

In the winter of 1895 when John Peters was twenty-eight he made the last payment on his farm. It was a cold February day when he did it, so cold that his mother, who for three winters had closed the big brick house in the village to be mistress of his, advised against his journey to the village for the necessary postal orders. So cold that Mary, teaching the district school a mile away, had taken matters into her own hands and dismissed the children at noon. The airtight stove around which they had crowded for their morning lessons was itself being vanquished by piercing drafts from insecure window frames and ill-fitting doors; the common water pail in its far corner was filmed with ice; and Mary's nerves were frayed by the continual stamping of numb, unwieldy feet and the continual blowing upon chilled fingers. Best, she thought, to start them on their ways while the scanty winter sunlight still prevailed. Shivering by the frosted window, she watched them, swathed and muffled, stumble down the snowy road toward farmhouses here and there, some fortunately near at hand, others two and three miles away through half-broken wood paths and beyond drifted hills. Before each of them there floated with every breath a thin wavering mist to be almost instantly captured and absorbed by the bitter cold. Mary herself was half-frozen by the time she had traversed the mile to John's driveway and hurried between the high walls of neatly shovelled snow to his back door and cheerful kitchen.

But there was no withstanding John's determination. Cold meant nothing to him, even today when the thermometer was fast approaching twenty-five below. Indeed, if anything, it sharpened his consuming desire to have the matter over and done with, completed, fulfilled at long length. He had dreamed for years after his slow, steady manner of dreaming of this day when he should own his farm, close his own barn doors at night upon his own snuffling, munching creatures. He had pictured it coming in the summer after haying was over, when his shorn fields after an August shower or two had become once more green and lively. He had thought they might even have an early picnic supper under his apple trees to celebrate the event. And after the supper—a supper of hot biscuits served with his own honey and his own blueberries and his own butter—he had thought he might take his pipe and walk all alone about his lands, bounding them with slow quiet strides.

He would begin, he had planned, with the eastern wood-lot, entering it from the country road over the brook which he had spanned by a bridge of logs and following its circuitous, bracken-edged path, through swampy land where one maple might even then show a bit of red, over sandy mounds where his spruce and pine grew, across ledges edged with sprawling juniper, through sunlit spaces of birch and beech. Then he would turn westward, mounting his northern boundary of open pasture-land where his cows stood all night after their milking or made dark imprints of themselves on the damp cropped grass and among the wet ferns. There at the high apex of his triangular pasture stood a great boulder shadowed by a beech. Once he had climbed to the top, he could see over all his possessions, fields, woods, and meadows, his white, low-roofed house and red barns beyond intervening slopes and misty hollows, perhaps even smoke from his own chimneys. He could see, too, the distant harbour stretching on to the Mt. Desert hills. Then he would turn south along his western line, walking now down through his descending fields, noting the condition of his fences and stone walls, feeling the spring of his own soil beneath his feet. One high field given now to oats though destined for a new orchard when he could manage it; two lower ones, the first, twenty acres of grass undulating in temperate mounds and easy dips, one of the best fully cleared fields in the county, the second shared by grass and gardens and ending with his farm buildings. At the foot of the high field, he had thought, he would mount his stone wall, sit there, perhaps, for some slow draws on his pipe and watch the low sun bathe the higher slopes and darken the hollows, elongate his straight beanpoles and suffuse the thick growth of his corn and potatoes. The air would be vibrant with the hum of insects; a thrush might even call from the thickets on the west; mist would hang over his lower meadows beyond his house, across the country road. His land would be still and secure beneath a clear, quiet sky, and he would go home in the gathering dusk, content.

But times had been hard and money scarce in late years. His dream for two Augusts had been deferred. Now it had come true in February on the coldest day of the year when his fields lay beneath feet of snow and when the smoke rose all day from his snug chimneys. That morning he had been surprised by a back payment on his wood, money which to his slow delight had made up the necessary two hundred dollars. It was all that remained of his debt, and he could not wait for mere weather.

At two o'clock he was on his way to the village in his old yellow sleigh. As he had harnessed in the stable, he had placed with a triumphant smile a belt of sleigh bells around the sleek back of his bay mare to supplement and increase those upon the thills. How they cut the frosty air as he drove out of the yard with a wave of his arm to his mother and Mary watching from the sitting room windows! How they multiplied themselves once he had left his yard, confined by walls of snow, the silvery echo of each bell leaping the muffled roadside thickets to linger in the thin, transparent air, chiming on over the hushed white slopes!

The country lay swathed and smothered in snow; his runners whined in the smooth, glistening ruts; his horse's well-shod feet cut with a crunching sound the packed surface of the road. No one else was abroad. He had his own land, the adjoining fields, the distant ridges to himself. The pale, clear sky gave no hope of release from cold; the earth lay passive and tranquil beneath it. The lowering sun moved southwestward in the completion of its brief day. Through an expanse of pasture-land it made maples and beeches rawboned and stark, casting dark blue shadows upon the uneven whiteness where rocks and underbrush lay concealed. Through a stretch of evergreens it touched the laden boughs of hemlocks which now and again, when the slight wind stirred, sent sliding from them with a sighing sound drifting clouds of snow crystals to catch the fading light.

John exulted in the cold, noting with excitement how Ginger's neck and shoulders were whitening as the frost transformed the warm breath from her nostrils, knowing that his own brows and lashes were stiff and white also. He thought as he thrashed his free arm now and again against his knees how uneventful and dull must be a state like California where soil was never frozen, never lay quiescent and waiting beneath the snow. Even Montana where his uncle had taken up land, land to be had for so little that it was in reality almost given away, must, he felt, be stupid in comparison with Maine. His uncle wrote of black, reckless soil so rich that it fell before the plough in clodless furrows promising acres of wheat with a minimum of labour. Such soil would not do for him, he concluded. He loved labour, the eternal battle with stubborn acres that must be mollified or outwitted some way or another. Even now under the snow he knew the land was stirring. That clump of maples on the hill above the village, gaunt and dead though they looked, were far beneath the surface of the ground feeling the first press of sap. In four weeks more he would start for his own high field with bit and auger, wooden spouts and pails, sure that he could trust the spring, no matter if the snow still prevailed. As he bent above the gray trunks of his maples, boring smooth round

holes deep enough to cut their swelling veins, he knew that his
neck and chest would feel warm and glowing within his flannel
shirt, that he within his own veins would feel the rush of returning
life. He felt within his great bearskin coat for his leather wallet
where his money lay and called the world good and the silent
earth, which, though it strove with man, was yet his companion,
the source of his well-being and his strength.

He found the village well-nigh deserted, the square piled with
snow from the sledges which had broken the road, the store windows caked with frost. Tying Ginger to the picket fence before the
post-office and covering her rimed sides with his fur robe, he
stamped into the dingy little building to rouse Joel Pendleton from
his snug chair by the stove in the stuffy inner office and to ask for
his postal orders. Joel was impressed. He had not written such
orders or received so much money for many months. John was
not averse, as he folded the blue slips within his letter to his uncle,
to telling him what such a stupendous act signified, and he
received Joel's congratulations with an exhilaration that warmed
his whole body so that he opened his fur coat and removed his
heavy cap. He knew that in spite of the cold-locked village the
information that John Peters at last owned his farm would travel
from house to house and be common property before another day
had passed. So elated was he, so bursting with contentment and
pride, that he forgot his usual reserve and smoked a pipe with Joel
sitting opposite him by the stove with his feet on the cracked old
fender. With no surprise at all he heard himself talking to Joel,
heard himself saying:

"People don't know what they're talking about when they say
a farm in these parts can't be made to pay. A farm'll pay all right if
a man's not afraid of working, and if he'll just take a chance now
and then and try new things. Now I've got my land paid for, every
cent, and don't owe for so much as a pitchfork, I'm going to

branch out a bit. I'm going to do more with apples. You can't expect trees most a century old to keep on doing things especially when they're all grass-choked and haven't been helped along for years. I'm going to fertilize my old orchard and start in grafting. And I'm going to set out new trees in my high field. I'm going to plough it and make it a real, up-to-date orchard like some I've read about out West. It makes me tired to hear folks say Maine land's all run out and that the West is the only place for the farmer. It's not the land that's run out, I say; it's the folks that think they're farming it, folks that aren't willing to work and to wait for things. And there's a lot in this reforestation, too. You can't cut and cut and expect the new growth to keep up with you. It isn't sense. When I can, I'm going to plant white pine and spruce in my lot and take care of them till they get going on their own."

The colour mounted in his face as he talked on, about a dairy herd and the chance for sheep which few farmers in the county seemed aware of. Joel Pendleton felt the laziness in his old veins stir in uneasy reproof.

"Youth," he thought. "That's what ails him, youth. Now if I was young again, I might take to the land myself." Aloud he said,

"Now you're free, John, and starting out fresh and on your own, like, you ought to think of marrying. A farmer needs a wife more than most men."

John was surprised at the lack of embarrassment he felt at the proposal.

"Maybe," he said. "There's time enough for that though. I'm in no hurry." He rose from his chair and shrugged himself into his greatcoat. "Tomorrow morning when I get up I'll be just starting out on my own. Every cent I earn from now on is mine now that letter's lying there ready for tomorrow's bag. I'm not likely to forget this day, Mr. Pendleton."

"No," said Joel, pulling himself in turn from his chair, "no, you ain't, and that's a fact. Suppose I stamp that letter here and now before your eyes. There! It goes into this bag here. You can know it's on its way when you bed down tonight. And I wish you luck, John."

John was adjusting the earcoverings of his cap in the outer office and putting on his mittens when the door opened to let in a blast of freezing air and Ellen Kimball in near-seal and a blue fascinator.

"John!" she cried, surprise and pleasure in her voice. "Well, I never! I thought you were buried up there and frozen, too. What's brought you down on a day like this? I've been hugging the stove all the afternoon till I couldn't stand it any longer. Freezing, I said to mother, is better than feeling so stupid you fall asleep."

"Lots," said John. "There's a lot of things brought me out, Ellen."

He stood and looked at Ellen as she asked for stamps at the tiny window and passed the day with Joel. The clock on the office wall said half-past three. He cleaned his stalls, milked, and bedded down on winter nights at five. But still he stood and looked at Ellen. Her cheeks were fresh and pink from the cold; her hair curled beneath her blue fascinator; her breath made a white mist even in the outer office. He had seen no one except Sarah and Mary Peters for days, and Ellen seemed suddenly desirable.

"This young man's paid for his farm, Ellen," proffered Joel through the opening in the office wall. "Brought me so much money I shan't rest easy in bed till I send it on to Washington. What do you think of that?"

"Well, I never!" said Ellen again. "Congratulations, John!"

She drew her hand from a blue mitten which matched her fascinator and extended it toward John. He took it and stood there holding it foolishly. In that moment he liked Ellen better than he had ever liked her in all his life. She seemed to be thinking of him and of all the hard work he had done to pay for his farm at last.

She seemed actually to be proud of him, and his heart quickened within him at the very idea of Ellen's being proud. He took off his cap which he had quite forgotten before and the colour flooded his face beneath his untidy hair.

"Thank you, Ellen," he stammered. "I do feel different. It's— it's a great feeling I've got."

"Come up to the house," said Ellen. "Mother'll be glad, too. There's fresh doughnuts and we'll make coffee. You'll need something before you drive back. It's not late, and your chores can wait a bit for once. Anyway it's light now till nearly six. You can drive me right home now. It's weeks since we've seen each other."

John went. He ate Mrs. Kimball's doughnuts and drank her good coffee by her sitting room fire. Mrs. Kimball, too, was glad for John. She said he was the most up and coming young man in the neighbourhood. Sitting there with her and Ellen, he talked and talked. Something seemed loosened inside him. The cold outside increased the cosiness within; and Ellen had even insisted generously on some oats for Ginger, standing snugly in the Kimball barn. And then suddenly, loth to go, he had thought of taking Ellen back with him to spend the night, perhaps even two nights with Mary and his mother.

"She can wrap up warm," he said to Mrs. Kimball. "It's not so cold really once you get started. Maybe you've got a flatiron for her to hold. They'll be awfully glad to see her, and—and it will be kind of a celebration for me."

Mrs. Kimball did not demur for long although she said it was a crazy notion. She said, too, that one simply couldn't keep pace with young folks nowadays. Nothing seemed to stump them, even twenty-five below zero. But Ellen had been dull enough, tired of knitting and crocheting and reading, and maybe a change would be good for her. She helped Ellen collect her things, placing in the meantime a soapstone on the top of the kitchen stove. John smoked a pipe while they made ready. He felt warm and expansive and so full of new strength and power that he did not know himself.

It was nearly five when they started northward up the snow-blocked hill, out into the open country. The sun had dropped below the firred ridges, but an orange glow prevailed from north to south. It was colder than ever. The runners of the sleigh swayed and whined, and John's bells filled the air with themselves and their wandering echoes. Ellen snuggled beside him deep beneath his fur robe, a soapstone at her feet, a flatiron in her lap. She was warm as toast, she said, and looked upon this as an adventure she had not had for months. She could not get over the thought of Mary's face when she should see her.

John for his part could not get over the engulfing satisfaction which flooded both mind and body. His thoughts were warm within him; he felt the good will of the whole world. His neighbours' homes had never looked so good to him, their chimneys smoking cosily, their overhanging eaves low in the fading light, their foundations banked high with boughs of fir beneath the snow. When they passed the wood-road that marked his eastern boundary, he felt a sense of possession that threatened to burst something inside him. He scanned the snowy path and, although the dusk was falling, saw upon it the unmistakable footprints of a fox leading away beneath the overhanging boughs. With the sight there came a genial feeling of kinship with all the wild creatures that were his tenants, beasts and birds which roamed or slept or in the spring would make homes in his hospitable trees and brush. They should never be molested, he said to himself, and the first thing he knew he was saying the same thing to Ellen beside him. She laughed in a kindly fashion and quite agreed. She had never been so companionable, he thought, and in the bitter cold when people were hugging their fires after seeing that their stock was safe and warm, what could be better than companionship?

The evening star had arisen when he drove Ellen through the walls of snow to his back door. His mother and Mary were glad to see her, more glad as they sensed his own pleasure in the surprise he had brought them. He whistled and sang as he went about his chores, secure in the thought that supper was being made ready for him in the kitchen. From his laden mows he threw down an extra supply of hay for his cattle and bedded them in deeper straw than usual. The streams of milk striking the bottoms of his pails beat in rhythm to his own excited heart. When he had finished and had carried his milk to the shed, he came back and stood in the door-way of his barn, listening quietly to the sidling and munching and champing going on in his stalls and stanchions, to the clink of chains and the rattle of wooden yokes, to the swish of tails and the stamping of contented feet. The cold within was dispelled by warm, fragrant breathing. No one there would suffer that night, he thought, no matter how the mercury fell. When he had closed his doors securely and turned toward the house through the path he had shovelled for himself through the snow, he thought how the cold deepened the glow from his windows. There was nothing comparable to the comfort and security a man felt when he saw his own lamplight across the snow from his own house.

Sarah Peters had an extra good supper that evening. She had planned it so that everything they ate had had its being in John's fields or barns or orchard. Ellen enlivened things indescribably, making an occasion out of an incident. He had never realized before how much fun and merriment Ellen had in her. He served the food himself with so little embarrassment that everyone was secretly startled. They sat around the table longer than usual and, after things were tidy again, drew their chairs about the Franklin stove in the sitting room where John's wood crackled and glowed.

The low-ceilinged room held the light and warmth snugly within itself. The women knitted or crocheted. Ellen was fashioning from pale blue wool a jacket for a baby soon to come in the village, and John wondered at the smallness of the sleeves she was just completing.

"They can't be large enough, Ellen," he said. "No baby in the world was ever so small as that. I don't believe it for a moment."

As he said it, he was surprised at his own daring in venturing on such a subject to Ellen. It must be, he said to himself in explanation, that he was emboldened by the way she seemed somehow to fit into his fireside, to look as though she belonged there.

Ellen was bold, also, feeling within herself a pleasant little tremor at her audacity as she answered him.

"Now what do you know about babies, John, I'd like to know?"

She wondered whatever her mother would have thought could she have heard such a rejoinder. That she would have considered it indelicate in the extreme, Ellen well knew. Therein, indeed, lay part of its allurement. She wondered, too, as she bent over her jacket with heightened colour, why one never expected or for that matter never received such social disapproval from Sarah Peters.

As for John, once he had become accustomed to the added familiarity he felt with Ellen, he watched the blue jacket and her fingers with ever-growing pleasure. Women ought always to knit or sew in the evenings, he thought, as he stretched out his long legs in his big chair and once more filled his pipe.

At nine he went upstairs with his mother to replenish the stove already lighted in the guest room where Ellen was to sleep. They had filled an old brass warming-pan now seldom used with embers from the fire downstairs. He stood in the doorway and watched Sarah Peters while she drew back the bed coverings to run the pan across the cold sheets and blankets. It gave one a comfortable feeling thus to prepare a room for a guest. He was glad his mother had insisted in the fall on fresh dimity curtains for the windows and on making braided mats for the old yellow floor whose wide boards creaked now in the cold.

When Ellen and Mary had gone upstairs and Sarah Peters was setting things right in the kitchen for the night, he lighted his lantern and went to the barn to see that there, too, all was well. He moved about his stalls and stanchions returning the patient stare of his creatures, stroking the sleek shoulders of his bay mare and thumping the thick red hide of his oxen. He was glad he had shingled his roof and repaired his clapboarding in the summer even though it had deferred his last payment. A farmer should not sleep comfortably at night if he knew that snow and undue wind could sift through his walls.

He blew out his lantern when he had once again closed his doors and stood without them looking up at the winter sky. The stars had never been brighter. There was Orion, his flaming belt and sword, with Betelgeuse forming his high shoulder and Rigel one of his ungainly knees. There was Aldebaran redder than usual as befitted the great eye of Taurus; there were the Pleiades so bright that one could almost imagine the presence of the seventh lost so long ago; there were the Twins and blazing Sirius, and behind far to the north the greater and lesser Bears and the familiar polar star.

Standing there beneath them, unconscious of the cold, he remembered how he had learned them, sometimes unwillingly, from Ellis on the rocking deck of the *Elizabeth*. There above the dark, tossing sea they had been but a sinister part of a life he hated and feared, suggesting to him only his homesickness in a wilderness of space. Here above his snow-covered fields and woods they became not so much removed from the earth by incomprehensible, undecipherable miles, as a part of the earth itself, of his land which with the rest of the earth moved beneath them. Throughout the round of the year he studied their varied shining for weather signs. By other signs which they afforded he planted his

corn and peas and oats, noting cautiously the position of the
moon within one or another of their constellations. Not that he
really believed in the signs—he had read and studied too much for
that—but they had a way of sticking in a farmer's mind, recurring
to him now and again when the time seemed ripe.

A snowy February for example, like this one, promised a fine
summer. Thunder in March was a bad sign for harvest. Stone walls
piled in October on the three days of the hunters' moon assured a
farmer of the friendliness of his neighbours for a full year at least.
One should never speak of secret matters in a field full of little
hills when the moon was waning. There was one old saw which
his uncle had taught him about a swarm of bees. He said it over to
himself with a smile out there beneath the stars:

*A swarm of bees in May*
*Is worth a load of hay.*
*A swarm of bees in June*
*Is worth a silver spoon.*
*A swarm of bees in July*
*Is not worth one fly.*

They were all simple things, these signs, so old that no one
could possibly trace them. Sometimes he thought they had been
given to the first farmers of the world to show the favour of earth
and sky toward them in those early days before the struggle for life
began, before man and earth knew enmity and violence. Like all
old things they should not be set aside carelessly, laughed at as useless and outworn. As for himself he always felt that such warnings
and predictions in some way connected him half-humorously, half-
reverently with the slow, tireless movements of heaven and earth
and lent thereby a dignity, even a grandeur, to his long days of toil.

## 2

Mary finished the winter term of school in John's district and stayed on for the spring which would complete her three years there among the country children. She had come immediately following her two years at Castine. She looked forward to the offer of a better school, but she was young, and even in rural Maine of the nineties experience was thought a necessary stepping-stone. Moreover, to live with John and her mother on his farm seemed for the time being at least the partial solution of financial problems arising from a depleted income in hard times. Sarah Peters closed the village house once the fall term had begun and opened it again when June had sent the children home for a summer in gardens and berry patches, farmhouse kitchens and hay fields.

In those three years life for Mary held a slow contentment in itself reassuring. Time as always was kind. Pleasures which she had thought closed for her because of their association with Hester again became loadstones, each attracting her in turn. Wood-lots flamed in October, were still in November, received in December their snows and in March the clinging mists which at once hid and nurtured their springing life. Fields held the mellow October sunlight, changing beneath it to the warm tans of Indian summer. Oaks purpled the distant hillsides, their more tenacious leaves fading slowly into the russet hues of early winter, paling before the first snows. Clouds were never the same from one day to another. As the days shortened in November, they had a way of forming harbours in the western sky, harbours landlocked in deepest blue or purple with waters of pale green or clearest yellow, which Mary saw as she came home from school along the westward-moving road.

"Valparaiso," she thought, "with its horns, or San Francisco golden in its own sunset, or Naples with Vesuvius beyond, or the great outer harbour of Batavia with its three inner ones." And so complete was the illusion in the still, windless air that she half expected to see the sails of a ship and then its black hull appearing in the far distance of the sky.

Weather in itself was exciting. She found herself wondering how anyone could be impervious to its mystery and its charm. The habit of waiting upon its changes, of watching it from day to day in the attempt to recognize its portents and be prepared for its vagaries, a habit which had become insensibly a part of her life at sea, she now transferred with growing consciousness to this new life close to the land. As John watched his creatures to see whether they sniffed the air or huddled back to back in a corner of the pasture, or listened to neighbourhood prognostications by aching corns or rheumatic knees, she studied the milk-white skies of early March, noting how birch trees whitened in capricious sunlight and how the wind made restive the pools of water covering the last silvery ice. The still, ancient prophecies of cloudless days slowly entered into her life and worked their gracious ways with her.

The country children whom she taught were a part of the earth also, trudging in the early morning with their dinner pails through pine woods and over pasture slopes, barefoot as soon as the May sun had warmed the soil. They had a spring in their brown, sinewy legs such as town and city children could never gather from stone pavements and plank sidewalks. They had wary eyes for birds' nests and sniffing noses for mayflowers and pennyroyal. They carried about with them proofs alike of their habitation and of their alliance therewith in their ineradicable, seemingly deep-rooted practice of chewing or eating whatever presented itself along their paths to school. They were forever rotating in their mouths or carrying between their teeth bits of fresh wood or bark, the tender tips of new balsam, checkerberry leaves, sweet fern and bayberry, sorrel, frost-bitten rose haws, the buds and even the blossoms of dandelions. Mary was constantly saying,

"Jimmy, what are you eating?"

"Just a piece of swamp-root, please, ma'am."

"Silas Ames, you know I will not have spruce gum chewed in school."

"It's not gum, ma'am. Honest. It's cherry bark. My mother says it's good for a cold."

To many of them books were rather extraneous things which they studied by force of necessity, droning out their lessons with minds on the ledgy playground or on the pasture brook which they would dam at recess or during the noon hour. They knew the country intimately rather than in detail; few of them were of the stuff of which naturalists are made; but they belonged to it, looked like it, smelled of it.

The smells in her schoolhouse, in fact, kept Mary amused when there was dearth of other entertainment. When she bent over the boys at their desks on spring mornings, she smelled barn smells, fresh milk, hayseed, manure, mingled with the scent of pine pitch which lingered on their fingers from the pricking of pine blisters and with that of the wood which they had carried into their mother's wood-boxes on their morning chores. In the winter when the windows were closed and smells unalleviated, one's nose could easily distinguish the manifold activities of barns and farmhouse kitchens. There were smells of soda-biscuits, flapjacks and doughnuts. Breakfasts were thus easily discerned. There were smells of lampwicks and soft soap, homemade sausage and apple butter, smells of wood smoke, horse liniments, spruce gum, ham and baked potatoes, apples, baked beans and johnny-cake and buttered popcorn. Colds brought more smells and made one keenly aware of the rigours of rural pharmacopoeia. Flannel chest protectors gave infallible proof of the plasters and poultices they had replaced, plasters of mustard and salt pork, hen's oil and duck's grease, boiled onions and flaxseed. Homemade cough syrups lingered in the warm, close air; and in February and March no child was without his odourous sulphur bag beneath flannel blouses and well-worn woolen frocks.

In a district of scattered farms the school was not large. There were twenty-three children in all, ranging in age from five to fifteen, bright children and dull children, plain children and now and then one so lovely that she seemed an emanation of the countryside, holding within her face and body all its gifts and graces. The bright ones, after they had mastered their Greenleaf's arithmetic, their Frye's geography, and their Montgomery's American history, would go to the Academy and thence perhaps to the normal school or even to college if enough money could be found somewhere. They would put on town clothes, have their hair cut in the prescribed fashion instead of around convenient kitchen bowls; they would lose their shyness; their parents would be proud of them, read their letters to neighbours. And always, wherever they went, they would hold within themselves something of the simplicity and indestructible value of their country heritage, being glad all their lives in familiar, homely foods, in the sight of farm animals and blossoming fruit trees. Others less sensitive, and thankful for escape would work in city kitchens, after an apprenticeship in summer cottages, or in city shops and factories, marrying any nondescript men who presented themselves, only providing they were not farmers. Still others would marry neighbouring boys and girls and in time inherit the family farms, spending their lives eagerly or with quiet content or merely with the negative patience of less quickened natures everywhere.

Mary liked teaching them, liked even the ingenuity required of her by the need of holding some twenty classes a day. Although there were no so-called "grades," the children were tenacious of their "places" in their books and of the progress they had made in previous terms. At fourteen it was better to do compound proportion, partial payments, and cube root alone than to review percentage with two twelve-year-olds and wait for them to catch up with one. Even the limited pedagogy dispensed by a normal school in the nineties must, she learned, wait upon necessity; in other words, one must cut one's pattern to fit one's cloth. Classes of one or two, therefore, did their examples on the wooden blackboards at the sides of the schoolroom while reading classes in quick succession read to her from the settee before her desk. Thus the long day sped on from nine o'clock to four with little time for anything except strict attention to the business at hand.

She liked, too, the meetings with their parents at Grange suppers or at other gatherings which were held now and again in the schoolhouse. There was something exciting, if a bit disarming, in being considered the Mentor of the neighbourhood, the dispenser of advice, the shaper of destinies. Her Saturday night beans and brown bread were eaten, in the spring and fall terms, now in one farmhouse, now in another according to the hospitable custom of the district; and she saw her children clean and shy during so stupendous an occasion as the entertainment of their teacher. On weekday evenings when she went to her room for reading and study, she stood by her window before lighting her own lamp and saw here and there on hilltops and deep within valleys the lighted panes of kitchens and sitting-rooms. Within those rooms, she knew, the best of her schoolroom bent above their books and slates while the younger and the less eager slept in the dark chambers above on feather beds beneath patchwork quilts.

The school, simple and poor as it was, held together like all schools of its kind a closely defined piece of country. The naming of such localities gave proof of that. They were called the Witham district, or District Number Ten, or the Willow Brook district. The country school was like the hub of a wheel, its radiating spokes culminating in homes here and there, the rim which held the widening spokes together some natural boundary, a circle of hills enclosing a valley, or the course of a stream shutting in a given territory. Such square miles of land held a common consciousness of which the school was the centre.

Some time in the near future such schools would go. She knew that from her reading. Districts would be consolidated. Better buildings would be erected, and the children gathered from miles around for better, more up-to-date instruction. Already, she knew, in other states richer and more progressive than Maine, these things were being done, supposedly to the best advantage of all concerned. But in the meantime she was not averse to teaching in this completely rural district, in a school not so much a part of a system as a centre and whole in itself, in whose life every home in the neighbourhood shared and to whose existence each contributed. One farmer filled the entryway with wood; another patched the roof; a third replaced a broken plank in the rickety stoop. There was more than a little to be gained, she concluded, from even such a humble seat of learning upon which the thought and the pride of a community converged. And when in the spring she received an offer to teach in the Academy, it was not without a feeling of regret that in late June she scrubbed her blackboards for the last time, locked her battered door, and went homeward down the ledgy schoolhouse hill among the chamomile and clover of its dishevelled, dusty playground.

3

Everyone said that Sarah Peters was far too young a woman to have a shock at fifty-eight. But she had it all the same, or perhaps more properly it had her, holding her helpless in its iron clutches. Perhaps, too, any other woman except herself would have paid more heed to its muttered threats of several years, to the queer pressure she had sometimes felt in her head, the sudden painful constrictions of her arms and hands which she had now and again suffered. She had not been unaware of these things nor entirely unsolicitous concerning them; but knowing the price she might pay for a confidential unearthing of them in the office of the village doctor, she had weighed the advantages and disadvantages of such procedure and concluded that silence was her best investment. She knew well what forty years' experience in the country had taught the doctor about shocks; they together with rheumatism and childbirth were his chief stock in trade; and it was her very respect for his knowledge which kept her from his office. She knew what he would tell her. Why pay him for it? He would tell her not to bend over a washtub or, worse, over a hot stove; not to eat too much or too hurriedly; not to go up and down stairs when it could be avoided; not to carry armfuls of wood or pails of water; not to bend over her peonies in the sun; not to fold the sheets and blankets which must be folded or to turn the mattresses which must be turned; in short, not to do any of the things which kept her life as well as her house in order. He would probably insist that someone be imported to do them for her, some woman who would be competent and insensitive, who would handle her East Indian china carefully yet briskly, who would dust her pictures without looking at them—someone with whom she could not find one honest word of fault. Lastly he would tell her not to get confused or upset in mind. Well, this last and most important prescription would be far easier of attainment if she kept away from him and his advice and within reason, of course, did as she had always done. She had never been one, she told herself, as suddenly tired without apparent cause, she rested now and then in mid-morning while Mary was at school, to turn the calm flow of her life topsy-turvy by some sudden decision of her own. All her years at sea had taught her to wait for things—for things one could neither hurry nor turn aside once they were started.

"You may as well keep your head," she said to herself every now and again in those years which had made her suspicious and watchful of her body. "Keep your head and bide your time."

Her time came one January morning in Mary's third year as teacher of English in the Academy. Her feet had been cold and numb all night long, and when she got out of her bed in the morning at her usual hour, they seemed strangely foreign to the floor. But she dressed and went downstairs, stamping them a bit irritably as she went about her kitchen. When she bent over her wood-box to get the one piece of wood she wanted for her fire, she felt suddenly faint and ill. Mary found her on the kitchen sofa between the two sunny eastern windows, the stick of wood still in her hand, and sent a boy who was passing for the doctor. In the fifteen minutes before he came Sarah Peters declared herself in need of nothing at all except to lie still and to have Mary put in its rightful place a certain bowl which had somehow been moved on the pantry shelf.

"This has been a long time coming," said the doctor as he bent over her. "I've seen it. I'm not blind. If you'd come to me, I might have staved it off a year or two."

"What's a year or two?" she asked in a thickened voice. She knew that strange things were slowly, irresistibly happening to her face and to her speech. "I began to live young. If I'd come to you, you'd only have spoiled these last years for me."

"Probably," said the doctor. "I don't blame you. Don't try to talk."

"There's no use to try," she muttered from somewhere deep within her tightening throat. "I—can't."

She was a beautiful woman and, as all beautiful persons ought to do, had always admired with a quiet, objective pleasure the fine carriage of her head and the clear firmness of her skin. Mary knew with anguish how it must torture her to feel the contours of her face being mercilessly drawn out of shape, assuming ugly, unnatural lines about her mouth and eyes. After a few days the paralysis of those muscles relaxed somewhat although she never again looked entirely natural; after a week she began to speak once more in a slow, faltering voice which came with effort from between her straining, distorted lips. She never walked again, nor could she so much as turn herself in bed or raise herself among her pillows. The stroke had made her right side useless, her right foot only the semblance of a foot which was moved about now and then like any other inanimate object in the changing of her position, her right hand placed here and there, at her side, across her breast, wherever it seemed best to place it. Sometimes Mary, coming suddenly into her mother's room, would see her holding the blue, lifeless hand in her firm left one, examining it for some hint of sensation which never came, studying it in half-amused surprise that a thing which looked so like a hand could do nothing that a hand should do.

But her mind remained untouched, becoming as the days unfolded themselves like some vast room, which, once cleared of useless lumber, swept, and put to rights, held now but light and space. The energies of her wasted body instead of leaving her seemed only to have transferred themselves or to have become transcended into new and magical forces of thought and power. Her memory glowed, transfiguring into the new reality of the present all that had enriched her past; her imagination created and re-created, enkindling stray, half-forgotten, half-grasped perceptions until the hours were not long enough for the thoughts and reflections which sprang into new life from depths and heights never

before seen within herself. Life now blossomed for her as never
before or perhaps rather gathered together, like the Angel of the
Resurrection, into one glorious harvest all its flowers and its fruits.
Thus illness became an unexplored mine of treasure, its outer
chambers of thought opening into inner fastnesses of spirit wherein
she knew the Tree of Life and heard the sound of living waters.

Fancy, too, lighted its candles, bringing laughter and gaiety out
of the most humdrum occurrences. She found herself laughing at
her own helplessness as over some trivial thing of no real consequence. Things which she had feared would cause her anxiety, the
sight of some one else handling her possessions, doing her work,
caring for her in intimate, humiliating ways, ceased suddenly to
trouble her at all. It was impossible to feel sorry for her. Mrs.
Kimball, bearing blanc-mange and condolence, went away irritated
at what she considered indecent cheerfulness and composure. After
all a sick-room was a sick-room and presumably imposed certain
seemly rules of behaviour on patient and caller alike. People might
as well save their sympathy, she confided to Ellen over the supper-
table, since it clearly was not wanted.

Mary, conscious that she was living daily in a house which
might be likened to that upper room in Jerusalem, tried to find
comparisons of what her mother's mind was like. She thought of
the watchfires in the *Agamemnon* of Aeschylus, blazing on their
high pyramids, of the golden apples in the Garden of Hesperides,
of the sure and steady flashes from lighthouse towers, of the
sunswept canvas of the ships she had watched with Mr. Gardiner.
During the short months of spring and summer she found it easy,
even inevitable, to be affectionate toward her mother. It was bod-
ies, not minds, she concluded, that built barriers between people,
all the manifold activities of hands and feet, forbidding manners
and inaccurate, too plentiful speech. Now that Sarah Peters' body
lay useless and her speech curtailed, her released mind ran to meet

that of her daughter in a companionship neither had known before. Mary read aloud the books she had always wanted to share, talked of this and that within them, revived memories she had been shy of reviving.

One Sunday at twilight in late May when the lilacs were in bloom above the gate and the tide was filling the harbour, they spoke of Jim Pendleton.

"I've thought of writing to him," said Mary, "and asking him to come. You'd like to see him, wouldn't you?"

"Yes."

"I'll write then. I'd like to see him myself."

"I have the address," said Sarah Peters, "in my desk upstairs."

"So have I. I asked his aunt for it yesterday."

"Are you sure you want to see him?"

"Perfectly sure. I'll tell him to bring his fiddle and play to you. I'll get out my music and practise up a bit so he won't be too irritated."

John, driving down each evening to sit for an hour with his mother before he went to say a long good-night to Ellen, accepted with slow surprise and relief the atmosphere of security and even of merriment in the brick house. He had dreaded to speak to his mother some weeks before of his new relationship with Ellen, but she had received his news calmly enough. She had wanted, she said, to see him safely settled in his own home with someone to care for him. Ellen, she was sure, would be the best of housekeepers, neat and thrifty and always pleasant to look at. No one could have been kinder to her, she said, than Ellen, more solicitous, more eager to help. If she entertained any misgivings at all about Ellen during the hours in the night when she lay awake because she did not want to bother the woman who cared for her to change her position in bed, she did not voice them to John or even to Mary. What was done was done and what would happen would happen.

John must run his own life in so far as he could. More than ever now she could not get away from the notion that mere events were as nothing compared to the way they were received, to the spirit which must steady and stay them on their course. John had his land which would ever be the source of his spirit. Ellen might fail him, but the land would not. He already carried about with him its gift, a simplicity which came from long communion with animals, with the mating and birth that went on in his pastures and barns, from long and devoted partnership with rain and sun. He would take Ellen in this same simplicity, which, Sarah Peters hoped, would be proof against the troubling of the petty claims of circumstance.

Mrs. Kimball was vastly relieved about John and Ellen. She had thought during the months of John's slow attendance that he was never coming to any point at all. He was an ambitious young man, she said to her neighbours, handsome, and steady as a clock. He could keep help for Ellen if he chose, and it was high time that she at twenty-eight should be married and settled. Of course, all things being equal, Mrs. Kimball secretly would have preferred a more exciting match for her daughter. For years she had cherished romantic dreams of Ellen's capturing now this young man, now that, of the growing summer colony, marrying wealth, position, and a New York home. But as the summers passed, each proving more conclusively that Maine must come in time to depend upon the outsider for her livelihood, it was slowly borne in, even upon Mrs. Kimball, that the line between sojourners and natives was yearly increasing in height and bulk. Young men from Fifth Avenue might admire Ellen's complexion in church, but they had not the slightest intention of inviting her upon their sailing-parties. Not for a moment that they discriminated against her socially; instead they simply never considered her at all. This fact, to a woman more thoughtful than Mrs. Kimball, might have been indicative if not prophetic of the future social history of half the coast in another generation. It might have suggested to her as it had already suggested to Sarah Peters how far less endurable to a locality as to an individual is unconscious unconcern than that which is conscious. But, since Mrs. Kimball was what she was, it suggested nothing at all except that as New York society was seemingly to be denied Ellen, she would best take John Peters if she could ever get him to the point of proposal. Now she had gotten him there, he meanwhile, after the manner of many men, believing himself to have been the complete master of the situation, Mrs. Kimball was settled in her own mind and happy. She put fine stitches in Ellen's wedding underwear by Sarah Peters' bed and talked long and volubly about the probable future of the young people.

Ellen also brought her sewing every other day or so. She looked fresh in her crisp cotton frocks and already matronly as she hemmed dish-towels in Sarah Peters' Boston rocker, now and then pausing from her sewing to rock serenely to and fro. She was full of plans for their home, rather definite plans perhaps, clear-cut and even now well established in her mind.

"I'm trying to get John to see the sense of using the sitting room for the dining room," she said to Sarah Peters. "That little dining room is too small and dark for any use. I like to eat where I can see what I'm eating myself. And I can't see any point of keeping the front room so shut up and sacred. People don't do that nowadays, I tell John. They use all their rooms, one the same as the other. What I plan to do, at least what I want to do when I once get him round to my way of thinking, is to use the dining room for a downstairs bedroom. We'll be able to keep a hired girl soon, I hope. The sitting room will make the prettiest dining room with flowers in the windows and the sun pouring in, and it's even more convenient to the kitchen. John," she concluded, looking a bit sharply at his mother, "John takes forever to make up his mind and forever more to change it, doesn't he?"

"Yes," said Sarah Peters, watching Ellen's capable, square hands with their blunt, strong fingers, "John's mind has never moved too quickly."

"Well," returned Ellen again a bit sharply, as she steadied her rocker and again took up her sewing, "I can't wait forever for it to move. He'll have to get used, I guess, to having it made up for him, at least in things like the dining room. That after all is just plain common sense as anyone can see."

Ellen had plenty of plain common sense. There it was inside her, almost a visible thing, solid and substantial and ever present like the black particles in granite. The only trouble with too much common sense, thought Sarah Peters, is that it doesn't leave enough room for other things.

Uncle Caleb also sat now and again in her pleasant room. He was growing more frail and uncertain with every month; and, with the calm knowledge he possessed of his faltering old bones and arteries, he had sold his house with its high-panelled wainscoting and the carvings his grandfather had made above each doorway to a prosperous merchant from Baltimore. Next year at this time, he told Sarah Peters, they would be settling in, enjoying the view from between his white pillars, burning in his back field the cultch of all sorts in his attic. He was glad to have things neatly attended to before he set out for whatever sort of port he was bound. Mary could have his money since he had outlived all his three children. There was not so much as he had hoped for.

His past had become more circumscribed with the years, but it still glowed sufficiently to allow him to spend one day in one place, another in another. Monday he spent in Shanghai where there was yellow fever; Tuesday he was dining with Captain Enright on birds'-nest soup in the cabin of the *Chrysolite* in

Hongkong; Wednesday he was a young man again, vastly proud in his first papers, lending aid in the devastated harbour of St. Peters to the survivors of the Martinique hurricane of 1831.

"What's the odds?" he said to Sarah Peters, settling his frayed black skull-cap with his mottled old fingers. "What's the odds, Sarah? Everything comes to an end one time or other. I ain't fig-urin' on what's happenin' to me after my last breath's blown. I ain't much concerned one way or another about that. I've had my life, I say, and by the great horned spoon I've used it! Young men nowadays can't have the life I've had, but what they don't know about, I suppose, won't ever hurt 'em. The world's changin', but it ain't changed me, thank God! And I ain't hankerin' to start on a new century, not I. I came in with this one, and I'm glad to go out with it. So what's the odds, I say?"

What, indeed, thought Sarah Peters, looking from her pillows far beyond the Mt. Desert Hills, her own memories warm and still within her. What, indeed?

4

One June evening just after supper Jim Pendleton came. Mary was gathering from the bushes by the doorway some boughs of syringa to arrange in her mother's fireplace when she saw him coming up the hill. He had sent no word in response to her letter, and his appearance surprised, even startled her. When she caught sight of him, he had just reached the church and stopped for a moment on the board sidewalk to look at it before again starting onward. Ten years slipped away as she saw him standing there, as she watched him swing his leg outward in the familiar way she remembered when once he resumed his climb.

She had just time to tell her mother, to rearrange her pillows, and to place the syringas in a jar of water before she heard the latch of the gate click. She went to the open door to meet him as he came up the flagstones of the path.

"Well, Mary?" he said half interrogatively, and then because there was clearly nothing else to be said until she had established what relationship she would, he said again, "Well?"

In the few moments that they stood there looking at each other before she extended her hand to him and then led the way through the hallway into her mother's room, Mary Peters underwent an experience in many ways similar to that which her mother had undergone years before in her cabin on the *Elizabeth*. She had expected at the sight of Jim Pendleton to feel pain, even bitterness, but she felt neither, and if sadness were present, it was rather a part of all sadness, of the *sunt lacrimae rerum* of the world, than any exactly defined sadness of her own. In place of the emotions she had expected she felt instead an odd sense of the fitness of things in having him standing there, as one is glad when a thing seems meet and right regardless of his own pleasure or his own discomfort therefrom. Hers was a nature in which thoughts were often as tangible as images or objects, and perhaps because he had for so long a time lived within her mind, even in the bringing of suffering, it suddenly seemed merely appropriate that he should now be standing on her door-rock. She did not speak to him, did not answer his interrogation in words; but he was conscious not only of her welcome but also of the abrupt disappearance of the awkwardness he had feared between them.

Had the least shred of bitterness remained within her, Mary told herself, it would have fled when once he greeted her mother. He had always had for Sarah Peters a gentleness accorded to no one else. Whenever he had been with her in the past, it had been as it were wrapped about him like an added garment; and now that she lay helpless before him and for the moment cruelly conscious of her drawn face and halting speech, the effulgence of it filled the room. His face worked with compassion and tenderness as he bent above her bed and kissed her misshapen lips, and Mary hurried into the next room to straighten the working of her own. Years afterward the remembrance of those moments remained with her to still the waves and the billows which he was to make pass over her.

He sat by Sarah Peters' bed and held her good hand for she wanted to feel the pressure of his own. He talked then, for once abandoning his silence, telling her of all the things which had happened to him in eight years, things which his infrequent and laconic letters had never told her. He had been about here and there, he said, when the Pendleton zest for wandering had come over him. He had played in ships' orchestras more or less; he could not say he shared his father's aversion to steam. He had fooled around with music mostly, had even composed a bit, light stuff which people liked and bought so that he had managed well enough so far as money was concerned. Just now he was with a company in New York which was experimenting with phonographs.

"There's a future in those things, I think," he said. "They sound wheezy and bad just now, but some day they're going to be better, with better records and better music. Some day before many more years people in places like this who like music are going to sit in their homes and hear it almost as it's played by great orchestras—I mean almost as though they were in New York or in London. I think perhaps I'll stick with this company. I can't seem to get much interest up in anything else."

Sarah Peters studied his face as he talked. Eight years had left their mark upon him. The lines about his nose and mouth had tightened and deepened, and although he was hardly over thirty, some streaks of gray had appeared in the hair above his temples. His father, she remembered, had grown gray while he was yet a

younger man. His eyes were still inscrutable although they soft-
ened while he talked with her. He still kept the fascination and
the odd appeal he had had as a boy, holding her yarn for her in
this very room. One could not be unconscious of his presence
whether one liked him or not; one might distrust him, be angry
or impatient with him, be ill at ease before his imperturbable gaze,
but there he was.

Mary, coming in an hour later to light the lamps, found herself not only conscious of him but hoping for his approval of her.
What there was about him sitting there which pervaded the house
and made such inroads upon her she did not know, but there it
was. He rose and lighted matches from his own box as she raised
and lowered the chimneys and adjusted the shades. Standing in the
middle of the room, he watched her as she drew the window curtains and closed her mother's door against the cool night air. She
knew that he was watching her every move.

"You're handsome, Mary," he said suddenly. "I always knew you
were good to look at, but I declare you're handsomer than ever."

"Nonsense!" she said, angry at her heart for jumping about
within her. "Don't be silly."

She sat down by the table beneath the light, and he still stood
regarding her. She wore a blue dress which brought colour into her
gray eyes. There was the same curious light about her face which
he remembered as a boy. For once she read his thoughts and knew
that at that moment they were both holding tenaciously the things
they had both known and loved—things at once far away and near
at hand. Colour suddenly flooded her neck and cheeks.

"I'm not silly," he said, edging quickly away from his own
mind. "Your mother will bear me out. And teaching doesn't seem
to have hurt you any, doesn't seem to have made a Miss Tapley out
of you." He sat down again, and, to Mary's relief, what had for a
moment held them together disappeared. "I'll bet," he resumed

more casually, "I'll bet you're glad you haven't boys like me to teach in the Academy."

"You *were* trying, Jim. I wouldn't stand you for a minute."

"I wouldn't blame you."

"Mother, you're tired. Jim's going back to the village to get his bag. I know you'll like to hear him moving about above your head."

He got his bag and stayed three days with Sarah Peters. He was good nature itself. He did all the odd jobs about the place that he had used to do when he was a boy. The woman who took care of her said she had never seen a man so handy about a house. When Mary came home from school at noon and at night, she found him sitting by her mother and knew he must carry back with him something secure and invulnerable. In the evenings he played for Sarah Peters, the things he had used to play and some of the music he himself had written. Mary played with him, surprised that he did not become irritated or sullen at her imperfect accompanying.

John came down to see him, brown from weeding and cultivating his furrows, comfortable and serene in his approaching marriage. Ten years of sun and rain, planting and harvest, had taken away from John any resentment he once had felt. His thoughts moved in a rhythmic groove from spring to fall and forward again to spring. There was no time or space now in John for the harbouring of rancour. Moreover, he was in love, swept at night by dreams about Ellen which he carried into the day, allowing his startled imagination its full sway as he went about his acres. Love at thirty-two, he had discovered, possessed powers and perceptions which young love could never grasp. He understood now things he had not then understood. His love had made John wise and kind and at the same time far less sure of himself when under its sway. He received Jim with the cordiality he was feeling these days for all the world, for all the men, women, animals and children therein;

and he received Jim's congratulations with even a bit of unconscious patronage. He owned his own farm which he would not exchange for all New York City; he had money in the bank; he hoped soon, he told himself as he smoked his pipe after supper, to be head of a family, and he could afford to be genial and gracious.

On the last evening of Jim's stay John brought Ellen to see him. Ellen's manner was a mixture of curiosity and easy assurance, amusing to Mary and Sarah Peters. She did not know all she would like to know about the past, and John was not one to divulge information which he wished to keep. Some time, she thought, she would get it out of him. Until then rumour excited her imagination far more than it disturbed her uncertain ethics, and she greeted Jim with the pleasing assumption that she was more attractive to him as an engaged woman than she had ever been before. No one knew better than he how to feed that illusion.

That last evening after John had taken Ellen home and gone back to the farm, the three of them talked late, speaking as they had never done of the things they had known in common. Mary did not know what had come over Jim Pendleton. He had never talked like this before. All puzzling, enigmatic things about him, things traceable to elements within him not their own, fell away from him. Tonight he belonged to the coast, was a sharer in its history and its heritage.

The past is precious to many but because of its very value communicable among few. Tonight it was communicable. It lay before them with all its graces, its guerdons, its benefactions. They had only to look at it lying there to know that it was alike their present and would be in one way or another their future. The old house closed it in with them, surrounded them with it. The long, free thoughts of four generations who had sailed all oceans lingered about its walls and wainscotings, adding faith to their own faith. Jim Pendleton forgot his phonographs, Sarah Peters her useless body, Mary her teaching. These things were at once pervaded yet transcended by the aspects of the larger realities they had known.

They talked of places they had seen and remembered for one reason or another.

"Once when I was just a kid," said Jim Pendleton, "we anchored for a night off the Azores. We'd had a hard voyage round from San Francisco and lost our course in a storm. I was fed up on the sea just then. I went to sleep on deck; it was hot and stuffy below and no one paid any attention to me. When I woke up, 'twas just before sunrise and for a minute I didn't know where I was. Then I saw we were in a little harbour below a village with mountains back of it. The village was sort of clinging to the hill- sides. It had fields about it, all pale green. I found out later they were pineapple fields and the village was Ponta Delgata. I don't know why it's always stuck in my head, but it has. Perhaps it was because the place seemed so still after all the slatting around we'd had. I never liked the sea much, at least I never thought I did, but a place like that sort of stays in a person's mind. You can't some- how get away from it and what it did to you. It kind of straightens things out—even years after."

As he spoke, Mary was again conscious of that half-disquiet- ing, half-secure unison of experience and spirit between herself and him. She thought of Cadiz and of how she, like him with Ponta Delgata, could somehow never get away from it.

They talked of winds, of weathering typhoons off the South China coast, of black gales off Cape Horn, of monsoons dry and wet, of the Trades.

"I keep thinking," said Sarah Peters, "of fair days when we ran before the Trades, days when everything seemed all right again no matter what had happened. I remember on my first voyage I was about ready to give up and stay at home until we once had caught them. Then everything seemed all right once more. Your father,

Mary, said then that the Trades kept many a sailor at sea. . . . I think about those days now."

They talked of the Sargasso on still days when ships without any steerageway at all yet dipped and rose again in mysterious accord with forces far beneath them.

"There was a robin there once," said Mary, "when I was thirteen. I fed it on the deck."

They talked of London Pool, its dark warehouses and the shadowy outlines of the ships there at night.

"There's something queer about those old ports," said Jim Pendleton, "London and Liverpool and Havre and all the rest. They don't change much somehow in spite of everything. I was fooling round a year ago in London, and I spent a lot of time around those piers and warehouses. They sort of keep things they've had no matter how things move on. It's kind of uncanny sometimes. The ships aren't there the way they used to be when we sailed in, but I swear you see them just the same, ghosts of all the ships that used to be there."

"When you've lived as long as I have," said Sarah Peters, "you'll know that there are some things that can't change. They stay just as they've always been. They stay in spite of everything even though they're only in your mind."

Mary dreamed that night of Cadiz almost exactly as she had dreamed the night she had come home. Mr. Gardiner was there again, and they walked together along its white wall in the sun above the sea.

Jim Pendleton left the next day while she was at school. She was glad he had not stayed to say good-bye to her.

5

Through late July and through all of August Mary helped John get his house ready for Ellen. They began as soon as haying was over, John hiring a man for his gardens and barns so that he could spend more time in the house. He repainted his floors and the woodwork of his rooms and whitewashed every ceiling. He chose the new paper for his walls himself.

Ellen thought his secrecy about a house she was to live in a crazy notion.

"If I'm going to live in it," she said, "I should think I could have a hand in selecting things. Suppose I don't like the way you've done it?"

"You will," said John.

She was irritated alike by his stubbornness and by her own submission to him, a submission which was usually the result not of argument but of John's rare and sudden kisses which left her so shaken and so eager for him that at the moment she was willing to consent to anything. Afterward, when she was feeling different, she was angry with herself for giving in to him. On his part he had yielded in the matter of the dining room. It was now no more, and its staring vacancy distressed him whenever he went into it. He had built after a design made by Mary a china closet into the corner of the sitting room, and its presence there marked once and for all the usage of the room.

"It does look nice, John," said Mary on the August morning that marked its completion, "and you've painted it beautifully. Ellen will be so excited when she sees her new dishes through all the panes of glass. And this room does make a lovely dining room with all the sun it gets in the morning and at noon." She looked up at him from the new sash curtains she was ruffling on their rods at one of the windows, and she read his face. "It was decent of you to make the change just for Ellen," she concluded. "I know you hated to do it."

He turned suddenly to survey the china closet before he answered her, and he stood with his back toward her as he spoke.

"Oh, it doesn't matter. I want her to have what she wants, of course. It's just that I'm foolish about making changes when they're not necessary. I sort of feel that a house kind of gets used to itself as it is and hates having its rooms all shifted round. And I suppose back of it is the feeling I've always had about the dining room. I never noticed 'twas dark and small the way Ellen says. I always remember how it was when I lived here the years you were at sea—how it used to feel to come back all tired from helping with the hay, get washed in the shed or at the pump, and then go in there for supper. Things tasted good. You could have all you wanted, and Aunt always had flowers on the table. 'Twas always light enough at supper. The sun streams right through that west window. . . . But it doesn't matter. I'll get used to this all right."

It was a long speech for John to make and Mary knew that only the depth and breadth of his feeling had allowed him to make it. She hurried with her curtains.

"Now I'm ready to help you upstairs with the border. That room will be done by night. We *are* making progress, John."

He followed her silently up the stairs and into the room which was to be Ellen's and his. The border of the wall-paper lay in tight rolls on the wooden bench he had constructed, and his paste and brushes were ready. She trimmed the edge of one roll with her scissors while he gave an extra stir to his paste.

"I'm sure I've never seen such lovely paper," she said, pausing in her cutting to survey the walls already covered. "The flowers on most wall-papers aren't life-like, but these are. The wild roses really are wild roses and so are the bachelors' buttons. Wherever did you find it, John?"

"Not in the village. I hunted and hunted, but there wasn't anything I liked—at least liked enough. I ordered it from a sample-book they had. They got it in Boston." He unrolled her trimmed border and spread it on the bench, slapping paste upon it with long strokes of his brush. "I like this border, too, with the trees in it. It sort of takes you out of the house someway. I kept thinking when I was hunting for what I wanted that it would be nice in winter to have flowers on the wall, ordinary flowers like these that we're used to. I hope Ellen likes it. I guess perhaps she isn't strong on being surprised though."

"Of course, she'll like it. No one could help liking it. And you've put it on so smoothly, like a regular paperhanger."

"Well," said John, moving his bench and pail into the hall so that he might better see the room, "it's saved a lot doing it ourselves. Only it wasn't just for that. I kind of thought I'd like to fix our house up all myself."

She looked at him with quick understanding. There was something a bit pathetic about him standing there in the room he had made ready for Ellen and himself with his own hands. John's hands, she knew, must always speak for him, say the things he could never say in words. The room was still and flooded with sunshine. A bee lost among the window panes buzzed about from one to another, dropping now and then with a thud against the white, freshly painted frames. John caught it in his handkerchief and then let it go through the open window at the front of the room. They stood there for a moment looking out at the open meadows beyond the country road and then at the garden before the house.

"Those tubs of geraniums up and down the walk are just right for this old house," said Mary. "And how they have blossomed! Ours are nothing in comparison. What have you done to them?"

"Just rich earth and some soapsuds now and then. That's all they need. I slipped them myself this spring so they would be fresh and new. They sort of brighten up a front yard out in the country like this."

"And those round marigold beds. I never saw such blossoms."

"I've kept at them a bit evenings," said John, "keeping the earth loose and giving them lots of water in dry weather. I chose marigolds especially for those beds instead of mixing a lot of stuff the way I've done before. They'll last almost to November in spite of frost. I want things to look bright for I expect Ellen's going to miss the village. She's not used to a quiet place the way I am."

They were married the fifteenth of September. The wedding was held quietly in Sarah Peters' room, a necessary concession which caused Mrs. Kimball real disappointment and Ellen, too, for that matter, although she had the decency to keep it to herself. Mrs. Kimball and Ellen had wanted a real wedding in the church with white ribbons stretched along the aisle, with bridesmaids, and the prettiest child in Petersport for ringbearer. John had wanted nothing at all but Ellen. Mrs. Kimball quieted her disappointment somewhat by a reception after the ceremony in her overstuffed parlours with Ellen and John standing under a bower of autumn leaves. Ellen's gifts were on display upstairs, the place of honour among them accorded a cut-glass punch bowl, the gift of Grace Wilbur and her husband, already returned to New York for the winter. Mrs. Kimball made everyone lift the punch bowl, and the oh's and ah's of astonishment assuaged somewhat her feeling that things were not just as she had wished. There were ice cream and cake and coffee, and each guest received a bit of wedding-cake in a white, heart-shaped box bought by mail order from Portland.

They went to Boston for a two weeks' honeymoon at the Parker House. This was a concession to Ellen and her mother, both of whom had a feeling for the fitness of things. John had not wanted to go anywhere. He could not see the sense in it himself. He had wanted to drive Ellen home in the new carriage he had bought for her as a wedding gift, over the quiet hill roads beneath the September stars. He had planned it all so often in his mind. He would show her the house he had made ready for her, and in the still dawn they would wake together with the sun rising late over the ridges and a new life begun for them both.

But he went to Boston all the same, making careful arrangements weeks ahead so that everything should go without a hitch. He took pride in Ellen's new clothes which she changed every day until no further changes were possible, and in the admiring stares she attracted from all sorts of persons as he guided her through the crowded streets. He took her to see the Minute Man at Lexington and Concord; he climbed Bunker Hill monument with her and saw the glass flowers at Harvard; and he spent his money recklessly on a bright day at Nantasket Beach, giving Ellen every amusement she craved and keeping to himself the longing he had to see her in blue gingham at their breakfast table.

6

As a matter of ironic fact, he had ample reason in the weeks and months that followed to recall his Boston honeymoon, so reluctantly granted to Ellen, not only with pleasure but also with a baffled sense of a stability which grew daily less stable. He actually wished at times as he went about his chores for the crowds on Summer Street where Ellen had actually told him she loved him while she was studying the autumn styles in a department store window. Once at home she was somehow different. It took John days even partially to forget her lack of eagerness over the house he had prepared for her. Details which he had planned so carefully she glanced at and forgot. His marigolds flamed unnoticed through October and November.

# The Land

She ran the house with an iron hand, irritated at the slightest
trace of disorder. No one could have been a better or a more trying
housekeeper. The country girl, whom she insisted upon hiring
once she had decided after a harried fortnight that the work was
too much for her unaided hands, found her none too easy a mistress. John, coming into the house at frequent intervals to see Ellen,
just to be assured that things were all right with her, found them
too often apparently all wrong. He grew slowly used to her complaints and impatient corrections and began to see the wisdom in
staying away except when he was summoned at meal-times.

As he went about his work during the weeks of late autumn
and early winter, getting things in shape both in barns and cellars
for snow and cold, he took refuge in the thought that she would
be different once they were together at night. Then her need of
him, which seemed during the day so often to be in abeyance or
even to have completely vanished, flamed in quick and passionate
demand. Yet in John's mind even their intimacy left something to
be desired. His dream of marriage had been of something more
than bodily dependence one upon the other; and he kept seeking
to discern in Ellen some trace of the tenderness and protection
which his very possession of her so engendered in himself. Waking
in the early morning beside her during those first weeks, hearing
her breathe in the stillness, searching in the half light for every line
and feature of her face, he thought with an intensity almost
painful how life had not enough days and weeks and years for him
to care for her, anticipate her wishes, spend himself in her service.
He was constantly being puzzled and disappointed in that she did
not seemingly carry into the morning some like impulse born of
her ecstasy and lovelier far than passion, something that should
betray itself in her hourly thought and care of him. But since she
betrayed little or nothing of the sort, only seeming at rare intervals
to preserve through the day some memory of what had been

between them, he grew at last inured to the situation thus forced upon him and decided that he must have been mistaken in his dreams and visions of a companionship at once gay and helpful. He could not, moreover, completely divorce from his mind the notion that life was managed somehow better, even lived more solicitously, among his creatures in his own pastures and barns.

Nor did Ellen from the start evince the interest he had hoped for in the multifarious affairs of the farm. Indeed, the farm seemed all of a piece to Ellen, a piece monotonous in its colouring, woven day by day of precisely the same fibres. Not for a moment could she see that for John no single thread was like any other thread—that pig-killing on the first snow meant a dark and sombre tone, which might well be counteracted by a good supper and a merry evening, that the birth of lambs or calves brought their far more joyous hues, that a January morning in the still woods with his axe suffused the whole fabric with light.

Out of his perplexity as he went about his land he devised schemes and gifts for her greater contentment and happiness, a hope forever lurking in the back of his mind that some one such surprise might work at least a momentary miracle. He spent more than he could afford in buying this and that, a butter-marker with her initials in place of the three acorns which his aunt had used for years and for which he himself had a foolish liking; a tasselled red whip to grace her carriage on her frequent journeys to the village; brackets for ivy and oxalis on either side of her dining room windows. He studied mail-order catalogues for these so that her surprise and pleasure might be more complete when the stage-driver should bring them into the yard. As he cleared his garden plots of frost-bitten leaves and stalks in that first bewildering fall, he planned to take her more often to church suppers and Academy entertainments, counting his own weariness and the sacrifice of his desire to stay at home a small price to pay if only they resulted in comfort and harmony.

# The Land

For as time went on, John found himself face to face with the acknowledgment, curious to his slow yet sensitive imagination, that what he now wanted most from Ellen was not satisfaction for his body, not even tenderness since that had been denied him, but rather the assurance from her of tranquillity and order within the four walls of his house. He knew, too, with an understanding that would not be set aside, that this want arose not so much out of his own need and desire as out of a sense of fairness he had toward the earth upon which he lived. He had suddenly discovered for himself out of those weeks and months of adjustment and concession that a farmer of all people ought to live harmoniously for the sake of rendering back to the earth from which he received his life something of the order which made that life possible. The tranquil symmetry of the seasons as he knew them, the methodical lengthening and shortening of days, the steady, rhythmical movements of moon and stars, growth and decay, depletion and replenishment—all the measured, temperate life he saw about him—made him want the life which earth daily afforded him to be temperate and measured also. It might be an odd notion, he said to himself, as he watched his creatures in their turn dependent upon him in league with the earth, a notion a man did not go about sharing with his fellows; but anyhow it had become securely lodged in his mind. He knew that whenever he came in at night from a long puttering day of setting things in order against the first heavy snow—repairing his stone walls, tightening his wire fences, placing a new timber here and there—he felt immeasurably more at peace with his world of soil and sky, rain and sun, if things were calm and equable in the house.

Once in a rare moment of confidence when Ellen had come home from a sewing-bee in the village full of this and that and more like herself as he had imagined her to be, he told her of his feeling, thinking she was in just the mood to see how he felt. As he talked while Ellen knitted, not looking at him at all, he felt rising within him a slow, choking mortification which scorched all the courage he had mustered and left him humiliated before her like a child who, in the hope of escaping punishment, has confessed to some wrong-doing. Her amused scorn was harder to bear than all her irritation and discontent over lesser matters. He escaped at length to his untroubled, placid stable, and after he had come in once more to find Ellen already gone to bed, he went to his old room below the sloping eaves of the ell which he had had as a boy. He was compelled to go there, not because he was angry or even hurt, but because he was suddenly afraid of Ellen, of her powers to wound not his feelings so much as the thoughts which had determined his life and dignified his work. It was the first time he had been away from her since their marriage six months before, and she was not one to overlook such treatment.

7

John Peters was not a great reader. The daily paper from Bangor and certain farm journals to which he subscribed usually sufficed for his two hours in the evening. But occasionally when Ellen was busy with her work-basket and conversation was not going too well, he picked up and became absorbed in the light fiction she drew out every fortnight from the Ladies' Social Library in the village. In these blithe books of untrammelled romance, current at the turn of the century, he now and again read incidents and dialogues quite unlike those he knew in his own life and yet alluring in their suggestion that, since they had presumably happened to other human beings, they might conceivably some day happen also to him. Sometimes he was moved beyond the approval of his practical, deliberate mind by certain

mellow and touching confidences given with apparent forethought by young wives to their susceptible and chivalrous husbands, moved so that he looked suddenly at Ellen's fair head bent
above her sewing and wondered whether he could respond in like
manner should she offer him any such entrancing announcement.

He was not, however, put to the test. It was not in Ellen's nature
to live alone with any such possibilities until the time should be
ripe and certain for their disclosure. Throughout January and
February she was fretted by fears and misgivings to which she gave
uneasy and frequent utterance quite unlike those of the heroines of
her favourite novels; by March she was again secure from dread and
to John's relief less irritable. In May she insisted on his driving her
to the office of the village doctor who bluntly confirmed her fears
and as bluntly offered his congratulations. Ellen's reply was a burst of
tears which so distressed John that for a fleeting moment he quite
unwittingly behaved like one of the heroes by putting his arm close
around her there in the doctor's dishevelled office.

"I can't go through with it," sobbed Ellen. "I know I can't."

"Nonsense!" said the doctor, giving John a sympathetic glance.
"I never heard such nonsense! A strong, healthy girl like you."

"It's all right, dear," said John, although he well knew it was
not all right, that nothing had been right for months.

Ellen sobbed on.

"Look here," said the doctor, "didn't you go to Boston a while
back? Didn't you see crowds and swarms of people on those streets
there? Of course, you did, thousands of 'em, every hour. Well, ever
one of 'em came into the world just as this baby's going to come
and just as you came yourself. You're no different from other folks
in these matters. Just you think about that and forget your fussing."

But Ellen did not forget from that moment onward. Their drive
home in the late May sunshine was the worst drive John had ever
undertaken. Ellen's sobs had given place to contentious upbraidings.

For the first time in his life John took no pleasure in a country white with blossoming fruit trees and quick with song sparrows and swollen streams, no pleasure in the wild plum and cherry foaming within the crevices of stone walls like lingering drifts of snow.

The summer was hot and dry. Water was scarce. Even the best and most unfailing of wells suffered depletion, and cisterns became as though they were not. Not a drop of rain fell throughout August, and the roadside dust lay thick upon yarrow and mayweed and hop-clover. Locusts shrilled in the air, adding their note of irritation to the general tension, or dropped with a whirring flop into the powdered and parched grass. Corn refused to fill its kernels with milk, and even the blueberries wrinkled and shrivelled beneath the sun. The night mists of the dog-days were sparse in moisture; garden truck was poor and tasteless; a bad harvest seemed a certainty.

John had his worries without the house as well as within, but the former were as nothing to the latter. Years of living beneath it had taught him the uselessness of cursing the weather. As the dry, unyielding skies of August bent over his land, he waited upon them just as his father had waited for days on end in the doldrums for so much as steerageway. Night after night he watched from the end of his driveway the thunder-heads rolling up from the south, azure clouds tipped with silver, gray-green clouds touched with gold, circling and billowing high into the heavens like coils and spirals of smoke from some mammoth, hidden chimneys below the horizon. For an hour they threatened, twisting and circling about in the pale evening sky, now casting a livid glare over the yellowing meadow grass, now muttering among themselves in inarticulate, defective rumblings of thunder. Thus they mocked and flouted the waterless earth, sending at last in place of rain some blasts of chill, dry air before they cleared the north and skulked away eastward to be lost over wide spaces of sea.

Balked thus again and again, John put upon dry cultivating his
dependence for any garden crop at all. He bent over his rows in
the heat, loosening the powdery soil until it was fine as sand about
the roots of corn and beans, beets and turnips. Whatever moisture
might come in from the sea between sunset and sunrise he was
bound to catch. Whenever rain came, he was resolved it should
not strike uselessly like pellets of fine shot against a baked soil,
beating away until it had runnelled the hillocks and weakened the
root holds. He fought aphids and slugs and cutworms, filled tin
cans with potato bugs. He seemed always, Ellen said, to be streaked
with soil, which lay in every crease of his face and arms and
hands. Often in the late afternoon he would take towel and soap
and clean clothes, skirt his grain field to the wood-lot, and bathe
in the soft water of the brook. It, too, was shrunken to half its size,
but there was a pool beneath a waterfall, a pool fringed with
meadow sweet and joe-pye-weed, where he could sit on the sandy
bottom and let a blue dragon-fly strike his bronzed shoulders and
water spiders skirt about him as he scrubbed himself.

The heat and the drought were hard on Ellen. She was white
and languid, with so little energy that John, pulsating with it,
became impatient in spite of himself over her very lassitude. She was
irritable, too, made so by the most unlooked-for causes. The blue
morning-glories on their strings by the kitchen windows annoyed
her because in a slight easterly breeze they tapped against the sill
and window-frame. John, cutting them back in unwilling compli-
ance with her demands, felt as though he were in turn demanding a
favour of the earth, a favour which set at naught all its labour in
their behalf. Escaping from her querulousness to his barn and fields,
he would an hour later, smitten in conscience by his remembrance
of the perspiration standing on her lips and forehead, return to the
house only to be met with increased disapproval.

Now and again through the long, trying summer Mrs. Kimball came for a week with Ellen. She immeasurably increased the weight of women which encumbered his house. She fussed over Ellen, making her more solicitous of herself, more fearful than ever. She expected her to have odd "cravings" for this food and that, and when she did not evince enough of them in mysterious succession, felt sure that things were not moving in their wonted course. Encouraged by her mother's expectations, Ellen did stir up within herself an overpowering desire for fresh peas, a desire which stripped John's thirsty vines, deprived his wallet of the money he had expected from previous and long-standing orders, and sent him to neighbouring gardens for more and yet more.

As September came on with rain at last, too late to save the summer vegetables, but a tardy mercy for the winter supply and for the pasturage, John Peters found himself steadily faced by an adversary of whose stealthy approach he had been for a full year uncomfortably aware. This adversary was his life with Ellen, and it was engaged in pushing him back to the wall where he must defend himself for the sake of the claim upon him of the other and larger life he knew. He knew his life with Ellen. Through and through he knew it. No longer bewildered by its transient ecstasy, he understood that their love was but brief desire and not a part of that other life, that succession of old and natural law which had made him its disciple when he was but a boy. Deep at the root of things, embedded in men and animals and greening trees, was this life, itself love, satisfying its own necessities, establishing its protections, spreading itself over the face of the earth in a boundless and measureless flood, receding and yet renewing itself, a thing so common, so permanent, so simple, that one might miss it through his very unapprehended familiarity with it. He had naturally expected his life with Ellen to be a part of this life, the only one he had known. On the contrary, for some reason which he could not fathom, the one was not only alien to the other but in actual combat with it.

Now the time had come when he must choose between them. On the one side was his life with Ellen, a life of constant adjustment to caprice and circumstance, a life of momentary passion which knew no fruits of the spirit, a circumscribed life of stubborn loyalty to a lost ideal. On the other was that life which by its very completeness and permanence allowed no adjustment. A man was not called upon to adjust himself to a concord of creation of which he was already himself a part. All that he must do was to recognize that partnership, a partnership upon which he was at once dependent and to which he contributed. If he maintained this larger loyalty, he knew well that he must look elsewhere than in his home for his peace and security. If he returned to that ancient covenant framed by long generations of men who had known the earth, he must find in his own fidelity to it whatever happiness was to be his. No longer would he attempt to understand humanity, which in the shape of Ellen so baffled and distressed him, but rather he would restore his tired mind to that plain, indestructible, universal life which had won his love and understanding even as a boy and to which until now he had given his unimpaired service.

He was never conscious of the day or the hour when he made his decision. Rather he found it already made for him during a fortnight in October which Ellen spent with her mother in Petersport. He never forgot those days, clear and lustral like a slow, deliberate plunge into cold, sunlit water. He went about his land engulfed in a sturdy content. His pumpkins lay in his shorn cornfields like great globes of gold. The hum of insects quavered in the still air. His cows stumbled leisurely across his pasture bars while the hunters' moon slowly changed from white to yellow in the eastern sky. He sat beneath his orchard trees, breathing the smell of his ripened fruit until long after his neighbours' lamps had gone out one by one, until the sky was pricked with fading stars.

Ellen upon her return found him as calm and immovable as the boulder at the apex of his triangular pasture. Thoughtful of her comfort, more tolerant than ever of her complaints, he was yet inaccessible in a way she was completely at a loss to comprehend. His very imperturbability in the face of what she felt disastrous, although it at first irritated her, had a way as it continued of quieting her worst fears. He had somehow grown as irresistible as the weather itself, and as she watched him going steadily about his common rounds, she felt creeping over her a strange feeling, compounded partly of reluctant respect, partly of fear, and not altogether unwholesome for her state of mind at the moment.

Perhaps this new feeling toward him tempered somewhat her opposition to his tenacious decision concerning the place of the baby's birth. She and her mother had determined upon Mrs. Kimball's house in the village where they could be sure that the doctor was near at hand and not at the mercy of a December snowstorm and where Ellen could be surrounded by houses and cheery people and not obliged to do her last waiting in the midst of a lonely, snowbound countryside. John had determined upon his own roof-trees. He wanted the baby from his very first cry to be established firmly in the place which would be his home. Deep within that pulsating kernel which was the life of John's nature, there was as a kind of nucleus the certainty that the place of a man's genesis has much to do with the continuity and stability not only of his ensuing days but of those of his children and his children's children. It was an old and perhaps baseless notion, already abandoned as senseless by the erection of city hospitals and soon to be doomed to death even in rural fastnesses when motor cars should afford quick transportation to the nearest up-to-date town. But at the turn of the century it was fast rooted in John Peters' mind, not to be gainsaid or set aside. It was perhaps the remnant of that Saxon heritage, yet to be discerned here and there in rural New England—that heritage which still fills one's heart at the sight of his own roof-slopes and lighted windows beneath them, making one still aware in the midst of a hurrying and changing world of the long, patient ritual of home.

John himself never entered or even passed by his father's brick house without being devoutly thankful that he had been born in the high chamber to the left of the white-panelled front door. In that very room four generations of men named Peters had seen the light. He could not be sufficiently grateful that he had been born there in that four-posted bed instead of on the high seas or in some outlandish port, quite unrelated to life as he had known it. In like manner he wanted his son to be born under his own rafters, in the room of its conception. Thus from the very start there would be established a relationship between the child and the timbers of his home, the sun which lighted its windows, the ground upon which it stood.

The question had caused such altercation during the summer and fall that it had been allowed to drop. In the hot August days John had actually feared that he might give way or at least insist as a compromise upon the house of his own birth. But after the fortnight in October there was the matter quite settled for him and needing only its firm disclosure to Ellen.

The disclosure was received better than he could have hoped. For one thing, Ellen was still under the spell of his new steadiness and composure. She had discovered in the few days since her return home that it was more than a little humiliating to beat one's head against a stone wall especially when more was to be gained by mutual concession. The Peterses, she concluded, were one and all a queer lot whom it was quite impossible to fathom. For another, John was willing and eager to grant her any compromise except the one and final settlement. Being herself, however, yielding to him was unthinkable without a last attempt at conquest.

"Suppose it's an awful storm," she ventured for the hundredth time at least. "You know what these roads can be like in December. Suppose we're out here all alone. Remember I've got to go through with it, not you."

"I don't know about that," said John quietly. "I expect it won't be easy for me."

Looking at him then, at his steady gaze upon her, Ellen was perhaps nearer an understanding of what went on inside him than she had ever been since their marriage.

"And we won't be alone," he continued. "I've seen to that. You don't think I want you to be afraid, Ellen? I've already written to Bangor for a nurse, a trained one, not one of these local women with all their whims and nostrums. She'll come whenever you want her, days ahead if you say so and stay on right with you."

"Oh," said Ellen, impressed in spite of herself. "But we're none of us certain about the time, you know. Suppose it came too early?"

"The doctor says it won't. I saw him in the village yesterday. He says things are going on just as they should. And I'm having a telephone put in, Ellen. I ordered it a week ago now that the line has gone through. The neighbours think I'm crazy, but I'm having it all the same. It won't take an hour with that to get the doctor here. And I won't have to leave you for a moment."

"Oh," said Ellen again. She had talked about a telephone, teased for one, ever since the construction of the line had begun a year ago, but she had found John as adamant against it. Now in spite of herself she was swept by visions of conversations with her village friends who could call her up through the central office if they were so unfortunate as to have no telephones in their own homes. She saw more invitations coming her way, a closer contact with village affairs, a quick avenue for the transmission of news.

"And I've decided," proceeded John, as quietly as ever, "not to be dependent on just one doctor. I got in touch with the best man in Bucksport yesterday, called him up from the village. He'll come if he's needed and glad to do it. So with all these precautions I don't think you ought to be afraid any longer, Ellen, of having the baby born in our own house."

Ellen said no more at the moment, and, indeed, was fairly reasonable in the complaints and objections which she felt called upon to make during November. She made them mostly to reassert her waning authority, to mitigate somewhat the uneasy feeling she had that John now held the mastery of things. And still she told herself as her time drew on, there were the telephone and the trained nurse and the Bucksport doctor, all distinct and expensive innovations for a Maine countryside. She took comfort in the information, eagerly purveyed by Mrs. Kimball, that the whole village was visibly impressed by the extraordinary preparations made by the young Peterses for their first baby.

## 8

The first snow came with the baby. The brown fields and untidy gardens had been waiting for it for weeks while the skies hung gray and cold above them. John heard the sharp spitting of the first stray flakes at three o'clock in the morning while he hurriedly built up the kitchen fire in response to Ellen's frightened announcement that her pains had already begun. The nurse in a gray wrapper over her white dress stood with him in the kitchen, warming her hands above the black stove covers outlined in the dim room by circles of red flame. She said there was no need either for worry or hurry. Women always, especially with their first, anticipated the event by hours and hours. She had been in the house a full week already, and had come to feel more sympathy for the tall, quiet young man who went so steadily about his ways than for her patient upstairs.

John was glad of the snow. When he had lighted his lantern and started for the barn earlier than usual, he took comfort in the quiet of its falling. His land was ready and waiting for its own long pregnancy beneath it. A day of falling snow evened out a man's mind as it relieved and evened the contours of road and hill. When he entered his barn, he was conscious of a hush within it as though his creatures with the sense of all their kind knew that the winter with its days and months of unruffled waiting was at last upon them. He left one of the doors open so that he might see in the slow dawn the dry flakes drifting down, might hear their muffled impact against the lifeless grasses which edged the doorway. In the smothered air the milk struck the bottom of his pails with a less metallic sound.

Once he had finished milking, he let his cows out into the barnyard while he cleaned their stalls, spreading fresh sawdust upon the knotted, moist, uneven floors. They stood together in a corner of the enclosure, their sides touching one another, while the sunless eastern skies grew slowly lighter. They were staring silently at the snow as though in patient resignation and acceptance of the winter, perhaps in mute understanding that things were happening as they always happened. Only two young heifers sniffed the air in a surprised fashion, edging uneasily about for a few minutes until they joined their more experienced elders in their corner by the gray log fence.

John drove early to the village for Mrs. Kimball. In spite of the nurse's advice the doctor had already been summoned by telephone in response to Ellen's excited and tearful demands. Coming from his placid stable across the yard which the snow was now whitening, John's heart had sunk within him before her fear and pain. His old tenderness came welling back upon him during the half-hour when he took the nurse's place, by her bed, an almost desperate tenderness, only now it was not merely for Ellen but for all who must suffer and fear. The nurse's reassurances were all in vain, and he harnessed his horse in an agony of regret and sympathy.

He met the doctor two miles out upon the road from the village, bumping along among the frozen ruts and paying small attention to his ambling old white mare. He had hitched his reins about his dashboard and was scanning his newspaper. They drew up for an exchange of greetings.

"I expect to spend the day at your house," said the doctor comfortably. "It's lucky there are no other youngsters on the way in these parts. That nurse of yours says there's no hurry, but your wife won't believe her. I hear she's in an awful stew. When she's had three or four, she'll get shaken down to it. How're you standing it yourself?"

John ignored the question. He was thinking of Ellen and wishing women could bring forth with the obedient acquiescence which he saw every year in his barns and fields. He could not bear to think of all the pain which birth had meant throughout the world. The doctor saw the anxiety drawing his face.

"Now you take it easy, young man. It's not your funeral any more than hers no matter what she says in an off-hour. By night this will all be over, and in two days she'll forget about it like all the rest."

"You better hurry along," said John, gathering up his reins. "She's really in a bad way."

"Plenty of time," said the doctor. "I was counting up this morning over my breakfast and this is only the seven hundredth baby over thirty-five years. They come thick and fast in this country."

He clucked to his horse and continued unconcernedly on his way. John going on his own did not know whether to be angry or encouraged by his apparent composure.

"And one thing more," called back the doctor through the gathering snow. "Don't be in any tearing hurry to get that mother of hers there. We've got women folks enough."

John did hurry with Mrs. Kimball, however. He found her in a state bordering on that of her daughter. He found her dressed and packed and ready for him on the door-rock of her white house. She said she had been walking the floor for an hour waiting for him. She said, too, that she should have been with Ellen for days before, that a girl needed her mother at this time more than at any other, and that if anything went wrong she should blame herself all her life long for not having come a week earlier, whether or no. John was very well aware of the implication in her last words. She said all these things and many more while John was stowing away her possessions in the back of the carriage. She was annoyed at his insistence that he should stop at the brick house to tell his mother things were started. What she said as they went northward into the country, he heard but vaguely. He was conscious only of driving through the quiet, windless storm with some disturbing force beside him quite at variance with all the forces which he knew.

Before, above, around him fell the snow from out the solemn, hushed sky—a pledge of warmth and security, a healer of scars, smoothing away the differences alike of land and of men, noiseless on the open road, sibilant among a clump of oaks, tapping upon the granite of boulders, mysterious, almost incredible in its coming year after year. Beside him sat Mrs. Kimball like some machine wound up and clicking away its brief life, unrelated, even at cross-purposes, with the earth and sky, fretting at the snow, filled with prognostications of evil and disaster, with prophecies and threats which even the snow could not muffle. When John deposited her at his back door at ten o'clock and turned his horse's head toward her stall, he felt as though it would take a full week of snow, falling steadily, to deaden the crass and intrusive actuality of her presence.

The day dragged on. Only the doctor, smoking his pipe during a half-hour's respite now and then in the barn with John, preserved his self-possession. His seven hundredth baby, at least in this stage of the game, was not resting heavily upon his mind. There were hours yet to wait, for he, he said, was not one to hurry nature. John, doing this or that in order to put some life into his body, which seemed to have nothing in it but a shaking and an emptiness, saw him coming through the snow.

"I don't think," said the doctor, leaning at ease against a stanchion, "that I'm for this everlasting stocking of trout streams. It used to be fun to fish in the Witham brook, used to take a day or so to land six of 'em. But last summer I snum if they weren't so thick you could see 'em nudging each other. Where's the sport in that, I ask you? And what's more, trout that's hatched and fed some sort of outlandish scientific stuff in those vats at the fish-hatchery, they don't have the flavour of the ones that are born and raised where they ought to be."

"How are things coming on in there?" asked John.

He was mending up an old work harness with hands that would not handle things as efficiently as usual.

"Fine as silk," said the doctor, "for six hours ahead of time. Her mother's fixing up some mess or other for her to take. Folks around here think there won't be a mouthful for a baby to eat unless the mother's crammed hours beforehand with corn meal and raisin gruel. 'Twon't hurt and 'twon't help, but it works off their energy, so it's all to the good. What you aiming to do, John, with this place here? Make a dairy farm out of it? You've got a better start at a herd than any man around."

John somehow could not get his mind onto a herd, but he did his best.

The two men ate their dinner by themselves in the kitchen. It was a boiled dinner, not too well prepared since three women all had had a nervous hand at it. The stove was flanked with clothes-horses bearing baby clothes and with chairs draped with sheets and blankets warming by the fire. As they ate, the doctor heartily, John hardly at all, they could hear at intervals Ellen's screams and her mother's high solicitude.

"Walk her around a bit," said the doctor to the harried nurse, calmly emptying the vinegar cruet upon his second helping of cabbage. "She's four hours to go yet at the very least. If she got up and grabbed the bedpost now and then, she'd be better off."

"She says she can't stand it," said the nurse, busying herself with the tea-kettle. "She wants some ether."

"Nonsense!" said the doctor. "She won't get it for some time yet. She's got to help herself a bit. I'll be up there just as soon as I've had my pipe. Who's running this show I'd like to know?"

In spite of the confusion in his mind John studied the doctor sitting so imperturbably in the warm kitchen, darkened by the falling snow. He had pushed his chair back against the wall between the windows and sat at an inclined angle calmly smoking his pipe. He had brought John into the world more than thirty years back and was not so young as he had been. He was a long, ungainly man with ill-fitting clothes and a shaggy gray head. He wore heavy shoes, one of which he tapped against the yellow floor in the rhythm of a tune which he was apparently singing to himself from somewhere in his gaunt old frame. His blue eyes were half-tired, half-humourous, and in the deep lines of his clean-shaven face lay numberless fights with rheumatism and fever and numberless quiet defeats when he had gone down, beaten by country consumption, shocks, and old age. His skin was bronzed and toughened, his stout hands also, and about him there clung a smell of his patient old horse and his moth-eaten laprobe. He knew things, John concluded, that all men ought to know, and he was glad to have him in his kitchen.

Ellen had what was known in country parlance as a tough time of it. The doctor's afternoon calls on John in the stable were shorter and at longer intervals.

"I understand," he said at four o'clock, just as John was thinking he would have to take up his position in the sitting room in spite of Mrs. Kimball's hourly banishments of him, "I understand, John, there's an automobile being brought here by some rusticator or other. Now what do you think of that? It'll make havoc along the roads with the horses. I can't say I care much about having old Nell scared out of her skin after so many years of taking it easy. But I guess they're coming all right, the infernal things. I guess nothing can stop 'em. Maybe you'll be ploughing with steam or gasoline before many years."

"Not I!" said John. He was wondering if it would be too upsetting to the cows if he milked them an hour earlier than usual. "How are things in there anyway?"

"Moving right along," said the doctor. "You stay where you are. The next time I come I'll likely bring you some news. Another two hours more will likely see us through."

But it was ten o'clock before things were over and John's son had come. Toward the end things did not go so well as they might. Even the doctor, now in his shirt sleeves rolled to the elbow, looked anxious. Ellen's screams echoed and re-echoed through the house. They penetrated the walls and the dark, snow-filled air even to the stable where John heard them when he had decided he could no longer pace the sitting room floor. They were not human screams, he thought. They began in unearthly moans, rising and rising into shrieks, dropping again into sobbing gasps that trembled and quavered away into momentary silence.

John's creatures heard them and stirred uneasily in their stalls and stanchions, rattling their chains and raising their heads in startled surprise.

When it was all over, John held his son by the kitchen fire while the others worked over Ellen. There was a smell of ether in the house. It mingled with the smell of blood and warm new flesh. John could not trust his shaking hands to undo the blankets that wrapped the baby. He sat mute and helpless by the fire, feeling only a stir now and then from the bundle in his arms.

In the snowy dawn he harnessed the doctor's white mare for him; the storm had ceased and the moon was riding high behind shining clouds. The land was white and still.

"Now get some sleep," said the doctor, hunching and bundling himself into the sagging seat of his worn top-buggy, "and don't go thinking she's had the worst time in the world. This is a Sunday school picnic to some I've seen, bad as it was. The Lord has His own ways, I suppose, and takes His own time, but I wish He wan't so sparing sometimes in grit and gumption."

When he had gone, his wagon wheels creaking through the snow, John stood on a rung of his mow-ladder, his head and shoulders half buried in the hay. Mrs. Kimball found him there at five o'clock. She had thrown a shawl about her shoulders and come out to find him. She had things to say to him that would not wait for a calmer and more propitious hour. She stood in the uncertain lantern light and said the things she had come out to say, bitter, vituperative things which came inexorably from her large mouth between her crowded teeth. She knew men, she said, their selfish demands, their thoughtlessness of consequences, their carelessness for the suffering of women. John had nearly lost Ellen, she said, her high, querulous tones piercing the hay-packed rafters. He would lose her for good and all if anything like this happened again.

Once she had returned to the house and an uneasy cock had begun to crow from the hen-house, John began to milk his cows, quite regardless of the fact that it was a full hour before the proper time.

9

The Peters' baby from the hour of his birth was all Kimball. Sarah Peters, scanning his face as he lay on her bed well swathed in the multiplicity of garments in vogue at the beginning of the century, could not find in his wide, round face a single trace of John or of any of his forbears on either side. Ellen was exhibiting him to his grandmother on the first warm day of spring. Ellen herself had "fleshened up" in country phrase and was well-nigh bursting from out a last year's cotton frock. She was proud of the resemblance of the baby to her side of the family with a possessive pride that went deeper than Sarah Peters had any idea of.

The baby was a placid, inactive child. He lay on his back with his wide, pale blue Kimball eyes staring at the ceiling. He had too flat a crown, Sarah Peters thought, and his colour was not of the best. Within or without him there was no sign of that mysterious sense of life which most babies possess.

Ellen remonstrated too lightly when he stolidly sucked his thumb as he seemed to be constantly doing.

"It's a bad habit, Ellen," said Sarah Peters. "You ought to tie up his hand so he can't get at it."

"Oh, he'll work out of it," returned Ellen. "If I do, he yells so I can't stand it. It's such a relief to have him quiet and without the colic. Every time he eats there's always colic. It seems to me I spend all my time these days jouncing him around to get gas out of his stomach. John says I give him too much to eat, but I say he's got to eat since he loses so much of it anyway. I tell John if he'll tend to feeding his calves and things, I'll tend to feeding the baby."

She glanced at Sarah Peters a bit uncomfortably, aware of something in the room besides a silence.

From the start Sarah Peters had not known much of John's and Ellen's life, its altercations and adjustments, where there were adjustments. Ellen had kept matters to herself largely for the reason that to her their life was not extraordinary. It went on well enough, she thought, as lives go. John, his mother knew, always kept matters to himself.

When he came in for Ellen and the baby, she noticed with a start how old and worn he looked. The hair on the left side of his head above his temple was thinning and showing the scar there.

"Did you get the paregoric, John?" asked Ellen.

"Yes," said John.

"Maybe there'll be some peace then tonight."

"The doctor says you're to go slow on it," said John. "It's not good for him."

Ellen began to dress the baby with various outer garments which she took one by one from the foot-board of the bed, his sacque, his long coat, his knitted, beribboned hood, his warm outside blanket.

"The doctor," she said as she worked, "doesn't know what I have to put up with. It's all very well for *him* to talk!"

John turned to his mother.

"Too bad about that porch those summer folks are sticking onto Uncle Caleb's house. They're spoiling it, taking away those old pillars for that new-fangled thing. I'm glad he doesn't have to see it. I hate to see those old places changed like that."

"Well, after all," said Ellen, wrestling impatiently with the baby's mittens, "it's their house, I suppose, bought and paid for, and what they do with it is their own business. And every bit of work they bring into this village, every dollar they spend here, helps us out, I say."

"I don't like to see changes like that either, John," said Sarah Peters quietly, "so I guess it's just as well I lie here where I can't see them."

Ellen was putting on her own hat and coat by the mirror in the hall when John told his mother the news he had brought her. She came back into the room with one long hat-pin in her mouth and the other in her hand. It was just like John, she thought, to save news like that and then to tell it where she could not have her real say out.

"I've got a surprise for you," John had been saying. "Ellis is coming next week to stay with us for a spell. He wrote me ten days back. He's quit sailing long ago, and I guess he's kind of high and dry from what I can gather, beached for good, I take it. I wrote and told him he was welcome to come and stay with us a while. He was good to me all those years, and I feel sorry for him."

"You—what?" cried Ellen, the hat-pin still in her mouth. "Well, I never, John!"

She stood in the middle of the room, staring at him, and he coloured visibly, not because of her but because of his mother looking at them.

"That old man?" continued Ellen, taking no pains to lower her voice. "He was old years ago when you used to sail in here. What'll we do with him, I'd like to know? It seems to me I have my hands full already."

Sarah Peters was aware as Ellen spoke not so much of all the things she was saying as of all the things she was not saying, of all the things she would say once they were started homeward. She knew that John had purposely made his announcement here in her room to spare himself, at least at the beginning, something of the disturbance that must follow it. She wished at that moment that she could keep John with her in his old room upstairs, away from all the discord and confusion he so hated.

Ellen pinned on her broad, flower-trimmed hat and seized the baby, intercepting John in his movement to take him.

"Well, I never!" she said again in place of a good-bye to Sarah Peters.

When she had started for the horse-block and the waiting carriage, John remained for a moment with his mother.

"I'm sorry Mary is late," said Sarah Peters. "She'll be sorry, too."

She saw that John was standing with his back toward her and knew that he was about to say something difficult for him to say. Her own words had been uttered only to make things easier for him.

"You mustn't mind Ellen," he said at last. "She's sort of upset with the baby and all. I should have asked her first, I suppose, before I wrote to him, but I thought 'twould be easier to have it all settled. If I could have afforded it, I'd have sent him money instead, but we're sort of hard up with the baby and last year being so bad, and I couldn't see any other way except to ask him. He always set a lot of store by us, you know. And he was good to me about all the animals I tried to keep on board the ship. Those old things that you remember sort of pull at you somehow. You know how 'tis. . . . But don't you worry, mother, it'll come out all right. Things do."

Sarah Peters might have worried as she listened to John's carriage wheels crunching up the gravelled ruts of the hill, had worry not left her long ago. In its place had come a pity for a certain seemingly inevitable unkindness in things themselves, a certain necessary sorrow and desolation in the circumstance of human existence, in the very manner by which men through some mischance had from the beginning lived their lives. She felt this pity for John and Ellen, for herself, for all other souls throughout the world. Since things were so, she thought, this sense of universal sympathy, this compassion for humanity, created of itself a certainty, a faith, without which men and women could not live, unconscious though they might be of its hourly alleviation.

She lay quietly in her bed as the spring sun went lower. She knew by the stillness of the gulls that the tide was full. She studied on the wall the faces of John's great-grandparents, painted in Antwerp one hundred years ago at the close of a prosperous voyage. John looked like his great-grandfather. She wondered if there were enough of John lying securely somewhere within his son to come out in the lines of his face as he grew older, obscured though it now was by the solid, unimaginative lineaments of the Kimballs.

## 10

Ellis was older both in years and in behaviour than even John had thought he could be. When he had pushed his doddering, rattling body up the gangplank of the Boston boat one warm July day and John had half lifted him to the high seat of the spring wagon, it seemed as though he ought to be tied there like a child in a highchair. He was shrivelled within a shabby black suit, the two flabby, sagging muscles, one on either side of his Adam's apple, rising insecurely above his celluloid collar. John could not see in him a single trace of the hearty, blue-clad, deliberate carpenter whom he had followed about the deck of the *Elizabeth*. He was deaf and shaky, and there was a constant trembling of his lower lip against his upper which, John knew, would be insufferably annoying to Ellen. John was on the point of repenting of his impulsive kindness a hundred times as he drove Ellis home with him, as he listened to the old man's palpitating reminiscences and half-tearful expressions of gratitude.

Ellis in point of sober fact would have exasperated a far more flexible nature than Ellen's. Not even the most objective and philosophic mind could have escaped irritation over his presence, and Ellen's mind was neither objective nor philosophic. Like many extremely old persons he had the vexing propensity toward ubiquity.

"He's always under foot," complained Ellen with complete justice on her part. "Why can't he keep out of my way?"

While she worked, he sat by the kitchen window whittling with his nerveless old fingers; while she washed the baby, he watched fascinated, standing at too close range for comfort; if she stayed too long upstairs, he appeared to see where she was. He was forever wanting to hold the baby against his old frame which smelled of age and stale tobacco. He dropped ashes from his filthy old pipe throughout the house, and as he smoked, his pipe kept up a clicking sound against his insecure false teeth.

"I have to bear the brunt of it," she said to John a dozen times a day. "You brought him here! Why can't you keep him outside with you?"

John tried to keep him outside, tried to devise chores for him. He fed the hens, leaving the hen-yard door open in the process so that they ran among the gardens. He filled the wood-boxes, dropping bark and dust over Ellen's clean kitchen floor. He tried to pile the wood in the shed, an avalanche of it falling and crushing one of his uncertain old feet. Raking up after the load, he left the fields untidy, bearded with hay. He was forever borrowing John's tools to tinker round at this and that, leaving them strewn about the place where they collected bits of rust upon their shiny steel.

His table manners were such as to be called intolerable even in the simplest of environments; his personal habits merited extreme reproach. Ellen steadfastly refused to enter the room in the ell which he occupied, and a daily combat ensued between her and the hired girl over its condition. On Saturday nights when

John superintended the old man's bath in the woodshed, filling the tub with hot water, even helping him to scrub himself, the atmosphere in the house pulsated with Ellen's anger over such a monstrous imposition.

Not for a moment did John blame Ellen for her exasperation or displeasure. It was only that he felt she ought to take Ellis as a kind of necessity, put upon them whether they would or no merely by untoward circumstance, which he, at least, for the sake of old association could not decently escape. Old age to John was simply a fact to be reckoned with deliberately, like the inevitable wearing out of land or the slow decay of tree trunks. He tried his utmost to shield Ellen from the old man, taking him whenever he could into the barns and fields, listening patiently in the summer evenings to his reminiscences as they sat in the orchard out of earshot of the house. His memory was failing him. He wandered garrulously from this port to that, forgetting the ships in which he had sailed, mixing hopelessly his dates, placing Hongkong in California and Valparaiso on the Suez Canal. He was forever expecting John's patient mind to set him right, get him straightened out and started clearly on his way once more. He wondered aloud hourly why God had seen fit to save him for such an old age; and John, stumbling wearily up the stairs to bed, sure of Ellen's upbraidings, wondered also.

Matters were close to the breaking-point when in early August the baby fell ill. Ellen, frightened out of her few remaining senses, traced the cause directly to the harassing presence of Ellis. She could not give the child proper food, she said, when she was so upset within her. On a hot morning after the baby had been fretful and feverish all night, she insisted on driving with him to the village to stay with her mother and to be near the doctor. John, secretly filled with relief at the thought of tolerating Ellis by himself, dropped his work and took them. On the way the baby stiffened in convulsions and by the time they reached the village was entirely ready for whatever ministrations the doctor could afford.

They were useless ministrations even though they were the fruit of long experience with overfed babies in a hot summer. The baby died late that afternoon. John, standing by the new telephone in his kitchen, heard the news through Mrs. Kimball's strident voice. He felt all the life go out of his legs as he heard it. For a moment he felt aggrieved, almost irritated, that the baby had not died in the house where, after so much dissension and expensive compromise, he had been born. It would have been a better rounding out of things, thought John, as the hired girl stood and stared at him, a colander of blueberries in her hand, if he had ended his brief life where he had begun it. He felt aggrieved, too, that the baby had died before he had even made the rounds of the farm in his father's arms. John had meant to take him once he was old enough to be out from under the constant domination of his mother. He had been cheated out of his son from the start, he said to himself, standing there in the silent kitchen, staring at the frightened girl, and he felt half angry about it.

When he had thought these odd thoughts for some still minutes, he went out into the yard. It was milking-time and Ellis was waiting for him. He had gathered the pails from where they had been placed in the sun on the granite curb around the well and was standing with them proudly, two in each of his shaking old hands. He liked to think he helped John with the milking. The pails were striking against each other in a dull clatter from his unsteady hold upon them.

"Do you mind, John," asked Ellis, "that sailor we had once on the *Elizabeth* who spit on that rock and ground his knife on it? Do you mind that, John? Where was that girl he was aiming for? Just where did she live, do you mind? I can't get it straight in my head."

"The baby's dead!" shouted John in Ellis' old ears.

He was shouting it not so much to Ellis as to the quiet evening sky above them, to his apple trees and beehives and green fields, to the meadow across the road over which floated a thin mist. He was shouting it to all his land which was to have been the baby's had he grown up.

"Dead, John!" cried Ellis, his old throat working up and down. "What do you mean? Dead? That little, measley thing? Dead? And I here going out to milk with you."

Ellis stumbled about talking to himself while John milked. He still stumbled about while John harnessed the horse to go to the village. When the last buckle was fastened and John was about to step into the wagon, Ellis put his hand, on which the veins stood out in great, crooked blue welts, on the rim of one of the front wheels.

"It's just come to my mind," he said. "It was in Valparaiso where that girl lived that did that sailor dirt."

They buried the baby the next day. It was the consensus of village opinion that so young a baby should not be accorded a funeral. About a funeral there was a certain connotation that one had really lived, at least through a respectable period of time. John made a box for it out of some new white pine he had, and Ellis took pride in planing the boards smooth and making a tiny bevelled edge about its cover, not so good as he might once have made it but quite good enough. They worked in the shed with the west wind blowing eastward through the open doors and the August grass swaying before it. While they worked, Ellis sang now and then, his cracked old voice missing some of the words:

*"The ship went sailing out over the bar*
*O Rio! O Rio!*
*Turn away, love, turn away*
*Away down Rio!"*

When they had put the baby in the box, John carried it beside him on the seat of his wagon to the churchyard. It was just at sundown. The tide was out, and the gulls were screaming their raucous, petulant screams so unworthy of the still even beauty of their flight. Ellen was quite too upset to be there, and her mother stayed with her. Ellis was there in his old blue jersey and tattered old sailor's cap which he held in his hand as John himself shovelled back the earth into the baby's grave. Mary stood beside Ellis. She had returned to the farm the night before with John to stay with them until Ellen should feel able to come back. She remembered even at that moment how it had been with Ellis that she had seen Cadiz years before. She shared with John his unspoken feeling about having the old man there. He had known three generations of Peterses, and, in spite of the changes wrought within and upon him, it was fitting that he should stand by the early grave of a fourth.

## 11

Ellen stayed with her mother in the village throughout the fall. She liked to be the cynosure of sympathetic eyes and thoughts. It had been hard for young Mrs. Peters, everyone said. These things invariably went more easily with men, any way you looked at it. They had their work to do and things to take up their minds. It was different with women. To have that which you had borne in such anguish snatched so pitilessly away from you was unbearable. The village was kind to Ellen, devising all manner of entertainment to keep her from brooding over her loss.

Mary remained through August and September with John and, even after the Academy opened, came to him for weekends. He liked having her in his house. He was sure of quiet evenings even with Ellis maundering about, growing more feeble and more

exasperating with every day. Mary had a way of "sluffing" him off
her mind, as they said in the country, of not having him rest too
heavily upon her consciousness. When things got too complicated,
she could laugh at him, which was in itself a remedy.

Moreover, her mind, quicker far than John's, had found a way
out against the day of Ellen's return, a return deferred, Ellen had
said definitely to John, until Ellis was out of the way. Mary had
found a decent home for Ellis, not far away, with people who
would be kind to him through what was likely to be his last winter. She had come to John's rescue with the offer of half his board
and keep. In November he was to be taken there. When an end
was in sight, thought John, as he hunted in vain for his tools or
found them rust-stained and battered in one unimaginable place
or another, a man could stand anything.

The autumn had never been more lovely. The weather was
firm and golden throughout October, the hills and ridges clear blue
in the morning, purple in the late afternoon. The colour, undevas-
tated by heavy rains, held its glory for weeks on end. There was a
slumbrous, drowsy atmosphere over the whole countryside. Driving
home with John on Friday nights through beech woods so still that
their very entrance seemed an intrusion, Mary felt how impossible
it was for certain thoughts to flourish in the spring. Memories, for
example, had no place there. The spring had no kinship with the
past. It was while October held as it were the whole year quietly
within its long embrace, allowing each month time to review its
past ecstasies, that one was called upon to remember.

Nor did spring hold anything in common with departure,
either with actual leave-takings among persons or with those van-
ishings, mental and emotional, with which the sensitive mind pre-
pares itself for winter. But in autumn departure lingered upon the
hills, certain, content, reassuring to those who saw it resting there.
Its voice was the final, plaintive notes of the thrushes at mid-day,

gathering to go, of the wild geese crying high in the skies at night, of the intermittent, thin quavering of the last crickets. Death in autumn, shorn of its ruthlessness and simple in its beauty, could not possibly take one by surprise.

When the first hard frosts of November had come, John began to put in motion a project he had cherished for years. He had coddled his idea, sure he knew what he was doing in spite of the discouraging prophecies of his neighbours. Mary liked to see it in his mind in the evening, glowing there. She knew he was depending on the earth to prove his faith in the face of men of less certainty and enterprise.

One of the nine elms which bordered his driveway, elms which as tiny trees his uncle had planted on the very day of John's birth as memorials to him, was obviously dying slowly from lack of room in which to grow. It stood out of line with those opposite, wedged into its own row as an unnecessary and unwanted fifth where four ought to be. John had felt sorry for it for years, and now that it was being literally sacrificed for want of space for its strangled roots, he had determined, not upon its destruction but upon its removal to a corner of his hayfield where it might spread its unimpeded roots throughout a full acre if it so desired. He was crazy, his neighbours said. Whoever heard of moving a tree already nearly thirty-five years old? And why such fuss over one elm when eight others would be left to shade his house and garden?

But John had dreamed for five winters of moving that tree, of saving for it the life it had striven so valiantly to keep. He liked to feel in partnership with other children of the earth. He had read and studied a good bit about moving trees, and he had used his common sense as well. He had thought as he lay in bed at night, a helpful thought often after a day of irritations, of how proud he would be could he in after years see that tree spreading its branches as it could not spread them now, sending out its great roots and its tiniest fibres through a whole corner of his field, shading his stone wall, adding beauty and symmetry to his land.

On a clear warm Saturday in mid-November he began his work with the crew of incredulous farmers whom he had engaged. First, a great hole in the field was dug and made ready, its tough top-soil broken, its rocks removed by crowbars. Next began the digging about the tree itself. John knew that within the veins of its greater roots the sap lay concealed, and his plan was not to disturb them more than was necessary. Only the small fibres stretching through the ground ten feet and more from the trunk should be severed. When this was done, a derrick should hoist the tree from its place, and his yoke of stout oxen should drag it by slow stages on high rollers prepared for it through the field to its new home. Once there, placed in position again by the derrick, the earth shovelled securely in and pressed down by a dozen stamping feet about even its smallest roots, he would guy it by wires to two pines standing conveniently some twenty feet away on either side. Nature, he thought, would do the rest. There would be the long winter for it to become accustomed to its new surroundings, held securely by its neighbours against high and sudden wind, and with the spring rains, if their work had been done well, its roots would swell and take hold upon the better, freer earth of the field.

As he worked, he felt a happiness and contentment steal over him, through his veins even into his hands and feet. He thought that if in the spring he could stand beneath his tree and see the unmistakable proofs of swelling buds, he could ask nothing better. New life sprang up within him anticipating the time.

The work went on apace; the great ditch about the tree deepened; already the men with their axes were severing the small rootfibres. The derrick was in position, the hoisting was soon to begin. Ellis was omnipresent, now here, now there, trying to wield an axe, stumbling about in the ditch, proving a nuisance to everyone. He had never seen a great tree moved and throughout the fall had begged the deferring of his own removal to his new home until the miracle had been accomplished.

"Land knows!" he had kept saying to John and Mary. "Land knows, I don't want to be impolite to them folks who've invited me, but I should like to see it moved. I truly should."

How it all happened no one ever really knew. One farmer said one thing, another another. But all seemed agreed that Ellis was standing directly beneath a great limb when the derrick began its upward pull. The agitated tree staggered and shook in trunk and branches; there was a fearful convulsion of the breaking earth about it, a rending sound of dislodged roots and stones. Something for years must have been eating away at its lowest limb, rendering it unable to bear the strain of any such upheaval as this. There was a tearing and a splintering as it broke away from the trunk, a sound which, penetrating even his deafness, caused Ellis just beneath to open his dull eyes in wonder. There was a confusion of shouting, hurrying men, crying this warning and that. There was John rushing beneath the falling limb to get stupid, tottering old Ellis, who was always, thought John, just where he ought not to be, out of the way in time.

But there was not time enough. It does not take a heavy limb, once dissevered, long to reach the ground. It got John and Ellis in their backs just as they were getting out from beneath it. Ellis had lost what wits he had, the men said, and, half-falling in his terror, had made it impossible for John to seize and carry him in time. The weight of the great branch crushed them both together. It was a quick death and a clean one.

Mary always remembered how quiet John's face was when the men had laid him on a grassy place beneath his orchard trees. There was no fear or worry on it anywhere. The men thought she was crazy when she told them to clear the limb away and go ahead then and there with the moving of the tree just as John had planned. They told their wives that night over their several supper tables that they had never gone through such an afternoon. But they did their work well nevertheless, even to replacing the disturbed soil about the tree in its new home, even to smoothing with their saws the great gash and tear which the falling branch had made in the gray elm bark.

The winter that year was kind with its snows which lay deep about the tree. The spring was slow and mild so that as the white drifts melted, the water seeped gradually through the earth. There was plenty of rain, too, in early March, warm rain for days on end. In April, Mary, watching day by day, saw the tree's swelling buds and in May the creeping cloud of new green spreading through its branches.

She told Sarah Peters about it with triumph in her face and voice.

# IV
## The Sea

1

Sarah Peters lived on in her bed in the brick house for four years after John's elm had first borne witness to his triumphant faith in earth, rain, and sun and in the thoughtful labour of men's careful hands. She remained as, for some inscrutable reason, she had come to be, both in body and in mind. She watched the mornings and the evenings of more than fourteen hundred days; mornings of fog and rain; hushed mornings of falling snow, clear mornings when the wind swept the leaves of her own elms into indescribable, tireless patterns of shade on her clipped garden grass; winter evenings of swift obscurity and summer ones lingering on in light. She was as unhurried as the days and nights themselves. She saw the tide fill the harbour, sweeping in from boundless waters without; she saw the schooners making in through the narrow channel and on spring mornings caught through the open windows the clumping of the staves and lumber stowed tightly between the railing of their decks. She smelled the acrid smell of flats at dead low water and saw the uneasy outlines of the gulls, gray and white against the muddy greens and browns. She watched the angular settlings of the small craft at anchor as the water left their sides and saw them three hours later rise again and float. Early, long before dawn, as she lay awake she heard the chug of motors ploughing the outer bay and knew how the fishermen sat in their dories, hunched figures, black and sleepy, their patient hands ready to measure out their baited trawls. As she lay there day after day, her respect for labour and for time increased within her, for labour which was the means of life and for time which quietly offered life a meaning and an end.

She said to herself again and again during those years how glad she was that she was not up and about a daily round of business. It would have been hard, she thought, to keep one's head before the now almost complete metamorphosis of the village and much of the coast. At least it would have been hard for *her*. By 1905 change had settled itself into comparative stability. The shipping except for desultory coastwise traffic was past; shipbuilding except in a few larger centres was over; and Maine, so far as its coastline was concerned, had given itself up to the inroads and the necessities of an alien population which afforded its sustenance during the summer months and excused its idleness during the winter.

Sarah Peters knew the village character better through sailing away from it for many years than if she had lived close at hand with it. She like others of her heritage and nurture had a perspective upon it that it could never have upon itself. She recognized that shrewdness native to the New England rural mind, a shrewdness steadily developed through two centuries and more by struggle with land and sea, by the necessity for thrift and quick thinking and the seizing of opportunity. She knew that, under the best of circumstances, under the mellowing influences of contact with other lands and other minds, that shrewdness lost itself in a humourous kind of wisdom; she knew, too, that under more narrowing influences it doubled back upon itself, became more acute, subtle, cunning even. She did not like to trust it against the temptations which would try it each summer as strangers with money in banks and pockets became dependent upon its services. Fishermen would turn from their fishing to the easier and more lucrative business of taking parties on the water for picnics on this island and that; storekeepers would raise their prices, secure in the thought that since people were able to pay more in the city during nine months of the year, they were equally able during three months to swell the tills of groceries and markets; carpenters and bricklayers after all must live through long and comparatively workless winters. Village youngsters would caddy on golf-links and at the end of the day count the tips in their pockets, calling such new and easy work as but fun

when compared with picking blueberries in the hot sun at so
many cents the quart. Girls and boys in the Academy who had
dreamed of college would glimpse suddenly the chance of earning
easy money on the grounds and in the homes of the palatial
estates now being built by village workmen. They would see a life
such as they had never known in their simple environments, a life
which in their inexperienced minds would breed either envy or
quite another sort of dreaming. Owners of land would put their
prices up and up as the demand exceeded the best supply, charg-
ing sums which would have lain forever upon the consciences of
their fathers and their grandfathers for rocky, barren acres if they
but provided a "view."

She saw it all coming, indeed much of it had come by 1905,
and understood without rancour and yet with misgiving that the
coast must pay dearly for it in the loss of a certain integrity, both
social and moral. For, as time went on, those who sojourned there
during the summer months would inevitably build their opinion of
coast character upon dealings with those with whom they came
most closely into contact rather than upon those who in times past
had lent to their coast a finer stamp and who even in times present
cherished its goodly, world-embracing heritage. Such persons, living quietly in their old homes and possessing a culture basically
comparable with any brought for a season from larger centres, were
relatively little known to dwellers of the summer colony in
Petersport or elsewhere. From the beginning of the influx there
had been, unfortunately enough, except in isolated cases almost no
association between the best of the native stock and those who
opened their homes in June and in late September steamed away
on the Boston boat or, as time went on, on the Bar Harbor
Express. Sarah Peters blamed neither for this since obviously neither was to blame. The native stock which she represented was self-
sufficient, taciturn, jealous of peace and security which was yearly

being inundated and destroyed; the strangers, as years went by and the old sea captains, once objects of curiosity, disappeared, were simply not interested. They had their own social life, often as diverse and as complicated as that lived during the winter in New York or Baltimore, and they had neither time nor inclination to discover what lay behind the face of Mary Peters, whom they saw in church, or whether the thoughts of the farmer's wife, from whom they bought their eggs and broilers, went beyond her hen yards. The situation was simply as it was, thought Sarah Peters, as she lay in her bed and watched the new automobile of the strangers in Uncle Caleb's house grinding up the hill in place of their carry-all of a year before. One could deplore it and the things it must trail in its wake without any active feeling of reproach.

For the most part her thoughts were not of things so near at hand. She had a score to settle, she concluded, in grateful remembrance before she went on, either into oblivion or into a new life, glimpses of which, she dared to believe, she had caught during her harvest of helplessness. She would not have had her life one whit different from what it had been, and no day passed without her thanksgiving. The very insensibility of her body, so much of the time unconscious that it was in a bed, brought with it its own freedom. Her mind could place it, unresisting, anywhere. She carried it, upright and beautiful and capable of ecstasy, through the months of her first voyage following immediately upon her wedding, a voyage from New York around the Cape of Good Hope to Sumatra and Java. She saw it sitting on the quarterdeck through warm tropical seas, felt it thrill to strange sights and sounds. She watched the fears which it had known calm themselves, become ironed out into a kind of fatalistic acceptance of whatever awaited it. She carried it through the sapphire waters of the Mediterranean in 1870 just after the new canal had been opened, saw Alexandria and Port Said, smelled their smells and heard their clatter. She

placed it contentedly for hours on end in the cabin of the
*Elizabeth* while the children did their lessons, remembering how
she had ravelled out old stockings for wool for darning when her
supply was exhausted and how John hated "The Psalm of Life."
She made it feel again the dash of spray on clear days of high,
favourable wind, the clinging dampness of fog, the extremes of
cold, and the beating, cruel sunlight of dirty Eastern harbours.
Again and again she made it climb the companionway in response
to a sudden cry from her husband so that it might see a passing
ship and feel the quick sense of fellowship in a common and
courageous enterprise. She left it, contented enough, in one place
or another while she remembered the people she had known,
people whom one never forgot because they had furnished admiration or curiosity or laughter—merchants and officers, this sailor
and that, the blue eyes of Mr. Gardiner blazing against steam while
he forgot to pass the potatoes. The world had been hers, she concluded, such a world as had dimmed and dulled regret into nothing at all and made even sorrow but a necessary complement to
life, without which one's days must go unfulfilled, even barren, to
the end of one's time.

When she had brought her body back to its bed after carrying
it here and there at will through a tangible world, again its very
insensibility freed her mind to range untrammelled another, less
tangible perhaps but in another sense more real. Here she dwelt
with thoughts rather than with people, things, and places—the
thoughts she had picked up here and there in her bright search
over many years, new thoughts brought to her from the books
that Mary read aloud. The wise in this world, she concluded, did
not place over-confidence in their own learning but rather drew
upon that of others more wise than they themselves. There were
hours, too, quite free of thoughts of any kind, hours when she was
teased out of thought by the all-pervading certainty of the clarity

and order of life of which only the greater part of mankind, too busy with its small affairs, seemed unaware. Such hours made clear to her the light of all the vanished ages, held before her eyes a golden branch amid the shadows.

She died at last on an October afternoon just as the full tide had turned to leave the harbour. She had been laughing with Mary over the bungling efforts of a schooner to make the landing before an unfavourable wind. Someone was sailing her who knew neither his ship nor her course.

"Bad seamanship," she said to Mary who was watching with her. "It would drive your father crazy."

Then things suddenly stopped within her, and she lay a bit lower in her pillows. The woman who had cared for her throughout her illness blamed herself. She had raised her too suddenly, she said. The doctor had warned her for months against it. But Mary, watching her mother's face relax slowly into its old familiar lines as the October sunlight streamed into the western room, could not see for a moment why it mattered in the least.

2

Jim came from New York the next day in response to Mary's telegram which had set village tongues wagging. Mary like her mother was forever unconscious of village tongues or perhaps instead completely unregardful of them. She had not hesitated for a moment before sending for Jim. She wanted him more than she wanted any one else, partly because he had loved her mother, largely because he and no one else held within himself the capacity for an understanding of what Sarah Peters had been and forever would be, the one understanding identical with Mary's own. He came for the funeral and stayed in the brick house with Mary and the woman who had cared for her mother and who was still reproachful of herself. He was tact and gentleness itself.

At the funeral he sat beside Mary in the room where as a boy he had held Sarah Peters' yarn for her. The tall clock ticked on in the hall as they waited for the house to fill with the people who walked up the flagstones, solemn people as curious as they were sad, people in dark clothes with rigid yet watchful faces. A village with death in its midst is always peculiarly cognizant of life.

Ellen Peters and Mrs. Kimball sat in the mourners' room with Jim and Mary and the woman who blamed herself for Sarah Peters' freedom. Ellen wore a black veil as did her mother, but they saw Jim Pendleton quite well for all that. Mrs. Kimball stiffened within her as she saw his arm across the back of Mary's chair. Ellen watched his dark, still face and thought how experienced he looked, how like a man of the world he seemed. She was far more conscious of him throughout the funeral than of Sarah Peters' body in its black coffin.

After the funeral he stayed on for two weeks in the village living with his aunt and uncle, who could not for their lives explain to themselves why they deferred to him after all the trouble he had caused them, why they felt half-afraid of him, in short why they let him stay with them at all. There he sat in their sitting room precisely as he had sat as a boy, taciturn yet agreeable, interested in their affairs, uncommunicative as to his own, smoking the cigarettes which they both despised. Mattie Pendleton gingerly emptied his stubs and ashes and cooked the things he liked, hating herself as she did so. She used her best china at every meal although she swore after each that she would never do it again. She heard herself urging him to sleep late in the morning, and, when he came down at eight o'clock, served the homemade sausage she had fried for him with many irritated pokings of her fork. She even sat opposite him while he ate, trying her utmost not to be pleased when he told her there had never been sausage like hers, wiggling her toes nervously within her old shoes as she tried in vain to discover why it was that she made such a confounded fool of herself. Later while he insisted upon washing his own dishes, telling her in the meanwhile how well he knew what a nuisance he had been as a boy and how sorry he was, she scorned her heart for its warming toward him even while she told herself that perhaps he had something in him after all. She excused him to her neighbours, consciously lying about the important position he held in New York business circles. At night when she lay in bed beside the sleeping Joel, she saw through the crack in her door the light from his room and wondered with all her old suspicion coming back whatever he could be up to all alone in there at such a ridiculous hour of the night.

Joel found himself also warming to his nephew's well-timed questions about this and that. Jim thought it remarkable, he said, that his uncle at seventy could keep everything in the post-office so straight in his mind, could know as much as he did about intricate postal affairs in Washington. Old Joel's deprecations grew daily weaker until before three days had passed he was endowing himself with a respect unknown in many years and Jim with an intelligence he had never before in his wildest moments accorded him. He even bragged about his nephew on store steps and in the village square, said that he had been maligned by people without half his good sense and that the trouble with Petersport folks was and always had been simply a lack of knowing a good thing when they saw it.

Jim ordered for his aunt and uncle from New York the latest thing in phonographs with a plentiful supply of new cylinder records which Mattie Pendleton handled with fear and awe, dropping each with care back into its cotton-lined box after she had played it evening after evening. She set the phonograph on her sitting room table and proudly asked her neighbours in to hear it.

Jim was gracious to them all, insinuating himself into their reluctant favour even while their perennial suspicion remained. He explained its workings, the making of its wax records while they watched with fascination the needle which brought out all the newest songs, sending them through the room from its pasteboard horn. Joel tapped his worn old slippers in time as it wound out "Arawana" and "The Saucy Little Bird on Nellie's Hat," and Mattie insecurely felt herself "growing soft" again as she listened. Jim sold half a dozen of the things before people knew they had ordered them, so expert was he in divulging their charm for winter evenings and in suggesting their indispensable assistance in keeping people, away from the larger life of the city, up with the swift changes in song hits.

"There's no reason why you folks down here shouldn't know the latest music," he said, as he helped the surprised women on with their coats after an hour of delighted listening. "People in the country often appreciate things more than those in the city. They've twice the intelligence, I find. The country's the place to live, I say, if you just have things like this to keep you from getting in a rut. By and by they'll go into all the schools, better and more improved ones than this. You wait and see. We're having records made now of things like Lincoln's Gettysburg Address and all the rest of the best stuff that everybody ought to know. You get educated while you think you're only being entertained. But don't buy till you get good and ready. I'm not down here to do business. I just want aunt and uncle to enjoy themselves this winter."

He divided his time circumspectly between Joel and Mattie Pendleton and Mary now alone in the brick house. He was different there. Had Mary seen and listened to him as he talked with his aunt's friends and neighbours, she would never have known him for the same person. He did not talk phonographs with her or song hits or business. As a matter of fact he did not talk much with her at all.

He did her gardening for her while she was at school, cutting back the frost-bitten stalks of her delphiniums and phlox, getting her borders ready for winter. He cut late marigolds and asters for her, arranging them with skillful fingers in bowls for the tables in the hall and sitting room. At night he covered the plants, which still blossomed, against the October frosts. Coming home in the late afternoon to the still house, she found these evidences of his presence and found, too, the stirring within herself of a life which had seemed dead during the hours at school. Reluctance and eagerness struggled within her as she now and again prepared supper for them both, arranging her table carefully, cooking the things he liked, dressing with care and forethought. When he came limping up the hill, she opened the door for him with much the same feeling that she had had when he had come four years ago, a sense of his presence being, if not meet and right, at least fitting and inevitable.

There are natures in the world which, often unconsciously, seek other natures because of peculiar, irresistible forces which bring them together, forces which may be evaded or escaped but which cannot be denied. Science may ascribe their being to laws of physics or chemistry or biology, but it cannot further account for them and their power. The more imaginative mind may interpret them less materially; the superstitious see in them the workings of fate. They may wreck or rebuild, bring remorse and ruin or the highest happiness according as they are balanced by caution and understanding; but the wise mind knows their existence and recognizes their power for what it is. Such a nature, discovering its complement, sometimes with fear and misgiving, realizes its fulfillment is at hand. Two such natures become one as inevitably as two streams converge in a common valley; and others, looking upon them know, either vaguely or surely according as they are attuned to life, that they hold in common something which surpasses and transcends friendship or companionship or even love. For an

extraordinary sympathy and understanding makes as it were two
parts into a single whole, forever outdistancing speech, rendering
explanations of thought or even of behaviour unnecessary, setting
at naught all practical considerations of this and that by which
most lives are governed.

Mary Peters at thirty-four felt these forces within her seeking
themselves in Jim Pendleton. She was not dazzled by him, not
even lonely for his companionship. She knew him for what he
was. She could hold him as though he were an object, quite at
arm's length, and look at him. She knew the qualities forever at
variance within him, compassion and carelessness, idleness and
vague ambition, generosity and selfishness. She knew what others
thought of him. Her heart had once been broken by him. But
there he was, holding within himself the anchorage for those
forces which at once nourished and consumed her life. These
forces defied analysis and scrutiny. They were. That was all.
Whether they were the result of a common experience, of influences larger than the life of some circumscribed community, she
did not know. Perhaps they were instead the causes which had
made possible the interpretations of those influences. She looked
at him and saw, not thoughts in common, not even experiences in
themselves, but rather the emotions which were the harvest or the
seed-time of such thoughts and such experiences. She looked at
him and felt reaching out toward her all that which had given,
which still gave meaning to her life—the swift understanding of
Cadiz and Ponta Delgata in the early morning, of fruit-laden boats
moving across clear water, of wind-filled sails and long hours of
idle waiting on a still sea. She knew that he knew all those things
which had quickened her, made her present and future but one
with her past. She knew, too, that this knowledge was not so much
born of a common experience as of that which had quickened the
experience itself. He saw things as only Mr. Gardiner had seen

them, although no one knew better than she that he was not of the stuff that had made Mr. Gardiner. And as she looked at him, sat opposite him at her table, and walked with him along the high shore roads, which gave glimpses of a more open sea, she knew, as she had known dimly four years ago in her mother's room, that for better or for worse her life was flowing into his.

There were other and more tangible elements, too, that supplemented the complemental forces between them. Each was alone, quite without ties of any sort, and neither was of the type which makes contacts with ease. Moreover, like most women everywhere toward that dependence forever in men, Mary felt a protective solicitude toward Jim Pendleton, undeserving of it as he might be. His lameness touched her even as it had done during her girlhood. His lack of stability, both physical and mental, drew upon her sympathy, making her imagine, even while she knew she was only imagining, that she could steer a better course for him than he could manage for himself. These arguments played the small part which mere arguments must ever play in a nature like her own. Beyond and above them was the fact that, because of certain identities in nature, she was a part of him and he of her.

It was characteristic of them both and of the feeling which was between them that they spoke little of it during those two weeks of renewed and renewing companionship. He came for her after school at night, carrying her books up the hill as he had done years before, both unregardful of the eyes and the busy minds of the village.

"Mary must be crazy, plain crazy," said Mrs. Kimball at breakfast, dinner, and supper to Ellen Peters who sat opposite her. "She's clear out of her head. She can't mean to throw herself away on a shiftless fellow like that."

Ellen sent a knowing look across the table at her mother.

"He has a way with women," she said. "He always had, and Mary's probably no different from the rest for all her stand-offishness."

"I don't know anything about his ways. I don't like him and never did from the day he came to your party till now. There are enough stories about him in this village to fill a book, and land knows what New York has to offer. And he's even got around Mattie Pendleton with his sly ways. She's even sticking up for him, did it to me myself in the post-office this morning. Someone ought to talk to Mary. Someone ought to tell her a few things if she can't see them for herself."

"If you mean yourself telling her," said Ellen, "you'd better take my advice and mind your own affairs. You'll only get snubbed for all your pains. She's queer and always was. They're all queer. I guess I know."

Jim walked with Mary through the early twilights of late October, hearing with her the frail snap of the leaves as they severed themselves from the trees to drift downward and fill the roadside ditches, watching the black outlines of swallows circling above the salt marshes and the dark blue of the hills darkening before the dusk. They sat in the sharp night air upon high pastures with the sea invisible before them, marked here and there by the lights of schooners at anchor. She stirred now and then to his kisses and more, when she was alone at night, to the knowledge of what lay before them both.

Nor was he for a moment unconscious of that knowledge which they shared in common. Only his knowledge was greater than her own even although he had not her powers of vision. He knew far better than she his chaotic, bewildered life through which he had been taken along by one impulse after another. He could not prophesy with any sense of security that this new anchorage would hold. He had nothing to offer her except an understanding, born of the fruits of a common past, and a love which, he now knew, had been hers from the beginning. Even had he been given to analysis of himself, it was futile to lay himself and his life before her. She knew enough of both, and he gave himself up, not without humility, to a new kind of intoxication—the realization that someone in the world knew his best and was supremely careless of his worst.

On the evening before his return to New York he brought her a gift, something which, he told her, he had bought for her three years back in an old music shop in Florence.

"It was hanging by a cord in the window of some place on the Ponte Vecchio," he said, "with the light upon it, and when I saw it, I knew it was yours, Mary, and nobody's else. I don't know why certain things belong to you, but they do."

It was a pocket fiddle of the seventeenth century, little more than a foot in length but complete in every detail. Fashioned of rosewood and inlaid with lines of ivory it was smooth to the touch, conveying to one's very hand the recognition of its life. It was shaped like a tiny boat, with rounded keel and pointed stern, and the four pale olive-wood stops which formed its prow were surmounted by a carved serpent's head. It was delicate and beautiful and old, and it held over one who saw and understood it the tyranny of all things old and exquisite. Lingering about it were the tunes and songs of centuries and the quick response it had brought from innumerable hearts. Mary stood holding it in the lamplit room, and Jim Pendleton thought he had never seen such radiance as that within her face.

"It used to be carried about by some wandering music master or strolling player half over the world, I suppose," he said, watching her as she held it. "They played them for dances and for the accompaniment of madrigals and all kinds of quaint songs. It's full of old stuff, that thing is—all the songs and dance tunes it's ever played. It's like the ships in London docks that can't for the life of them lose the places they've sailed to."

Her eyes shone brighter and brighter as she held the little fiddle. He had never seen such eyes, he thought.

"It's like the flutes in Arcadia," she said, "that they played under the beech trees, Daphnis and Tityrus and all the rest. It takes time away so that you don't know there is such a thing. It's older than three hundred years, Jim. You feel its age just holding it. It even gets into your hands."

He still looked at her, realizing again with the same surprise she always engendered in him how like his gift she was herself.

"That's why it belongs to you," he said. "You're old, Mary. There's nothing new about you. That's why you're different from everybody else. You're full of old places and old thoughts. Don't you understand? That's why you can't be touched or—or frightened by new, untried things. That's why you're too patient with a man like me." He took the fiddle from her hands. "You ought to live with things like this," he finished suddenly, "not with someone like me. I've got too much of the new in me. I'm always off on some tangent or another. You know that. I'll hurt you. You know that, too."

"Yes," she said. "I know that, too. But it doesn't matter. I've never paid much attention to the future."

"You don't have to," he persisted, "because you carry yours along with you. But I can't carry mine. It's always carrying me. Even loving you probably won't hold me, no matter how it seems now. It didn't hold my father, and I've more than my father to reckon with."

"I know," she said again. "I've gone over it a hundred times and it always comes out the same way. It's like the problems in geometry I used to do here at this table that had only one way of being solved. When I'd finished with them, I always piled my books and papers in one corner, and there they were."

Jim Pendleton still stood and watched her. All his life passed before him as he did so, the tides which had carried him hither and yon, the storms which others had weathered for him, the disasters here and there which others as well as he had paid for.

"It's not too late, Mary, even now," he said. "I can't stay here without you, but I can go away. Sometimes the best way to meet a thing is to run away from it. The trouble with me is I haven't run away half enough. All you have to do is to tell me to go. It's you who has to decide just as it's always been, but I wish you'd tell me to go, Mary."

She still smiled at him.

"I can't decide," she said. "I've never really decided anything. We don't come from people who do decide things. They've always been settled for us. Things always open up before me, and now this has opened. I'll take what comes. There's too much of each of us in the other for me to tell you to go."

He played the pocket fiddle for her that evening, drawing its tiny bow across its strings. She sat radiant on the sofa beside him, careless of his misgivings, conscious only that for a third time her life was being fulfilled within her.

3

He went back to New York the next day. He walked the decks of the Boston boat until long past midnight, so black-browed and silent that all the other passengers commented upon him, wondering who he was and what was causing him such evident confusion. In Boston he sent a telegram to a woman in New York who had been impatiently waiting a fortnight for news of his whereabouts and his return. She met his train in the late afternoon, angry at his neglect, fearful of his new and inexplicable manner toward her. They sat for hours after dinner in a downtown restaurant which he laconically refused to leave for a more congenial and private environment. When it was over and the woman convinced for the time being that he was through, he sent her home in a cab (she prophesying that in a week he would think better of his nonsense) and went himself to his own rooms.

They were dishevelled rooms, clean as a puzzled and irascible landlady could make them but dishevelled for all that, littered with music paper and scores, which she did not dare disturb, hung about with decrepit old instruments of one sort or another, which she did not dare to touch no matter how much dust they collected, strewn with books in unfamiliar languages. During his frequent and curious absences she often nosed about his possessions, trying to discover what manner of man he was and failing completely. For two years now she had been on the point of telling him to take himself and his silly belongings out of her house, but just when she was trembling on the nervous verge of her announcement, he had always done some unexpected thing which made her change her distraught mind. Once he had brought her some flowers. You could not really tell a man to leave your house when he stood before you with his arms full of flowers. And times out of number he had been kind to her brother, who swept the hall and steps and who was a bit rickety in his head. Moreover, there was something about Mr. Pendleton, even when he actually did nothing for you, even when he was careless and sullen to the point of driving one crazy, that worked on your feelings, mad as he made you. Mrs. Higgins herself did not know what it was, but Miss Crosby, an elderly spinster whom she also housed, did, as far as one could know.

"I'm sure I don't know why I keep him," said Mrs. Higgins to Miss Crosby when she had closed the door of Miss Crosby's single upon them and sat down on Miss Crosby's sanitary cot to quiet her shaking knees. "I'm sure I don't!"

"It's charm, Mrs. Higgins," Miss Crosby would say, "and there's no telling about charm. Some few folks like him have it and more like you and me don't. You'll never send him off. I disapprove of him with every ounce of conscience and decency I have in me, but he's got charm all the same, I tell you."

That night he did not go to bed at all in spite of Mrs. Higgins' warning on the wall about the wasting of gas. He wanted to utilize to the utmost his new determination while he still had it. He sat at his disordered desk, going through a plethora of letters and papers, photographs, odds and ends of knick-knacks. In the morning his wastebasket was piled high as well as a generous portion of the floor around it. After he was well out of the house at nine o'clock, Mrs. Higgins did her utmost to piece some of the letters together, but without much success. Those written in a foreign tongue were beyond her anyway, and he had taken great care to tear the others into pieces so small that they defied reassembling.

His firm, none too pleased with his absence at a busy time of year, was mollified by the order sheets which he brought back with him. There was no telling about Pendleton. Once you were done up with him and ready to tell him to quit, he came back at you with more business than stable fellows of three times his calibre could possibly muster up in twice the time.

"Apparently you're a success in the rural fastnesses," said his sales manager. "I didn't suppose there was a cent to be squeezed out of those Maine villages."

"There's a lot of things you don't know about Maine villages," returned Jim Pendleton, his tired mind a confusion of emotions. "It's lucky I'm a success with them for I'm going to be your sole representative there in less than a year's time."

4

By the first of November Petersport had drawn itself closely within itself and was ready for the winter. The summer cottages were closed, locked and banked and boarded. Their sightless eyes stared seaward from cove and headland; and fishermen, coming in on the afternoon tide with a poor catch, commented upon the wealth and leisure which they represented, swapped yarns about their owners, and said it was a queer world which gave some men so much and made others bend their backs and callous their hands for so little. Golf links were shaggy in their desertion, grew brown and cold beneath the sullen skies of November. Village boys and girls wandered about the gravelled driveways of one residence or another, gathered whatever late flowers still survived, and on dark evenings made love on deserted verandas facing the sea. And now that the visitors were gone and money in store tills had been carried to the nearest bank or stored away in places of safe keeping, the village turned to its own sequestered ways.

The atmosphere at church on Sunday mornings regained its ease and composure now that embarrassing differences in clothes and manners were no longer in evidence. The ministers need be no longer conscious of frayed frock coats and inadequate sermons. Singers in the choir felt no necessity for apology. Church suppers started again on Thursday evenings, although now in the wake of progress a fifteen-cent charge was laid upon them. They were preceded as always by sewing for the August sale. Lodges reopened, farmers driving in from the country to attend their meetings and bringing their wives to the corresponding societies for women, the Rebekahs and the Eastern Star. Ellen Peters enjoyed her part in these organizations. She looked well, had a good memory, and knew how to conduct the ceremonies assigned to her with ease and impressiveness.

Life had opened again for Ellen after a seemly interim, and she relished her experiences as delegate to this and that conclave through the county. Ellen was still young and good to look upon. She had a keen Kimball eye out for whatever might turn up and a keener one to make things turn up if they seemed a bit slow or reluctant. Ellen was a born manager, her mother said proudly to Ellen and to others. She must not for a moment think that anything was over and done for her. Her warning was quite unnecessary. Ellen might not dream dreams or see visions, but she had her plans and knew her needs. She kept herself well to windward with a weather eye always scanning the horizon.

It was a cold winter of late snow but plentiful when it came. The roads until well into January were frozen and rutty with pockets of surface ice. On late December mornings Mary Peters, starting for the Academy with feet that responded to her eager heart, saw the steam rising from the icy water into the icier air, pale blue clouds of vapour at first even with the sea and then disseminating into thin wraiths of mist. By Christmas the harbour was frozen, the islands set in jagged ice-cakes broken by the tides; by January the sheet of ice was extending toward more open water. Wood was cut on the larger islands then and brought by ox-sledges across the white expanse. The sea and the earth became one.

The snow came after Christmas was some weeks past, drifting down then for days on end as though to make up for its negligence. Mary watched it muffling her rose bushes in mounds of white, pencilling the black stems of her lilacs. She never could have enough snow, she thought, just as this winter she never seemed to have enough of anything. The new abundance within filled her classrooms and the quiet rooms of the brick house. As she sat by her table at night, preparing her lessons for school, reading, or writing to Jim Pendleton, she wondered if the four walls of an old house could actually keep within themselves something of

the life they had known. Could persons so endow objects which
they loved with such thoughts and feelings that the objects took
upon themselves new significance and meaning, not alone to those
who had known them best but to others as well? Could thoughts
linger on in the places in which they had been thought so that
one was actually conscious of their presence as she seemed to be?
Or was it only her imagination which conceived the peace and
the plenitude she was constantly aware of?

"I swear," she wrote Jim Pendleton, "that the little fiddle is
reliving all its life before my very eyes. I keep it on the little table in
the corner of the sitting room, and every time I come in, I'm conscious of it whether I see it or not and even when I've forgotten all
about it. Anyone but you would think me crazy, I'm sure, but I
know hundreds of things about it to tell you when you come."

The village was sharply cognizant of the frequency of her letters to Jim and of the comparative infrequency of his to her. He had
begged her to write him often; he needed her letters, he said, and it
was not difficult to grant his request. As for his to her, she knew too
well his ineptitude at writing, the difficulty he had in placing
thoughts on paper, and she was satisfied with the brief replies he
made to her own thoughts, little as they told her about himself. She
kept always an abiding sense of his understanding. Besides, there was
more than a little of him in the rooms in which she lived.

She thought more often of Hester during that winter than she
had thought in years. Hester had left herself in the brick house in
a hundred ways. There was a pitcher she had loved to dry, a squat
white pitcher with fat blue dots like calico and a quaint humour
all its own. There was the old highchair in the kitchen in which
she had loved to sit, laughing at this and that, and there were days
of wind and sun like herself. No shred of bitterness or even of
regret shadowed Mary's thoughts of her. With her own love for
Jim Pendleton flooding her mind and stirring her senses, she felt

more close to Hester, understanding her brief and tragic passion as she had never before understood it. If the spirits of those who had gone remained in touch with those on earth whom they had loved, she knew there could be no resentment in Hester's spirit. She had been the embodiment of light and merriment, and Mary felt crowding back upon her through those winter days all the old and new graces of her companionship.

The manifold activities of village and country life, those old and simple means of livelihood, took upon themselves through her awakened eyes fresh interest and value. Nothing escaped her. When the men cut the ice in February, she watched the oxen holding back the laden sledges on the high slope of the hill, their arching necks held taut within their jangling yokes, their hind legs bent and bowed from exertion, their fore legs stiff and unyielding as they gripped the snowy road. The ice from quick and early freezing on still nights before the snow had come was clearer than she had ever remembered it, great square blocks of light piled upon one another, catching the sun in prismatic hues. The sledges creaked and swayed down the hill from morning till night, their bells clear as the ice itself; and when they returned empty with chips of ice clinging to their worn boards, the children when school was out hitched their sleds to chains and poles and were drawn up the hill to coast downward on the packed, shining surface of the snow. In February, too, the smelt tents littered the harbour ice, tiny canvas houses smoking cosily on cold clear mornings from their squat chimneys; and on Saturday the boys speared frost fish through the holes they had made below the mill-dam where the ice was thin.

There was a certain morning in early April which she was always to remember, not so much because she saw it as because she heard and felt its meaning. It was a morning of scant sunlight through fog and mist, a morning when roads ran with water and

every ditch had a sound of its own. As she walked to school, she
heard the rush of the released brook tumbling over the dam and
the high, raucous shrieks of the saw-mill now returned to work.
The smell of freshly sawn lumber filled the air; the harbour ice,
obscured by fog, was, cracking before the incoming tide. Fog filled
the outer bay, dense and white, hiding the Mt. Desert hills and the
nearby headlands and ridges. Rocks along the roadside gleamed
dark and wet through the dimness, and every bush and twig was
beaded with trembling drops.

There had been far more lovely mornings before, but never
one, she thought, with such a sense of returning life and motion.
Her blood raced strangely within her. She could feel it in her very
fingers keeping pace with the steady hiss of crumbling snow, inundated by runnels of water. It was a morning one felt rather than
saw, felt so keenly that one did not need one's eyes at all. She had
known numberless days like this at sea, fog-wrapped days when
sound and motion had taken the place of sight; and as she walked
down the hill on the board sidewalk, she felt it spring like the
deck beneath her feet.

She wrote about that morning to Jim Pendleton, and he, reading this and other of her letters in his disorderly rooms at Mrs.
Higgins', allowed himself to believe that she had enough life for
them both.

5

They were married in early July just when Sarah Peters' crimson peonies were at their best below the front windows of the
brick house. Mary, smiling to herself as she crossed off the possibility of this guest and that, had asked no one to her wedding
except the country woman who had cared for her mother. The

minister might bring his own second witness, she wrote Jim Pendleton, if he could find one who was willing to come.

Mrs. Kimball was torn between resentment and relief when no invitation was forthcoming to her and Ellen. She had been in a state of nervous apprehension from the moment when rumour followed fast upon Mary's resignation from the Academy, a state which kept her out of her kitchen for hours on end while she communicated it to her neighbours.

"If anyone's to be asked," she announced a dozen times a day, "it's sure to be Ellen and I, and I suppose Joel and Mattie. For all I know, they'll be fools enough to go. He's completely pulled the wool over their eyes. But I tell Ellen I can't countenance such goings-on, and if I went, I'd be countenancing it. After all's said and done, principles are principles, and the time comes when you have to stand up for them."

Ellen from the start had not shared her mother's consternation.

"In my opinion," she said, "you're crossing a bridge you'll never have to come to. Mary isn't going to ask either of us, so you may as well help me with the strawberries instead of getting so worked up you can't stay at home. Besides, I can't for the life of me see why everybody's in such a stew. I've always rather liked Jim Pendleton myself. Say what you will, he's got a way with him that most men don't have."

Mrs. Kimball, dressed to go out, widened her large mouth before Ellen's terse remarks and steadied herself by the kitchen sink.

"Well, I never!" she cried at Ellen. "Well, I never did! I never supposed I'd hear a thing like that from a daughter of mine!"

Ellen was hulling strawberries at the kitchen table. Their red stains brought out the whiteness of her capable hands. In a clean blue apron she was freshness and composure itself.

"Calm down, mother," she said. "Times have changed since you were young, or at least you think they have even if they haven't. Men have to sow a few wild oats in my opinion to make them fit to live with. If John had sown a few, I'd probably have had an easier time with him."

"Ellen!" screamed Mrs. Kimball again. She did not know what was getting into Ellen. "I declare I never heard such talk!"

"Didn't you?" asked Ellen.

She carried the colander of hulled berries to the sink and washed them there, wielding the pump vigorously with her strong right hand, moving the berries about with her left to be sure she had them clean. Her mother still stared at her.

"Besides, they're not young. They're both of them old enough to know better even if they have been encouraged in this nonsense from the start. It's dangerous, they say, to blame the dead, but Sarah Peters began this years ago by having him in her house for days on end. If people get what they deserve, she ought to be resting uneasy in her grave this minute."

"They don't," said Ellen with wisdom rare for her. She continued with rarer wisdom. "And Sarah Peters isn't uneasy wherever she is. She never was uneasy. That's one difference between you and she, mother. Give her what she deserves, I say. She—she was a fine woman, and you know it."

Mrs. Kimball took off her hat suddenly and sat down by the kitchen table. It was a warm day, and she had all at once discovered that she could not follow Ellen.

"Yes," she said, "I suppose she was. I've never held anything against her. Come to all of this, she might have been Jim Pendleton's mother herself if it hadn't been for those wild oats you're encouraging."

Ellen finished washing the berries. She emptied them from the colander into a yellow bowl and began to measure out sugar for them in a tin measuring cup.

"He might have had a worse fate," she said quietly. "And now suppose we let him alone. Maybe he'll wake up this village a bit and Mary, too, when it comes to that. It won't hurt her any. She needs waking up. And take it from me, we don't need to worry about any invitation to their wedding."

The minister brought his wife as a necessary second witness, and her days for a fortnight thereafter were upset by a multiplicity of eager callers. It had been simple enough, she told them, with the house clean and full of flowers. It was a beautiful day and the sun was all over everything. They were married in the room in which Sarah Peters had lain for so many years. The minister's wife had had an uncanny feeling that Sarah Peters herself was present since so much of her seemed left within the room. They had stood before the fireplace beneath the portrait of Mary's great-grandparents, painted, somebody said, in some foreign port at least a hundred years ago. Mary had worn a blue dress of some thin stuff; the minister's wife actually thought she had seen it in church the summer before. Of course, some might think she should have worn black for her mother, but since she had chosen curiously enough not to wear black at all since her mother's death, why put it on for a wedding when things surely ought to be bright and cheerful?

She had looked lovely in a way it was hard to explain, not exactly handsome but so kind of shining you kept staring at her to try to discover what it was in her face that so sort of lighted her up. The bridegroom looked nice, too, although he wore nothing in particular that she could remember, just a suit of some sort, gray, she thought. Contrary to all she had heard about him, for she had come to Petersport since his youth, he seemed nice and quiet enough, and as tactful and polite as anyone could want. He was handsome, too, in spite of his lameness and a certain foreign look about him. No, she could not see that he was nervous or restless. He acted perfectly calm to her.

The service was simple enough, just the necessary questions and answers, and they both looked at each other as they answered which the minister's wife thought nice and unusual; in fact, she said, they looked at each other so intently and with such an air of shutting the whole world out, that she felt almost a bit in the way herself. No, there was no kiss. Probably they were saving that until they were alone, which, according to her opinion, was much the nicest way to do.

After the wedding, which was just at sundown, they all went into the dining room and had the most delicious supper which Mary served herself with her husband to help her. They five sat at the table as though they had always sat there, she said, and the talk was the easiest imaginable. Jim Pendleton must have been all over the world, she thought, for he knew more things about more places than even her husband, who as a young man had been in the foreign mission field. And after supper he showed them all kinds of curious things, musical instruments mostly from every country under the sun, some apparently as old as the hills. The queer thing about it was they didn't seem to be in any hurry to be alone. It seemed instead as though they had been alone together for ages.

She must admit, she said, that she had a comfortable, good feeling as she left them there in the doorway at twilight, and her husband shared her sentiments. Whatever people might say, they seemed to belong to each other more than most couples seemed to belong.

"And we have plenty of them in this parsonage," she said expansively, "from all over the county. There's hardly a week without one at least. I've been ready to cry over some I've seen and signed my name to in this very room, girls who ought to have been married months back—you know what I mean—and fellows looking as though they were standing up to be shot instead of married."

She wished she could explain just what it was that seemed to make this marriage different from most, just what it was that she had been aware of between Mary Peters and Jim Pendleton. It almost seemed, she concluded, feeling foolish as she said it, as though each of them were giving the other what each had already.

"What I mean, I guess," she said, "is that they won't have to get acquainted with each other the way most married folks do. At least, it don't seem as if they would."

And she, for one, was going to stop nosing around in other folks' business. It was surely not her province as a minister's wife to speak evil of her neighbours, no matter what talk reached her ears. Moreover, she was convinced beyond a doubt that Jim and Mary Pendleton were suited to each other, and she was ready to prophesy their complete happiness no matter what anyone might say.

6

Her prophecies were amply fulfilled during the first months in the brick house. Jim Pendleton was at once enlarged and steadied by Mary's love. He had never known a love like it, complete in its selflessness, untiring in its solicitude, with seemingly no demands or exactions. There was no curtailing of his freedom except as his new environment in itself curtailed it. She gave him, he thought then, everything that he had ever wanted, a passion which knew no withholding, a delight in things and experiences which he had sought vainly in all other persons he had known, a tolerance of his moods, a humour forever flying to meet his own.

The determination also of the minister's wife to let bygones be bygones had its influence upon her neighbours, already urged on by lively curiosity. They called upon the Pendletons in twos and threes, their eyes prepared to take in everything, their tongues ready for quick release once they had left the flagstone walk. They found a quiet, tranquil hostess and a host who was geniality itself. Unlike his wife, at least unlike her attitude in times past, he seemed not at all averse to being drawn into village affairs. Ellen, coming by herself a fortnight after the wedding and looking unusually attractive in a new suit and hat, somewhat archly proposed his participation in a musicale to be given in the fall. He was at once eager and cooperative. Within fifteen minutes his quick mind had planned Ellen's program for her. He even accompanied her to the gate after she had reluctantly declined Mary's invitation to supper, and stood there laughing with her over this and that.

"Ellen hasn't changed much," he said to Mary upon his return to the sitting-room. "She's about as she was at her birthday party twenty years ago."

He had never asked about John and Ellen, largely because, Mary thought, he probably knew about them. Knowing Ellen, one would be likely to know about her and John.

"I remember that party," he continued, "and how you helped me with the games I didn't understand. There was a girl there named Grace Wilbur. What's become of her?"

"She's still here summers. She married a New York man. They have a big place on the outer bay. I haven't seen her in years except now and again in church. They say she married very well."

"I'd expect that of her," he said. "She seemed to know how to look out for herself."

She caught something then in his face and voice which she sometimes caught and which, she knew, had nothing to do with him and her. She had known from the beginning that there had been, would always be, things which had nothing to do with him and her.

She maintained a patience with his disorderly ways which he had neither expected nor for that matter deserved. In the early weeks of their marriage she received with apparent pleasure all the odds and ends of his possessions which he had had sent on from New York, books, more old instruments, packing cases filled with music. She cleared an upstairs room of its furniture so that he might have it for all such things which belonged especially to him.

"Studios they call such places now," she said. "This will be your studio, Jim, where you can get away when you like from Petersport and me."

She sat for hours on the floor on rainy afternoons while he unpacked his things, showing her this and that: his *viola d'amore* with beautiful sloping shoulders, a back of thinnest pear-tree wood, and tiny sympathetic under-strings for overtones; another with purfling inlaid with ebony and ivory and a fingerboard of intricate checked design; an Italian *cetera* with a circular sound-hole below its delicate bridge, a sound-hole carved like the rose-window of a cathedral by curious, eager hands dead long ago; a lyra guitar with pointed, spreading wings like those of swallows at rest; a walking-stick and flute all in one. He explained their history to her, where he had bought them, and their use.

"I've spent a fortune on these things," he said, half in apology, half in explanation. "I haven't much money, Mary. Probably I should have told you that long ago."

"It doesn't matter. What's money? I haven't much myself."

"Any other man would have told you. The trouble is I never think of money when I'm with you."

"We've got a roof over our heads, a fairly good one when it comes to that."

"I know, but it's your roof, not mine. Decent men rather want to look after their wives. At least that's the Maine idea, and I don't even know how I'll get on with this phonograph agency down here. I suppose there's a limit to people in these outlying parts, and anyway, you can't expect everyone to buy a phonograph. I wouldn't have one of the darned things in the house myself."

She laughed. She could never get used to the discrepancy between her husband's odd business and her husband himself.

Jim was not poor at business when he stuck to it. The trouble was he was as desultory and erratic about business as he was about everything else. He drove about the country now and then with his uncle's old horse, leaving home in the morning and returning at any hour that suited his convenience or his fancy. He talked with farmers in their barn doorways and in spite of himself enjoyed the way country girls had of looking at him and remembering him afterward with quickened glances when they met him in the village. Within a year he knew everyone within a radius of twenty miles and was a welcome guest at all country dinner tables. He sold phonographs, too, choosing with care the records to play on the sample he always carried, knowing precisely what would suit this woman and that, collecting with easy nonchalance his down payments, seemingly careless about the necessary balance. Mary rarely asked him about his excursions. Sometimes he told her; more often, as the months and years went on, he did not. She knew with a clarity of mind which never failed her that the man she lived with and loved was not the man whom the farmers and their wives and daughters knew.

There were always the days and the evenings when, except for some hours in the village about the stores and post-office, he was at home. On such days he helped her with her housework, read to her while she sewed, dickered about upstairs with his music. He was always composing something or other which was never completed, trying it over on the piano, good-naturedly irritated because it would not come out as he wanted, dropping it finally to take it up months afterward or, more likely, to forget it altogether. On such days she was always conscious that he belonged to her and, for that time at least, wanted to belong to no one else. Between them then lay what had brought them together, untouched, secure in spite of insecurity. She was his anchorage much as her mother had been, the full tide which kept him afloat and which would always return to lift and steady him.

She reckoned with his inevitable restlessness, knowing that with all her love she could not keep it from him. When days in the country did not suffice, or longer jaunts in the automobile, which to the amazement of Petersport he bought the fourth year of their marriage, failed to dispel a certain feverishness in him, she proposed a journey to New York to see his firm and get new points for his business. He always protested while she was packing his bag for him, but he went all the same, saying good-bye to her a little miserably, throwing himself completely upon her patient knowledge.

The days after his return were always memorable. He stayed at home then or took her with him through the country. He could never seem to get enough of her during those days. He laughed with her over this and that, replanned the trip to Europe they were always planning, anticipated her thoughts and wishes, looked at her with renewed understanding of all they held in common. At these times she experienced such a fresh baptism of her spirit that all disturbing traits in him became again as though they were not. She had no regrets, she thought, as they wound along this road and that, eating their supper on some beach or headland below the circling gulls, watching the sunlight upon a sleepy heron in some quiet cove, returning to the silent house to be together at night.

7

Jim became increasingly popular in village circles. He was what the Maine coast has always called "good company." He knew precisely how to talk, when he was in a talking mood, with all sorts and types of people. He would sit for hours on store platforms on summer evenings or on store counters in the winters in desultory gossip or in chat about this and that, local politics, the crops, the fishing, the summer people. Men liked him even while, as they said to one another, they kept an eye upon him. He was nice to children, taking them fishing for flounders in his rowboat, coasting with them on winter evenings, telling them fascinating stories of his life at sea. They one and all adored him, his kindness toward them and their confidence in him tending to lessen the suspicions of their mothers. The very fact that he was an outsider, a man of wider than village experience, bred an uneasy attraction toward him. He attended church on Sunday mornings and even took upon himself the directing of the choir, an overture which was swift in winning him widespread approval. And as time went on without any of the varied catastrophes which had been prophesied, people began to regard him as a fixture among them, ceased to talk so incessantly about him, and accepted him more or less as one of themselves, yet always with certain reservations both mental and moral.

He joined two of the village lodges, going with some inward amusement through their ceremonies, laughing now and then with Mary over their seriousness and their lavish suppers. Ellen was an avid lodge woman. She held this office and that, was always in great demand as a delegate here and there, cooked, as only Ellen could cook, all manner of provender for the refreshments which invariably accompanied a meeting. She was always heading committees and somehow always seemed to manage it so that Jim was on her committee whatever it might be. Jim sometimes drove her in his automobile to this village and that where there were installations or some other sort of conclave. After all, if one were going to live in a community, he said to Mary, not without an embarrassment which she was quick to detect, one might as well enter at least partially into the life of it. Mary had not the slightest objection, she said; she thought it was exactly the thing for him to do.

She spoke truly when she told him she had no objections. After all, she said wisely to herself, why harbour, or worse express, objections when they would have been but futile? Objections were material, tangible things. They required the bandying about of words, meant discussions and arguments, which she had always disliked and avoided. They would raise obstacles between that which she gave to him and he to her. She knew that only by letting him go his many and diverse ways could she keep the unison of spirit between them. She had known always that his was a nature of conflicts, of ill-assorted parts each with its demands which must be reckoned with and allowed some measure of satisfaction, whereas hers was a nature peculiarly whole, maintained and animated by thoughts and impressions which knew relatively little divergence. And yet she knew, too, that somewhere within those inharmonious parts that made Jim Pendleton was that accord with herself which had brought and which still kept them together. This she relied upon with a faith and a vision which allowed no frustration.

As the years went on, she found herself faced by certain practical necessities of life which demanded common sense and ingenuity. The rural phonograph business died a natural death after three years of spasmodic pursuit. Various other agencies were as short-lived and expensive as they were unsuccessful. A position as pianist in a village orchestra which played for dances in neighbouring towns and country districts lent its services in quelling restlessness but was not particularly lucrative. From its journeyings here and there it brought, moreover, uneasy rumours to her ears, rumours which were never full-fledged but which rather came indirectly, bearing their own suggestions in glances and pregnant silences on the part of interested and sympathetic neighbours. To these she steadfastly declined to give undue credence.

She began to advertise herself as a tutor to the children of summer residents by placing a notice in June on the new

bulletin-board in the post-office, now superintended by a younger
man than old Joel. Parents were surprised as well as relieved to
learn that there was a woman in the village who could teach Latin
and geometry and English and a man who knew French, if he
could be induced to stay in one place long enough to teach it.
Mary gave lessons at her sitting-room table to boys and girls who
had neglected the advantages of their smart schools during the
winter. Some were idle, recalcitrant and spoiled; others were intel-
ligent enough to appreciate her. These latter told their families at
the luncheon-table that Mrs. Pendleton was a far better teacher
than any they had had during the winter and that she had a house
full of beautiful old things from all sorts of queer places. Their
mothers called on her at the end of the season, partly to pay for
her services, partly to see her much-talked-of house.

For by 1912 the rage for antiques was beginning, a rage which
in fifteen years was to deplete the old coast houses and families of
their rightful possessions, nurture dishonesty in collectors of all sorts,
and immeasurably widen the gulf between native and sojourner.
Mary's visitors found their eyes straying from her face, which they
thought undeniably superior, and her advice concerning the minds
of their children to the furnishings of her rooms, her tall clock in
the hall which had marked off the lives of four generations of
Peterses, her mirrors, her ladder-backed chairs, the Currier and Ives
upon her walls, the copper lustre and sandwich glass visible through
the glass doors of her dining-room cupboard. They managed to
convey to her in a well-bred manner that there was a growing
demand for anything she might find superfluous and that they
themselves were not averse to making her offers for this and that.

"I suppose you know there are museum pieces in this house,
Mrs. Pendleton. Of course, I don't suppose you'd ever want to part
with any of them. You have your own sentiments naturally toward
old family things. But if at any time you should—"

Mary did not wait for the time, for she knew it would never come. Necessity in her life had always set aside decision. She went first to her attic, exploring corners stored with old furniture, looking through trunks and chests. There were things there, spool-beds, chests of drawers, andirons, a warming-pan or two, mute reminders of Peterses who had used them long ago. There were china dogs, mop-eared and staring, spreading porcelain vases with flutings of gold leaf, candle-moulds, demi-Johns, ships' lanterns, mirror frames. There were pieces of shell-work under glass, odds and ends of foreign embroideries, some ships cunningly contrived in bottles, a child's tea-set quite intact, which, she remembered, her grandmother had received as a birthday present in Calcutta and which she herself had been allowed to use once on some state occasion when she was remaining over a voyage at home. She would sell these first, she concluded. After all, there was no one to leave them to, and their departure would make no inroads upon her rooms downstairs. She sold them to Jewish dealers, dark, impatient, callous men with dirty money in their wallets, who drove hard bargains and argued insufferably with her over the things she would not sell them. The news that she was ridding herself of her possessions travelled rapidly by some sort of underground railway, and the following summer there was hardly a week without its eager would-be purchaser.

Certain women from the city who opened tea-rooms and gift-shops along the coast began to supplement the Jewish dealers. Their cleverly contrived signs brought more customers if there were antiques to be examined as well as tea to be consumed on the verandas of the cottages and old farmhouses which they had bought. They were more pleasant to talk with, appreciative, interested even in the things she would not part with. But they were persistent also, returning after she had thought they were gone for good, persuading her to take even from the downstairs rooms this and that, whose absence would not be particularly noticeable.

"There's one thing you can be glad about, Mrs. Pendleton," they said, as they stowed away their new acquisitions on the back seats of their high Ford cars. "These won't go into some dirty downtown junk shop in New York to be pawed over by people who don't know or care anything about them. We sell directly to customers who really want them for their own homes and who know their value. Anyway, it's nicer, isn't it, to have the things one cares for go to people who'll appreciate their full value, who'll know what they've meant in the past?"

Jim made no comments upon her new venture. He always managed to be out of the house if possible when such bargainings were going on. She understood his irritation when he missed this and that, the small inlaid table in the hall which had brought her twenty-five dollars, the old sofa between the kitchen windows which, she told him, had as a matter of fact always been in her way. When he looked at her after these discoveries, she saw in his eyes the knowledge that his prophecies of eight years ago on the night when he had brought her the little fiddle were being fulfilled. She saw, too, staring at her the more bitter admission of his failure and defeat. After such moments she found herself forever casting about in her mind for some way to save him from his own disillusionment.

They had their hours still of mutual dependence and larger understanding. She knew that he loved her, that he had found in her and still found the one anchorage for him against capricious winds and overwhelming tides. She understood precisely as he understood, only without his bitterness, that the things which had captured, which would always capture his roving fancy—notions of easy money, unworthy amusements, women here and there— were but troublings of surface water. They still had their days together, days when he threw himself pathetically upon her forbearance, hurting her as he could never hurt her by his waywardness. Ponta Delgata was always there for him, obscured and mist-hung at times as it might be. Cadiz was always there for her, undimmed and shining.

But she knew also that surface waters can devastate, and her thoughts continued to cast about for some way to save him from himself.

8

The winter of 1913 and 1914 was a hard one for Petersport. The village had not known in years so much sickness. Whooping-cough followed measles, and colds among the older inhabitants seemed constantly developing into pneumonia. The doctor, himself no longer young, hardly knew what it was to get a full night's sleep, and his successor to Old Nell had quite forgotten what it used to be like to have her harness off her shaggy back. The doctor drove through all weathers to this farmhouse and that, over frozen roads in his rickety old buggy, through snow drifts in his smelly old sleigh. He was in such haste that he could not take his newspaper along as usual; and no sooner had he returned home than he set out again on village calls.

Mrs. Kimball caught a cold in late February, largely, Ellen declared, because of her frenzied precautions to avoid it. The cold lingered, tenacious of its comfortable lodging in Mrs. Kimball's large frame, adamant against hot lemonade, feet-soakings, and generous dosings of all local remedies. Mrs. Kimball's panic did not encourage or hasten its departure. She knew she was going to die, she said a dozen times a day; she had had a feeling since the August sale that she would never live to see another; and the doctor, studying his thermometer one cold night in the Kimball kitchen, was beginning to give heed to her forebodings.

Ellen in a red-flannel wrapper watched him as he replaced the thermometer in his vest pocket. Ellen was not at her best as a nurse. She was obviously nervous herself, and she did not like the blunt way the doctor always took with her.

"I've had an afternoon of it," she said. "She's been talking about the August sale for hours, thinks she's there selling fancy work."

"That August sale," observed the doctor, "causes enough delirium in this village among *well* folks."

There was something in his manner that made Ellen more nervous.

"Is she worse?" she asked him. "If she is, I'm sure I don't know what I'll do here all alone."

"Well," said the doctor, "there's a lot of people alone with sick folks just now in this village. The last woman who can nurse anyone was placed long ago."

"I asked you if she was worse," said Ellen again. He really was trying, she thought, had been ever since she could remember anything about him.

The doctor proceeded to light his pipe.

"I guess perhaps I'll stay around a bit," he said, taking a chair by the kitchen table. "You give her the stuff I've mixed in that glass, and we'll see how she acts to it. Just keep your head, Ellen. Nobody else wants it."

Ellen was ready to scream at him with irritation.

"I wish you'd answer my question," she said. "It's no good putting me off. I guess I know she's sick better than any one else. Is she worse, I asked you?"

"Seventy-two's a bad age for pneumonia," said the doctor, puffing speculatively at his pipe, "and she hasn't got the shape for it either. There's not enough space between her lungs and her stomach, and her heart's kicking up a bit."

"Pneumonia!" cried Ellen. "This is the first time I've heard of that. You've never said she had pneumonia!"

"She's had it for four days," said the doctor, "and it's about time we knew what its plans are, one way or another. Now don't you get all flustered, Ellen. It won't do any good. I'll go around later and get Mary Pendleton to come over and stay tonight. She'll keep her head and be here in case you need anybody."

Ellen stood in the middle of the kitchen floor, the tumbler in her hand. With all her nervous dread she was wishing she dared tell the doctor to suggest Jim's coming also. It would give her confidence, she thought, just to have a man in the house. But, she decided, she did not dare tell him. He was a shrewd old fellow with a keen eye out for the implications of things, an eye which Ellen did not care just then to face.

"There's one thing," she warned him, moving toward the door. "Don't for heaven's sake let her know she's in any danger. If she is, don't ever let on to her. She couldn't stand it for a minute."

"That's one idea," said the doctor, "that I've never entertained, not for the fraction of a second."

Jim came with Mary at midnight. He sat with Ellen on the sofa in the sitting-room while Mary took her turn with Mrs. Kimball. The doctor had been hurriedly called away for someone in even worse straits. Jim was kind to Ellen, and she liked to have him beside her. Now that she was in such trouble, there seemed to be no reason why his manner toward her should not be the affectionate one which in times past she had sometimes uneasily felt she should repulse more than she was given to repulsing.

Mrs. Kimball died suddenly at two o'clock while Mary was sitting by her bed. She died more quietly than she had ever lived, with the least fuss she had ever made about anything. Even the August sale had gone clean out of her mind two hours before the end.

The doctor was not surprised when Jim had fetched him from another village house.

"Pneumonia is the old people's friend," he said to the three of them in the Kimball sitting room.

He wondered as he said the words how often he had said them in his long years of practice. They always filled in awkward moments when one had to say something or other.

## 9

Jim and Mary rallied round Ellen in her trouble. Ellen was the sort of person who expected rallying round. Added to her sorrow, she said, were more problems than she could ever solve alone and unaided. There was that great house in the village in which she positively rattled round all by herself. And besides there was the farm, badly rented since John's death to people who did not keep things up as they should. It made her positively crazy to see things at such loose ends, the lawn uncared for, the garden grown up to grass, machinery left out in all weathers. She asked Jim now and then to drive her up there, so that she might see how ill-kept the place was and get his advice on what she should do.

She could not sleep at night from worrying about all that was on her mind. Moreover, although she knew everyone thought she was foolish, she was uneasy all alone. It was awful to go to bed late enough so that she thought she could sleep through the night and then to wake at two or three o'clock, nervous as a cat. Mary came to the rescue occasionally during the spring and summer by asking her to sleep at the brick house. People said she must be out of her head to do such a thing, blind as a bat, they said, but she did it all the same.

Ellen was at her best on the evenings she was with the Pendletons. All the brittle, designing things which were a part of Ellen's nature seemed to be absent then. She could not do enough to show her gratitude to Jim and Mary. She was quiet and subdued at supper and later in the sitting room, gossiped less about her neighbours, seemed genuinely interested in things larger than herself. Seeing her there, Mary was always remembering her as she was at John's house on the cold night when he had brought her home with him after he had made his last payment on his land. She wondered if there were perhaps not another side to Ellen which nothing in her life had hitherto brought out. Had she been born off Singapore in the *Nautilus* where Mary had superseded her, would that have made a difference to Ellen?

In her own house she could not have callers enough. She urged them to bring their sewing and sit with her on the porch in the warm afternoons. They helped take up her time, she said, and gave her something to think about. Jim had the habit of running in to see her when he went down each morning for the mail. Her neighbours watched him as he limped up the walk to her neat back door and always knew to the minute just what time it was when he came out again. When they came to see her later with their work-bags and mentioned him cautiously, perhaps a bit expectantly, Ellen was at once nonchalant and evasive.

Jim went to New York just after the war had started. He had been uneasy for days in early August, reading the papers eagerly, ordering one from New York so that he might know better just what was going on in Europe. To Mary during those weeks he seemed to belong less to the coast than ever, less to the Pendletons, less even to her. She knew why he was going to the city. She was sorry for the wretchedness that drew his face as he said good-bye to her, but she was glad as she went about her work that circumstances had at last found a way out for him.

Given three days to prepare herself, she was not in the least surprised or seemingly disturbed when he came home and told her what he had decided to do. He sat opposite her at the late supper she had prepared and told her quickly as though he wanted above everything else to have things over and done with.

"I'm going to France," he said. "Some other men I know are going. They want extras over there for ambulances and hospitals and things, and they say I'll work in especially well because I know the language and the country. It's the best thing I can do, Mary—for both of us. You know that as well as I. There's no use—going into things, I suppose?"

She poured him another cup of tea. "No," she said, "not the least use in the world. I'm glad you're going."

"What'll you do here?"

"I'll go back to teaching for a year anyway. I went to see the school board yesterday. I heard there was a vacancy they weren't expecting. They say they're glad to have me. That will take care of me all right. You don't need to worry."

"I've never had to worry about you. Maybe if I had, things would have been different."

"No, they wouldn't."

He turned away from her, staring into the fire she had lighted.

"It'll take money, I suppose, at least some to get me started. But maybe it's cheap at the price."

"I've got money. I sold the old secretary yesterday from the back living room. It brought a big price. Grace Wilbur bought it, Mrs. Hawley. She said she'd wanted it ever since she saw it three years ago while I was teaching her daughter."

He hitched uneasily in his chair, and drummed with his fingers upon the table.

"That's the last thing I wanted you to do, Mary," he said a bit testily.

"It's the last thing I wanted to do myself. But sometimes things have to be faced precisely as they are."

"That can't be hard for you or at least not a new thing. You've faced them for eight years precisely as they are. That's why, I suppose, it's no use to talk about them. I can't tell you anything you don't know already."

"No, dear," she said, smiling at him. "Whatever we do, let's not talk."

He started to leave the table, crumpling his napkin absent-mindedly into his pocket in a habit peculiar to him. She held out her hand for it, and he gave it to her, meeting her eyes for the moment.

"There's one thing I've got to ask," he said. "Please tell me the truth. Are you sorry, Mary?"

It was the last time he saw the old familiar light flooding her face.

"No," she said. "I'm not sorry. I'll never be sorry all my life. You can depend on that."

She carried the dishes to the kitchen. He did not help her as usual. As she washed them, she saw him through the open doorway in the dim light of her mother's room. He was standing with his hands sunk deep in his pockets and his back toward her below the old portrait from Antwerp. Before she had finished, he called to her.

"I think I'll walk down and tell Ellen," he said. "I told the stage-driver coming home, and she's bound to hear of it before bed-time. She might be—a bit upset if I didn't tell her myself."

10

Jim Pendleton never got to France. On the night before he was to leave he drove Ellen Peters to a lodge installation fourteen miles away. There did not seem to be any other way for her to get there, he told Mary, and he had promised weeks earlier to take her. They never reached the installation. Where they went in the interim no one ever knew. Certain inhabitants of Petersport, also in the town to which they had been bound, had seen them there somewhat past midnight, evidently on the point of starting for home. The same persons, driving their teams and singles along the homeward road, found their overturned and wrecked automobile at the bottom of a steep hill six miles from Petersport. It had struck, evidently with terrific force, the piles of a bridge leading across a salt marsh which the tide filled when it was high. The driver, they concluded at the hastily summoned and equally hastily dismissed inquest, had either lost his head completely and driven straight into disaster, or else at the moment, being completely engrossed in other matters, had had no head to lose. People in general were inclined toward the latter view of the situation.

He, they thought, was killed instantly, a calamity in itself odd since drivers were usually the ones to escape injury. They found him curved around the third pile of the open bridge, an unpleas-ant sight enough even in the uncertain light just before dawn. Ellen Peters lay in a gully opposite, within three feet of the incoming tide. When they lifted her, she was seemingly conscious enough both to cry out and to explain little. She did not know what had happened, she said, or why anything should have hap-pened. She was sure they were going along safely and quietly enough. She had bones enough broken to take one hospital a year to mend those that could be mended. One hip was smashed beyond the hope of its ever holding her up again.

Those who had driven ahead through the early morning to tell Mrs. Pendleton said they had never seen a woman like her. They found her up and about her house at six o'clock. If she was anxious over the fact that her husband had not returned, she did not show it, nor did she appear shocked or surprised when they told her what they had to tell. Naturally they made it as easy as they could, not for a moment suggesting by their manner the strangeness of her husband's absence from her on the night before he was to leave for France.

## 11

Mary Pendleton sold the brick house in 1917 to some new summer residents from Cleveland. She might have afforded to live in it, but she could never afford to keep it up. Like all old houses it was constantly requiring attention, new shingles, underpinning here and there, work on trees and garden. She got what she thought a good price for it, which she was in no position to decline. She might have done even better could she have held on a little longer until the added prosperity following the war years had begun. But she was glad to get what she did.

She managed the sale of Ellen's house for her also. That went to a shrewd village woman who opened it as a boarding-house for students in music. Petersport had steadily grown as a summer musical centre. The leader of a New York quartet, well known throughout the country, had opened a summer course for students in stringed instruments and had lured thereto all sorts of young people, Jews and Italians and what not, who must be fed and housed somewhere. The proceeds from the two sales made quite a respectable sum for Mary and Ellen.

For Mary could not see herself deserting Ellen in the crisis that had befallen her. Ellen was not in the least resigned to the invalidism that faced her all her life. This and that woman had taken care of her since she had come from the hospital and been placed in a wheel-chair in her living-room. One and all annoyed Ellen. They could not keep house to suit her, were no cooks comparable to herself; they went out too much, were awkward and hasty in waiting on her and in helping her from her chair to her bed at night. Mary alone satisfied her, did not get on her nerves. It was Ellen who conceived and furthered the idea of their both selling out and going to the farm in which, since John had made no will, Mary herself held a part.

It would be quiet at the farm, Ellen said, and away from things which she was now completely out of anyway. The summer people who thronged the village annoyed her because they paid no attention to her; and she was completely fed up on her neighbours. Those who wanted to see her, and they were few enough, she said, could surely drive five or six miles to do so, especially since even Petersport natives now had cars of their own. The constant scraping of violins in practice from the houses which rented rooms got on her nerves. She had never cared for music anyway. They could keep chickens on the farm, sell eggs and broilers, and maybe have something of a garden as well. And she could be where she had once been happy. For by some extraordinary concatenations within her own mind, amusing to Mary in spite of herself, Ellen had actually become convinced that she had been happy during her married life.

What was more, their money would go further there than in the village, she said, now that prices were so high for even the neccssities. They would not need to look so well, keep so dressed up. With careful planning they had enough to live on. She would really try, she said, crying a bit as she did so, not to be too much of a nuisance to Mary. No one understood better than she that she had ruined Mary's life, though, God knew, she had been innocent of meaning to do so. She hoped Mary knew that. And no one knew so well as she that Mary was the only soul living whom she cared for, and who could be of any service to her.

After hours of such talk from Ellen, Mary had no alternative
to offer. Ellen's life stretched ahead of her, probably years of existence, barren, meagre, unsatisfied, because of Ellen herself. Her
own life was none of these things wherever it was spent. It was
still free and stable. It did not matter at all where she lived.

She spent days again in getting John's house ready for Ellen.
She had the shaggy grass in the neglected garden cut and mown;
she painted tubs for other geraniums along the path leading to the
front door; she sowed marigolds and zinnias, nasturtiums and
morning-glories. She had the house newly painted and the old
rooms freshened and put to rights. From the brick house she
brought the things she could not bear to sell and arranged them in
the rooms she had set apart particularly for herself—her mother's
four-posted bed, sundry chairs, tables, and chests of drawers, all the
books, the Antwerp portrait, Sarah Peters' East Indian china. She
sold the farm machinery she would not want or need, arranged
with a nearby farmer to take over their field space and with a
good-natured boy, whose father had once been a pupil of hers, to
do their chores. She bought a cow, a horse for necessary journeys
to town; she repaired and enlarged the old chicken-house. She
might even keep bees, she thought. She liked the notion of honey
being slowly made from the blossoms on John's apple trees; and
she had never outgrown her pleasure in seeing the sunlight stream
through a glass jar of it on the breakfast table.

By the late spring of 1918 they were moved and settled. Ellen
had her wheel-chair by the front windows of the sitting-room where
she could see the garden and whatever passing there was along the
road before the house. The meadows stretched beyond the road,
green and waving, bright with buttercups and daisies, hawk-weed
and Queen Anne's lace. Ellen could wheel herself easily into the
sunny dining room which she had once so desired. The old dining
room which John had liked as a boy was now her bedroom. She still

complained of its lack of sunshine although she said sensibly enough that it did not matter much since she was in it only to sleep.

Mary had the upstairs rooms to herself. She kept the sunny front one, which had been John's and Ellen's, for her sitting room, placing in it her books, her father's logs, the Antwerp portrait, the pictures of the ships in which the Peterses had sailed. She wished she could glimpse the sea from its windows but was daily grateful for the boulder in John's high field from the top of which the whole harbour stretched distantly before her to the Mt. Desert hills. They were very snug and comfortable, she thought, once she was through with the moving and the settling, and she had always liked the country.

The land would still hold its being, its indestructible sustenance of mind as well as of body; the hills would still retain their security. There would be daily surprises in sky and wind and weather. The violet of the awakening birches in April, spreading mist-like over the ridges, would be only less beautiful than their bare purple splendour of late autumn. There would be still days in October when the yellow leaves of beech and the scarlet of maple would glow with inner light. There would be corn pricking the wet May soil and sleepy, rotund pumpkins strewing its untidy field when the year had run its course. The snow would come. John's elm, now shadowing his field after fifteen years of robust life, would flower in the spring. Such things as these, she knew, did not exist by and for themselves.

Ellen did her utmost to be reasonable and decent. She could use her hands, and she used them almost hourly in knitting and crocheting for some Portland agency which paid her for her work. She made numberless jackets and socks for babies, hoods and carriage robes. She braided rug rags, yards upon yards of tight and even braiding, which Mary sewed into rugs. These brought good prices from summer people once they had learned where such work could be obtained, and their visits to the farmhouse always afforded Ellen exciting interruptions in long and quiet days. Being Ellen, she had her hours of bitterness, of querulous complainings against her fate, but taken by and large she was far more amenable than Mary had hoped for or imagined.

Even had she been more trying, it would not have mattered so much to Mary. She was forever conscious that she lived two lives, the effulgence of one so irradiating the pale light of the other that it was often dimmed or put completely out of sight. There was her life with Ellen, material, tangible, restrictive, its demands continuous even when they were pleasantly made; and there was her life without Ellen, omnipresent as Ellen was. Whether this other life was one of voluntary or involuntary abstraction (possessions which will ever be the most intact and sound of social virtues) she could not have said. She knew only that she was constantly aware of it within and without her, in her thoughts, in the things she loved and valued, in her past which had placed its own imperishable perception upon thoughts and things. She could perform her daily tasks for Ellen, menial, sometimes ugly and humiliating, and yet herself be anywhere under the sun. She could talk trivialities with Ellen for hours on end without being for a moment touched by one of them. She lived what most would call, what, indeed, most did call, a gruelling and circum-scribed existence, knowing full well it might go on for years; and yet, true to her heritage, she was forever a spectator of it rather than a sharer in it, knowing better that it had no power to make the least inroad upon the other and larger life she knew.

## 12

Her first summer in the country held for her a surprising wealth, a plenitude and richness which she had never before adequately realized and which succeeding summers only deepened and glorified. Summer in a village, rural as it might be, held nothing in comparison. In the open country, close to, even upon the teeming and ripening earth, the summer months were known with a difference. She had lived before upon the farm through the serenity of autumn, through the cold solemnity of winter, through the expectancy of spring, but never before had she experienced in all its intimacy the width and the depth of summer, its lavish pageantry, the alchemy of its life and strength.

She was up early in the morning, two hours before Ellen was awake. She saw the burst of early light upon the hills and fields, the dew upon the grass. She caught the prodigality of life itself, which, having climbed the high, slow staircase of the year to its very top, now flung itself upon a waiting world. Earth, she understood, revealed in summer secrets magical enough to give to men and women who lived upon it the life of the Immortals.

She worked in the garden in the morning freshness, turning the cool, damp soil about the roots of her flowers, crumbling it in her hands. The summer birds put into their singing a contented fullness absent in the spring. Their families were reared and off, sweeping over the high grass for the flies which sparkled on timothy and redtop. Purple finches filled the air with their ecstasies; tree swallows and bluebirds and wrens quarrelled over her birdhouses; thrushes called from thickets far into the August mornings and white-throats sounded from distant pasture slopes their plaintive whistles. Later when her work was done in the house and the sun was hot and high she worked again, her knees against the warm earth whose rhythm she could feel entering her very body. Even the thick, pulsating stalks of weeds put life into her hands as she pulled them from the heavy soil—sorrel and plantain, shepherd's purse and chickweed, Roman wormwood with its acrid scent, the tenacious strangling roots of red clover crunching as they left the ground. Women, she thought, belonged on the earth even more than men. She could not stand with hoe and rake as most men stood in their garden rows. She wanted rather to feel beneath her knees and hands the grass and soil.

The hours of every day in summer rose as it were to a veritable peak of almost feverish activity. It was as though they had not time enough to fling abroad their manifold life. The air itself streamed with energy, mounting through the hours of the morning to the hot noons of July and August when for a single hour, as though under a full tide, the land lay beneath it bathed in light and strength. In this hour on July noons the haymakers rested under the trees, smoking their pipes or sleeping with their broad-brimmed straw hats across their faces. The grass lay in swaths beneath the sun, and the swallows circled above it looking for insects to pierce with their sharp beaks.

As she gathered wild strawberries, separating them carefully from the tangled grass of field and meadow, she became aware of the life in the grass itself, in the thickness of its stiff points and in the plumed sprays of that which flowered. She became aware, too, of all the living things which leapt about within it or drifted in the air above it, flies and bees and butterflies. She saw the light concentrated for an instant upon wing textures and glowing scales. Such a luxury and splendour of very being, such an elasticity of growth, she had never known before.

In summer even the nights were alive. The travailling earth knew no rest in its labour. Mist rose from the warm, sun-drenched fields into the cool air. The garden soil steamed from within and caught the dew which fell from without upon it. Through July nights whip-poor-wills called and answered one another, their sharp cries keeping the pastures awake. Fireflies gleamed over the fields and among the trees suggesting warmth and light in their fitful shining. Over the marsh land beyond the meadows will-o'-the-wisps now

and again glowed among the cat-tails and rushes. The stars were
low and bright. In August the insects hummed and trilled through
the night air. The sun, bursting over the ridges, found a sleepless
land ever increasing in life and strength.

The most common of July roadsides quivered all day in its
prodigal growth. Wild roses covered the rocks and flaming day
lilies blossomed in the damp ditches. Meadow-sweet and steeple-
bush, sarsaparilla and ferns, blackberries, St. John's wort, and
loosestrife flourished in a confusion of plenty from the most
unpromising of soil. Fireweed and evening primroses bent their
gaudy spikes before the light wind. Even the baked clay and sand
bordering the road flowered in yarrow and may-weed and clover.
Elder flaunted its scarlet cones among the thickets where thrushes
scurried and sang.

Summer, she learned, knew no bounds, no self-restraint. It was
the only season with a scent of its own and a sound. It could not
be contained, could not offer itself only to the eyes. In its brief but
overwhelming life it must use all means to enforce its immortality
upon all in unison with it. She smelled the ferns in their lush
growth in roadside ditches, by log fences, and by the brown, sunshot pools of the pasture brooks. In the night she drew in the
scent of dew-laden hay, so different from that which lay beneath
the sun; in the morning she smelled the hot, sweet scent of
syringas and the moist heavy smell of the garden loam after a
night of August showers. The warmed pastures in early afternoon
filled the shimmering air with the breath of pennyroyal and bayberry, ripe blueberries and juniper, fir balsam and checkerberry.

As to the sound of summer, that was peculiar unto itself. She
was forever trying to explain it, and it was forever eluding her. It
was no sound which could be discerned or labelled, not the midsummer hum over the hayfields, not the sound of wind in the full
trees or swinging grass, not the whirr of insects or the hum of bees

and wasps. It was instead a tremor in the air itself, a vibration almost visible to the eye as well in multitudinous motes and rays of light, a resonance which seemed to come from the very earth under the fervour of the sunlight. She thought sometimes of the tiny sympathetic strings on the old *viola d'amore*, once in her house, which provided overtones for the strings above them. The vibrations from earth to air were such strings, she concluded, only instead of overtones they were undertones, and yet distinct to one who listened.

The air of winter held no such sound. In itself it was soundless. Sleigh-bells might echo within it, branches might creak or crack, the snow might fill it with all healing sounds; but the cold air itself received no vibrations from a frozen earth. In autumn the dying earth was voiceless to the air; in spring its voice was stirring, yet unborn. But in summer the life within it came forth in a thousand pulsating rhythms to meet the light and heat that played upon it.

She sat in meadows and pastures and heard this sound filling the air. And summer which had seemed to her before the least of the seasons, the most obvious, the least suggestive, became to her the proof of immortality, the spur to faith and hope, the fulfillment of life itself.

## 13

In the early nineteen-twenties a veritable passion for hooked rugs swept the coast from Kittery to New Brunswick and Nova Scotia. Towns and villages were combed to their outskirts. The most rural of housewives in gray farmhouses miles from main-travelled roads grew accustomed to automobiles bumping over the rocks in their pasture lanes, to hearing unfamiliar voices in city accents saying at their back doors,

"I just called to see if by any chance you had one or two of the old hooked rugs for sale. I'm trying to find some for my summer cottage."

Rugs which lay on the yellow floors of their shabby parlours and which their grandmothers had made, rugs frayed and torn in their kitchens and bedrooms, rugs relegated as useless to barn lofts and outhouses—any rugs brought a price, absurd to the buyer who now and then stifled a qualm or two, bewildered in its generosity to persons who had practically no ready money at all. Black rugs with long-eared yellow dogs upon them brought a glint into the eye of the purchaser, who never allowed herself to be over-enthusiastic; rugs in squares and triangles, grays and blacks and whites outlined in red, were also in great demand; rugs with a centre of roses, rugs with kittens lapping milk, any rug at all, tattered though it might be, which had a ship upon it. To many of the owners the strange part of it was that the older the rug, the more enthusiasm was evinced over it. Dollar bills, two-dollar bills, sometimes even a five-dollar bill crossed the rickety thresholds of country doors, making their receivers rejoice and determine to purchase a congoleum from the fascinating pages of Sears Roebuck or Montgomery Ward.

Many of the rugs never saw the floors of the summer cottages for which they had presumably been purchased. They were instead washed and mended by expert hands and put up for sale in gift-shops and tea-rooms, at flower shows or summer bazaars, where they brought ten, twenty, even thirty times their purchase price. The names of their makers, even of their designers, who had sat over their frames and tables in the mid-eighteen hundreds, were irretrievably lost. On the whole, it did not matter much, the original buyers said to themselves as they mended the frayed edges. In most cases their owners did not know enough to appreciate them and in their hearts much preferred congoleum.

## Mary Peters

Once the supply of old rugs was exhausted, enterprising Maine housewives began to make new ones. Braided rugs were for the time superseded. Frames were hauled with great clatter from attic corners; piece-bags and closets and chests were ransacked for material which when washed could be cut or torn into rags fit for hooking. Designs might be had in plenty from cheap magazines circulated freely throughout the countryside, *The Maine Farmer, Farm and Home, The Farmer's Wife*. Furthermore in certain neighbourhoods there were discovered old copies of *Godey* and of *Harper's Bazaar*, all of which gave up their treasures throughout a village. Occasionally a woman could and did make her own designs to the envy of her neighbours and much to the distinct advantage of her own pocketbook.

Mary Pendleton, refusing quietly when the besiegers struck her driveway to sell the rugs her grandmother had hooked on land and sea, decided to spend some winter months in hooking those which she would gladly sell. She and Ellen, tenaciously set against the depletion of their principal, needed money always to eke out a slender income. Mary required no magazines to stir her ready imagination. She could make her own designs. She made them; and before one summer was past, she had become known for her rugs in a dozen summer colonies along the coast.

Through the tiny squares of the burlap stretched upon her frames, she drew with her hook the first fifteen years of her life, translating into rug rags the things she had known and loved. She hooked a merchant ship on a dark blue sea, no staid ship but one with sails set before a wind which became visible even as one looked upon them. She hooked a flight of birds moving above a gray ocean toward a distant point of land. She hooked the port of San Francisco with the mountains of the Coast Range beyond it and the palms of the Java coast beneath a tropical moon. Under her fingers Valparaiso rose on its hills above its horned harbour.

She hooked sampans laden with bright-coloured fruits, manned by squat men in bamboo hats, and moving across the brown and muddy waters of Chinese river-mouths. She hooked lighthouses, red-sailed fishing craft in foreign ports, surf breaking upon a reef.

Her callers were amazed at the variety of her subjects and at her skill.

"Extraordinary, Mrs. Pendleton!" they said. "But what we want to know is where on earth you got your ideas, way off up here."

"Out of her own head," interrupted Ellen then. "She went to sea when she was a child. I thought everyone knew that Mary had gone to sea."

"To sea?" they said. "I didn't know there were actually people left nowadays even in Maine who had been to sea. Then that old town there is an actual place. Just imagine that! Don't forget that, my dear, when we show our rug this winter."

Once in a cold January when they were completely shut in by snow and Ellen's fate sat more bitterly than usual upon her, Mary hooked above a blue sea a red-roofed village, its church and huddled houses clinging to high hills above them. Beyond it were pineapple fields of pale green. In a way all her own she shaded her colours so that one somehow caught the idea that it was early morning over the strange, foreign little town.

"That's a good one," said Ellen watching it grow day by day. "In my opinion that's the best one yet. It ought to fetch a top price. What is that town anyway?"

"Just a place I heard of once years ago."

"Hasn't it a name?"

"Not that I know of," said Mary. "If it has, I've forgotten it."

This rug she refused to sell in spite of Ellen's excited comments upon it to eager purchasers. She did not even show it, if she could help herself, but kept it in her own room beside her bed.

She became an expert in dyeing bits of wool, working hours to get the exact shade she needed. When her piece-bags and closets were exhausted of old material, she bought odds and ends from the factories and coloured them to suit herself. The knuckles of her fingers and the palms of her hands grew rough and calloused by hook and burlap, but she had never in her life felt more free.

After she had been for two years at her work she began upon a rug which she meant to work on at odd moments for any length of time, not anxious as to its completion. She cleared a room in the ell of its furniture and erected there a larger frame than she had ever used, a frame with cross pieces and understops to hold it closely together, for she needed above all space for this hooking. Once her design was made, she began her work, giving a few minutes or an hour or two a day as she could. It was pleasant to work alone in the low western room with the afternoon sun streaming in across the ridges and open fields. The wool she used was the best she could procure, new wool which she bought undyed and dyed herself to be sure she had the exact colour.

From the brown burlap the sea rose slowly, deep blue as the Atlantic neared the Mediterranean, and set here and there by all manner of ships, their rigging as complete as she could make it. There arose, too, as time went on, a high, white city above a white wall which kept out the sea—a city of towers and domes and minarets, so outlined in darker wools, so shaded with bits of pale blue and palest yellow, that one not only saw their relation to one another but received as well the indelible impression that the city was bathed in sunlight. Three years went into its making, odds and ends of days when she could leave Ellen by herself, hours stolen from the hooking of the rugs that had been ordered. When it was done, she spread it upon the floor of her sitting-room below the Antwerp portrait and the pictures of sailing ships.

## 14

There was hardly a day in July and August when people did not come to look at rugs and often leave their orders for the winter. Times were good and money was freely spent. Ellen was happier in the summer. Persons who returned after one visit often brought her delicacies, flowers, fruit, and books, and she got from their presence and their gifts not only the attention she craved but things, she said, to think about all winter.

One afternoon in September when they had thought most visitors had gone for good, Mrs. Hawley, she who had been Grace Wilbur, drove her automobile into their driveway. She had come, both to make a charitable call on Ellen, which she sometimes did, and to order some rugs for her daughter who was to be married in the spring. Mrs. Hawley was a handsome woman, well set up, well dressed. She managed this interlude in the multifarious affairs of her day with hasty good nature.

"Barbara's gone and got herself engaged," she said to Ellen after she had placed her order. She said it with an inclusive glance at Mary who had once taught Barbara her summer Latin. "She went to Harvard to some house party or other last November and completely lost her heart to a young law student there. It's terrible to bring up children nowadays! You just never know what they are about one minute of the time, especially if you live the life I have to. I guess this young man's all right enough. Mr. Hawley and I like him, though we'd made up our minds rather that she'd marry a New York man. His family comes from Boston, though I think his father said they came from Maine originally—way back some time. Gardiner's his name. His father's out there in the car. Mr. Hawley met him in Bar Harbor last week and asked him over for the weekend since he thought we might as well begin to get acquainted. And then whatever did he do but go back to New

York and leave him on my hands? He's all right but rather quiet, and I'm at my wits' end to know what to talk to him about."

"Bring him in here if you like," said Ellen. "Maybe he'd like to see the rugs."

"I'm afraid he'd like them too well. He's daft on ships and things, and we really can't stay. Some people in his family, I believe, used to go to sea. Suppose you come out and meet him, Mrs. Pendleton, while I have my little visit out with Ellen. You went to sea yourself, didn't you? Anyway, I know your husband did."

Mary went to meet Mr. Gardiner. He had already left the car and was looking appreciatively at the beautiful lines of the old house. He was a tall man of fifty with clear blue eyes and a fine head. He seemed completely at home with Mary once he had looked at her.

They went across the yard together and through the orchard to a bench under the yellowing trees. The apples were ripe above them and the ground strewn with windfalls.

"Maybe you can help me out," he said. "Mrs. Hawley says you used to live in the village. You taught her daughter, I think, one summer. My father had a younger brother who sailed as first officer with a man from here, Peters the name was. I was just a youngster then, and I barely remember him. He was a fine fellow, went to Harvard, but couldn't for the life of him keep away from the sea. He was lost off San Francisco in 1886, and the captain, too. I remember how impressed my father was with a letter the captain's wife wrote him. I've tried to get a line on things ever since I came two days ago—that's one reason I came, in fact—but this summer colony keeps one rushing even in September. One might far better live on Park Avenue."

Mary Pendleton's heart quickened as she told him. She might have been fourteen again, she thought, reading Shakespeare on the quarterdeck in the sun. She told him all about young Mr. Gardiner, his hatred of steam, the geranium in his cabin, even about the robin in the Sargasso. The years slipped away from her as though they were not. She talked not of the past but of the present.

"I loved him as a little girl," she said simply, unsurprised at her saying it to someone who should have been a stranger. "I loved him as I've never loved anyone all my life."

Until that moment she had not known how true it was.

The man who sat beside her in the orchard felt as though he had known her always. She represented what his people had represented, knew what his people had known. Half-forgotten pride in his own heritage came beating back upon him. They talked of ships and of what their voyages over the earth had meant to those who voyaged in them and to the towns and villages from whence they came.

"My grandfather sailed himself when he was young," he said. "That's why he had nothing to say when his last son threw up school-mastering for the sea. Sailing made men, he always said, as nothing else could make them."

It might have been Mr. Gardiner himself speaking in the creaking cabin below the noisy tumbler rack. She heard again through the open ports the continual wash of the sea, the whine of stout new cordage, the whistle of the wind through taut and straining sails. She smelt again the smell of tar and hemp and salt.

"And now I see that it made women, too," he concluded quietly.

"I'm sorry the coast has had to change so," he continued after a moment, "sorry that these things are only memories." He looked at her with quick perception. "It must be hard for you to see strangers in your old houses, to have your village overrun by outsiders. I don't suppose people who come here, like Mrs. Hawley for instance, know much about the history of a place like this even though they take up their residence here to escape city taxes. Perhaps they don't even care much."

"No," she said, "I'm afraid they don't. They're not really to blame, I suppose. They have their own interests, and they don't come largely from New England. Still it would be helpful all around and save a lot of misunderstanding if they knew a bit more about the best of us." She smiled at him. "If you asked Mrs. Hawley, for instance, what sort of people Petersport had produced even in its best days, you wouldn't get a very flattering account of us, I'm afraid, or a very truthful one for that matter. To most summer people the coast of Maine has no existence apart from themselves. That's the hard thing about the whole situation."

"My son is going to marry Mrs. Hawley's daughter."

"Maybe then your son can show Mrs. Hawley, if he's at all like you or like the Mr. Gardiner I knew."

He hesitated.

"I don't know about my son," he said. "But perhaps when he comes here next summer, a woman like you could teach him. You seem to know the things that all people ought to know, but don't."

Mrs. Hawley felt nervous after half an hour with Ellen. She could not imagine what had become of Mrs. Pendleton and her guest. She had a dinner-party, she said, and twelve miles to drive before seeing to her table and getting dressed besides. When she saw them returning beneath the orchard trees, she was both amused and irritated.

"What can they have found to say to each other all this time?" she said to Ellen. "I really didn't bring him up here to start a lifelong friendship."

She was at the door to meet them.

"I hate to hurry you," she said to Mr. Gardiner, "but there's a dinner, you know."

"I hate to be hurried," said Mr. Gardiner pleasantly. "As a matter of fact, I can't be until I've seen some things Mrs. Pendleton is showing me upstairs."

"Can you beat that?" asked Mrs. Hawley returning to the sitting room and Ellen.

Ellen was irritated also. She had not enjoyed her role as hostess to an uneasy guest, who was obviously thinking of everyone and everything except Ellen herself.

"Mary's clean daft at times," she said to Grace Wilbur. "Folks don't know all I have to put up with. She has her good points, I'll admit, but sometimes she goes clear out of her head."

Mrs. Hawley at last got Mr. Gardiner away. He had little or nothing to say to her as they sped toward the village and then along the shore road home. Dinner was late that evening, and she was embarrassed and apologetic as they sat down at last to her brilliantly lighted table just as the harvest moon rose over the still waters of the bay.

"You must blame Mr. Gardiner and not me, however," she said, doing her best by easy banter to conceal her annoyance. "He became so enamoured up in the country by a local Maud Muller that I thought I'd never tear him away."


15


Ellen was in such a state of nerves when Mrs. Hawley's car had rounded the end of the driveway that she declared she would eat no supper. It was thoughtless of Mary, she said, to leave her so long with Grace Wilbur who patronized her anyway and always had, and rather unbecoming in a woman of Mary's age to talk so long with a perfect stranger and then take him upstairs to see the Lord knew what. She was so wrought up now she should not sleep a wink and wanted only to be left alone to pull herself together if she could, though she knew very well she couldn't.

Once Ellen had finished all she had to say, Mary went out the back door and through the lower field northward. It was a beautiful still evening, the sky clear except for some low-lying dark clouds against the pale yellow of the west. There was not the slightest breath of wind. As she climbed the high field toward the boulder, she heard the tremulous hum of crickets filling the air. From the top of the great rock she could see the distant harbour, the quiet, full waters of the outer bay stretching on toward the blue Mt. Desert hills. A schooner was lying there, all her sails set to advantage her slow course shoreward. The last rays of sunlight caught them, and they glowed for some moments on the still sea.

Mary Pendleton wanted for nothing as she sat there. Her life that afternoon had been rounded into a perfect circle, complete and fulfilled. She had nothing to regret, everything to remember with gratitude. Most people were wrong about life, she thought. It was not a struggle against temptation as she had been taught in church. Nor was it a search for truth as the philosophers said, or even for happiness, much as humanity craved happiness. It was rather a kind of waiting—a waiting upon the graciousness and the bounty of the things which had been, in order that the things to come might find one free and unafraid.

She watched from the boulder the darkening of the hills, the paling of the harbour water. The sails of the schooner were lost in the fading light. She saw the mist rise from fields and meadows. Those who had written the books which she loved were right. Earth was still the ancient lifegiver, and the broad-backed sea the dispenser of many gifts.

## The End

# Reading Group Discussion

# Reading Group Discussion

## *About this book:*

*Mary Peters*, published in 1934, is the first installment of Mary Ellen Chase's Maine trilogy. It was followed by *Silas Crockett* in 1935, and *Windswept*—her most acclaimed novel—in 1941. These three novels established her reputation as one of the country's leading regional novelists, in the honored tradition of Sarah Orne Jewett and Willa Cather. This novel is imbued with Chase's intimate understanding of the New England way of life and her belief in the powerful influence of Maine's seafaring heritage.

Mary Peters comes from a long line of sea captains, and is born on her father's ship off Singapore. She spends the first fifteen years of her life on the *Elizabeth*, until her return to the small village of Petersport, Maine. The reader follows Mary and her family as they live through years of tumultuous change—and no small amount of personal tragedy—always keeping within them the strength gained from a life at sea.

*Mary Peters* was conceived twenty-five years before Chase began to create the fictional village of Petersport. Inspiration for the novel came from Chase's grandmother, Eliza, who often shared stories about life at sea, equally weighted with joy and fear. Chase greatly admired Eliza, and named her heroine after her great-great-grandmother; but while her own family members may have provided inspiration, Chase maintained that her characters were not based on actual people, but were a blend of many.

Chase believed that a novel should portray life as it was actually lived; thus, *Mary Peters* is rooted in the real-life history of Maine during the late nineteenth and early twentieth centuries. Chase fills her work with intimate descriptions of the natural world, both at sea and on land, and includes details about the education, morals, and village life of the time. She captures the pervasive changes wrought by the Industrial Revolution, when the coastal people stood on the brink of a new world—slowly turning from the glorious era of sail to serving the incoming tide of wealthy summer vacationers.

Even more important than creating a record of the past, however, was Chase's desire to immortalize its spirit and honor its virtues. In her biography of Mary Ellen Chase, Elienne Squire wrote:

"The most valuable elements in her work stem from her sure knowledge of the circumscribed life she had known. She discovered in the demise of a region not only a meaningful relationship to twentieth-century realities, but the source of a country's strength and ongoing spiritual heritage. Chase carried the chronicle forward, elevating the regional novel to its highest level by paying homage to the past." [Squire, *A Lantern in the Wind: The Life of Mary Ellen Chase*, page 94]

With *Mary Peters*, Mary Ellen Chase makes a rich contribution to Maine literature. She not only tells the story of the Peters family—she offers an elegy for a lost way of life, and in so doing, captures the heart of the Maine coast and its people.

### Discussion Questions:

1) A central theme in *Mary Peters* is the importance of memory, as evidenced in the opening epigraph from *The Brothers Karamazov*: "You must know that there is nothing higher and stronger and more wholesome and good for life than some good memory, especially a memory of childhood." The first chapter of the novel opens with the lines: "Mary Peters first saw Cadiz in 1880. She was nine years old then." How does memory play a role in several of the characters' lives? How does it impact their choices? How important is memory in your own lives?

2) "A childhood spent largely at sea 'might help to form a mind and an imagination invulnerable against time, chance, and tragedy.' " [Squire, *A Lantern in the Wind*, page 94] How is Mary Peters invulnerable to the tragedies that she faces in life? Even though they had the same experience in their early years, John's path was quite different; why do you think this is so?

3) The Industrial Revolution and its aftermath inspired Chase to write more than one novel, in an effort to preserve the history of this important era. *Mary Peters* has been praised by critics as "magnificent, a social document of lasting value." [Squire, *A Lantern in the Wind*, page 97] Do you think the novel successfully transports the reader? What did you learn about this place and time that you didn't know before reading the novel? How does Chase balance her goal of preserving the past with moving the plot forward?

4) The years following the Industrial Revolution brought huge changes to the Maine coast. Young people were tempted by the thought of an easier way of life, and turned from world travel to the more limited lifestyle of working for summer residents. Was their choice inevitable? How is Maine a microcosm of the post-industrialized nation? Are there any parallels in today's society?

5) Chase can be compared to other well-known Maine authors (Sarah Orne Jewett, Elisabeth Ogilvie, Ruth Moore), particularly when it comes to her descriptions of setting. Chase had an abiding love for the Maine landscape, and her characters demonstrate this same attachment. The setting becomes a character in its own right as she evokes life on the sea, in a small village, and on a farm. Explain the importance of setting in this novel. Is the background even more important than the human characters in

some respects? How does the setting influence certain characters and help determine their futures? How does the background contribute to the overall mood and flow of the story? Invite volunteers to read their favorite descriptive passages to the group.

6) *Mary Peters* is divided into four sections: The Sea, The Village, The Land, and then, a return to The Sea. Why do you think Chase structured the novel this way? Why does she use this elliptical return to the sea at the end? Which characters best represent each of these sections?

7) One of the most poignant characters in the novel is Mary's brother, John Peters. What is his role in the novel? Explain his relationship with Ellen Kimball. Why do you think Chase allows such heartache and tragedy to enter into the story? What do you think Chase hoped to symbolize with the transplanting of John's tree?

8) Sarah Peters is an intriguing personality, and one of the strongest female characters in Maine literature. Her acceptance of the inevitability of fate is at the core of her character. How does Mary Peters carry on her mother's legacy? What is it that allows Mary to forgive Jim for Hester's tragedy, and to nurse Ellen with such forbearance at the end of the novel? Why do John Peters and Ellen Kimball not possess the same ability?

9) Like Sarah, Mary Peters is a strong female protagonist, and from a young age, she is self-reliant. Discuss the feminist overtones in the novel, particularly in light of the fact that the women in the novel are universally stronger than the men. Was Chase ahead of her time with these views? What seem to be the strengths that Chase valued most—and why are these most often exhibited in her female characters?

10) Sarah Peters has progressive views of sexuality and relationships, and she is fiercely independent. She cautions her children against being swayed by village gossip and public opinion, particularly where the Pendleton men are concerned. Does this element, quite shocking at the time, strengthen Chase's work? Why do you think the Kennebunk Library banned the novel?

11) Mary Peters develops passionate attachments to those she loves (Mr. Gardiner, Hester, Jim Pendleton). Compare these different relationships, and Mary's role in each of them. Why is Mary so drawn to Jim Pendleton? And later, knowing his weakness, why does she go forward with their marriage?

12) In her later years, Mary claims that the man she loved most in her life was Mr. Gardiner, her teacher on board her father's ship. They were truly matched in terms of intellect and sentiment, and in some ways, she compared all men to him throughout her life. When she meets Mr. Gardiner's nephew, those feelings return. Is there a hint of a future relationship with the nephew? Would that be necessary for Mary's sense of fulfillment?

13) A critic wrote that Mary Ellen Chase created "one-note characters" that allowed no room for pity. Chase responded by saying· "You criticize me because I do not arouse 'pity.' But pity is precisely what I want to avoid. No one of my characters is pitiable. That is just the point. They, the best, are meant to be triumphant . . ." [Squire, pages 97–98] Does Chase succeed in her attempt to portray the inherent dignity of her characters, despite showing their weaknesses? Are her characters multilayered? Which character do you admire most?

14) In a 1961 lecture to fellow authors, Chase outlined her belief that a novel was not merely a story, but should contain an "evaluation of life." Chase felt that modern literature lacked an awareness of "noble themes and heroic characters," and blamed this on an ever-increasing reliance on psychotherapy. Compare our twenty-first-century realities—television therapists, dysfunctional relationships, blaming others for life's difficulties—with the way of life presented in Chase's work. In our post–9/11 world, what can we learn from novels such as *Mary Peters*?

### For Further Reading:

Chase, Evelyn Hyman. *Feminist Convert: A Portrait of Mary Ellen Chase*. Santa Barbara: John Daniel and Co., 1988.

Chase, Mary Ellen. *Silas Crockett*. New York: Macmillan, 1935.

Chase, Mary Ellen. *Windswept*. New York: Macmillan, 1941.

Squire, Elienne. *A Lantern in the Wind: The Life of Mary Ellen Chase*, Santa Barbara: Fithian Press, 1995.

Westbrook, Perry D. *Mary Ellen Chase*. New York: Twayne Publishers, 1965.